W9-CDC-635

THE ENORMOUS ROOM

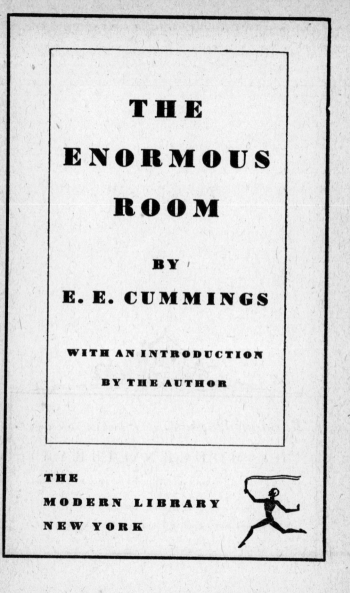

THE
ENORMOUS
ROOM

BY

E. E. CUMMINGS

WITH AN INTRODUCTION

BY THE AUTHOR

THE
MODERN LIBRARY
NEW YORK

Random House IS THE PUBLISHER OF

THE MODERN LIBRARY

BENNETT A. CERF · DONALD S. KLOPFER · ROBERT K. HAAS

Manufactured in the United States of America

Printed by Parkway Printing Company   Bound by H. Wolff

E. E. CUMMINGS
(1894-   )

A NOTE ON THE AUTHOR OF "THE ENORMOUS ROOM"

During the War, Edward Estlin Cummings enlisted in the Norton-Harjes Ambulance Corps. With no charge against him, he was confined in a concentration camp in La Ferté Macé, France. It was there that he gathered material for his first and most successful book. Since the War, E. E. Cummings has been identified with an almost hieroglyphic form of verse and with painting that pushes abstraction beyond the abstract. He has been the terror of typesetters, an enigma to book reviewers and the special target of all the world's literary philistines.

BIBLIOGRAPHY

THE ENORMOUS ROOM (1922)
TULIPS AND CHIMNEYS (1923)
XLI POEMS (1925)
& (1925)
IS 5 (1926)
HIM (1927)
———— (1930)
VIVA (1931)
EIMI (1932)

CONTENTS

		PAGE
	INTRODUCTION	vii
	FOREWORD	xi
CHAPTER		
I.	I BEGIN A PILGRIMAGE	I
II.	EN ROUTE	23
III.	A PILGRIM'S PROGRESS	37
IV.	LE NOUVEAU	61
V.	A GROUP OF PORTRAITS	113
VI.	APOLLYON	147
VII.	AN APPROACH TO THE DELECTABLE MOUNTAINS	176
VIII.	THE WANDERER	216
IX.	ZOO-LOO	231
X.	SURPLICE	254
XI.	JEAN LE NÈGRE	269
XII.	THREE WISE MEN	294
XIII.	I SAY GOOD-BYE TO LA MISÈRE	313

INTRODUCTION

Don't be afraid.

—But I've never seen a picture you painted or read a word you wrote—

So what?

So you're thirty-eight?

Correct.

And have only just finished your second novel?

Socalled.

Entitled ee-eye-em-eye?

Right.

And pronounced?

"A" as in a, "me" as in me; accent on the "me".

Signifying?

Am.

How does Am compare with The Enormous Room?

Favorably.

They're not at all similar, are they?

When The Enormous Room was published, some people wanted a war book; they were disappointed. When Eimi was published, some people wanted Another Enormous Room; they were disappointed.

Doesn't The Enormous Room really concern war?

It actually uses war: to explore an inconceivable vastness which is so unbelievably far away that it appears microscopic.

When you wrote this book, you were looking through war at something very big and very far away?

When this book wrote itself, I was observing a negligible portion of something incredibly more distant than any sun; something more unimaginably huge than the most prodigious of all universes—

Namely?

The individual.

Well! And what about Am?

Some people had decided that The Enormous Room wasn't a just-war book and was a class-war book, when along came Eimi—aha! said some people; here's another dirty dig at capitalism.

And they were disappointed.

Sic.

Do you think these disappointed people really hated capitalism?

I feel these disappointed people unreally hated themselves—

And you really hated Russia.

Russia, I felt, was more deadly than war; when nationalists hate, they hate by merely killing and maiming human beings; when internationalists hate, they hate by categorying and pigeonholing human beings.

So both your novels were what people didn't expect.

Eimi is the individual again; a more complex individual, a more enormous room.

By a—what do you call yourself? painter? poet? playwright? satirist? essayist? novelist?

Artist.

But not a successful artist, in the popular sense?

Don't be silly.

Yet you probably consider your art of vital consequence—

Improbably.

—To the world?

To myself.

What about the world, Mr. Cummings?

I live in so many: which one do you mean?

I mean the everyday humdrum world, which includes me and you and millions upon millions of men and women.

So?

Did it ever occur to you that people in this socalled world of ours are not interested in art?

Da da.

Isn't that too bad!

How?

If people were interested in art, you as an artist would receive wider recognition—

Wider?

Of course.

Not deeper.

Deeper?

Love, for example, is deeper than flattery.

Ah—but (now that you mention it) isn't love just a trifle oldfashioned?

I dare say.

And aren't you supposed to be ultramodernistic?

I dare say.

But I dare say you don't dare say precisely why you consider your art of vital consequence—

Thanks to I dare say my art I am able to become myself.

Well well! Doesn't that sound as if people who weren't artists couldn't become themselves?

Does it?

What do you think happens to people who aren't artists? What do you think people who aren't artists become?

I feel they don't become: I feel nothing happens to them; I feel negation becomes of them.

Negation?

You paraphrased it a few moments ago.

How?

"This socalled world of ours."

Labouring under the childish delusion that economic forces don't exist, eh?

I am labouring.

Answer one question: do economic forces exist or do they not?

Do you believe in ghosts?

I said economic forces.

So what?

Well well well! Where ignorance is bliss . . . Listen, Mr. Lowercase Highbrow—

Shoot.

—I'm afraid you've never been hungry.

Don't be afraid.

E. E. CUMMINGS

New York
1932

FOREWORD (1922)

'FOR THIS MY SON WAS DEAD, AND IS ALIVE AGAIN; HE WAS LOST AND IS FOUND.'

He was lost by the Norton-Harjes Ambulance Corps.

He was officially dead as a result of official misinformation.

He was entombed by the French Government.

It took the better part of three months to find him and bring him back to life with the help of powerful and willing friends on both sides of the Atlantic. The following documents tell the story.

104 IRVING STREET,
CAMBRIDGE, *December* 8, 1917.

President Woodrow Wilson,
White House,
Washington, D.C.

MR. PRESIDENT:

It seems criminal to ask for a single moment of your time. But I am strongly advised that it would be more criminal to delay any longer calling to your attention a crime against American citizenship in which the French Government has persisted for many weeks—in spite of constant appeals made to the American Minister at Paris; and in spite of subsequent action taken by the State Department at Washington, on the initiative of my friend Hon. —.

The victims are two American ambulance drivers,

Edward Estlin Cummings of Cambridge, Mass., and
W— S— B—.

More than two months ago these young men were
arrested, subjected to many indignities, dragged across
France like criminals, and closely confined in a Concentration Camp at La Ferté Macé; where according to
latest advices they still remain,—awaiting the final action
of the Minister of the Interior upon the findings of a
Commission which passed upon their cases as long ago
as October 17.

Against Cummings both private and official advices
from Paris state that there is no charge whatever. He
has been subjected to this outrageous treatment solely
because of his intimate friendship with young B—, whose
sole crime is,—so far as can be learned,—that certain
letters to friends in America were misinterpreted by an
over-zealous French censor.

It only adds to the indignity and irony of the situation
to say that young Cummings is an enthusiastic lover of
France, and so loyal to the friends he has made among
the French soldiers, that even while suffering in health
from his unjust confinement, he excuses the ingratitude
of the country he has risked his life to serve, by calling
attention to the atmosphere of intense suspicion and distrust that has naturally resulted from the painful experience which France has had with foreign emissaries.

Be assured, Mr. President, that I have waited long—
it seems like ages—and have exhausted all other available
help before venturing to trouble you.

1. After many weeks of vain effort to secure effective
action by the American Ambassador at Paris, Richard
Norton of the Norton-Harjes Ambulance Corps, to
which the boys belonged, was completely discouraged,
and advised me to seek help here.

2. The efforts of the State Department at Washington
resulted as follows:

i. A cable from Paris saying there was no charge against Cummings and intimating that he would speedily be released.

ii. A little later a second cable advising that Edward Estlin Cummings had sailed on the Antilles and was reported lost.

iii. A week later a third cable correcting this cruel error, and saying the Embassy was renewing efforts to locate Cummings—apparently still ignorant even of the place of his confinement.

After such painful and baffling experiences, I turn to you,—burdened though I know you to be, in this world crisis, with the weightiest task ever laid upon any man.

But I have another reason for asking this favour. I do not speak for my son alone; or for him and his friend alone. My son has a mother,—as brave and patriotic as any mother who ever dedicated an only son to a great cause. The mothers of our boys in France have rights as well as the boys themselves.

My boy's mother had a right to be protected from the weeks of horrible anxiety and suspense caused by the inexplicable arrest and imprisonment of her son. My boy's mother had a right to be spared the supreme agony caused by a blundering cable from Paris saying that he had been drowned by a submarine. (An error which Mr. Norton subsequently cabled that he had discovered six weeks before.) My boy's mother and all American mothers have a right to be protected against all needless anxiety and sorrow.

Pardon me, Mr. President, but if I were president and your son were suffering such prolonged injustice at the hands of France; and your son's mother had been needlessly kept in Hell as many weeks as my boy's mother has,—I would do something to make American citizenship as sacred in the eyes of Frenchmen as Roman citizenship was in the eyes of the ancient world. Then it was enough to ask the question, 'Is it lawful to scourge a man that is a Roman, and uncondemned?' Now, in France, it seems lawful to treat like a condemned criminal a man that is an American, uncondemned and admittedly innocent!

Very respectfully,

EDWARD CUMMINGS

This letter was received at the White House. Whether it was received with sympathy or with silent disapproval, is still a mystery. A Washington official, a friend in need and a friend indeed in these trying experiences, took the precaution to have it delivered by messenger. Otherwise, fear that it had been 'lost in the mail' would have added another twinge of uncertainty to the prolonged and exquisite tortures inflicted upon parents by alternations of misinformation and official silence. Doubtless the official stethoscope was on the heart of the world just then; and perhaps it was too much to expect that even a post-card would be wasted on private heart-aches.

In any event this letter told where to look for the missing boys,—something the French Government either could not or would not disclose, in spite of constant pressure by the American Embassy at Paris and constant efforts by my friend Richard Norton, who was head of the Norton-Harjes Ambulance organization from which they had been abducted.

Release soon followed, as narrated in the following letter to Major — of the Staff of the Judge Advocate General in Paris.

February 20, 1921.

MY DEAR MR. —

Your letter of January 30th, which I had been waiting for with great interest ever since I received your cable, arrived this morning. My son arrived in New York on January 1st. He was in bad shape physically as a result of his imprisonment: very much under weight, suffering from a bad skin infection which he had acquired at the concentration camp. However, in view of the extraordinary facilities which the detention camp offered for acquiring dangerous diseases, he is certainly to be congratulated on having escaped with one of the least harmful. The medical treatment at the camp was quite in keeping with the general standards of sanitation there; with the result that it was not until he began to receive competent surgical treatment after his release and on board ship that there was much chance of improvement. A month of competent medical treatment here seems to have got rid of this painful reminder of official hospitality. He is, at present, visiting friends in New York. If he were here, I am sure he would join with me and with his mother in thanking you for the interest you have taken and the efforts you have made.

W— S— B— is, I am happy to say, expected in New York this week by the S.S. Niagara. News of his release and subsequently of his departure came by cable. What you say about the nervous strain under which he was living, as an explanation of the letters to which the authorities objected, is entirely borne out by first-hand information. The kind of badgering which the youth received was enough to upset a less sensitive temperament. It speaks volumes for the character of his environment that such treatment aroused the resentment of only one of his companions, and that even this manifestation of normal human sympathy was regarded as 'suspicious.' If you are right in characterizing B—'s condition as more or less hysterical, what shall we say of the conditions which made possible the treatment which he and his friend received? I am glad B— wrote the very sensible and manly letter to the Embassy, which you mention.

After I have had an opportunity to converse with him, I shall be in better position to reach a conclusion in regard to certain matters about which I will not now express an opinion.

I would only add that I do not in the least share your complacency in regard to the treatment which my son received. The very fact that, as you say, no charges were made and that he was detained on suspicion for many weeks after the Commission passed on his case and reported to the Minister of the Interior that he ought to be released, leads me to a conclusion exactly opposite to that which you express. It seems to me impossible to believe that any well-ordered Government would fail to acknowledge such action to have been unreasonable. Moreover, 'detention on suspicion' was a small part of what actually took place. To take a single illustration, you will recall that after many weeks' persistent effort to secure information, the Embassy was still kept so much in the dark about the facts, that it cabled the report that my son had embarked on The Antilles and was reported lost. And when convinced of that error, the Embassy cabled that it was renewing efforts to locate my son. Up to that moment, it would appear that the authorities had not even condescended to tell the United States Embassy where this innocent American citizen was confined; so that a mistaken report of his death was regarded as an adequate explanation of his disappearance. If I had accepted this report and taken no further action, it is by no means certain that he would not be dead by this time.

I am free to say, that in my opinion no self-respecting Government could allow one of its own citizens, against whom there has been no accusation brought, to be subjected to such prolonged indignities and injuries by a friendly Government without vigorous remonstrance. I regard it as a patriotic duty, as well as a matter of personal self-respect, to do what I can to see that such remonstrance is made. I still think too highly both of my own Government and of the Government of France to believe that such an untoward incident will fail to receive the serious attention it deserves. If I am wrong, and American citizens must expect to suffer such indignities and injuries at the hands of other Governments without any effort at remonstrance and redress by their own Government, I believe the public ought to know the humiliating truth. It will make interesting reading. It remains for my son to determine what action he will take.

I am glad to know your son is returning. I am looking forward with great pleasure to conversing with him.

I cannot adequately express my gratitude to you and to other friends for the sympathy and assistance I have received. If any expenses have been incurred on my behalf or on behalf of my son, I beg you to give me the pleasure of reimbursing you. At best, I must always remain your debtor.

> With best wishes,
> Sincerely yours,
> EDWARD CUMMINGS

I yield to no one in enthusiasm for the cause of France. Her cause was our cause and the cause of civilization; and the tragedy is that it took us so long to find it out. I would gladly have risked my life for her, as my son risked his and would have risked it again had not the departure of his regiment overseas been stopped by the Armistice.

France was beset with enemies within as well as without. Some of the 'suspects' were members of her official household. Her Minister of Interior was thrown into prison. She was distracted with fear. Her existence was at stake. Under such circumstances excesses were sure to be committed. But it is precisely at such times that American citizens most need and are most entitled to the protection of their own Government.

EDWARD CUMMINGS

THE ENORMOUS ROOM

I

I BEGIN A PILGRIMAGE

We had succeeded, my friend B. and I, in dispensing with almost three of our six months' engagement as *Conducteurs Volontaires, Section Sanitaire Vingt-et-Un, Ambulance Norton Harjes, Croix Rouge Américaine,* and at the Moment which subsequent experience served to capitalize had just finished the unlovely job of cleaning and greasing (*nettoyer* is the proper word) the own private flivver of the *chef de section,* a gentleman by the convenient name of Mr. A. To borrow a characteristic cadence from Our Great President: the lively satisfaction which we might be suspected of having derived from the accomplishment of a task so important in the saving of civilization from the clutches of Prussian tyranny was in some degree inhibited, unhappily, by a complete absence of cordial relations between the man whom fate had placed over us and ourselves. Or, to use the vulgar American idiom, B. and I and Mr. A. didn't get on well. We were in fundamental disagreement as to the attitude which we, Americans, should uphold toward the poilus in whose behalf we had volunteered assistance, Mr. A. maintaining 'you boys want to keep away from those dirty Frenchmen' and 'we're here to show those bastards how they do things in America,' to which we answered by seizing every opportunity for fraternization. Inasmuch as eight dirty Frenchmen were attached to the section in various capacities (cook, provisioner, chauffeur,

3

mechanician, etc.), and the section itself was affiliated
with a branch of the French army, fraternization was
easy. Now when he saw that we had not the slightest
intention of adopting his ideals, Mr. A. (together with
the *sous-lieutenant* who acted as his translator—for the
chef's knowledge of the French language, obtained during
several years' heroic service, consisted for the most part
in 'Sar var,' 'Sar marche,' '*Deet donk moan vieux*') confined his efforts to denying us the privilege of acting as
conducteurs, on the ground that our personal appearance
was a disgrace to the section. In this, I am bound to say,
Mr. A. was but sustaining the tradition conceived origi-
nally by his predecessor, a Mr. P., a Harvard man, who
until his departure from *Vingt-et-Un* succeeded in
making life absolutely miserable for B. and myself. Before leaving this painful subject I beg to state that, at
least as far as I was concerned, the tradition had a firm
foundation in my own predisposition for uncouthness
plus what *Le Matin* (if we remember correctly) cleverly
nicknamed *La Boue Héroïque*.

Having accomplished the *nettoyage* (at which we were
by this time adepts, thanks to Mr. A.'s habit of detailing
us to wash any car which its driver and *aide* might consider too dirty a task for their own hands) we proceeded
in search of a little water for personal use. B. speedily
finished his ablutions. I was strolling carelessly and solo
from the cook-wagon toward one of the two tents—
which protestingly housed some forty huddling Americans by night—holding in my hand an historic *morceau
de chocolat*, when a spic not to say span gentleman in a
suspiciously quiet French uniform allowed himself to be
driven up to the *bureau* by two neat soldiers with tin
derbies, in a Renault whose painful cleanliness shamed

my recent efforts. This must be a general at least, I
thought, regretting the extremely undress character of
my uniform, which uniform consisted of overalls and a
cigarette.

Having furtively watched the gentleman alight and
receive a ceremonious welcome from the *chef* and the
aforesaid French lieutenant who accompanied the section
for translatory reasons, I hastily betook myself to one of
the tents, where I found B. engaged in dragging all his
belongings into a central pile of frightening proportions.
He was surrounded by a group of fellow-heroes who
hailed my coming with considerable enthusiasm. 'Your
bunky's leaving,' said somebody. 'Going to Paris,' volunteered a man, who had been trying for three months to
get there. 'Prison, you mean,' remarked a confirmed op-
timist whose disposition had felt the effects of the French
climate.

Albeit confused by the eloquence of B.'s unalterable
silence, I immediately associated his present predicament
with the advent of the mysterious stranger, and forthwith
dashed forth bent on demanding from one of the tin-
derbies the high identity and sacred mission of this personage. I knew that with the exception of ourselves every
one in the section had been given his *permission de sept
jours*—even two men who had arrived later than we and
whose turn should subsequently have come after ours. I
also knew that at the headquarters of the Ambulance, 7
rue François premier, *se trouvait* Monsieur Norton, the
supreme head of the Norton Harjes fraternity, who had
known my father in other days. Putting two and two
together I decided that this potentate had sent an emissary
to Mr. A. to demand an explanation of the various and
sundry insults and indignities to which I and my friend

had been subjected, and more particularly to secure our long-delayed *permission*. Accordingly I was in high spirits as I rushed toward the *bureau*.

I didn't have to go far. The mysterious one, in conversation with *monsieur le sous-lieutenant*, met me halfway. I caught the words: 'And Cummings [the first and last time that my name was correctly pronounced by a Frenchman], where is he?'

'Present,' I said, giving a salute to which neither of them paid the slightest attention.

'Ah yes,' impenetrably remarked the mysterious one in positively sanitary English. 'You shall put all your baggage in the car, at once'—then, to tin-derby-the-first, who appeared in an occult manner at his master's elbow— '*Allez avec lui, chercher ses affaires, de suite.*'

My *affaires* were mostly in the vicinity of the cuisine, where lodged the *cuisinier, mécanicien, menuisier*, etc., who had made room for me (some ten days since) on their own initiative, thus saving me the humiliation of sleeping with nineteen Americans in a tent which was always two-thirds full of mud. Thither I led the tin-derby, who scrutinized everything with surprising interest. I threw *mes affaires* hastily together (including some minor accessories which I was going to leave behind; but which the t-d bade me include) and emerged with a duffle-bag under one arm and a bed-roll under the other, to encounter my excellent friends the dirty Frenchmen aforesaid. They all popped out together from one door, looking rather astonished. Something by way of explanation as well as farewell was most certainly required, so I made a speech in my best French:

'Gentlemen, friends, comrades—I am going away immediately and shall be guillotined to-morrow.'

—'Oh hardly guillotined I should say,' remarked t-d, in a voice which froze my marrow despite my high spirits; while the cook and carpenter gaped audibly and the mechanician clutched a hopelessly smashed carburetter for support.

One of the section's *voitures*, a F.I.A.T., was standing ready. General Nemo sternly forbade me to approach the Renault (in which B.'s baggage was already deposited) and waved me into the F.I.A.T. bed, bed-roll and all; whereupon t-d leaped in and seated himself opposite me in a position of perfect unrelaxation which, despite my aforesaid exultation at quitting the section in general and Mr. A. in particular, impressed me as being almost menacing. Through the front window I saw my friend drive away with t-d number 2 and Nemo; then, having waved hasty farewell to all *les Américains* that I knew—3 in number—and having exchanged affectionate greetings with Mr. A. (who admitted he was very sorry indeed to lose us), I experienced the jolt of the clutch—and we were off in pursuit.

Whatever may have been the forebodings inspired by t-d number 1's attitude, they were completely annihilated by the thrilling joy which I experienced on losing sight of the accursed section and its asinine inhabitants—by the indisputable and authentic thrill of going somewhere and nowhere under the miraculous auspices of some one and no one—of being yanked from the putrescent banalities of an official non-existence into a high and clear adventure, by a *deus ex machina* in a grey-blue uniform and a couple of tin-derbies. I whistled and sang and cried to my *vis-à-vis*: 'By the way, who is yonder distinguished gentleman who has been so good as to take my friend and me on this little promenade?'—to which, between lurches of the groaning F.I.A.T., t-d replied awesomely, clutching at the window for the benefit of his equilibrium: 'Monsieur le Ministre de Sûreté de Noyon.'

Not in the least realizing what this might mean, I grinned. A responsive grin, visiting informally the tired cheeks of my confrère, ended by frankly connecting his worthy and enormous ears which were squeezed into oblivion by the oversize casque. My eyes, jumping from those ears, lit on that helmet and noticed for the first time an emblem, a sort of flowering little explosion, or hair-switch rampant. It seemed to me very jovial and a little absurd.

'We're on our way to Noyon, then?'

T-d shrugged his shoulders.

Here the driver's hat blew off. I heard him swear, and saw the hat sailing in our wake. I jumped to my feet as the F.I.A.T. came to a sudden stop, and started for the ground—then checked my flight in mid-air and landed on the seat, completely astonished. T-d's revolver, which had hopped from its holster at my first move, slid back into its nest. The owner of the revolver was muttering something rather disagreeable. The driver (being an American of *Vingt-et-Un*) was backing up instead of retrieving his cap in person. My mind felt as if it had been thrown suddenly from fourth into reverse. I pondered and said nothing.

On again—faster, to make up for lost time. On the correct assumption that t-d does not understand English, the driver passes the time of day through the minute window:

'For Christ's sake, Cummings, what's up?'

'You got me,' I said, laughing at the delicate *naïveté* of the question.

'Did y' do something to get pinched?'

'Probably,' I answered importantly and vaguely, feeling a new dignity.

'Well, if you didn't, maybe B — did.'

"Maybe,' I countered, trying not to appear enthusiastic. As a matter of fact I was never so excited and proud. I was, to be sure, a criminal! Well, well, thank God that settled one question for good and all—no more *section sanitaire* for me! No more Mr. A. and his daily lectures on cleanliness, deportment, etc. In spite of myself I started to sing. The driver interrupted:

'I heard you asking the tin lid something in French. Whadhesay?'

'Said that gink in the Renault is the head cop of Noyon,' I answered at random.

'GOOD-NIGHT. Maybe we'd better ring off, or you'll get in wrong with'—he indicated t-d with a wave of his head that communicated itself to the car in a magnificent skid; and t-d's derby rang out as the skid pitched t-d the length of the F.I.A.T.

'You rang the bell then,' I commended—then to t-d: 'Nice car for the wounded to ride in,' I politely observed. T-d answered nothing. . . .

Noyon.

We drive straight up to something which looks unpleasantly like a feudal dungeon. The driver is now told to be somewhere at a certain time, and meanwhile to eat with the Head Cop, who may be found just around the corner—(I am doing the translating for t-d)—and, oh yes; it seems that the Head Cop has particularly requested the pleasure of this distinguished American's company at *déjeuner*.

'Does he mean me?' the driver asked innocently.

'Sure,' I told him.

Nothing is said of B. or me.

Now, cautiously, t-d first and I a slow next, we descend. The F.I.A.T. rumbles off, with the distinguished one's backward-glaring head poked out a yard more or less, and that distinguished face so completely surrendered to mystification as to cause a large laugh on my part.

'*Vous avez faim?*'

It was the erstwhile-ferocious speaking. A criminal, I remembered, is somebody against whom everything he says and does is very cleverly made use of. After weighing the matter in my mind for some moments I decided at all cost to tell the truth, and replied:

'I could eat an elephant.'

Hereupon t-d led me to the Kitchen Itself, set me to eat upon a stool, and admonished the cook in a fierce voice:

'Give this great criminal something to eat in the name of the French Republic!'

And for the first time in three months I tasted Food.

T-d seated himself beside me, opened a huge jack-knife, and fell to, after first removing his tin-derby and loosening his belt.

One of the pleasantest memories connected with that irrevocable meal is of a large, gentle, strong woman who entered in a hurry, and seeing me cried out:

'What is it?'

'It's an American, my mother,' t-d answered through fried potatoes.

'*Pourquoi qu'il est ici?*' The woman touched me on the shoulder, and satisfied herself that I was real.

'The good God is doubtless acquainted with the explanation,' said t-d pleasantly. 'Not myself being the—'

'Ah, *mon pauvre,*' said this very beautiful sort of woman. 'You are going to be a prisoner here. Every one of the prisoners has a *marraine,* do you understand? I am their *marraine.* I love them and look after them. Well, listen: I will be your *marraine,* too.'

I bowed, and looked around for something to pledge her in. T-d was watching. My eyes fell on a huge glass of red *pinard.* 'Yes, drink,' said my captor, with a smile. I raised my huge glass.

'*A la santé de ma marraine charmante.*'

—This deed of gallantry quite won the cook (a smallish, agile Frenchman), who shovelled several helps of potatoes on my already empty plate. The tin-derby approved also: 'That's right, eat, drink, you'll need it later perhaps.' And his knife guillotined another delicious hunk of white bread.

At last, sated with luxuries, I bade adieu to my *marraine* and allowed t-d to conduct me (I going first, as always) upstairs and into a little den whose interior boasted two mattresses, a man sitting at the table, and a newspaper in the hands of the man.

'*C'est un Américain,*' t-d said by way of introduction. The newspaper detached itself from the man, who said: 'He's welcome indeed: make yourself at home, Mr. American'—and bowed himself out. My captor immediately collapsed on one mattress.

I asked permission to do the same on the other, which favour was sleepily granted. With half-shut eyes my Ego lay and pondered: the delicious meal it had just enjoyed;

what was to come; the joys of being a great criminal . . . then, being not at all inclined to sleep, I read *Le Petit Parisien* quite through, even to *Les Voies Urinaires*.

Which reminded me—and I woke up t-d and asked: 'May I visit the *vespasienne?*'

'Downstairs,' he replied fuzzily, and readjusted his slumbers.

There was no one moving about in the little court. I lingered somewhat on the way upstairs. The stairs were abnormally dirty. When I re-entered, t-d was roaring to himself. I read the journal through again. It must be about three o'clock.

Suddenly t-d woke up, straightened and buckled his personality, and murmured, 'It's time, come on.'

Le bureau de Monsieur de Ministre was just around the corner, as it proved. Before the door stood the patient F.I.A.T. It was ceremoniously informed by t-d that we would wait on the steps.

Well! Did I know any more?—the American driver wanted to know.

Having proved to my own satisfaction that my fingers could still roll a pretty good cigarette, I answered: 'No,' between puffs.

The American drew nearer and whispered spectacularly: 'Your friend is upstairs. I think they're examining him.' T-d got this; and though his rehabilitated dignity had accepted the 'makin's' from its prisoner, it became immediately incensed:

'That's enough,' he said sternly.

And dragged me *tout-à-coup* upstairs, where I met B. and his t-d coming out of the *bureau* door. B. looked peculiarly cheerful. 'I think we're going to prison all right,' he assured me.

Braced by this news, poked from behind by my t-d, and waved on from before by M. le Ministre himself, I floated vaguely into a very washed, neat, business-like and altogether American room of modest proportions, whose door was immediately shut and guarded on the inside by my escort.

Monsieur le Ministre said:

'Lift your arms.'

Then he went through my pockets. He found cigarettes, pencils, a jack-knife, and several francs. He laid his treasures on a clean table and said: 'You are not allowed to keep these. I shall be responsible.' Then he looked me coldly in the eye and asked if I had anything else.

I told him that I believed I had a handkerchief.

He asked me: 'Have you anything in your shoes?'

'My feet,' I said, gently.

'Come this way,' he said frigidly, opening a door which I had not remarked. I bowed in acknowledgment of the courtesy, and entered room number 2.

I looked into six eyes which sat at a desk.

Two belonged to a lawyerish person in civilian clothes, with a bored expression, plus a moustache of dreamy proportions with which the owner constantly imitated a gentleman ringing for a drink. Two appertained to a splendid old dotard (a face all ski-jumps and toboggan-slides), on whose protruding chest the rosette of the Legion pompously squatted. Numbers five and six had reference to Monsieur, who had seated himself before I had time to focus my slightly bewildered eyes.

Monsieur spoke sanitary English, as I have said.

'What is your name'—'Edward E. Cummings.'—'Your second name?'—'E-s-t-l-i-n,' I spelled it for him.—'How do you say that?'—I didn't understand.—'How do you say your name?'—'Oh,' I said; and pronounced it. He explained in French to the moustache that my first name was Edouard, my second 'A-s-tay-l-ee-n,' and my third 'Say-u-deux m-ee-n-zhay-s'—and the moustache wrote it all down. Monsieur then turned to me once more:

'You are Irish?'—'No,' I said, 'American.'—'You are Irish by family?'—'No, Scotch.'—'You are sure that there was never an Irishman in your parents?'—'So far as I know,' I said, 'there never was an Irishman there.'—'Perhaps a hundred years back?' he insisted.—'Not a chance,' I said decisively. But Monsieur was not to be denied: 'Your name it is Irish?'—'Cummings is a very old Scotch name,' I told him fluently; 'it used to be Comyn. A Scotchman named The Red Comyn was killed by Robert Bruce in a church. He was my ancestor and a very well-known man.'—'But your second name, where have you got that?'—'From an Englishman, a friend of my father.' This statement seemed to produce a very favourable impression in the case of the rosette, who murmured: '*Un ami de son père, un anglais, bon!*' several times. Monsieur, quite evidently disappointed, told the moustache in French to write down that I denied my Irish parentage; which the moustache did.

'What does your father in America?'—'He is a minister of the Gospel,' I answered. 'Which church?'—'Unitarian.' This puzzled him. After a moment he had an inspiration: 'That is the same as a Free Thinker?'—I explained in French that it wasn't and that *mon père* was a holy man. At last Monsieur told the moustache to write, Protestant; and the moustache obediently did so.

From this point our conversation was carried on in French, somewhat to the chagrin of Monsieur, but to the joy of the rosette and with the approval of the moustache. In answer to questions, I informed them that I was a student for five years at Harvard (expressing great surprise that they had never heard of Harvard), that I had come to New York and studied painting, that I had enlisted in New York as *conducteur volontaire,* embarking for France shortly after, about the middle of April.

Monsieur asked: 'You met B — on the *pacquebot?*' I said I did.

Monsieur glanced significantly around. The rosette nodded a number of times. The moustache rang.

I understood that these kind people were planning to make me out the innocent victim of a wily villain, and could not forbear a smile. *C'est rigolo,* I said to myself; they'll have a great time doing it.

'You and your friend were together in Paris?' I said 'Yes.' 'How long?' 'A month, while we were waiting for our uniforms.'

A significant look by Monsieur, which is echoed by his confrères.

Leaning forward, Monsieur asked coldly and carefully: 'What did you do in Paris?' to which I responded briefly and warmly, 'We had a good time.'

This reply pleased the rosette hugely. He wagged his head till I thought it would have tumbled off. Even the moustache seemed amused. Monsieur le Ministre de Sûreté de Noyon bit his lip. 'Never mind writing that down,' he directed the lawyer. Then, returning to the charge:

'You had a great deal of trouble with Lieutenant A.?'

I laughed outright at this complimentary nomenclature. 'Yes, we certainly did.'

He asked: 'Why?'—so I sketched 'Lieutenant' A. in vivid terms, making use of certain choice expressions with which one of the 'dirty Frenchmen' attached to the section, a *Parisien*, master of *argot*, had furnished me. My phraseology surprised my examiners, one of whom (I think the moustache) observed sarcastically that I had made good use of my time in Paris.

Monsieur le Ministre asked: Was it true (*a*) that B. and I were always together and (*b*) preferred the company of the attached Frenchmen to that of our fellow-Americans?—to which I answered in the affirmative. Why? he wanted to know. So I explained that we felt that the more French we knew and the better we knew the French, the better for us; expatiating a bit on the necessity for a complete mutual understanding of the Latin and Anglo-Saxon races if victory was to be won.

Again the rosette nodded with approbation.

Monsieur le Ministre may have felt that he was losing his case, for he played his trump card immediately: 'You are aware that your friend has written to friends in America and to his family very bad letters.' 'I am not,' I said.

In a flash I understood the motivation of Monsieur's visit to *Vingt-et-Un*: the French censor had intercepted some of B.'s letters, and had notified Mr. A. and Mr. A.'s translator, both of whom had thankfully testified to the bad character of B. and (wishing very naturally to get rid of both of us at once) had further averred that we were always together and that consequently I might properly be regarded as a suspicious character. Whereupon they had received instructions to hold us at the section until Noyon could arrive and take charge—hence our failure to obtain our long overdue *permission*.

'Your friend,' said Monsieur in English, 'is here a short while ago. I ask him if he is up in the aeroplane flying over

Germans will he drop the bombs on Germans and he say no, he will not drop any bombs on Germans.'

By this falsehood (such as it happened to be) I confess that I was nonplussed. In the first place, I was at the time innocent of third-degree methods. Secondly: I remembered that, a week or so since, B., myself and another American in the section had written a letter which, on the advice of the *sous-lieutenant* who accompanied *Vingt-et-Un* as translator, we had addressed to the Under-Secretary of State in French Aviation, asking that inasmuch as the American Government was about to take over the Red Cross (which meant that all the *sections sanitaires* would be affiliated with the American, and no longer with the French Army) we three at any rate might be allowed to continue our association with the French by enlisting in l'Esquadrille Lafayette. One of the 'dirty Frenchmen' had written the letter for us in the finest language imaginable, from data supplied by ourselves.

'You write a letter, your friend and you, for French aviation?'

Here I corrected him: there were three of us, and why didn't he have the third culprit arrested, might I ask? But he ignored this little digression, and wanted to know: Why not American aviation?—to which I answered: Ah, but as my friend has so often said to me, the French are after all the finest people in the world.

This double-blow stopped Noyon dead, but only for a second.

'Did your friend write this letter?'—'No,' I answered truthfully.—'Who did write it?'—'One of the Frenchmen attached to the section.'—'What is his name?'—'I'm sure I don't know,' I answered; mentally swearing that what-

ever might happen to me, the scribe should not suffer. 'At
my urgent request,' I added.

Relapsing into French, Monsieur asked me if I would
have any hesitation in dropping bombs on Germans? I
said no, I wouldn't. And why did I suppose I was fitted
to become aviator? Because, I told him, I weighed 135
pounds and could drive any kind of auto or motor-cycle.
(I hoped he would make me prove this assertion, in which
case I promised myself that I wouldn't stop till I got to
Munich; but no.)

'Do you mean to say that my friend was not only trying
to avoid serving in the American Army but was contemplating treason as well?' I asked.

'Well, that would be it, would it not?' he answered
coolly. Then, leaning forward once more, he fired at me:
'Why did you write to an official so high?'

At this I laughed outright. 'Because the excellent *sous-
lieutenant* who translated when Mr. Lieutenant A.
couldn't understand advised us to do so.'

Following up this sortie, I addressed the moustache:
'Write this down in the testimony—that I, here present,
refuse utterly to believe that my friend is not as sincere a
lover of France and the French people as any man living!
—Tell him to write it,' I commanded Noyon stonily. But
Noyon shook his head, saying: 'We have the very best
reason for supposing your friend to be no friend of
France.' I answered: 'That is not my affair. I want my
opinion of my friend written in; do you see?' 'That's rea-
sonable,' the rosette murmured; and the moustache wrote
it down.

'Why do you think we volunteered?' I asked sarcastically, when the testimony was complete.

Monsieur le Ministre was evidently rather uncomfortable. He writhed a little in his chair, and tweaked his chin three or four times. The rosette and the moustache were exchanging animated phrases. At last Noyon, motioning for silence and speaking in an almost desperate tone, demanded:

'*Est-ce-que vous détestez les boches?*'

I had won my own case. The question was purely perfunctory. To walk out of the room a free man I had merely to say yes. My examiners were sure of my answer. The rosette was leaning forward and smiling encouragingly. The moustache was making little *oui*'s in the air with his pen. And Noyon had given up all hope of making me out a criminal. I might be rash, but I was innocent; the dupe of a superior and malign intelligence. I would probably be admonished to choose my friends more carefully next time, and that would be all. . . .

Deliberately, I framed the answer:

'*Non. J'aime beaucoup les français.*'

Agile as a weasel, Monsieur le Ministre was on top of me: 'It is impossible to love Frenchmen and not to hate Germans.'

I did not mind his triumph in the least. The discomfiture of the rosette merely amused me. The surprise of the moustache I found very pleasant.

Poor rosette! He kept murmuring desperately: 'Fond of his friend, quite right. Mistaken of course, too bad, meant well.'

With a supremely disagreeable expression on his immaculate face the victorious minister of security pressed his victim with regained assurance: 'But you are doubtless aware of the atrocities committed by the boches?'

'I have read about them,' I replied cheerfully.

'You do not believe?'

'*Ça se peut.*'

'And if they are so, which of course they are' (tone of profound conviction), 'you do not detest the Germans?'

'Oh, in that case, of course anyone must detest them,' I averred with perfect politeness.

And my case was lost, for ever lost. I breathed freely once more. All my nervousness was gone. The attempt of the three gentlemen sitting before me to endow my friend and myself with different fates had irrevocably failed.

At the conclusion of a short conference I was told by Monsieur:

'I am sorry for you, but due to your friend you will be detained a little while.'

I asked: 'Several weeks?'

'Possibly,' said Monsieur.

This concluded the trial.

Monsieur le Ministre conducted me into room number 1 again. 'Since I have taken your cigarettes and shall keep them for you, I will give you some tobacco. Do you prefer English or French?'

Because the French (*paquet bleu*) are stronger and because he expected me to say English, I said 'French.'

With a sorrowful expression Noyon went to a sort of book-case and took down a blue packet. I think I asked for matches, or else he had given back the few which he found on my person.

Noyon, t-d and the grand criminal (alias I) now descended solemnly to the F.I.A.T. The more and more mystified *conducteur* conveyed us a short distance to what was obviously a prison-yard. Monsieur le Ministre watched me descend my voluminous baggage.

This was carefully examined by Monsieur at the *bureau* of the prison. Monsieur made me turn everything topsy-

turvy and inside-out. Monsieur expressed great surprise
at a huge *coquille*: where did I get it?—I said a French
soldier gave it to me as a souvenir.—And several *têtes
d'obus*?—Also souvenirs, I assured him merrily. Did Monsieur suppose I was caught in the act of blowing up the
French Government, or what exactly?—But here are a
dozen sketch-books, what is in them?—Oh, Monsieur,
you flatter me: drawings.—Of fortifications?—Hardly;
of poilus, children, and other ruins.—Ummmm. (Monsieur examined the drawings and found that I had spoken
the truth.) Monsieur puts all these trifles into a small
bag, with which I had been furnished (in addition to the
huge duffle-bag) by the generous *Crois Rouge*. Labels
them (in French): 'Articles found in the baggage of
Cummings and deemed inutile to the case at hand.' This
leaves in the duffle-bag aforesaid: my fur coat, which I
brought from New York, my bed and blankets and bed-
roll, my civilian clothes, and about twenty-five pounds
of soiled linen. 'You may take the bed-roll and the folding
bed into your cell'—the rest of my *affaires* will remain in
safe keeping at the *bureau*.

'Come with me,' grimly croaked a lank turnkey-creature.

Bed-roll and bed in hand, I came along.

We had but a short distance to go; several steps in fact.
I remember we turned a corner and somehow got sight
of a sort of square near the prison. A military band was
executing itself to the stolid delight of some handfuls of
ragged *civiles*. My new captor paused a moment; perhaps
his patriotic soul was stirred. Then we traversed an alley
with locked doors on both sides, and stopped in front of
the last door on the right. A key opened it. The music
could still be distinctly heard.

The opened door showed a room, about sixteen feet short and four feet narrow, with a heap of straw in the further end. My spirits had been steadily recovering from the banality of their examination; and it was with a genuine and never-to-be-forgotten thrill that I remarked, as I crossed what might have been the threshold: '*Mais, on est bien ici.*'

A hideous crash nipped the last word. I had supposed the whole prison to have been utterly destroyed by earthquake, but it was only my door closing. . . .

II

EN ROUTE

I PUT the bed-roll down. I stood up.

I was myself.

An uncontrollable joy gutted me after three months of humiliation, of being bossed and herded and bullied and insulted. I was myself and my own master.

In this delirium of relief (hardly noticing what I did) I inspected the pile of straw, decided against it, set up my bed, disposed the roll on it, and began to examine my cell.

I have mentioned the length and breadth. The cell was ridiculously high; perhaps ten feet. The end with the door in it was peculiar. The door was not placed in the middle of this end, but at one side, allowing for a huge iron can waist-high which stood in the other corner. Over the door and across the end, a grating extended. A slit of sky was always visible.

Whistling joyously to myself, I took three steps which brought me to the door end. The door was massively made, all of iron or steel I should think: It delighted me. The can excited my curiosity. I looked over the edge of it. At the bottom reposefully lay a new human *t . . d.*

I have a sneaking mania for wood-cuts, particularly when used to illustrate the indispensable psychological crisis of some out-worn romance. There is in my possession at this minute a masterful depiction of a tall, bearded, horrified man who, clad in an anonymous rig of goat-

skins, with a fantastic umbrella clasped weakly in one
huge paw, bends to examine an indication of humanity
in the somewhat cubist wilderness whereof he had fancied
himself the owner . . .

It was then that I noticed the walls. Arm-high they
were covered with designs, mottoes, pictures. The drawing
had all been done in pencil. I resolved to ask for a pencil
at the first opportunity.

There had been Germans and Frenchmen imprisoned in
this cell. On the right wall, near the door-end, was a long
selection from Goethe, laboriously copied. Near the other
end of this wall a satiric landscape took place. The technique of this landscape frightened me. There were houses,
men, children. And there were trees. I began to wonder
what a tree looks like, and laughed copiously.

The back wall had a large and exquisite portrait of a
German officer.

The left wall was adorned with a yacht, flying a number
—13. 'My beloved boat' was inscribed in German underneath. Then came a bust of a German soldier, very ideal-
ized, full of unfear. After this, a masterful crudity—a
doughnut-bodied rider, sliding with fearful rapidity
down the acute back-bone of a totally transparent
sausage-shaped horse who was moving simultaneously in
five directions. The rider had a bored expression as he
supported the stiff reins in one fist. His further leg assisted
in his flight. He wore a German soldier's cap and was
smoking. I made up my mind to copy the horse and rider
at once, so soon that is as I should have obtained a pencil.

Last, I found a drawing surrounded by a scrolled motto.
The drawing was a potted plant with four blossoms. The
four blossoms were elaborately dead. Their death was
drawn with a fearful care. An obscure deliberation was

exposed in the depiction of their drooping petals. The pot tottered very crookedly on a sort of table, as near as I could see. All around ran a funereal scroll. I read: '*Mes dernières adieux à ma femme aimée, Gaby.*' A fierce hand, totally distinct from the former, wrote in proud letters above: '*Tombé pour désert. Six ans de prison—dégradation militaire.*'

It must have been five o'clock. Steps. A vast cluttering of the exterior of the door—by whom? Whang opens the door. Turnkey-creature extending a piece of *chocolat* with extreme and surly caution. I say '*Merci*' and seize *chocolat*. Klang shuts the door.

I am lying on my back, the twilight does mistily bluish miracles through the slit over the whang-klang. I can just see leaves, meaning tree.

Then from the left and way off, faintly, broke a smooth whistle, cool like a peeled willow-branch, and I found myself listening to an air from Pétrouchka, Pétrouchka, which we saw in Paris at the Châtelet, *mon ami et moi* . . .

The voice stopped in the middle—and I finished the air. This code continued for a half-hour.

It was dark.

I had laid a piece of my piece of *chocolat* on the window-sill. As I lay on my back, a little silhouette came along the sill and ate that piece of a piece, taking something like four minutes to do so. He then looked at me, I then smiled at him, and we parted, each happier than before.

My *cellule* was cool, and I fell asleep easily.

(Thinking of Paris.)

. . . Awakened by a conversation whose vibrations I clearly felt through the left wall:

Turnkey-creature: 'What?'

A mouldily mouldering molish voice, suggesting putrefying tracts and orifices, answers with a cob-webbish patience so far beyond despair as to be indescribable: *'La soupe.'*

'Well, the soup, I just gave it to you, Monsieur Savy.'

'Must have a little something else. My money is *chez le directeur.* Please take my money which is *chez le directeur* and give me anything else.'

'All right, the next time I come to see you to-day I'll bring you a salad, a nice salad, Monsieur.'

'Thank you, Monsieur,' the voice mouldered.

Klang!—and says the t-c to somebody else; while turning the lock of Monsieur Savy's door; taking pains to raise his voice so that Monsieur Savy will not miss a single word through the slit over Monsieur Savy's whang-klang:

'That old fool! Always asks for things. When supposest thou will he realize that he's never going to get anything?'

Grubbing at my door. Whang!

The faces stood in the doorway, looking me down. The expression of the faces identically turnkeyish, i.e., stupidly gloating, ponderously and imperturbably tickled. Look who's here, who let that in.

The right body collapsed sufficiently to deposit a bowl just inside.

I smiled and said: 'Good morning, sirs. The can stinks.'

They did not smile and said: 'Naturally.' I smiled and said: 'Please give me a pencil. I want to pass the time.' They did not smile and said: 'Directly.'

I smiled and said: 'I want some water, if you please.' They shut the door, saying 'Later.'

Klang and footsteps.

I contemplate the bowl, which contemplates me. A glaze of greenish grease seals the mystery of its contents.

I induce two fingers to penetrate the seal. They bring me up a flat sliver of *choux* and a large, hard, thoughtful, solemn, uncooked bean. To pour the water off (it is warmish and sticky) without committing a nuisance is to lift the cover off *Ça Pue*. I did.

Thus leaving beans and cabbage-slivers. Which I ate hurryingly, fearing a ventral misgiving.

I pass a lot of time cursing myself about the pencil, looking at my walls, my unique interior.

Suddenly I realize the indisputable grip of nature's humorous hand. One evidently stands on *Ça Pue* in such cases. Having finished, panting with stink, I stumble on the bed and consider my next move.

The straw will do. Ouch, but it's Dirty.—Several hours elapse ...

Stepsandfumble. Klang. Repetition of promise to Monsieur Savy, etc.

Turnkeyish and turnkeyish. Identical expression. One body collapses sufficiently to deposit a hunk of bread and a piece of water.

'Give your bowl.'

I gave it, smiled and said: 'Well, how about that pencil?' 'Pencil?' T-c looked at T-c.

They recited then the following word: 'To-morrow.' Klangandfootsteps.

So I took matches, burnt, and with just 60 of them wrote the first stanza of a ballad. To-morrow I will write the second. Day after to-morrow the third. Next day the refrain. After—oh, well.

My whistling of Pétrouchka brought no response this evening.

So I climbed on *Ça Pue*, whom I now regarded with

complete friendliness; the new moon was unclosing sticky wings in dusk, a far noise from near things.

I sang a song the 'dirty Frenchmen' taught us, *mon ami et moi.* The song says *Bon soir, Madame de la Lune.* . . . I did not sing out loud, simply because the moon was like a mademoiselle, and I did not want to offend the moon. My friends: the silhouette and *la lune,* not counting *Ça Pue,* whom I regarded almost as a part of me.

Then I lay down, and heard (but could not see) the silhouette eat something or somebody . . . and saw, but could not hear, the incense of *Ça Pue* mount gingerly upon the taking air of twilight.

The next day.—Promise to M. Savy. Whang. 'My pencil?'—'You don't need any pencil, you're going away.' —'When?'—'Directly.'—'How directly?'—'In an hour or two: your friend has already gone before. Get ready.'

Klangandsteps.

Every one very sore about me. *Je m'en fous pas mal,* however.

One hour I guess.

Steps. Sudden throwing of door open. Pause.

'Come out, American.'

As I came out, toting bed and bed-roll, I remarked: 'I'm sorry to leave you,' which made T-c furiously to masticate his unsignificant moustache.

Escorted to *bureau,* where I am turned over to a very fat gendarme.

'This is the American.' The v-f-g eyed me, and I read my sins in his pork-like orbs. 'Hurry, we have to walk,' he ventured sullenly and commandingly.

Himself stooped puffingly to pick up the segregated sack. And I placed my bed, bed-roll, blankets, and ample pelisse under one arm, my 150-odd lb. duffle-bag under the other; then I paused. Then I said, 'Where's my cane?'

The v-f-g hereat had a sort of fit, which perfectly became him.

I repeated gently: 'When I came to the *bureau* I had a cane.'

'*Je m'en fous de ta canne,*' burbled my new captor frothily, his pink evil eyes swelling with wrath.

'I'm staying,' I replied calmly, and sat down on a curb, in the midst of my ponderous trinkets.

A *foule* of gendarmes gathered. One didn't take a cane with one to prison (I was glad to know where I was bound, and thanked this communicative gentleman); or criminals weren't allowed canes; or where exactly did I think I was, in the Tuileries? asks a rube movie-cop personage.

'Very well, gentlemen,' I said. 'You will allow me to tell you something.' (I was beet-coloured.) '*En Amérique on ne fait pas comme ça.*'

This haughty inaccuracy produced an astonishing effect, namely, the prestidigitatorial vanishment of the v-f-g. The v-f-g's numerous confrères looked scared and twirled their whiskers.

I sat on the curb and began to fill a paper with something which I found in my pockets, certainly not tobacco.

Splutter-splutter-fizz-poop—the v-f-g is back, with my great oak-branch in his raised hand, slithering opprobria and mostly crying: 'Is that huge piece of wood what you call a cane? Is it? It is, is it? What? How? What the—' so on.

I beamed upon him and thanked him, and explained that a 'dirty Frenchman' had given it to me as a souvenir, and that I would now proceed.

Twisting the handle in the loop of my sack, and hoisting the vast parcel under my arm, I essayed twice to boost

it on my back. This to the accompaniment of Hurry
HurryHurryHurryHurryHurryHurry . . . The third
time I sweated and staggered to my feet, completely
accoutred.

Down the road. Into the *ville*. Curious looks from a
few pedestrians. A driver stops his wagon to watch the
spider and his outlandish fly. I chuckled to think how
long since I had washed and shaved. Then I nearly fell,
staggered on a few steps and set down the two loads.

Perhaps it was the fault of the strictly vegetarian diet.
At any rate I couldn't move a step farther with my
bundles. The sun sent the sweat along my nose in tickling
waves. My eyes were blind.

Hereupon I suggested that the v-f-g carry part of one
of my bundles with me, and received the answer: "I am
doing too much for you as it is. No gendarme is supposed
to carry a prisoner's baggage."

I said then: 'I'm too tired.'

He responded: 'You can leave here anything you don't
care to carry further; I'll take care of it.'

I looked at the gendarme. I looked several blocks
through him. My lip did something like a sneer. My hands
did something like fists.

At this crisis, along comes a little boy. May God bless all
males between seven and ten years of age in France.

The gendarme offered a suggestion, in these words:
'Have you any change about you?' He knew of course
that the sanitary official's first act had been to deprive me
of every last cent. The gendarme's eyes were fine. They
reminded me of . . . never mind. 'If you have change,'
said he, 'you might hire this kid to carry some of your
baggage.' Then he lit a pipe which was made in his own
image, and smiled fattily.

But herein the v-f-g had bust his milk-jug. There is a slit of a pocket made in the uniform of his criminal on the right side, and completely covered by the belt which his criminal always wears. His criminal had thus outwitted the gumshoe fraternity.

The gosse could scarcely balance my smaller parcel, but managed after three rests to get it to the station platform; here I tipped him something like two cents (all I had) which, with dollar-big eyes he took, and ran.

A strongly-built, groomed apache smelling of cologne and onions greeted my v-f-g with that affection which is peculiar to gendarmes. On me he stared cynically, then sneered frankly.

With a little tooty shriek, the funny train tottered in. My captors had taken pains to place themselves at the wrong end of the platform. Now they encouraged me to HurryHurryHurry.

I managed to get under the load and tottered the length of the train to a car especially reserved. There was one other criminal, a beautifully-smiling, shortish man, with a very fine blanket wrapped in a waterproof oilskin cover. We grinned at each other (the most cordial salutation, by the way, that I have ever exchanged with a human being) and sat down opposite one another—he, plus my baggage which he helped me lift in, occupying one seat; the gendarme-sandwich, of which I formed the *pièce de résistance*, the other.

The engine got under way after several feints; which pleased the Germans so that they sent seven scout planes right over the station, train, us *et tout*. All the French anticraft guns went off together for the sake of sympathy; the guardians of the peace squinted cautiously from their respective windows, and then began a debate

on the number of the enemy while their prisoners smiled
at each other appreciatively.

'*Il fait chaud*,' said this divine man, prisoner, criminal,
or what not, as he offered me a glass of wine in the form
of a huge tin cup overflowed from the *bidon*, in his
slightly unsteady and delicately made hand. He is a Belgian. Volunteered at beginning of war. *Permission* at
Paris, overstayed by one day. When he reported to his
officer, the latter announced that he was a deserter—'I
said to him, "It is funny. It is funny I should have come
back, of my own free will, to my company. I should have
thought that being a deserter I would have preferred to
remain in Paris." ' The wine was terribly cold, and I
thanked my divine host.

Never have I tasted such wine.

They had given me a chunk of war-bread in place of
blessing when I left Noyon. I bit into it with renewed
might. But the divine man across from me immediately
produced a sausage, half of which he laid simply upon my
knee. The halving was done with a large keen poilu's
couteau.

I have not tasted a sausage since.

The pigs on my either hand had by this time overcome
their respective inertias and were chomping cheek-mur-
dering chunks. They had quite a lay-out, a regular picnic-
lunch elaborate enough for kings or even presidents. The
v-f-g in particular annoyed me by uttering alternate
chompings and belchings. All the time he ate he kept his
eyes half-shut; and a mist overspread the sensual meadows
of his coarse face.

His two reddish eyes rolled devouringly toward the
blanket in its waterproof roll. After a huge gulp of wine
he said thickly (for his huge moustache was crusted with

saliva-tinted half-moistened shreds of food), 'You will have no use for that *machine, là-bas*. They are going to take everything away from you when you get there, you know. I could use it nicely. I have wanted such a piece of *caoutchouc* for a great while, in order to make me an *imperméable*. Do you see?" (Gulp. Swallow.)

Here I had an inspiration. I would save the blanket-cover by drawing these brigands' attention to myself. At the same time I would satisfy my inborn taste for the ridiculous. 'Have you a pencil?' I said. 'Because I am an artist in my own country, and will do your picture.'

He gave me a pencil. I don't remember where the paper came from. I posed him in a pig-like position, and the picture made him chew his moustache. The apache thought it very droll. I should do his picture too, at once. I did my best; though protesting that he was too beautiful for my pencil, which remark he countered by murmuring (as he screwed his moustache another notch), 'Never mind, you will try.' Oh, yes, I would try all right, all right. He objected, I recall, to the nose.

By this time the divine 'deserter' was writhing with joy. 'If you please, Monsieur,' he whispered radiantly, 'it would be too great an honour, but if you could—I should be overcome . . .'

Tears (for some strange reason) came into my eyes.

He handled his picture sacredly, criticized it with precision and care, finally bestowed it in his inner pocket. Then we drank. It happened that the train stopped and the apache was persuaded to go out and get his prisoner's *bidon* filled. Then we drank again.

He smiled as he told me he was getting ten years. Three years at solitary confinement was it, and seven working in a gang on the road? That would not be so bad. He wishes he was not married, had not a little child. 'The bachelors are lucky in this war'—he smiled.

Now the gendarmes began cleaning their beards, brushing their stomachs, spreading their legs, collecting their baggage. The reddish eyes, little and cruel, woke from the trance of digestion and settled with positive ferocity on their prey. 'You will have no use . . .'

Silently the sensitive, gentle hands of the divine prisoner undid the blanket-cover. Silently the long, tired, well-shaped arms passed it across to the brigand at my left side. With a grunt of satisfaction the brigand stuffed it in a large pouch, taking pains that it should not show. Silently the divine eyes said to mine: 'What can we do, we criminals?' And we smiled at each other for the last time, the eyes and my eyes.

A station. The apache descends. I follow with my numerous *affaires*. The divine man follows me—the v-f-g him.

The blanket-roll containing my large fur-coat got more and more unrolled; finally I could not possibly hold it.

It fell. To pick it up, I must take the sack off my back.

Then comes a voice, 'Allow me, if you please, monsieur' —and the sack has disappeared. Blindly and dumbly I stumbled on with the roll; and so at length we come into the yard of a little prison; and the divine man bowed under my great sack . . . I never thanked him. When I turned, they'd taken him away, and the sack stood accusingly at my feet.

Through the complete disorder of my numbed mind flicker jabbings of strange tongues. Some high boy's voice is appealing to me in Belgian, Italian, Polish, Spanish, and

—beautiful English. 'Hey, Jack, give me a cigarette, Jack...'

I lift my eyes. I am standing in a tiny oblong space. A sort of court. All around, two-story wooden barracks. Little crude staircases lead up to doors heavily chained and immensely padlocked. More like ladders than stairs. Curious hewn windows, smaller in proportion than the slits in a doll's house. Are these faces behind the slits? The doors bulge incessantly under the shock of bodies hurled against them from within. The whole dirty *nouveau* business about to crumble.

Glance one.

Glance two: directly before me. A wall with many bars fixed across one minute opening. At the opening a dozen, fifteen, grins. Upon the bars hands, scraggy and bluishly white. Through the bars stretchings of lean arms, incessant stretchings. The grins leap at the window, hands belonging to them catch hold, arms belonging to the hands stretch in my direction... an instant; then new grins leap from behind and knock off the first grins which go down with a fragile crashing like glass smashed: hands wither and break, arms streak out of sight, sucked inward.

In the huge potpourri of misery a central figure clung, shaken but undislodged. Clung like a monkey to central bars. Clung like an angel to a harp. Calling pleasantly in a high boyish voice: 'O Jack, give me a cigarette.'

A handsome face, dark, Latin smile, musical fingers strong.

I waded suddenly through a group of gendarmes (they stood around me watching with a disagreeable curiosity my reaction to this). Strode fiercely to the window.

Trillions of hands.

Quadrillions of itching fingers.

The angel-monkey received the package of cigarettes politely, disappearing with it into howling darkness. I heard his high boy's voice distributing cigarettes. Then he leapt into sight, poised gracefully against two central bars, saying, 'Thank you, Jack, good boy' ... 'Thanks, *merci, gracias* ...' a deafening din of gratitude reeked from within.

'Put your baggage in here,' quoth an angry voice. 'No, you will not take anything but one blanket in your cell, understand.' In French. Evidently the head of the house speaking. I obeyed. A corpulent soldier importantly led me to my cell. My cell is two doors away from the monkey-angel, on the same side. The high boy-voice, centralized in a torrent-like halo of stretchings, followed my back. The head himself unlocked a lock. I marched coldly in. The fat soldier locked and chained my door. Four feet went away. I felt in my pocket, finding four cigarettes. I am sorry I did not give these also to the monkey—to the angel. Lifted my eyes, and saw my own harp.

III

A PILGRIM'S PROGRESS

THROUGH the bars I looked into that little and dirty lane whereby I had entered; in which a sentinel, gun on shoulder, and with a huge revolver strapped at his hip, monotonously moved. On my right was an old wall overwhelmed with moss. A few growths stemmed from its crevices. Their leaves are of a refreshing colour. I felt singularly happy, and carefully throwing myself on the bare planks sang one after another all the French songs which I had picked up in my stay at the ambulance; sang La Madelon, sang AVec avEC DU, and *Les Galiots sont Lourds dans l'Sac*—concluding with an inspired rendering of *La Marseillaise,* at which the guard (who had several times stopped his round in what I choose to interpret as astonishment) grounded arms and swore appreciatively. Various officials of the jail passed by me and my lusty songs; I cared no whit. Two or three conferred, pointing in my direction, and I sang a little louder for the benefit of their perplexity. Finally out of voice I stopped.

It was twilight.

As I lay on my back luxuriously I saw through the bars of my twice padlocked door a boy and a girl about ten years old. I saw them climb on the wall and play together, obliviously and exquisitely, in the darkening air. I watched them for many minutes; till the last moment of light failed; till they and the wall itself dissolved in a common mystery, leaving only the bored silhouette of

the soldier moving imperceptibly and wearily against a
still more gloomy piece of autumn sky.

At last I knew that I was very thirsty; and leaping up
began to clamour at my bars. '*Quelque chose à boire, s'il
vous plaît.*' After a long debate with the sergeant of
guards, who said very angrily: 'Give it to him,' a guard
took my request and disappeared from view, returning
with a more heavily armed guard and a tin cup full of
water. One of these gentry watched the water and me,
while the other wrestled with the padlock. The door being
minutely opened, one guard and the water painfully entered. The other guard remained at the door, gun in readiness. The water was set down, and the enterer assumed a
perpendicular position which I thought merited recognition; accordingly I said '*Merci*' politely, without getting
up from the planks. Immediately he began to deliver a
sharp lecture on the probability of my using the tin cup
to saw my way out; and commended haste in no doubtful
terms. I smiled, asked pardon for my inherent stupidity
(which speech seemed to anger him) and guzzled the so-
called water without looking at it, having learned something from Noyon. With a long and dangerous look at
their prisoner, the gentlemen of the guard withdrew,
using inconceivable caution in the re-locking of the door.

I laughed and fell asleep.

After (as I judged) four minutes of slumber, I was
awakened by at least six men standing over me. The darkness was intense, it was extraordinarily cold. I glared at
them and tried to understand what new crime I had
committed. One of the six was repeating: 'Get up, you
are going away. *Quatre heures.*' After several attempts I
got up. They formed a circle around me; and together
we marched a few steps to a sort of storeroom, where

my great sack, small sack, and overcoat were handed to me. A rather agreeably voiced guard then handed me a half-cake of *chocolat*, saying (but with a tolerable grimness): '*Vous en aurez besoin, croyez-moi.*' I found my stick, at which 'piece of furniture' they amused themselves a little until I showed its use, by catching the ring at the mouth of my sack in the curved end of the stick and swinging the whole business unaided on my back. Two new guards—or rather gendarmes—were now officially put in charge of my person; and the three of us passed down the lane, much to the interest of the sentinel, to whom I bade a vivid and unreturned adieu. I can see him perfectly as he stares stupidly at us, a queer shape in the gloom, before turning on his heel.

Toward the very station whereat some hours since I had disembarked with the Belgian deserter and my former escorts, we moved. I was stiff with cold and only half awake, but peculiarly thrilled. The gendarmes on either side moved grimly, without speaking; or returning monosyllables to my few questions. Yes, we were to take the train. I was going somewhere, then? '*B'en sûr.*'—'Where?' —'You will know in time.'

After a few minutes we reached the station, which I failed to recognize. The yellow flares of lamps, huge and formless in the night mist, some figures moving to and fro on a little platform, a rustle of conversation: everything seemed ridiculously suppressed, beautifully abnormal, deliciously insane. Every figure was wrapped with its individual ghostliness; a number of ghosts each out on his own promenade, yet each for some reason selecting this unearthly patch of the world, this putrescent and uneasy gloom. Even my guards talked in whispers. 'Watch him, I'll see about the train.' So one went off into

the mist. I leaned dizzily against the wall nearest me
(having plumped down my baggage) and stared into the
darkness at my elbow, filled with talking shadows. I recognized *officiers anglais* wandering helplessly up and down,
supported with their sticks; French lieutenants talking to
each other, here and there; the extraordinary sense-bereft
station-master at a distance looking like a cross between a
jumping-jack and a goblin; knots of *permissionnaires*
cursing wearily or joking hopelessly with one another or
stalking back and forth with imprecatory gesticulations.
'*C'est d'la blague. Sais-tu, il n'y a plus de trains?*'—'*Le
conducteur est mort, j'connais sa sœur.*'—'*J'suis foutu,
mon vieux.*'—'*Nous sommes tous perdus, dis-donc.*'—
'*Quelle heure?*'—'*Mon cher, il n'y a plus d'heures, le
gouvernement français les défend.*' Suddenly burst out of
the loquacious opacity of dozen handfuls of *Algériens,*
their feet swaggering with fatigue, their eyes burning apparently by themselves—faceless in the equally black
mist. By threes and fives they assaulted the goblin who
wailed and shook his withered fist in their faces. There
was no train. It had been taken away by the French Government. 'How do I know how the poilus can get back
to their regiments on time? Of course you'll all of you be
deserters, but is it my fault?' (I thought of my friend, the
Belgian, at this moment lying in a pen at the prison which
I had just quitted by some miracle) . . . One of these fine
people from uncivilized, ignorant, unwarlike Algeria was
drunk and knew it, as did two of his very fine friends who
announced that as there was no train he should have a
good sleep at a farm-house hard by, which farm-house one
of them claimed to espy through the impenetrable night.
The drunk was accordingly escorted into the dark, his
friends' abrupt steps correcting his own large slovenly

procedure out of earshot. . . . Some of the Black People sat down near me, and smoked. Their enormous faces, wads of vital darkness, swooped with fatigue. Their vast gentle hands lay noisily about their knees.

The departed gendarme returned, with a bump, out of the mist. The train for Paris would arrive *de suite*. We were just in time, our movements had so far been very creditable. All was well. It was cold, eh?

Then with the ghastly miniature roar of an insane toy the train for Paris came fumbling cautiously into the station. . . .

We boarded it, due caution being taken that I should not escape. As a matter of fact I held up the would-be passengers for nearly a minute by my unaided attempts to boost my uncouth baggage aboard. Then my captors and I blundered heavily into a compartment in which an Englishman and two Frenchwomen were seated. My gendarmes established themselves on either side of the door, a process which woke up the Anglo-Saxon and caused a brief gap in the low talk of the women. Jolt—we were off.

I find myself with a *française* on my left and an *anglais* on my right. The latter has already uncomprehendingly subsided into sleep. The former (a woman of about thirty) is talking pleasantly to her friend, whom I face. She must have been very pretty before she put on the black. Her friend is also a *veuve*. How pleasantly they talk, of *la guerre*, of Paris, of the bad service; talk in agreeably modulated voices, leaning a little forward to each other, not wishing to disturb the dolt at my right. The train tears slowly on. Both the gendarmes are asleep, one with his hand automatically grasping the handle of the door. Lest I escape. I try all sorts of positions, for I find myself very tired. The best is to put my cane between my legs and rest my chin on it; but even that is uncomfortable, for the Englishman has writhed all over me by this time and is snoring creditably. I look him over; an Etonian, as I guess. Certain well-bred-well-fedness. Except for the position—well, *c'est la guerre*. The women are speaking softly. 'And do you know, my dear, that they had raids again in Paris? My sister wrote me.'—'One has excitement always in a great city, my dear.'—

Bump, slowing down. BUMP-BUMP.

It is light outside. One sees the world. There is a world still, the *gouvernement français* has not taken it away, and the air must be beautifully cool. In the compartment it is hot. The gendarmes smell worst. I know how I smell. What polite women.

Enfin, nous voilà. My guards awoke and yawned pretentiously. Lest I should think they had dozed off. It is Paris.

Some *permissionnaires* cried 'Paris.' The woman across from me said 'Paris, Paris.' A great shout came up from every insane drowsy brain that had travelled with us—a fierce and beautiful cry, which went the length of the train. . . . Paris where one forgets, Paris which is Pleasure, Paris in whom our souls live, Paris the beautiful, Paris *enfin*.

The Englishman woke up and said heavily to me: 'I say, where are we?'

'Paris,' I answered, walking carefully on his feet as I made my baggage-laden way out of the compartment. It was Paris.

My guards hurried me through the station. One of them (I saw for the first time) was older than the other, and rather handsome with his Van Dyck blackness of curly beard. He said that it was too early for the *métro*, it was closed. We should take a car. It would bring us to the other *Gare* from which our next train left. We should hurry. We emerged from the station and its crowds of crazy men. We boarded a car marked something. The conductress, a strong, pink-cheeked, rather beautiful girl in black, pulled my baggage in for me with a gesture which filled all of me with joy. I thanked her, and she smiled at me. The car moved along through the morning.

We descended from it. We started off on foot. The car was not the right car. We would have to walk to the station. I was faint and almost dead from weariness and I stopped when my overcoat had fallen from my benumbed arm for the second time: 'How far is it?' The older gendarme returned briefly, '*Vingt minutes.*' I said to him: 'Will you help me carry these things?' He thought, and told the younger to carry my small sack filled with papers. The latter grunted, '*C'est défendu.*' We went a little farther, and I broke down again. I stopped dead, and said: 'I can't go any farther.' It was obvious to my escorts that I couldn't, so I didn't trouble to elucidate. Moreover, I was past elucidation.

The older stroked his beard. 'Well,' he said, 'would you care to take a *fiacre?*' I merely looked at him. 'If you wish to call a *fiacre*, I will take out of your money, which I have here and which I must not give to you, the necessary sum, and make a note of it, subtracting from the original amount a sufficiency for our fare to the *Gare*. In that case we will not walk to the *Gare*, we will in fact ride.'

'*S'il vous plaît*,' was all I found to reply to this eloquence.

Several *fiacres libres* had gone by during the peroration of the law, and no more seemed to offer themselves. After some minutes, however, one appeared and was duly hailed.

Nervously (he was shy in the big city) the older asked if
the *cocher* knew where the *Gare* was. '*Laquelle?*' demanded the *cocher* angrily. And when he was told—
'*Naturellement, je connais, pourquoi pas?*' we got in; I
being directed to sit in the middle, and my two bags and
fur coat piled on top of us all.

So we drove through the streets in the freshness of the
full morning, the streets full of a few divine people who
stared at me and nudged one another, the streets of Paris
... the drowsy ways wakening at the horse's hoofs, the
people lifting their faces to stare.

We arrived at the *Gare*, and I recognized it vaguely.
Was it D'Orleans? We dismounted, and the tremendous
transaction of the fare was apparently very creditably
accomplished by the older. The *cocher* gave me a look and
remarked whatever it is Paris *cochers* remark to Paris
fiacre-horses, pulling dully at the reins. We entered the
station and I collapsed comfortably on a bench; the
younger, seating himself with enormous pomposity at
my side, adjusted his tunic with a purely feminine gesture
expressive at once of pride and nervousness. Gradually
my vision gained in focus. The station has a good many
people in it. The number increases momently. A great
many are girls. I am in a new world—a world of chic
femininity. My eyes devour the inimitable details of
costume, the inexpressible nuances of pose, the indescribable *démarche* of the midinette. They hold themselves
differently. They have even a little bold colour here and
there on skirt or blouse or hat. They are not talking about
la guerre. Incredible. They appear very beautiful, these
Parisiennes.

And simultaneously with my appreciation of the crisp
persons about me comes the hitherto unacknowledged

appreciation of my uncouthness. My chin tells my hand
of a good quarter inch of beard, every hair of it stiff with
dirt. I can feel the dirt-pools under my eyes. My hands are
rough with dirt. My uniform is smeared and creased in a
hundred thousand directions. My puttees and shoes are
prehistoric in appearance. . . .

My first request was permission to visit the *vespasienne*.
The younger didn't wish to assume any unnecessary re-
sponsibilities; I should wait till the older returned. There
he was now. I might ask him. The older benignly granted
my petition, nodding significantly to his fellow-guard, by
whom I was accordingly escorted to my destination and
subsequently back to my bench. When we got back the
gendarmes held a consultation of terrific importance; in
substance, the train which should be leaving at that moment (six something) did not run to-day. We should
therefore wait for the next train, which leaves at twelve-
something-else. Then the older surveyed me, and said
almost kindly: 'How would you like a cup of coffee?'—
'Much,' I replied sincerely enough.—'Come with me,' he
commanded, resuming instantly his official manner. 'And
you' (to the younger) 'watch his baggage.'

Of all the very beautiful women whom I had seen the
most very beautiful was the large and circular lady who
sold a cup of perfectly hot and genuine coffee for *deux
sous*, just on the brink of the station, chatting cheerfully
with her many customers. Of all the drinks I ever drank,
hers was the most sacredly delicious. She wore, I remember, a tight black dress in which enormous and benignant
breasts bulged and sank continuously. I lingered over my
tiny cup, watching her swift big hands, her round nodding face, her large sudden smile. I drank two coffees,
and insisted that my money should pay for our drinks.

Of all the treating which I shall ever do, the treating of
my captor will stand unique in pleasure. Even he half
appreciated the sense of humour involved; though his
dignity did not permit a visible acknowledgment thereof.

Madame la vendeuse de café, I shall remember you for
more than a little while.

Having thus consummated breakfast, my guardian
suggested a walk. Agreed. I felt I had the strength of ten
because the coffee was pure. Moreover, it would be a nov-
elty, *me promener sans* 150-odd pounds of baggage. We
set out.

As we walked easily and leisurely the by this time well-
peopled *rues* of the vicinity, my guard indulged himself in
pleasant conversation. Did I know Paris much? He knew
it all. But he had not been in Paris for several (eight was
it?) years. It was a fine place, a large city to be sure. But
always changing. I had spent a month in Paris while waiting for my uniform and my assignment to a *section sanitaire?* And my friend was with me? H-mmm-mm.

A perfectly typical runt of a Paris bull eyed us. The
older saluted him with infinite respect, the respect of a
shabby rube deacon for a well-dressed burglar. They
exchanged a few well-chosen words, in French of course.
'What ya got there?'—'An American.'—'What's wrong
with him?'—'H-mmm'—mysterious shrug of the shoulders followed by a whisper in the ear of the city thug.
The latter contented himself with 'Ha-aaa'—plus a look
at me which was meant to wipe me off the earth's face (I
pretended to be studying the morning meanwhile). Then
we moved on, followed by ferocious stares from the Paris
bull. Evidently I was getting to be more of a criminal
every minute; I should probably be shot to-morrow, not
(as I had assumed erroneously) the day after. I drank the

morning with renewed vigour, thanking heaven for the coffee, Paris; and feeling complete confidence in myself. I should make a great speech (in *Midi* French). I should say to the firing squad: 'Gentlemen, *c'est d'la blague, tu sais? Moi, je connais la sœur du conducteur.*' ... They would ask me when I preferred to die. I should reply, 'Pardon me, you wish to ask me when I prefer to become immortal?' I should answer: 'What matter? *Ça m'est égal, parce qu'il n'y a plus d'heures—le gouvernement français les défend.*'

My laughter surprised the older considerably. He would have been more astonished had I yielded to the well-nigh irrepressible inclination, which at the moment suffused me, to clap him heartily upon the back.

Everything was *blague*. The *cocher*, the *café*, the police, the morning, and least and last the excellent French government.

We had walked for a half-hour or more. My guide and protector now inquired of an *ouvrier* the location of the *boucheries*. 'There is one right in front of you,' he was told. Sure enough, not a block away. I laughed again. It was eight years all right.

The older bought a great many things in the next five minutes: *saucisse, fromage, pain, chocolat, pinard rouge.* A bourgeoise with an unagreeable face and suspicion of me written in headlines all over her mouth served us with quick hard laconicisms of movement. I hated her and consequently refused my captor's advice to buy a little of everything (on the ground that it would be a long time till the next meal), contenting myself with a cake of chocolate—rather bad chocolate, but nothing to what I was due to eat during the next three months. Then we retraced our steps, arriving at the station after several

mistakes and inquiries, to find the younger faithfully
keeping guard over my two *sacs* and overcoat.

The older and I sat down, and the younger took his
turn at promenading. I got up to buy a Fantasio at the
stand ten steps away, and the older jumped up and escorted
me to and from it. I think I asked him what he would
read? and he said 'Nothing.' Maybe I bought him a journal. So we waited, eyed by every one in the *Gare*, laughed
at by the officers and their *marraines*, pointed at by sinewy
dames and decrepit *bonshommes*—the centre of amusement for the whole station. In spite of my reading I felt
distinctly uncomfortable. Would it never be Twelve?
Here comes the younger, neat as a pin, looking fairly
sterilized. He sits down on my left. Watches are osten-
tatiously consulted. It is time. *En avant*. I sling myself
under my bags.

'Where are we going now?' I asked the older. Curling
the tips of his moustachios, he replied 'Mah-say.'

Marseilles! I was happy once more. I had always wanted
to go to that great port of the Mediterranean, where one
has new colours and strange customs, and where the
people sing when they talk. But how extraordinary to
have come to Paris—and what a trip lay before us. I was
much muddled about the whole thing. Probably I was
to be deported. But why from Marseilles? Where was
Marseilles, anyway? I was probably all wrong about its
location. Who cared, after all? At least we were leaving
the pointings and the sneers and the half-suppressed
titters. . . .

Two fat and respectable *bonshommes*, the two gendarmes, and I, made up one compartment. The former
talked an animated stream, the guards and I were on the
whole silent. I watched the liquidating landscape and

dozed happily. The gendarmes dozed, one at each door. The train rushed lazily across the earth, between farmhouses, into fields, along woods . . . the sunlight smacked my eye and cuffed my sleepy mind with colour.

I was awakened by a noise of eating. My protectors, knife in hand, were consuming their meat and bread, occasionally tilting their *bidons* on high and absorbing the thin streams which spurted therefrom. I tried a little *chocolat*. The *bonshommes* were already busy with their repast. The older gendarme watched me chewing away at the *chocolat*, then commanded, 'Take some bread.' This astonished me, I confess, beyond anything which had heretofore occurred. I gazed mutely at him, wondering whether the *gouvernement français* had made away with his wits. He had relaxed amazingly: his cap lay beside him, his tunic was unbuttoned, he slouched in a completely undisciplined posture—his face seemed to have been changed for a peasant's, it was almost open in expression and almost completely at ease. I seized the offered hunk and chewed vigorously on it. Bread was bread. The older appeared pleased with my appetite; his face softened, still more, as he remarked: 'Bread without wine doesn't taste good,' and proffered his *bidon*. I drank as much as I dared and thanked him: '*Ça va mieux.*' The *pinard* went straight to my brain, I felt my mind cuddled by a pleasant warmth, my thoughts became invested with a great contentment. The train stopped; and the younger sprang out carrying the empty *bidons* of himself and his confrère. When they and he returned, I enjoyed another *coup*. From that moment till we reached our destination at about eight o'clock the older and I got on extraordinarily well. When the gentlemen descended at their station he waxed almost familiar. I was in excellent spirits; rather drunk; extremely tired. Now that the two guardians and myself were alone in the compartment, the curiosity which had hitherto been stifled by etiquette and pride of capture came rapidly to light. Why was I here, anyway? I seemed well enough to them.—Because my friend had written some letters, I told them.—But I had done nothing myself?—I explained that *nous étions toujours ensemble, mon ami et moi;* that was the only reason which I knew of.—It was very funny to see how this explanation improved matters. The older in particular was immensely relieved.—I would without doubt, he said, be set free immediately upon my arrival. The French Government didn't keep people like me in prison.—They fired some questions about America at me, to which I imaginatively replied. I think I told the younger that the average height of buildings in America was nine hundred metres. He stared and shook his head doubtfully, but I convinced him in the end. Then in my turn I asked questions, the first being: Where was my friend?—It seems that my friend had left Gré (or whatever it was) the morning of the day I had entered it.—Did they know where my friend was going?—They couldn't say. They had been told that he was very dangerous.—So we talked on and on: How long had I studied French? I spoke very well. Was it hard to learn English?—

Yet when I climbed out to relieve myself by the roadside one of them was at my heels.

Finally watches were consulted, tunics buttoned, hats donned. I was told in a gruff voice to prepare myself; that we were approaching the end of our journey. Looking at the erstwhile participants in conversation, I scarcely knew them. They had put on with their caps a positive ferocity of bearing. I began to think that I had dreamed the incidents of the preceding hours.

We descended at a minute, dirty station which possessed the air of having been dropped by mistake from the bung of the *gouvernement français*. The older sought out the station-master, who having nothing to do was taking a siesta in a miniature waiting-room. The general countenance of the place was exceedingly depressing; but I attempted to keep up my spirits with the reflection that after all this was but a junction, and that from here we were to take a train for Marseilles herself. The name of the station, Briouse, I found somewhat dreary. And now the older returned with the news that our train wasn't running to-day, and that the next train didn't arrive till early morning, and should we walk? I could check my great *sac* and overcoat. The small *sac* I should carry along —it was only a step, after all.

With a glance at the desolation of Briouse, I agreed to the stroll. It was a fine night for a little promenade; not too cool, and with a promise of a moon stuck into the sky. The *sac* and coat were accordingly checked by the older; the station-master glanced at me and haughtily grunted (having learned that I was an American); and my protectors and I set out.

I insisted that we stop at the first café and have some wine on me. To this my escorts agreed, making me go ten paces ahead of them, and waiting until I was through before stepping up to the bar—not from politeness, to be sure, but because (as I soon gathered) gendarmes were not any too popular in this part of the world, and the sight of two gendarmes with a prisoner might inspire the habitués to attempt a rescue. Furthermore, on leaving the café (a desolate place if I ever saw one, with a fearful *pa-*

tronne) I was instructed sharply to keep close to them but on no account to place myself between them, there being sundry villagers to be encountered before we struck the high road to Marseilles. Thanks to their forethought and my obedience the rescue did not take place, nor did our party excite even the curiosity of the scarce and soggy inhabitants of the unlovely town of Briouse.

The high road won, all of us relaxed considerably. The *sac* full of suspicious letters which I bore on my shoulder was not so light as I had thought, but the kick of the Briouse *pinard* thrust me forward at a good clip. The road was absolutely deserted; the night hung loosely around it, here and there tattered by attempting moonbeams. I was somewhat sorry to find the way hilly, and in places bad underfoot; yet the unknown adventure lying before me, and the delicious silence of the night (in which our words rattled queerly like tin soldiers in a plush-lined box) boosted me into a condition of mysterious happiness. We talked, the older and I, of strange subjects. As I suspected, he had been not always a gendarme. He had seen service among the Arabs. He had always liked languages and had picked up Arabian with great ease—of this he was very proud. For instance—the Arabian way of saying 'Give me to eat' was this; when you wanted wine you said so and so; 'Nice day' was something else. He thought I could pick it up inasmuch as I had done so creditably with French. He was absolutely certain that English was much easier to learn than French, and would not be moved. Now what was the American language like? I explained that it was a sort of *Argot*-English. When I gave him some phrases he was astonished—'It sounds like English!' he cried, and retailed his stock of English phrases for my approval. I tried hard to get his intonation of the Arabian, and he helped me on the difficult sounds. America must be a strange place, he thought. . . .

After two hours' walking, he called a halt, bidding us rest. We all lay flat on the grass by the roadside. The moon was still battling with clouds. The darkness of the fields on either side was total. I crawled on hands and knees to the sound of silver-trickling water and found a little spring-fed stream. Prone, weight on elbows, I drank heavily of its perfect blackness. It was icy, talkative, minutely alive.

The older presently gave a perfunctory 'alors'; we got up; I hoisted my suspicious utterances upon my shoulder, which recognized the renewal of hostilities with a neuralgic throb. I banged forward with bigger and bigger feet. A bird, scared, swooped almost into my face. Occasionally some night-noise pricked a futile minute hole in the enormous curtain of soggy darkness. Uphill now. Every muscle thoroughly aching, head spinning, I half-straightened my no longer obedient body; and jumped: face to face with a little wooden man hanging all by itself in a grove of low trees.

The wooden body clumsy with pain burst into fragile legs with absurdly large feet and funny writhing toes; its little stiff arms made abrupt, cruel, equal angles with the road. About its stunted loins clung a ponderous and jocular fragment of drapery. On one terribly brittle shoulder the droll lump of its neckless head ridiculously lived. There was in this complete silent doll a gruesome truth of instinct, a success of uncanny poignancy, an unearthly ferocity of rectangular emotion.

For perhaps a minute the almost obliterated face and mine eyed one another in the silence of intolerable autumn.

Who was this wooden man? Like a sharp, black, mechanical cry in the spongy organism of gloom stood the coarse and sudden sculpture of his torment; the big mouth of night carefully spurted the angular actual language of his martyred body. I had seen him before in the dream of some mediæval saint with a thief sagging at either side, surrounded with crisp angels. To-night he was alone; save for myself, and the moon's minute flower pushing between slabs of fractured cloud.

I was wrong, the moon and I and he were not alone. . . . A glance up the road gave me two silhouettes at pause. The gendarmes were waiting. I must hurry to catch up or incur suspicion by my sloth. I hastened forward, with a last look over my shoulder . . . the wooden man was watching us.

When I came abreast of them, expecting abuse, I was surprised by the older's saying quietly, 'We haven't far to go,' and plunging forward imperturbably into the night.

Nor had we gone a half-hour before several dark squat forms confronted us: houses. I decided that I did not like houses—particularly as now my guardians' manner abruptly changed; once more tunics were buttoned, holsters adjusted, and myself directed to walk between and keep always up with the others. Now the road became thoroughly afflicted with houses, houses not however so large and lively as I had expected from my dreams of Marseilles. Indeed we seemed to be entering an extremely small and rather disagreeable town. I ventured to ask what its name was. 'Mah-say' was the response. By this I was fairly puzzled. However, the street led us to a square, and I saw the towers of a church sitting in the sky; between them the round, yellow, big moon looked im-

mensely and peacefully conscious . . . no one was stirring
in the little streets, all the houses were keeping the moon's
secret.

We walked on.

I was too tired to think. I merely felt the town as a
unique unreality. What was it? I knew—the moon's picture of a town. These streets with their houses did not
exist, they were but a ludicrous projection of the moon's
sumptuous personality. This was a city of Pretend, created
by the hypnotism of moonlight.—Yet when I examined
the moon she too seemed but a painting of a moon, and
the sky in which she lived a fragile echo of colour. If I
blew hard the whole shy mechanism would collapse gently
with a neat, soundless crash. I must not, or lose all.

We turned a corner, then another. My guides conferred
concerning the location of something, I couldn't make
out what. Then the older nodded in the direction of a
long, dull, dirty mass not a hundred yards away, which
(as near as I could see) served either as a church or a
tomb. Toward this we turned. All too soon I made out
its entirely dismal exterior. Grey, long, stone walls, surrounded on the street side by a fence of ample proportions and uniformly dull colour. Now I perceived that
we made toward a gate, singularly narrow and forbid-
ding, in the grey, long wall. No living soul appeared to
inhabit this desolation.

The older rang at the gate. A gendarme with a revolver
answered his ring; and presently he was admitted, leaving
the younger and myself to wait. And now I began to realize that this was the gendarmerie of the town, into which
for safe-keeping I was presently to be inducted for the
night. My heart sank, I confess, at the thought of sleeping in the company of that species of humanity which I

had come to detest beyond anything in hell or on earth. Meanwhile the doorman had returned with the older, and I was bidden roughly enough to pick up my baggage and march. I followed my guides down a corridor, up a stair-case, and into a dark, small room where a candle was burning. Dazzled by the light and dizzied by the fatigue of my ten- or twelve-mile stroll, I let my baggage go; and leaned against a convenient wall, trying to determine who was now my tormentor.

Facing me at a table stood a man of about my own height, and as I should judge about forty years old. His face was seedy, sallow and long. He had bushy, semi-circular eyebrows which drooped so much as to reduce his eyes to mere blinking slits. His cheeks were so fur-rowed that they leaned inward. He had no nose, properly speaking, but a large beak of preposterous widthlessness, which gave his whole face the expression of falling gravely downstairs, and quite obliterated the unimportant chin. His mouth was made of two long uncertain lips which twitched nervously. His cropped black hair was rumpled, his blouse, from which hung a *croix de guerre*, unbut-toned; and his unputteed shanks culminated in bed-slippers. In physique he reminded me a little of Ichabod Crane. His neck was exactly like a hen's: I felt sure that when he drank he must tilt his head back as hens do in order that the liquid may run down their throats. But his method of keeping himself upright, together with certain spasmodic contractions of his fingers and the nervous 'uh-ah, uh-ah,' which punctuated his insecure phrases like uncertain commas, combined to offer the suggestion of a rooster; a rather moth-eaten rooster, which took itself tremendously seriously and was showing-off to an imaginary group of admiring hens situated somewhere in the background of his consciousness.

'*Vous êtes uh-ah l'am-é-ri-cain?*'

'*Je suis américain,*' I admitted.

'*Eh-bi-en uh-ah uh-ah*—We were expecting you.' He surveyed me with great interest.

Behind this seedy and restless personage I noted his absolute likeness, adorning one of the walls. The rooster was faithfully depicted *à la* Rembrandt at half-length in the stirring guise of a fencer, foil in hand, and wearing enormous gloves. The execution of this masterpiece left something to be desired; but the whole betokened a certain spirit and verve, on the part of the sitter, which I found difficulty in attributing to the being before me.

'*Vous êtes uh-ah KEW-MANGZ?*'

'What?' I said, completely baffled by this extraordinary dissyllable.

'*Comprenez vous fran-çais?*'

'*Un peu.*'

'*Bon. Alors, vous vous ap-pel-lez KEW-MANGZ, n'est-ce-pas? Edouard KEW-MANGZ.*'

'Oh,' I said, relieved, 'yes.' It was really amazing, the way he writhed around the G.

'*Comment ça se prononce en anglais?*'

I told him.

He replied benevolently, somewhat troubled, 'uh-ah uh-ah uh-ah—*Pour-quoi êtes vous ici, KEW-MANGS?*'

At this question I was for one moment angrier than I had ever before been in all my life. Then I realized the absurdity of the situation, and laughed.—'*Sais pas.*'

The questionnaire continued:

'You were in the Red Cross?'—'Surely, in the Norton Harjes Ambulance, *Section Sanitaire Vingt-et-Un.*'—

'You had a friend there?'—'Naturally.'—'*Il a écrit, votre ami, des bê-tises, n'est-ce-pas?*'—'So they told me. *N'en sais rien.*'—'What sort of a person was your friend?'—'He was a magnificent person, always *très gentil* with me.' —(With a queer pucker the fencer remarked) 'Your friend got you into a lot of trouble though.'—(To which I replied with a broad grin) '*N'importe,* we are *cama-rades.*'

A stream of puzzled uh-ahs followed this reply. The fencer or rooster or whatever he might be finally, picking up the lamp and the lock, said: '*Alors, viens avec moi, KEW-MANGS.*' I started to pick up the *sac,* but he told me it would be kept in the office (we being in the office). I said I had checked a large *sac* and my fur overcoat at Briouse, and he assured me they would be sent on by train. He now dismissed the gendarmes, who had been listening curiously to the examination. As I was conducted from the *bureau* I asked him point-blank: 'How long am I to stay here?'—to which he answered, '*Oh, peut-être un jour, deux jours, je ne sais pas.*'

Two days in a gendarmerie would be enough, I thought. We marched out.

Behind me the bed-slippered rooster uh-ahingly shuf-fled. In front of me clumsily gambolled the huge imita-tion of myself. It descended the terribly worn stairs. It turned to the right and disappeared. . . .

We were standing in a chapel.

The shrinking light which my guide held had become suddenly minute; it was beating, senseless and futile, with shrill fists upon a thick enormous moisture of gloom. To the left and right through lean oblongs of stained glass burst dirty burglars of moonlight. The clammy, stupid distance uttered dimly an uncanny conflict—the mutter-

less tumbling of brutish shadows. A crowding ooze bat-
tled with my lungs. My nostrils fought against the
monstrous atmospheric slime. which hugged a sweet unpleasant odour. Staring ahead, I gradually disinterred the
pale carrion of the darkness—an altar, guarded with the
ugliness of unlit candles, on which stood inexorably the
efficient implements for eating God.

I was to be confessed, then, of my guilty conscience,
before retiring? It boded well for the morrow.

. . . the measured accents of the fencer said: *'Prenez
votre paillasse.'* I turned. He was bending over a formless
mass in one corner of the room. The mass stretched half-
way to the ceiling. It was made of mattress-shapes. I
pulled at one—burlap, stuffed with prickly straw. I got it
on my shoulder. *'Alors.'* He lighted me to the doorway
by which we had entered. (I was somewhat pleased to
leave the place.)

Back, down a corridor, up more stairs; and we are confronted by a small scarred pair of doors from which hung
two of the largest padlocks I had ever seen. Being unable
to go further, I stopped; he produced a huge ring of keys.
Fumbled with the locks. No sound of life: the keys rattled in the locks with surprising loudness; the latter with
an evil grace yielded—the two little miserable doors swung
open.

Into the square blackness I staggered with my *paillasse*.
There was no way of judging the size of the dark room
which uttered no sound. In front of me was a pillar. 'Put
it down by that post, and sleep there for to-night, in the
morning *nous allons voir*,' directed the fencer. 'You won't
need a blanket,' he added; and the doors clanged, the
light and fencer disappeared.

I needed no second invitation to sleep. Fully dressed,

I fell on my *paillasse* with a weariness which I never felt before or since. But I did not close my eyes: for all about me there rose a sea of most extraordinary sound . . . the hitherto empty and minute room became suddenly enormous: weird cries, oaths, laughter, pulling it sideways and backward, extending it to inconceivable depth and width, telescoping it to frightful nearness. From all directions, by at least thirty voices in eleven languages (I counted as I lay Dutch, Belgian, Spanish, Turkish, Arabian, Polish, Russian, Swedish, German, French—and English) at distances varying from seventy feet to a few inches, for twenty minutes I was ferociously bombarded. Nor was my perplexity purely aural. About five minutes after lying down I saw (by a hitherto unnoticed speck of light which burned near the doors which I had entered) two extraordinary looking figures—one a well-set man with a big, black beard, the other a consumptive with a bald head and sickly moustache, both clad only in their knee-length chemises, hairy legs naked, feet bare— wander down the room and urinate profusely in the corner nearest me. This act accomplished, the figures wandered back, greeted with a volley of ejaculatory abuse from the invisible co-occupants of my new sleeping-apartment; and disappeared in darkness.

I remarked to myself that the gendarmes of this gendarmerie were peculiarly up in languages, and fell asleep.

IV

LE NOUVEAU

'*Vous ne voulez pas de café?*'

The threatening question recited in a hoarse voice woke me like a shot. Sprawled half on and half off my *paillasse*, I looked suddenly up into a juvenile pimply face with a red tassel bobbing in its eyes. A boy in a Belgian uniform was stooping over me. In one hand a huge pail a third full of liquid slime. I said fiercely: '*Au contraire, je veux bien.*' And collapsed on the mattress.

'*Pas de quart, vous?*' the face fired at me.

'*Comprends pas,*' I replied, wondering what on earth the words meant.

'English?'

'American.'

At this moment a tin cup appeared mysteriously out of the gloom and was rapidly filled from the pail, after which operation the tassel remarked: 'Your friend here,' and disappeared.

I decided I had gone completely crazy.

The cup had been deposited near me. Not daring to approach it, I boosted my aching corpse on one of its futile elbows and gazed blankly around. My eyes, wading laboriously through a dank atmosphere, a darkness gruesomely tactile, perceived only here and there lively patches of vibrating humanity. My ears recognized English, something which I took to be Low German and which was Belgian, Dutch, Polish, and what I guessed to be Russian.

Trembling with this chaos, my hand sought the cup. The cup was not warm; the contents, which I hastily gulped, was not even tepid. The taste was dull, almost bitter, clinging, thick, nauseating. I felt a renewed interest in living as soon as the deathful swallow descended to my abdomen, very much as a suicide who changes his mind after the fatal dose. I decided that it would be useless to vomit. I sat up. I looked around.

The darkness was rapidly going out of the sluggish, stinking air. I was sitting on my mattress at one end of a sort of room, filled with pillars; ecclesiastical in feeling. I already perceived it to be of enormous length. My mattress resembled an island: all around it, at distances varying from a quarter of an inch to ten feet (which constituted the limit of distinct vision) reposed startling identities. There was blood in some of them. Others consisted of a rind of bluish matter sustaining a core of yellowish froth. From behind me a chunk of hurtling spittle joined its fellows. I decided to stand up.

At this moment, at the far end of the room, I seemed to see an extraordinary vulture-like silhouette leap up from nowhere. It rushed a little way in my direction crying hoarsely 'Corvée d'eau!'—stopped, bent down at what I perceived to be a *paillasse* like mine, jerked what was presumably the occupant by the feet, shook him, turned to the next, and so on up to six. As there seemed to be innumerable *paillasses*, laid side by side at intervals of perhaps a foot with their heads to the wall on three sides of me, I was wondering why the vulture had stopped at six. On each mattress a crude imitation of humanity, wrapped ear-high in its blanket, lay and drank from a cup like mine and spat long and high into the room. The ponderous reek of sleepy bodies undulated toward me from three directions. I had lost sight of the vulture in a kind of insane confusion which arose from the further end of the room. It was as if he had touched off six high explosives. Occasional pauses in the minutely crazy din were accurately punctuated by exploding bowels; to the great amusement of innumerable somebodies, whose precise whereabouts the gloom carefully guarded.

I felt that I was the focus of a group of indistinct recumbents who were talking about me to one another in many incomprehensible tongues. I noticed beside every pillar (including the one beside which I had innocently thrown down my *paillasse* the night before) a good-sized pail, overflowing with urine, and surrounded by a large irregular puddle. My *paillasse* was within an inch of the nearest puddle. What I took to be a man, an amazing distance off, got out of bed and succeeded in locating the pail nearest to him after several attempts. The invisible recumbents yelled at him in six languages.

All at once a handsome figure arose from the gloom at my elbow. I smiled stupidly into his clear, hardish eyes. And he remarked pleasantly:

'Your friend's here, Johnny, and wants to see you.'

A bulge of pleasure swooped along my body, chasing aches and numbness, my muscles danced, nerves tingled in perpetual holiday.

B. was lying on his camp-cot, wrapped like an Eskimo in a blanket which hid all but his nose and eyes.

'Hello, Cummings,' he said smiling. 'There's a man here who is a friend of Vanderbilt and knew Cézanne.'

I gazed somewhat critically at B. There was nothing particularly insane about him, unless it was his enthusiastic excitement, which might almost be attributed to my jack-in-the-box manner of arriving. He said: 'There are people here who speak English, Russian, Arabian. There are the finest people here! Did you go to Gré? I fought rats all night there. Huge ones. They tried to eat me. And from Gré to Paris? I had three gendarmes all the way to keep me from escaping, and they all fell asleep.'

I began to be afraid that I was asleep myself. 'Please be frank,' I begged. 'Strictly *entre nous:* am I dreaming, or is this a bug-house?'

B. laughed, and said: 'I thought so when I arrived two days ago. When I came in sight of the place a lot of girls waved from the window and yelled at me. I no sooner got inside than a queer-looking duck whom I took to be a nut came rushing up to me, and cried: *"Trop tard pour la soupe!"*—This is *Camp de Triage de la Ferté Macé*, Orne, France, and all these fine people were arrested as *espions*. Only two or three of them can speak a word of French, and that's *soupe!'*

I said: 'My God, I thought Marseilles was somewhere on the Mediterranean Ocean, and that this was a gen-darmerie.'

'But this is M-a-c-é. It's a little mean town, where everybody snickers and sneers at you if they see you're a prisoner. They did at me.'

'Do you mean to say we're *espions* too?'

'Of course!' B. said enthusiastically. 'Thank God! And in to stay. Every time I think of the *section sanitaire*, and A. and his thugs, and the whole rotten red-taped *Croix Rouge*, I have to laugh. Cummings, I tell you this is the finest place on earth!'

A vision of the *Chef de Section Sanitaire Vingt-et-Un* passed through my mind. The doughy face. Imitation-English-officer swagger. Large calves, squeaking puttees.

The daily lecture: 'I doughno what's th' matter with you fellers. You look like nice boys. Well-edjucated. But you're so dirty in your habits. You boys are always kickin' because I don't put you on a car together. I'm ashamed to do it, that's why. I doughwanta give this section a black eye. We gotta show these lousy Frenchmen what Americans are. We gotta show we're superior to 'em. Those bastards doughno what a bath means. And you fellers are always hangin' round, talkin' with them dirty frog-eaters that does the cookin' and the dirty work round here. How d'you boys expect me to give you a chance? I'd like to put you fellers on a car; I wanta see you boys happy. But I don't dare to, that's why. If you want me to send you out, you gotta shave and look neat, and *keep away from them dirty Frenchmen*. We Americans are over here to learn them lousy bastards something.'

I laughed for sheer joy.

A terrific tumult interrupted my mirth. *'Par ici!'*— 'Get out of the way, you dam Polak!'—'M'sieu', M'sieu'.' —'Over here!'—*'Mais non!'*—'Gott-er-dummer!' I turned in terror to see my *paillasse* in the clutches of four men who were apparently rending it in as many directions.

One was a clean-shaved youngish man with lively eyes, alert and muscular, whom I identified as the man who had called me 'Johnny.' He had hold of a corner of the mattress and was pulling against the possessor of the opposite corner: an incoherent personage enveloped in a buffoonery of amazing rags and patches, with a shabby head on which excited wisps of dirty hair stood upright in excitement, and the tall, ludicrous, extraordinary, almost noble figure of a dancing bear. A third corner of the *paillasse* was rudely grasped by a six-foot combination of yellow hair, red hooligan face, and sky-blue trousers; assisted by the undersized tasselled mucker in Belgian uniform, with a pimply rogue's mug and unlimited impertinence of diction, who had awakened me by demanding if I wanted coffee. Albeit completely dazed by the uncouth vocal fracas, I realized in some manner that these hostile forces were contending, not for the possession of the mattress, but merely for the privilege of presenting the mattress to myself.

Before I could offer any advice on this delicate topic, a childish voice cried emphatically beside my ear: *'Met-tez la pail-lasse ici! Qu'est le que vous al-lez faire? C'est pas la peine de dé-chi-rer une pail-lasse!'*—at the same moment the mattress rushed with cobalt strides in my direction, propelled by the successful efforts of the Belgian uniform and the hooligan visage, the clean-shaven man and the incoherent bear still desperately clutching their respective corners; and upon its arrival was seized with surprising strength by the owner of the child's voice—a fluffy little gnome-shaped man with a sensitive face which had suffered much—and indignantly deposited beside B.'s bed in a space mysteriously cleared for its reception. The gnome immediately kneeled upon it and fell to carefully smoothing certain creases caused by the recent conflict, exclaiming slowly, syllable by syllable: *'Mon Dieu. Main-te-nant, c'est mieux. Il ne faut pas faire des choses comme ça.'* The clean-shaven man regarded him loftily with folded arms, while the tassel and the trousers victoriously inquired if I had a cigarette?—and upon receiving one apiece (also the gnome, and the clean-shaven man, who accepted his with some dignity) sat down without much ado on B.'s bed—which groaned ominously in protest—and hungrily fired questions at me. The bear meanwhile, looking as if nothing had happened, adjusted his ruffled costume with a satisfied air and (calmly gazing into the distance) began with singularly delicate fingers to stuff a stunted and ancient pipe with what appeared to be a mixture of wood and manure.

I was still answering questions, when a gnarled voice suddenly threatened, over our heads: '*Balai? Vous. Tout le monde Propre. Surveillant dit. Pas moi, c'est-ce pas?*' —I started, expecting to see a parrot.

It was the silhouette.

A vulture-like figure stood before me, a demoralized broom clenched in one claw or fist: it had lean legs cased in shabby trousers, muscular shoulders covered with a rough shirt open at the neck, knotted arms, and a coarse, insane face crammed beneath the visor of a cap. The face consisted of a rapid nose, drooping moustache, ferocious watery small eyes, a pugnacious chin, and sunken cheeks hideously smiling. There was something in the ensemble at once brutal and ridiculous, vigorous and pathetic.

Again I had not time to speak; for the hooligan in azure trousers hurled his butt at the bear's feet, exclaiming: 'There's another for you, Polak!'—jumped from the bed, seized the broom, and poured upon the vulture a torrent of *Gott-verdummers*, to which the latter replied copiously and in kind. Then the red face bent within a few inches of my own, and for the first time I saw that it had recently been young—'I say I do your sweep for you,' it translated pleasantly. I thanked it; and the vulture, exclaiming, '*Bon. Bon. Pas moi. Surveillant. Harree faire pour tout le monde.* Hee, hee'—rushed off, followed by Harree and the tassel. Out of the corner of my eye I watched the tall, ludicrous, extraordinary, almost proud figure of the bear stoop with quiet dignity, the musical fingers close with a singular delicacy upon the moist, indescribable eighth-of-an-inch of tobacco.

I did not know that this was a Delectable Mountain. . . .

The clean-shaven man (who appeared to have been completely won over by his smoke) and the fluffy gnome, who had completed the arrangement of my *paillasse,* now entered into conversation with myself and B.; the clean-shaven one seating himself in Harree's stead, the gnome declining (on the ground that the bed was already sufficiently loaded) to occupy the place left vacant by the tassel's exit, and leaning against the drab, sweating, poisonous wall. He managed, however, to call our attention to the shelf at B.'s head which he himself had constructed, and promised me a similar luxury *tout de suite.* He was a Russian, and had a wife and *gosse* in Paris. '*Je m'ap-pelle Monsieur Au-guste à votre ser-vice*'—and his gentle pale eyes sparkled. The clean-shaven talked distinct and absolutely perfect English. His name was Fritz. He was a Norwegian, a stoker on a ship. 'You mustn't mind that feller that wanted you to sweep. He's crazy. They call him John the *Baigneur.* He used to be the *baigneur.* Now he's *Maître de Chambre.* They wanted me to take it—I said, "F— it, I don't want it." Let him have it. That's no kind of a job, every one complaining and on top of you morning till night. "Let them that wants the job take it," I said. That crazy Dutchman's been here for two years. They told him to get out and he wouldn't, he was too fond of the booze' (I jumped at the slang) 'and the girls. They took it away from John and give it to that little Ree-shar feller, that doctor. That was a swell job he had, *baigneur,* too. All the bloody liquor you can drink and a girl every time you want one.

He ain't never had a girl in his life, that Ree-shar feller.'
His laughter was hard, clear, cynical. 'That Pompom, the
little Belgian feller was just here, he's a great one for the
girls. He and Harree. Always getting *cabinot*. I got it
twice myself since I been here.'

All this time the enormous room was filling gradually
with dirty light. In the further end six figures were
brooming furiously, yelling to each other in the dust
like demons. A seventh, Harree, was loping to and fro
splashing water from a pail and enveloping everything
and everybody in a ponderous and blasphemous fog of
Gott-verdummers. Along three sides (with the exception,
that is, of the nearer end, which boasted the sole door)
were laid, with their lengths at right angles to the walls,
at intervals of three or four feet, something like forty
paillasses. On each, with half a dozen exceptions (where
the occupants had not yet finished their coffee or were on
duty for the *corvée*), lay the headless body of a man
smothered in its blanket, only the boots showing.

The demons were working toward our end of the
room. Harree had got his broom and was assisting.
Nearer and nearer they came; converging, they united
their separate heaps of filth in a loudly stinking single
mound at the door. Brooms were stacked against the
wall in the corner. The men strolled back to their *paillasses*.

Monsieur Auguste, whose French had not been able to
keep pace with Fritz's English, saw his chance, and pro-
posed '*Main-te-nant que la Chambre est tout propre, allons faire une pe-tite pro-me-nade, tous les trois.*' Fritz
understood perfectly, and rose, remarking as he fingered
his immaculate chin, 'Well, I guess I'll take a shave before
the bloody *planton* comes'—and Monsieur Auguste, B.
and I started down the room.

It was in shape oblong, about 80 feet by 40, unmistakably ecclesiastical in feeling—two rows of wooden
pillars, spaced at intervals of fifteen feet, rose to a vaulted
ceiling 25 or 30 feet above the floor. As you stood with
your back to the door, and faced down the room, you
had in the near right-hand corner (where the brooms
stood) six pails of urine. On the right-hand long wall,
a little beyond the angle of this corner, a few boards
tacked together in any fashion to make a two-sided
screen four feet in height marked the position of a *cabinet
d'aisance,* composed of a small coverless tin pail identical with the other six, and a board of the usual design
which could be placed on the pail or not as desired. The
wooden floor in the neighbourhood of the booth and
pails was of a dark colour, obviously owing to the con-
tinual overflow of their contents.

The right-hand long wall contained something like
ten large windows, of which the first was commanded by
the somewhat primitive *cabinet.* There were no other windows in the remaining walls; or they had been carefully
rendered useless. In spite of this fact, the inhabitants had
contrived a couple of peep-holes—one in the door-end
and one in the left-hand long wall; the former commanding the gate by which I had entered, the latter a portion
of the street by which I had reached the gate. The block-
ing of all windows on three sides had an obvious significance: *les hommes* were not supposed to see anything
which went on in the world without; *les hommes* might,
however, look their fill on a little washing-shed, on a
corner of what seemed to be another wing of the building,
and on a bleak, lifeless, abject landscape of scrubby
woods beyond—which constituted the view from the ten
windows on the right. The authorities had miscalculated

a little in one respect: a merest fraction of the barb-wire
pen which began at the corner of the above-mentioned
building was visible from these windows, which windows
(I was told) were consequently thronged by fighting men
at the time of the girls' promenade. A *planton*, I was also
told, made it his business, by keeping *les femmes* out of
this corner of their *cour* at the point of the bayonet, to
deprive them of the sight of their admirers. In addition,
it was *pain sec* or *cabinot* for any of either sex who were
caught communicating with each other. Moreover the
promenades des hommes et des femmes occurred at,
roughly speaking, the same hour, so that an *homme* or
femme who remained upstairs on the chance of getting
a smile or a wave from his or her girl or lover lost the
promenade thereby. . . .

We had in succession gazed from the windows, crossed
the end of the room, and started down the other side,
Monsieur Auguste marching between us—when suddenly
B. exclaimed in English, 'Good morning! How are you
to-day?' And I looked across Monsieur Auguste, anticipating another Harree or at least a Fritz. What was my
surprise to see a spare majestic figure of manifest refinement, immaculately apparelled in a crisp albeit collarless
shirt, carefully mended trousers in which the remains of
a crease still lingered, a threadbare but perfectly fitting
swallow-tail coat, and newly varnished (if somewhat ancient) shoes. Indeed for the first time since my arrival at
La Ferté I was confronted by a perfect type: the apotheosis
of injured nobility, the humiliated victim of perfectly
unfortunate circumstances, the utterly respectable gentleman who has seen better days. There was about him,
moreover, something irretrievably English, nay even pathetically Victorian—it was as if a page of Dickens was

shaking my friend's hand. 'Count Bragard, I want you to
meet my friend Cummings'—he saluted me in modulated
and courteous accents of indisputable culture, gracefully
extending his pale hand. 'I have heard a great deal about
you from B., and wanted very much to meet you. It is a
pleasure to find a friend of my friend B., some one congenial and intelligent in contrast to these swine'—he indicated the room with a gesture of complete contempt. 'I
see you were strolling. Let us take a turn.' Monsieur
Auguste said tactfully, '*Je vais vous voir tout à l'heure,
mes amis*,' and left us with an affectionate shake of the
hand and a side-long glance of jealousy and mistrust at
B.'s respectable friend.

'You're looking pretty well to-day, Count Bragard,' B.
said amiably.

'I do well enough,' the count answered. 'It is a frightful
strain—you of course realize that—for anyone who has
been accustomed to the decencies, let alone the luxuries, of
life. This filth'—he pronounced the word with indescribable bitterness—'this herding of men like cattle—they
treat us no better than pigs here. The fellows drop their
dung in the very room where they sleep. What is one to
expect of a place like this? *Ce n'est pas une existence*'—
his French was glib and faultless.

'I was telling my friend that you knew Cézanne,' said
B. 'Being an artist he was naturally much interested.'

Count Bragard stopped in astonishment, and withdrew
his hands slowly from the tails of his coat. 'Is it possible!'
he exclaimed, in great agitation. 'What an astonishing
coincidence! I am myself a painter. You perhaps noticed
this badge'—he indicated a button attached to his left
lapel, and I bent and read the words: On War Service.
'I always wear it,' he said with a smile of faultless sorrow,

and resumed his walk. 'They don't know what it means here, but I wear it all the same. I was a special representative for the *London Sphere* at the front in this war. I did the trenches and all that sort of thing. They paid me well; I got fifteen pounds a week. And why not? I am an R.A. My speciality was horses. I painted the finest horses in England, among them the King's own entry in the last Derby. Do you know London?' We said no. 'If you are ever in London, go to the' (I forget the name) 'Hotel—one of the best in town. It has a beautiful large bar, exquisitely furnished in the very best taste. Anyone will tell you where to find the— It has one of my paintings over the bar: Straight-jacket' (or some such name) 'The Marquis of — 's horse, who won last time the race was run. I was in America in 1910. You know Cornelius Vanderbilt perhaps? I painted some of his horses. We were the best of friends, Vanderbilt and I. I got handsome prices, you understand, three, five, six thousand pounds. When I left, he gave me this card—I have it here somewhere—' he again stopped, sought in his breast-pocket a moment, and produced a visiting card. On one side I read the name 'Cornelius Vanderbilt'—on the other, in bold handwriting—'to my very dear friend Count F. A. de Bragard' and a date. 'He hated to have me go.'

I was walking in a dream.

'Have you your sketch-books and paints with you? What a pity. I am always intending to send to England for mine, but you know—one can't paint in a place like this. It is impossible—all this dirt and these filthy people— it stinks! Ugh!'

I forced myself to say: 'How did you happen to come here?'

He shrugged his shoulders. 'How indeed, you may well

ask! I cannot tell you. It must have been some hideous mistake. As soon as I got here I spoke to the *Directeur* and to the *Surveillant*. The *Directeur* said he knew nothing about it; the *Surveillant* told me confidentially that it was a mistake on the part of the French Government; that I would be out directly. He's not such a bad sort. So I am waiting: every day I expect orders from the English Government for my release. The whole thing is preposterous. I wrote to the Embassy and told them so. As soon as I set foot outside this place, I shall sue the French Government for ten thousand pounds for the loss of time it has occasioned me. Imagine it—I had contracts with countless members of The Lords—and the war came. Then I was sent to the front by the *Sphere*—and here I am, every day costing me dear, rotting away in this horrible place. The time I have wasted here has already cost me a fortune.'

He paused directly in front of the door and spoke with solemnity: 'A man might as well be dead.'

Scarcely had the words passed his lips when I almost jumped out of my skin, for directly before us on the other side of the wall arose the very noise which announced to Scrooge the approach of Marley's ghost—a dismal clanking and rattling of chains. Had Marley's transparent figure walked straight through the wall and up to the Dickensian character at my side, I would have been less surprised than I was by what actually happened.

The doors opened with an uncanny bang and in the bang stood a fragile, minute, queer figure, remotely suggesting an old man. The chief characteristic of the apparition was a certain disagreeable nudity which resulted from a complete lack of all the accepted appurtenances and prerogatives of old age. Its little stooping body, helpless and brittle, bore with extraordinary difficulty a head of

absurd largeness, yet which moved on the fleshless neck
with a horrible agility. Dull eyes sat in the clean-shaven
wrinkles of a face neatly hopeless. At the knees a pair of
hands hung, infantile in their smallness. In the loose
mouth a tiny cigarette had perched and was solemnly
smoking itself.

Suddenly the figure darted at me with a spiderlike en-
tirety.

I felt myself lost.

A voice said mechanically from the vicinity of my feet:
'*Il vous faut prendre des douches*'—I stared stupidly. The
spectre was poised before me; its averted eyes contemplated the window. 'Take your bath,' it added as an after-
thought, in English—'come with me.' It turned suddenly.
It hurried to the doorway. I followed. Its rapid, deadly,
doll-like hands shut and skilfully locked the doors in a
twinkling. 'Come,' its voice said.

It hurried before me down two dirty flights of narrow,
mutilated stairs. It turned left, and passed through an
open door.

I found myself in the wet sunless air of morning.

To the right it hurried, following the wall of the building. I pursued it mechanically. At the corner, which I had
seen from the window upstairs, the barbed-wire fence
eight feet in height began. The thing paused, produced a
key, and unlocked a gate. The first three or four feet of
wire swung inward. He entered, I after him.

In a flash the gate was locked behind me, and I was
following along a wall at right angles to the first. I strode
after the thing. A moment before I had been walking in a
free world: now I was again a prisoner. The sky was still
over me, the clammy morning caressed me; but walls of
wire and stone told me that my instant of freedom had

departed. I was in fact traversing a lane no wider than the gate; on my left, barbed-wire separated me from the famous *cour* in which *les femmes se promènent*—a rectangle about 50 feet deep and 200 long, with a stone wall at the farther end of it and otherwise surrounded by wire; —on my right, grey sameness of stone, the ennui of the regular and the perpendicular, the ponderous ferocity of silence. . . .

I had taken automatically some six or eight steps in pursuit of the fleeing spectre when, right over my head, the grey stone curdled with a female darkness; the hard and the angular softening in a putrescent explosion of thick wriggling laughter. I started, looked up, and encountered a window stuffed with four savage fragments of crowding Face: four livid, shaggy disks focusing hungrily; four pairs of uncouth eyes rapidly smouldering; eight lips shaking in a toothless and viscous titter. Suddenly above and behind these terrors rose a single horror of beauty—a crisp, vital head, a young ivory actual face, a night of firm, alive, icy hair, a white large frightful smile.

. . . The thing was crying two or three paces in front of me: 'Come!' The heads had vanished as by magic.

I dived forward; followed through a little door in the wall into a room about fifteen feet square, occupied by a small stove, a pile of wood, and a ladder. He plunged through another even smaller door, into a bleak rectangular place, where I was confronted on the left by a large tin bath and on the right by ten wooden tubs, each about a yard in diameter, set in a row against the wall. 'Undress,' commanded the spectre. I did so. 'Go into the first one.' I climbed into a tub. 'You shall pull the string,' the spectre said, hurriedly throwing his cigarette into a corner. I stared upward, and discovered a string dangling from a kind of reservoir over my head: I pulled: and was saluted by a stabbing crash of icy water. I leaped from the tub. 'Here is your napkin. Make dry yourself'—he handed me a piece of cloth a little bigger than a handkerchief. 'Hurree.' I donned my clothes, wet and shivering and altogether miserable. 'Good. Come now!' I followed him, through the room with the stove, into the barb-wire lane. A hoarse shout rose from the yard—which was filled with women, girls, children, and a baby or two. I thought I recognized one of the four terrors who had saluted me from the window, in a girl of 18 with a soiled, slobby body huddling beneath its dingy dress; her bony shoulders stifled in a shawl upon which excremental hair limply spouted; a huge empty mouth; and a red nose, sticking between the bluish cheeks that shook with spasms of coughing. Just inside the wire a figure reminiscent of Gré, gun on shoulder, revolver on hip, moved monotonously.

The apparition hurried me through the gate and along the wall into the building, where instead of mounting the stairs he pointed down a long gloomy corridor with a square of light at the end of it, saying rapidly, 'Go to the promenade'—and vanished.

With the laughter of the Five still ringing in my ears, and no very clear conception of the meaning of existence, I stumbled down the corridor, bumping squarely into a beefy figure with a bull's neck and the familiar revolver, who demanded furiously: '*Qu'est-ce que vous faites là? Nom de Dieu!*'—'*Pardon. Les douches,*' I answered, quelled by the collision.—He demanded in wrathy French, 'Who took you to the *douches*?'—For a moment I was at a complete loss—then Fritz's remark about the new *baigneur* flashed through my mind: 'Ree-shar,' I answered calmly.—The bull snorted satisfactorily. 'Get into the *cour* and hurry up about it,' he ordered.—'*C'est par là?*' I inquired politely.—He stared at me contemptuously without answering; so I took it upon myself to use the nearest door, hoping that he would have the decency not to shoot me. I had no sooner crossed the threshold when I found myself once more in the welcome air; and not ten paces away I espied B. peacefully lounging, with some thirty others, within a *cour* about one quarter the size of the women's. I marched up to a little dingy gate in the barbed-wire fence, and was hunting for the latch (as no padlock was in evidence) when a scared voice cried loudly, '*Qu'est-ce que vous faites là!*' and I found myself stupidly looking into a rifle. B., Fritz, Harree, Pompom, Monsieur Auguste, The Bear, and last but not least Count de Bragard immediately informed the trembling *planton* that I was a *Nouveau* who had just returned from the *douches* to which I had been escorted by Monsieur Reeshar, and that I should be admitted to the *cour* by all means. The cautious watcher of the skies was not however to be fooled by any such fol-de-rol and stood his ground. Fortunately at this point the beefy *planton* yelled from the doorway, 'Let him in.' And I was accordingly let in, to the gratification of my friends, and against the better judgment of the guardian of the *cour*, who muttered something about having more than enough to do already.

I had not been mistaken as to the size of the men's yard: it was certainly not more than twenty yards deep and fifteen wide. By the distinctness with which the shouts of *les femmes* reached my ears, I perceived that the two *cours* adjoined. They were separated by a stone wall ten feet in height, which I had already remarked (while en route to *les douches*) as forming one end of the *cour des femmes*. The men's *cour* had another stone wall slightly higher than the first, and which ran parallel to it; the two remaining sides, which were properly ends, were made by the familiar *fil-de-fer barbelé*.

The furniture of the *cour* was simple: in the middle of the further end, a wooden sentry-box was placed just inside the wire; a curious contrivance, which I discovered to be a sister to the booth upstairs, graced the wall on the left which separated the two *cours*, while further up on this wall a horizontal iron bar projected from the stone at a height of seven feet and was supported at its other end by a wooden post, the idea apparently being to give the prisoners a little taste of gymnastic; a minute wooden shed filled the right upper corner and served secondarily as a very partial shelter for *les hommes* and primarily as a stable for an extraordinary water-wagon, composed of a wooden barrel on two wheels with shafts which could not possibly accommodate anything larger than a diminutive donkey (but in which I myself was to walk not infrequently, as it proved); parallel to the second stone wall, but at a safe distance from it, stretched a couple of iron girders serving as a barbarously cold seat for any unfortunate who could not remain on his feet the entire time; on the ground close by the shed lay amusement devices numbers 2 and 3—a huge iron cannon-ball and the six-foot iron axle of a departed wagon—for testing the strength of the prisoners and beguiling any time which might lie heavily on their hands after they had regaled themselves with the horizontal bar; and finally, a dozen mangy apple-trees, fighting for their very lives in the angry soil, proclaimed to all the world that the *cour* itself was in reality a *verger*.

'Les pommiers sont pleins de pommes;
Allons au verger, Simone.' . . .

A description of the *cour* would be incomplete without
an enumeration of the manifold duties of the *planton* in
charge, which were as follows: to prevent the men from
using the horizontal bar, except for chinning, since if you
swung yourself upon it you could look over the wall into
the women's *cour*; to see that no one threw anything over
the wall into said *cour*; to dodge the cannon-ball which
had a mysterious habit of taking advantage of the slope
of the ground and bounding along at a prodigious rate of
speed straight for the sentry-box; to watch closely anyone
who inhabited the *cabinet d'aisance*, lest he should make
use of it to vault over the wall; to see that no one stood
on the girders, for a similar reason; to keep watch over
anyone who entered the shed; to see that every one urinated properly against the wall in the general vicinity of
the *cabinet*; to protect the apple-trees into which well-
aimed pieces of wood and stone were continually flying
and dislodging the sacred fruit; to mind that no one
entered or exited by the gate in the upper fence without
authority: to report any signs, words, tokens, or other
immoralities exchanged by prisoners with girls sitting in
the windows of the women's wing (it was from one of
these windows that I had recently received my salutation),
also names of said girls, it being *défendu* to exhibit any
part of the female person at a window while the males
were on promenade; to quell all *rixes* and especially to
prevent people from using the wagon axle as a weapon of
defence or offence; and last, to keep an eye on the *balayeur*
when he and his wheelbarrow made use of a secondary

gate situated in the fence at the further end, not far from
the sentry-box, to dump themselves.

Having acquainted me with the various *défendus* which
limited the activities of a man on promenade, my friends
proceeded to enliven the otherwise somewhat tedious
morning by shattering one after another all rules and
regulations. Fritz, having chinned himself fifteen times,
suddenly appeared astride of the bar, evoking a repri-
mand; Pompom bowled the *planton* with the cannon-ball,
apologizing in profuse and vile French; Harree the Hollander tossed the wagon-axle lightly half the length of
the *cour*, missing The Bear by an inch; The Bear bided
his time and cleverly hurled a large stick into one of the
holy trees, bringing to the ground a withered apple for
which at least twenty people fought for several minutes;
and so on. The most open gestures were indulged in for
the benefit of several girls who had braved the official
wrath and were enjoying the morning at their windows.
The girders were used as a race-track. The beams sup-
porting the shed-room were shinned. The water-wagon
was dislocated from its proper position. The *cabinet* and
urinal were misused. The gate was continually admitting
and emitting persons who said they were thirsty, and
must get a drink at a tub of water which stood around the
corner. A letter was surreptitiously thrown over the wall
into the *cour des femmes*.

The *planton* who suffered all these indignities was a
solemn youth with wise eyes situated very far apart in a
mealy expressionless ellipse of face, to the lower end of
which clung a piece of down, exactly like a feather sticking to an egg. The rest of him was fairly normal with the
exception of his hands, which were not mates; the left
being considerably larger, and made of wood.

I was at first somewhat startled by this eccentricity; but soon learned that with the exception of two or three, who formed the *Surveillant's* permanent staff and of whom the beefy one was a shining example, all the *plantons* were supposed to be unhealthy; they were indeed *réformés* whom *le gouvernement français* sent from time to time to La Ferté and similar institutions for a little outing, and as soon as they had recovered their health under these salubrious influences they were shipped back to do their bit for world-safety, democracy, freedom, etc., in the trenches. I also learned that of all the ways of attaining *cabinot* by far the simplest was to apply to a *planton*, particularly to a permanent *planton*, say the beefy one (who was reputed to be peculiarly touchy on this point) the term *embusqué*. This method never failed. To its efficacy many of *les hommes*, and more of the girls (by whom the *plantons*, owing to their habit of taking advantage of the weaker sex at every opportunity, were even more despised) attested by not infrequent spasms of consumptive coughing, which could be plainly heard from the further end of one *cour* to the other.

In a little over two hours I learned an astonishing lot about La Ferté itself: it was a co-educational receiving station whither were sent from various parts of France (*a*) males suspected of *espionnage* and (*b*) females of a well-known type *qui se trouvaient dans la zone des armées*. It was pointed out to me that the task of finding such members of the human race was *pas difficile*: in the case of the men, any foreigner would do, provided his country was neutral (e.g. Holland): as for the girls, inasmuch as the armies of the Allies were continually retreating, the *zone des armées* (particularly in the case of Belgium) was always including new cities, whose *petites femmes* became

automatically subject to arrest. It was not to be supposed
that all the women of La Ferté were *putains;* there were
a large number of *femmes honnêtes,* the wives of prisoners, who met their husbands at specified times on the floor
below the men's quarters, whither man and woman were
duly and separately conducted by *plantons.* In this case
no charges had been preferred against the women; they
were voluntary prisoners, who had preferred to freedom
this living in proximity to their husbands. Many of them
had children; some babies. In addition there were certain
femmes honnêtes whose nationality, as in the case of the
men, had cost them their liberty; Margherite the *blanchis-
seuse,* for example, was a German.

La Ferté Macé was not, properly speaking, a prison,
but a *Porte* or *Camp de Triage:* that is to say, persons sent
to it were held for a Commission, composed of an official,
an *avocat,* and a *capitaine de gendarmerie,* which inspected the camp and passed upon each case in turn for
the purpose of determining the guiltiness of the suspected
party. If the latter were found guilty by the commission,
he or she was sent off to a regular prison camp *pour la
durée de la guerre;* if not guilty, he or she was (in theory)
set free. The Commission came to La Ferté once every
three months. It should be added that there were *prisonniers* who had passed the Commission two, three, four
and even five times, without any appreciable result; there
were *prisonnières* who had remained in La Ferté a year,
and even eighteen months.

The authorities at La Ferté consisted of the *Directeur,*
or general overlord, the *Surveillant,* who had the *plantons*
under him and was responsible to the *Directeur* for the
administration of the camp, and the *Gestionnaire* (who
kept the accounts). As assistant, the *Surveillant* had a

mail clerk who acted as translator on occasion. Twice a
week the camp was visited by a regular French army
doctor (*médecin major*) who was supposed to prescribe
in severe cases and to give the women venereal inspection
at regular intervals. The daily routine of attending to
minor ailments and injuries was in the hands of Monsieur
Ree-shar (Richard), who knew probably less about medi-
cine than any man living and was an ordinary *prisonnier*
like all of us, but whose impeccable conduct merited cosy
quarters. A *balayeur* was appointed from time to time by
the *Surveillant*, acting for the *Directeur*, from the inhabitants of La Ferté, as was also a cook's assistant. The
regular cook was a fixture, and a *boche* like the other fix-
tures, Margherite and Richard. This fact might seem
curious were it not that the manner, appearance and
actions of the *Directeur* himself proved beyond a shadow
of a doubt that he was all which the term *boche* could
possibly imply.

'He's a son of a bitch,' B. said heartily. 'They took me
up to him when I came two days ago. As soon as he saw
me he bellowed: "*Imbécile et inchrétien!*"; then he called
me a great lot of other things, including Shame of my
country, Traitor to the sacred cause of liberty, Contemp-
tible coward and Vile, sneaking spy. When he got all
through I said, "*Je ne comprends pas le français.*" You
should have seen him then.'

Separation of the sexes was enforced, not, it is true,
with success, but with a commendable ferocity. The punishments for both men and girls were *pain sec* and *cabinot*.

'What on earth is *cabinot?*' I demanded.

There were various *cabinots*: each sex had its regular
cabinot, and there were certain extra ones. B. knew all
about them from Harree and Pompom, who spent nearly

all their time in the *cabinot*. They were rooms about nine feet square and six feet high. There was no light and no floor, and the ground (three were on the ground floor) was always wet and often a good many inches under water. The occupant on entering was searched for tobacco, deprived of his or her *paillasse* and blanket, and invited to sleep on the ground on some planks. One didn't need to write a letter to a member of the opposite sex to get *cabinot*, or even to call a *planton embusqué*—there was a woman, a foreigner, who, instead of sending a letter to her embassy through the *bureau* (where all letters were read by the mail clerk to make sure that they said nothing disagreeable about the authorities or conditions of La Ferté) tried to smuggle it outside, and *attrapait vingt-huit jours de cabinot*. She had previously written three times, handing the letters to the *Surveillant*, as per regulations, and had received no reply. Fritz, who had no idea why he was arrested and was crazy to get in touch with his embassy, had likewise written several letters, taking the utmost care to state the facts only and always handing them in; but he had never received a word in return. The obvious inference was that letters from a foreigner to his embassy were duly accepted by the *Surveillant*, but rarely if ever left La Ferté.

B. and I were conversing merrily à propos the God-sent miracle of our escape from *Vingt-et-Un*, when a benign-faced personage of about fifty with sparse greyish hair and a Benjamin Franklin expression appeared on the other side of the fence, from the direction of the door through which I had passed after bumping the beefy bull. '*Planton*,' it cried heavily to the wooden-handed one. '*Deux hommes pour aller chercher l'eau.*' Harree and Pompom were already at the gate with the archaic water-wagon, the former pushing from behind and the latter in the shafts. The guardian of the *cour* walked up and opened the gate for them, after ascertaining that another *planton* was waiting at the corner of the building to escort them on their mission. A little way from the *cour*, the stone wall which formed one of its boundaries (and which ran parallel to the other stone wall dividing the two *cours*) met the prison building; and here was a huge double-door, twice padlocked, through which the water-seekers passed on to the street. There was a sort of hydrant up the street a few hundred yards, I was told. The cook (Benjamin F. that is) required from three to six wagonfuls of water twice a day, and in reward for the labour involved in its capture was in the habit of giving a cup of coffee to the captors. I resolved that I would seek water at the earliest opportunity.

Harree and Pompom had completed their third and final trip and returned from the kitchen, smacking their lips and wiping their mouths with the backs of their hands. I was gazing airily into the muddy sky, when a roar issued from the doorway:

'*Montez les hommes!*'

It was the beefy-necked. We filed from the *cour*, through the door, past a little window which I was told belonged to the kitchen, down the clammy corridor, up the three flights of stairs, to the door of The Enormous Room. Padlocks were unlocked, chains rattled, and the door thrown open. We entered. The Enormous Room received us in silence. The door was slammed and locked behind us by the *planton*, whom we could hear descending the gnarled and filthy stairs.

In the course of a half-hour, which time as I was informed intervened between the just-ended morning

promenade and the noon meal which was the next thing
on the programme, I gleaned considerable information
concerning the daily schedule of La Ferté. A typical day
was divided by *planton*-cries as follows:

(1) '*Café*.' At 5.30 every morning a *planton* or *plantons* mounted to the room. One man descended to the
kitchen, got a pail of coffee, and brought it up.

(2) '*Corvée d'eau*.' From time to time the occupants of
the room chose one of their number to be '*maître de
chambre*,' or roughly speaking Boss. When the *planton*
opened the door, allowing the coffee-getter to descend,
it was the duty of the *maître de chambre* to rouse a certain
number of the men (generally six, the occupants of the
room being taken in rotation), who forthwith carried the
pails of urine and excrement to the door. Upon the arrival
of coffee, the *maître de chambre* and his crew 'descended'
said pails, together with a few clean pails for water, to
the ground floor; where a *planton* was in readiness to
escort them to a sort of sewer situated a few yards beyond
the *cour des femmes*. Here the full pails were dumped:
with the exception, occasionally, of one or two pails of
urine which the *Surveillant* might direct to be thrown
on the *Directeur's* little garden in which it was rumoured
he was growing a rose for his daughter. From the sewer
the *corvée* gang were escorted to a pump, where they
filled their water pails. They then mounted to the room,
where the emptied pails were ranged against the wall beside the door, with the exception of one which was returned to the *cabinet*. The water pails were placed hard
by. The door was now locked, and the *planton* descended.

While the men selected for *corvée* had been performing
their duties the other occupants had been enjoying coffee.
The *corvée* men now joined them. The *maître de chambre*

usually allowed about fifteen minutes for himself and his crew to consume their breakfast. He then announced:

(3) '*Nettoyage de Chambre.*' Some one sprinkled the floor with water from one of the pails which had been just brought up. The other members of the crew swept the room, fusing their separate piles of filth at the door. This process consumed something like a half-hour.

(4) The sweeping completed, the men had nothing more to do till 7.30, at which hour a *planton* mounted, announcing '*A la promenade les hommes.*' The *corvée* crew now carried down the product of their late labours. The other occupants descended or not directly to the *cour*, according to their tastes; morning promenade being optional. At 9.30 the *planton* demanded:

(5) '*Montez les hommes.*' Those who had taken advantage of the morning stroll were brought upstairs to the room, the *corvée* men descended the excrement which had accumulated during promenade, and everybody was thereupon locked in for a half-hour, or until ten o'clock, when a *planton* again mounted and cried:

(6) '*A la soupe les hommes.*' Every one descended to a wing of the building opposite the *cour des hommes*, where the noon meal was enjoyed until 10.30 or thereabouts, when the order:

(7) '*Tout le monde en haut*' was given. There was a digestive interval of two and a half hours spent in the room. At one o'clock a *planton* mounted, announcing:

(8) '*Les hommes à la promenade*' (in which case the afternoon promenade was a matter of choice) or '*Tout le monde en bas,*' whereat every one had to descend, willy-nilly, '*plucher les pommes*'—potatoes (which constituted the *pièce de résistance* of '*la soupe*') being peeled and sliced on alternate days by the men and the girls. At 3.30:

(9) *'Tout le monde en haut'* was again given, the world mounted, the *corvée* crew descended excrement, and every one was then locked in till 4, at which hour a *planton* arrived to announce:

(10) *'A la soupe,'* that is to say the evening meal, or dinner. After dinner anyone who wished might go on promenade for an hour; those who wished might return to the room. At eight o'clock the *planton* made a final inspection and pronounced:

(11) *'Lumières éteintes.'*

The most terrible cry of all, and which was not included in the regular programme of *planton*-cries, consisted of the words:

'A la douche les hommes'—when all, sick, dead and dying not excepted, descended to the baths. Although *les douches* came only once in *quinze jours*, such was the terror they inspired that it was necessary for the *planton* to hunt under *paillasses* for people who would have preferred death itself.

Upon remarking that *corvée d'eau* must be excessively disagreeable, I was informed that it had its bright side, viz. that in going to and from the sewer one could easily exchange a furtive signal with the women who always took pains to be at their windows at that moment. Influenced perhaps by this, Harree and Pompom were in the habit of doing their friends' *corvées* for a consideration. The girls, I was further instructed, had their *corvée* (as well as their meals) just after the men; and the miraculous stupidity of the *plantons* had been known to result in the co-incidence of the two.

At this point somebody asked me how I had enjoyed my *douche?*

I was replying in terms of unmeasured opprobrium

when I was interrupted by that gruesome clanking and
rattling which announced the opening of the door. A
moment later it was thrown wide, and the beefy-neck
stood in the doorway, a huge bunch of keys in his paw,
and shouted:

'*A la soupe les hommes.*'

The cry was lost in a tremendous confusion, a reckless
thither-and-hithering of humanity, every one trying to
be at the door, spoon in hand, before his neighbour. B.
said calmly, extracting his own spoon from beneath his
paillasse, on which we were seated: 'They'll give you yours
downstairs, and when you get it you want to hide it or
it'll be pinched'—and in company with Monsieur
Bragard, who had refused the morning promenade, and
whose gentility would not permit him to hurry when it
was a question of such a low craving as hunger, we joined
the dancing, roaring throng at the door. I was not too
famished myself to be unimpressed by the instantaneous
change which had come over The Enormous Room's occupants. Never did Circe herself cast upon men so bestial
an enchantment. Among these faces convulsed with utter
animalism I scarcely recognized my various acquaintances.
The transformation produced by the *planton*'s shout was
not merely amazing; it was uncanny, and not a little
thrilling. These eyes bubbling with lust, obscene grins
sprouting from contorted lips, bodies unclenching and
clenching in unctuous gestures of complete savagery, convinced me by a certain insane beauty. Before the arbiter
of their destinies some thirty creatures, hideous and authentic, poised, cohering in a sole chaos of desire; a fluent
and numerous cluster of vital inhumanity. As I contemplated this ferocious and uncouth miracle, this
beautiful manifestation of the sinister alchemy of hunger,

I felt that the last vestige of individualism was about utterly to disappear, wholly abolished in a gambolling and wallowing throb.

The beefy-neck bellowed:

'*Est-ce que vous êtes tous ici?*'

A shrill roar of language answered. He looked contemptuously around him, upon the thirty clamouring faces each of which wanted to eat him—puttees, revolver and all. Then he cried:

'*Allez, descendez.*'

Squirming, jostling, fighting, roaring, we poured slowly through the doorway. Ridiculously. Horribly. I felt like a glorious microbe in huge, absurd din irrevocably swathed. B. was beside me. A little ahead Monsieur Auguste's voice protested. Count Bragard brought up the rear.

When we reached the corridor nearly all the breath was knocked out of me. The corridor being wider than the stairs allowed me to inhale and look around. B. was yelling in my ear:

'Look at the Hollanders and the Belgians! They're always ahead when it comes to food!'

Sure enough: John the Bathman, Harree and Pompom were leading this extraordinary procession. Fritz was right behind them, however, and pressing the leaders hard. I heard Monsieur Auguste crying in his child's voice:

'*Si tout-le-monde veut marcher dou-ce-ment nous allons ar-ri-ver plus tôt! Il faut pas faire comme ça!*'

Then suddenly the roar ceased. The mêlée integrated. We were marching in orderly ranks. B. said:

'The *Surveillant!*'

At the end of the corridor, opposite the kitchen window, there was a flight of stairs. On the third stair from the bottom stood (teetering a little slowly back and forth, his lean hands joined behind him and twitching regularly, a *képi* tilted forward on his cadaverous head so that its visor almost hid the weak eyes sunkenly peering from under droopy eyebrows, his pompous rooster-like body immaculately attired in a shiny uniform, his puttees sleeked, his *croix* polished)—The Fencer. There was a renovated look about him which made me laugh. Also his pose was ludicrously suggestive of Napoleon reviewing the armies of France.

Our column's first rank moved by him. I expected it to continue ahead through the door and into the open air, as I had myself done in going from *les douches* to *le cour;* but it turned a sharp right and then sharp left, and I perceived a short hall, almost hidden by the stairs. In a moment I had passed the Fencer myself and entered the hall. In another moment I was in a room, pretty nearly square, filled with rows of pillars. On turning into the hall the column had come almost to a standstill. I saw now that the reason for this slowing-down lay in the fact that on entering the room every man in turn passed a table and received a piece of bread from the chef. When B. and I came opposite the table the dispenser of bread smiled pleasantly and nodded to B., then selected a large hunk and pushed it rapidly into B.'s hands with an air of doing something which he shouldn't. B. introduced me, whereupon the smile and selection was repeated.

'He thinks I'm a German,' B. explained in a whisper, 'and that you are a German too.' Then aloud, to the cook: 'My friend here needs a spoon. He just got here this morning and they haven't given him one.'

The excellent person at the bread table hereupon said to me: 'You shall go to the window and say I tell you to

ask for spoon and you will catch one spoon'—and I broke
through the waiting line, approached the kitchen-window,
and demanded of a roguish face within:

'*Une cuillère, s'il vous plait.*'

The roguish face, which had been singing in a high
faint voice to itself, replied critically but not unkindly:

'*Vous êtes un nouveau?*'

I said that I was, that I had arrived late last night.

It disappeared, reappeared, and handed me a tin spoon
and cup, saying:

'*Vous n'avez pas de tasse?*'—'*Non,*' I said.

'*Tiens. Prends ça. Vite.*' Nodding in the direction of
the *Surveillant,* who was standing all this time on the
stairs behind me.

I had expected from the cook's phrase that something
would be thrown at me which I should have to catch, and
was accordingly somewhat relieved at the true state of
affairs. On re-entering the *salle à manger* I was greeted by
many cries and wavings, and looking in their direction
perceived *tout le monde* uproariously seated at wooden
benches which were placed on either side of an enormous
wooden table. There was a tiny gap in one bench where a
place had been saved for me by B. with the assistance of
Monsieur Auguste, Count Bragard, Harree and several
other fellow-convicts. In a moment I had straddled the
bench and was occupying the gap, spoon and cup in hand,
and ready for anything.

The din was perfectly terrific. It had a minutely large
quality. Here and there, in a kind of sonal darkness, solid
sincere unintelligible absurd wisps of profanity heavily
flickered. Optically the phenomenon was equally remarkable: seated waggingly swaying corpse-like figures, swaggering, pounding with their little spoons, roaring hoarse

unkempt. Evidently *Monsieur le Surveillant* had been forgotten. All at once the roar bulged unbearably. The roguish man, followed by the *chef* himself, entered with a suffering waddle, each of them bearing a huge bowl of steaming something. At least six people immediately rose, gesturing and imploring: '*Ici*'—'*Mais non, ici*'—'*Mettez le ici*—'

The bearers plumped their burdens carefully down, one at the head of the table and one in the middle. The men opposite the bowls stood up. Every man seized the empty plate in front of him and shoved it into his neighbour's hand; the plates moved toward the bowls, were filled amid uncouth protestations and accusations—'*Mettez plus que ça*'—'*C'est pas juste, alors*'—'*Donnez-moi encore des pommes*'—'*Nom de Dieu, il n'y en a pas assez*'—'*Cochon, qu'est-ce qu'il veut?*'—'Shut up'—'*Gottverdummer*'—and returned one by one. As each man received his own, he fell upon it with a sudden guzzle. Eventually, in front of me, solemnly sat a faintly-smoking urine-coloured circular broth, in which soggily hung half-suspended slabs of raw potato. Following the example of my neighbours, I too addressed myself to *La Soupe*. I found her luke-warm, completely flavourless. I examined the hunk of bread. It was almost bluish in colour; in taste mouldy, slightly sour. 'If you crumb some into the soup,' remarked B., who had been studying my reactions from the corner of his eye, 'they both taste better.' I tried the experiment. It was a complete success. At least one felt as if one were getting nourishment. Between gulps I smelled the bread furtively. It smelled rather much like an old attic in which kites and other toys gradually are forgotten in a gentle darkness.

B. and I were finishing our soup together when behind

and somewhat to the left there came the noise of a lock
being manipulated. I turned and saw in one corner of the
salle à manger a little door, shaking mysteriously. Finally
it was thrown open, revealing a sort of minute bar and a
little closet filled with what appeared to be groceries and
tobacco; and behind the bar, standing in the closet, a
husky competent-looking lady. 'It's the canteen,' B. said.
We rose, spoon in hand and breadhunk stuck on spoon,
and made our way to the lady. I had, naturally, no money;
but B. reassured me that before the day was over I should
see the *Gestionnaire* and make arrangements for drawing
on the supply of ready cash which the gendarmes who
took me from Gré had confided to the *Surveillant's* care;
eventually I could also draw on my account with Norton-
Harjes in Paris; meantime he had *quelques sous* which
might well go into *chocolat* and cigarettes. The large lady
had a pleasant quietness about her, a sort of simplicity,
which made me extremely desirous of complying with
B.'s suggestion. Incidentally I was feeling somewhat uncertain in the region of the stomach, due to the unique
quality of the lunch which I had just enjoyed, and I
brightened at the thought of anything as solid as *chocolat*.
Accordingly we purchased (or rather B. did) a *paquet
jaune* and a cake of something which was not Menier.
And the remaining *sous* we squandered on a glass apiece
of red acrid *pinard*, gravely and with great happiness
pledging the hostess of the occasion and then each other.

With the exception of ourselves hardly anyone patron-
ized the canteen, noting which I felt somewhat con-
spicuous. When, however, Harree, Pompom and John the
Bathman came rushing up and demanded cigarettes my
fears were dispelled. Moreover the *pinard* was excellent.

'Come on! Arrange yourselves!' the bull-neck cried

hoarsely as the five of us were lighting up; and we joined the line of fellow-prisoners with their breads and spoons, gaping, belching, trumpeting fraternally, by the door-way.

'*Tout le monde en haut!*' this *planton* roared.

Slowly we fled through the tiny hall, past the stairs (empty now of their Napoleonic burden), down the corridor, up the creaking, gnarled, damp flights, and (after the inevitable pause in which the escort rattled chains and locks) into The Enormous Room.

This would be about ten-thirty.

Just what I tasted, did, smelled, saw and heard, not to mention touched, between ten-thirty and the completion of the evening meal (otherwise the four-o'clock soup) I am quite at a loss to say. Whether it was that glass of *pinard* (plus or rather times the astonishing exhaustion bequeathed me by my journey of the day before) which caused me to enter temporarily the gates of forgetfulness, or whether the sheer excitement attendant upon my ultra-novel surroundings proved too much for an indispensable part of my so-called mind—I do not in the least know. I am fairly certain that I went on afternoon promenade. After which I must surely have mounted to await my supper in The Enormous Room. Whence (after the due and proper interval) I doubtless descended to the clutches of *La Soupe Extraordinaire* . . . yes, for I perfectly recall the cry which made me suddenly to re-enter the dimension of distinctness . . . and, by Jove, I had just finished a glass of *pinard* . . . when we heard—

'*A la promenade,*' . . . we issued *en queue*, firmly grasping our spoons and bread, through the dining-room door. Turning right we were emitted, by the door opposite the kitchen, from the building itself into the open air. A few steps and we passed through the little gate in the barb-wire fence of the *cour*.

Greatly refreshed by my second introduction to the canteen, and with the digestion of the somewhat extraordinary evening meal apparently assured, I gazed almost intelligently around me. Count Bragard had declined the evening promenade in favour of The Enormous Room, but I perceived in the crowd the now familiar faces of the three Hollanders—John, Harree and Pompom—likewise of The Bear, Monsieur Auguste, and Fritz. In the course of the next hour I had become, if not personally, at least optically, acquainted with nearly a dozen others.

One was a queer-looking, almost infantile man of perhaps thirty-five who wore a black vest, a pair of threadbare pants, a collarless striped shirt open at the neck with a gold stud therein, a cap slightly too large pulled down so that the visor almost hid his prominent eyebrows if not his tiny eyes, and something approximating sneakers. His expression was imitative and vacant. He stuck to Fritz most of the time, and took pains—when a girl leaned from her window—to betray a manliness of demeanour which contrasted absurdly with his mentor's naturally athletic bearing. He tried to speak (and evidently thought he spoke) English, or rather English words; but with the exception of a few obscenities pronounced in a surprisingly natural manner his vocabulary gave him considerable difficulty. Even when he and Fritz exchanged views, as they frequently did, in Danish, a certain linguistic awkwardness persisted; yielding the impression that to give or receive an idea entailed a tremendous effort of the intelligence. He was extremely vain, and indeed struck poses whenever he got a chance. He was also good-natured—stupidly so. It might be said of him

that he never knew defeat; since if, after staggering a few
moments under the weight of the bar which Fritz raised
and lowered with ease fourteen times under the stimulus
of a female gaze, the little man fell suddenly to earth
with his burden, not a trace of discomfiture could be
seen upon his small visage—he seemed, on the contrary,
well pleased with himself, and the subsequent pose which
his small body adopted demanded congratulations. When
he stuck his chest up or out, he looked a trifle like a ban-
tam rooster. When he tagged Fritz he resembled a rather
brittle monkey, a monkey on a stick perhaps, capable of
brief and stiff antics. His name was Jan.

On the huge beam of iron, sitting somewhat beautifully all by himself, I noticed somebody with pink cheeks
and blue eyes, in a dark suit of neatly kept clothes, with
a small cap on his head. His demeanour, in contrast to
the other occupants of the *cour,* was noticeably incon-
spicuous. In his poise lived an almost brilliant quietness.
His eyes were remarkably sensitive. They were apparently
anxious not to see people and things. He impressed me at
once by a shyness which was completely deerlike. Possibly he was afraid. Nobody knew him or anything about
him. I do not remember when we devised the name, but
B. and I referred to him as The Silent Man.

Somewhat overawed by the animals Harree and Pompom (but nevertheless managing to overawe a goodly
portion of his fellow-captives), an extraordinary human
being paced the *cour.* On gazing for the first time directly
at him I experienced a feeling of nausea. A figure inclined
to corpulence, dressed with care, remarkable only above
the neck—and then what a head! It was large, and had a
copious mop of limp hair combed back from the high
forehead—hair of a disagreeable blonde tint, dutch-cut

behind, falling over the pinkish soft neck almost to the shoulders. In this pianist's or artist's hair, which shook *en masse* when the owner walked, two large and outstanding and altogether brutal white ears tried to hide themselves. The face, a cross between classic Greek and Jew, had a Reynard expression, something distinctly wily and perfectly disagreeable. And equally with the hair blonde moustache—or rather moustachios projectingly important—waved beneath the prominent nostrils, and served to partially conceal the pallid mouth, weak and large, whose lips assumed from time to time a smile which had something almost fœtal about it. Over the even weaker chin was disposed a blonde goatee. The cheeks were fatty. The continually perspiring forehead exhibited innumerable pinkish pock-marks. In conversing with a companion this being emitted a disgusting smoothness, his very gestures were oily like his skin. He wore a pair of bloated wristless hands, the knuckles lost in fat, with which he smoothed the air from time to time. He was speaking low and effortless French, completely absorbed in the developing ideas which issued fluently from his moustachios. About him there clung an aura of cringing. His hair, whiskers and neck looked as if they were trick neck, whiskers and hair, as if they might at any moment suddenly disintegrate, as if the smoothness of his eloquence alone kept them in place.

We called him Judas.

Beside him, clumsily keeping the pace but not the step, was a tallish effeminate person whose immaculate funereal suit hung loosely upon an aged and hurrying anatomy. He wore a black big cap on top of his haggard and remarkably clean-shaven face, the most prominent feature of which was a red nose which sniffed a little now and then as if its owner was suffering from a severe cold. This person emanated age, neatness and despair. Aside from the nose, which compelled immediate attention, his face consisted of a few large planes loosely juxtaposed and registering pathos. His motions were without grace. He had a certain refinement. He could not have been more than forty-five. There was worry on every inch of him. Possibly he thought that he might die. B. said, 'He's a Belgian, a friend of Count Bragard, and his name is Monsieur Pet-airs.' From time to time Monsieur Petairs remarked something delicately and pettishly in a gentle and weak voice. His Adam's-apple, at such moments, jumped about in a longish, slack, wrinkled, skinny neck which was like the neck of a turkey. To this turkey the approach of Thanksgiving inspired dread. From time to time M. Petairs looked about him sidewise as if he expected to see a hatchet. His hands were claws, kind, awkward and nervous. They twitched. The bony and wrinkled things looked as if they would like to close quickly upon a throat.

B. called my attention to a figure squatting in the middle of the *cour* with his broad back against one of the more miserable trees. This figure was clothed in a remarkably picturesque manner: it wore a dark sombrero-like hat with a large drooping brim, a bright red gipsy shirt of some remarkably fine material with huge sleeves loosely falling, and baggy corduroy trousers whence escaped two brown shapely naked feet. On moving a little I discovered a face—perhaps the handsomest face that I have ever seen, of a gold brown colour, framed in an amazingly large and beautiful black beard. The features were finely formed and almost fluent, the eyes soft and extraordinarily sensitive, the mouth delicate and firm beneath a black moustache which fused with the silky and

wonderful darkness falling upon the breast. The face
contained a beauty and dignity which, as I first saw it,
annihilated the surrounding tumult without an effort.
Around the carefully formed nostrils there was something almost of contempt. The cheeks had known suns
of which I might not think. The feet had travelled
nakedly in countries not easily imagined. Seated gravely
in the mud and noise of the *cour,* under the pitiful and
scraggly *pommier* ... behind the eyes lived a world of
complete strangeness and silence. The composure of the
body was graceful and Jove-like. This being might have
been a prophet come out of a country nearer to the sun.
Perhaps a god who had lost his road and allowed himself
to be taken prisoner by *le gouvernement français.* At
least a prince of a dark and desirable country, a king over
a gold-skinned people, who would return when he wished
to his fountains and his houris. I learned upon inquiry
that he travelled in various countries with a horse and
cart and his wife and children, selling bright colours to
the women and men of these countries. As it turned out,
he was one of The Delectable Mountains; to discover
which I had come a long and difficult way. Wherefore I
shall tell you no more about him for the present, except
that his name was Joseph Demestre.

We called him The Wanderer.

I was still wondering at my good luck in occupying the
same miserable yard with this exquisite personage when
a hoarse, rather thick voice shouted from the gate:
'*L'américain!*'

It was a *planton,* in fact the chief *planton* for whom
all ordinary *plantons* had unutterable respect and whom
all mere men unutterably hated. It was the *planton* into

whom I had had the distinguished honour of bumping shortly after my visit to *le bain*.

The Hollanders and Fritz were at the gate in a mob, all shouting 'Which' in four languages.

This *planton* did not deign to notice them. He repeated roughly '*L'américain.*' Then, yielding a point to their frenzied entreaties: '*Le nouveau.*'

B. said to me, 'Probably he's going to take you to the *Gestionnaire*. You're supposed to see him when you arrive. He's got your money and will keep it for you, and give you an allowance twice a week. You can't draw more than 20 francs. I'll hold your bread and spoon.'

'Where the devil is the American?' cried the *planton*.

'*Me voici.*'

'Follow me.'

I followed his back and rump and holster through the little gate in the barbed-wire fence and into the building, at which point he commanded 'Proceed.'

I asked 'Where?'

'Straight ahead,' he said angrily.

I proceeded. 'Left!' he cried. I turned. A door confronted me. '*Entrez,*' he commanded. I did. An unremarkable-looking gentleman in a French uniform, sitting at a sort of table. '*Monsieur le médecin, le nouveau.*' The doctor got up. 'Open your shirt.' I did. 'Take down your pants.' I did. 'All right.' Then, as the *planton* was about to escort me from the room: 'English?' he asked with curiosity. 'No,' I said, 'American.' '*Vraiment*'—he contemplated me with attention. 'South American are you?' 'United States,' I explained. '*Vraiment*'—he looked curiously at me, not disagreeably in the least. '*Pourquoi vous êtes ici?*' 'I don't know,' I said, smiling pleasantly, 'except that my friend wrote some letters which were intercepted by the French censor.' 'Ah!' he remarked. '*C'est tout.*'

And I departed. 'Proceed!' cried the Black Holster. I retraced my steps, and was about to exit through the door leading to the *cour*, when 'Stop! *Nom de Dieu!* Proceed!'

I asked 'Where?' completely bewildered.

'Up,' he said angrily.

I turned to the stairs on the left, and climbed.

'Not so fast there,' he roared behind me.

I slowed up. We reached the landing. I was sure that the *Gestionnaire* was a very fierce man—probably a lean slight person who would rush at me from the nearest door, saying 'Hands up' in French, whatever that may be. The door opposite me stood open. I looked in. There was the *Surveillant* standing, hands behind back, approvingly regarding my progress. I was asking myself, Should I bow? when a scurrying and a tittering made me look left, along a dark and particularly dirty hall. Women's voices . . . I almost fell with surprise. Were not these shadows faces peering a little boldly at me from doors? How many girls were there—it sounded as if there were a hundred—

'*Qu'est-ce que vous foutez*,' etc., and the *planton* gave me a good shove in the direction of another flight of stairs. I obligingly ascended; thinking of the *Surveillant* as a spider, elegantly poised in the centre of his nefarious web, waiting for a fly to make too many struggles. . . .

At the top of this flight I was confronted by a second hall. A shut door indicated the existence of a being directly over the *Surveillant's* holy head. Upon this door, lest I should lose time in speculating, was in ample letters inscribed:

GESTIONNAIRE.

I felt unutterably lost. I approached the door. I even started to push it.

'*Attends, Nom de Dieu.*' The *planton* gave me another shove, faced the door, knocked twice, and cried in accents of profound respect: '*Monsieur le Gestionnaire*'—after which he gazed at me with really supreme contempt, his neat pig-like face becoming almost circular.

I said to myself: This *Gestionnaire*, whoever he is, must be a very terrible person, a frightful person, a person utterly without mercy.

From within a heavy, stupid, pleasant voice lazily remarked:

'*Entrez.*'

The *planton* threw the door open, stood stiffly on the threshold, and gave me the look which *plantons* give to eggs when *plantons* are a little hungry.

I crossed the threshold, trembling with (let us hope) anger.

Before me, seated at a table, was a very fat personage with a black skull-cap perched upon its head. Its face was possessed of an enormous nose, on which pince-nez precariously roosted; otherwise said face was large, whiskered, very German and had three chins. Extraordinary creature. Its belly, as it sat, was slightly dented by the table-top, on which table-top rested several enormous tomes similar to those employed by the recording angel on the Day of Judgement, an ink-stand or two, innumerable pens and pencils, and some positively fatal-looking papers. The person was dressed in worthy and semi-dismal clothes amply cut to afford a promenade for the big stomach. The coat was of that extremely thin black material which occasionally is affected by clerks and dentists and more often by librarians. If ever I looked

upon an honest German jowl, or even upon a caricature
thereof, I looked upon one now. Such a round, fat, red,
pleasant, beer-drinking face as reminded me only and
immediately of huge meerschaum pipes, Deutsche Verein
mottos, sudsy seidels of Wurtzburger, and Jacob Wirth's
(once upon a time) brachwurst. Such pin-like pink merry
eyes as made me think of Kris Kringle himself. Such extraordinarily huge reddish hands as might have grasped
six seidels together in the Deutsche Küche on 13th Street.
I gasped with pleasurable relief.

Monsieur le Gestionnaire looked as if he was trying
very hard, with the aid of his beribboned glasses and
librarian's jacket (not to mention a very ponderous gold
watch-chain and locket that were supported by his copious equator), to appear possessed of the solemnity
necessarily emanating from his lofty and responsible office. This solemnity, however, met its Waterloo in his
frank and stupid eyes, not to say his trilogy of cheerful
chins—so much so that I felt like crying 'Wie gehts!' and
cracking him on his huge back. Such an animal! A contented animal, a bulbous animal; the only living hippopotamus in captivity, fresh from the Nile.

He contemplated me with a natural, under the circumstances, curiosity. He even naïvely contemplated me. As
if I were hay. My hay-coloured head perhaps pleased him,
as a hippopotamus. He would perhaps eat me. He grunted,
exposing tobacco-yellow tusks, and his tiny eyes twit-
tered. Finally he gradually uttered, with a thick accent,
the following extremely impressive dictum:

'*C'est l'américain.*'

I felt much pleased, and said, '*Oui, j'suis américain,
Monsieur.*'

He rolled half over backwards in his creaking chair

with wonderment at such an unexpected retort. He studied my face with a puzzled air, appearing slightly embarrassed that before him should stand *l'américain* and that *l'américain* should admit it, and that it should all be so wonderfully clear. I saw a second dictum, even more profound than the first, ascending from his black vest. The chain and fob trembled with anticipation. I was wholly fascinated. What vast blob of wisdom would find its difficult way out of him? The bulbous lips wiggled in a pleasant smile.

'*Voo parlez français.*'

This was delightful. The *planton* behind me was obviously angered by the congenial demeanour of *Monsieur le Gestionnaire*, and rasped with his boot upon the threshold. The maps to my right and left, maps of France, maps of the Mediterranean, of Europe even, were abashed. A little anæmic and humble biped whom I had not previously noted, as he stood in one corner with a painfully deferential expression, looked all at once relieved. I guessed, and correctly guessed, that this little thing was the translator of La Ferté. His weak face wore glasses of the same type as the hippopotamus's, but without a huge black ribbon. I decided to give him a tremor; and said to the hippo, '*Un peu, Monsieur,*' at which the little thing looked sickly.

The hippopotamus benevolently remarked, '*Voo parlez bien,*' and his glasses fell off. He turned to the watchful *planton:*

'*Voo poovez aller. Je vooz appelerai.*'

The watchful *planton* did a sort of salute and closed the door after him. The skull-capped dignitary turned to his papers and began mouthing them with his huge

hands, grunting pleasantly. Finally he found one, and
said lazily:

'*De quel endroit que vous êtes?*'

'*De Massachusetts,*' said I.

He wheeled round and stared dumbly at the weak-
faced one, who looked at a complete loss, but managed to
stammer simperingly that it was a part of the United
States.

'UH.' The hippopotamus said.

Then he remarked that I had been arrested, and I
agreed that I had been arrested.

Then he said: 'Have you got any money?' and before
I could answer clambered heavily to his feet and, leaning
over the table before which I stood, punched me gently.

'Uh,' said the hippopotamus, sat down, and put on his
glasses.

'I have your money here,' he said. 'You are allowed
to draw a little from time to time. You may draw 20
francs, if you like. You may draw it twice a week.'

'I should like to draw 20 francs now,' I said, 'in order
to buy something at the canteen.'

'You will give me a receipt,' said the hippopotamus.
'You want to draw 20 francs now, quite so.' He began,
puffing and grunting, to make handwriting of a peculiarly large and somewhat loose variety.

The weak face now stepped forward, and asked me
gently: 'Hugh er a merry can?'—so I carried on a brilliant conversation in pidgin-English about my relatives
and America until interrupted by:

'Uh.'

The hip had finished.

'Sign your name here,' he said, and I did. He looked
about in one of the tomes and checked something oppo-

site my name, which I enjoyed seeing in the list of in-
mates. It had been spelled, erased, and re-spelled several
times.

Monsieur le Gestionnaire contemplated my signature.
Then he looked up, smiled, and nodded recognition to
some one behind me. I turned. There stood (having long
since noiselessly entered) the Fencer Himself, nervously
clasping and unclasping his hands behind his back and
regarding me with approval, or as a keeper regards some
rare monkey newly forwarded from its habitat by Hagen-
beck.

The hip pulled out a drawer. He found, after hunting,
some notes. He counted two off, licking his big thumb
with a pompous gesture, and having recounted them
passed them heavily to me. I took them as a monkey
takes a coco-nut.

'Do you wish?'—the *Gestionnaire* nodded toward me,
addressing the Fencer.

'No, no,' the Fencer said bowingly. 'I have talked to
him already.'

'Call that *planton!*' cried *Monsieur le Gestionnaire*,
to the little thing. The little thing ran out dutifully and
called in a weak voice *'Planton!'*

A gruff but respectful *'Oui'* boomed from below-stairs.
In a moment the *planton* of *plantons* had respectfully
entered.

'The promenade being over, you can take him to the
men's room,' said the *Surveillant*, as the hippo (immensely relieved and rather proud of himself) collapsed
in his creaking chair.

Feeling like a suit-case in the clutches of a porter, I
obediently preceded my escort down two flights, first
having bowed to the hippopotamus and said *'Merci'*—to

which courtesy the Hippo paid no attention. As we went along the dank hall on the ground floor, I regretted that no whispers and titters had greeted my descent. Probably the furious *planton* had seen to it that *les femmes* kept their rooms in silence: We ascended the three flights at the farther end of the corridor, the *planton* of all *plantons* unlocked and unbolted the door at the top landing, and I was swallowed by The Enormous Room.

I made for B., in my excitement allowing myself to wave the bank-notes. Instantly a host had gathered at my side. On my way to my bed—a distance of perhaps thirty feet—I was patted on the back by Harree, Pompom and Bathhouse John, congratulated by Monsieur Auguste, and saluted by Fritz. Arriving, I found myself the centre of a stupendous crowd. People who had previously had nothing to say to me, who had even sneered at my unwashed and unshaven exterior, now addressed me in terms of more than polite interest. Judas himself stopped in a promenade of the room, eyed me a moment, hastened smoothly to my vicinity, and made a few oily remarks of a pleasant nature. Simultaneously by Monsieur Auguste, Harree and Fritz I was advised to hide my money and hide it well. There were people, you know . . . who didn't hesitate, you understand . . . I understood, and to the vast disappointment of the clamorous majority reduced my wealth to its lowest terms and crammed it in my trousers, stuffing several trifles of a bulky nature on top of it. Then I gazed quietly around with a William S. Hart expression calculated to allay any undue excitement. One by one the curious and enthusiastic faded from me, and I was left with the few whom I already considered my friends; with which few B. and myself proceeded to while away the time remaining before *Lumières Eteintes*.

Incidentally, I exchanged (in the course of the next two hours) a considerable mass of two-legged beings for a number of extremely interesting individuals. Also, in that somewhat limited period of time, I gained all sorts of highly enlightening information concerning the lives, habits and likes of half a dozen of as fine companions as it has ever been my luck to meet or, so far as I can now imagine, ever will be. In prison one learns several million things—if one is *l'américain* from *Mass-a-chu-setts*. When the ominous and awe-inspiring rattle on the farther side of the locked door announced that the captors were come to bid the captives good night, I was still in the midst of conversation and had been around the world a number of times. At the clanking sound our little circle centripetally disintegrated, as if by sheer magic: and I was left somewhat dizzily to face a renewal of reality.

The door shot wide. The *planton's* almost indistinguishable figure in the doorway told me that the entire room was dark. I had not noticed the darkness. Somebody had placed a candle (which I recalled having seen on a table in the middle of the room when I looked up once or twice during the conversation) on a little shelf hard by the *cabinet*. There had been men playing at cards by this candle—now everybody was quietly reposing upon the floor along three sides of The Enormous Room. The *planton* entered. Walked over to the light. Said something about everybody being present, and was answered by a number of voices in a more or less profane affirmative. Strutted to and fro, kicked the *cabinet*, flashed an electric torch, and walked up the room examining each *paillasse* to make sure it had an occupant. Crossed the room

at the upper end. Started down on my side. The white
circle was in my eyes. The *planton* stopped. I stared stupidly and wearily into the glare. The light moved all
over me and my bed. The rough voice behind the glare
said:

'*Vous êtes le nouveau?*'

Monsieur Auguste, from my left, said quietly:

'*Oui, c'est le nouveau.*'

The holder of the torch grunted, and (after pausing
a second at B.'s bed to inspect a picture of perfect innocence) banged out through the door, which whanged to
behind him and another *planton* of whose presence I had
been hitherto unaware. A perfect symphony of '*Bonne-
nuit's*', '*Dormez-bien's*' and other affectionate admonitions greeted the exeunt of the authorities. They were
advised by various parts of the room in divers tongues to
dream of their wives, to be careful of themselves in bed,
to avoid catching cold, and to attend to a number of personal wants before retiring. The symphony gradually
collapsed, leaving me sitting in a state of complete wonderment, dead tired and very happy, upon my *paillasse*.

'I think I'll turn in,' I said to the neighbouring darkness.

'That's what I'm doing,' B.'s voice said.

'By God,' I said, 'this is the finest place I've ever been
in my life.'

'It's the finest place in the world,' said B.'s voice.

'Thank Heaven, we're out of A.'s way and the——
Section Sanitaire,' I grunted as I placed my boots where
a pillow might have been imagined.

'Amen,' B.'s voice said.

'*Si vous met-tez vos chaus-sures en des-sous de la pail-*

lasse,' Monsieur Auguste's voice said, *'vous al-lez bien dor-mir.'*

I thanked him for the suggestion, and did so. I reclined in an ecstasy of happiness and weariness. There could be nothing better than this. To sleep.

'Got a *gottverdummer* cigarette?' Harree's voice asked of Fritz.

'No bloody fear,' Fritz's voice replied coolly.

Snores had already begun in various keys at various distances in various directions. The candle flickered a little, as if darkness and itself were struggling to the death, and darkness were winning.

'I'll get a chew from John,' Harree's voice said.

Three or four *paillasses* away, a subdued conversation was proceeding. I found myself listening sleepily.

'Et puis,' a voice said, *'je suis réformé. . . .'*

V

A GROUP OF PORTRAITS

WITH the reader's permission I beg, at this point of my narrative, to indulge in one or two extrinsic observations.

In the preceding pages I have described my Pilgrim's Progress from the Slough of Despond, commonly known as *Section Sanitaire Vingt-et-Un* (then located at Germaine) through the mysteries of Noyon, Gré and Paris to the *Porte de Triage de La Ferté Macé*, Orne. With the end of my first day as a certified inhabitant of the latter institution a definite progression is brought to a close. Beginning with my second day at La Ferté a new period opens. This period extends to the moment of my departure and includes the discovery of The Delectable Mountains, two of which—The Wanderer, and I shall not say the other—have already been sighted. It is like a vast grey box in which are laid helter-skelter a great many toys, each of which is itself completely significant apart from the always unchanging temporal dimension which merely contains it along with the rest. I make this point clear for the benefit of any of my readers who have not had the distinguished privilege of being in jail. To those who have been in jail my meaning is at once apparent; particularly if they have had the highly enlightening experience of being in jail with a perfectly indefinite sentence. How, in such a case, could events occur and be remembered otherwise than as individualities distinct from Time Itself? Or, since one day and the

next are the same to such a prisoner, where does Time
come in at all? Obviously, once the prisoner is habituated
to his environment, once he accepts the fact that speculation as to when he will regain his liberty cannot possibly shorten the hours of his incarceration and may very
well drive him into a state of unhappiness (not to say
morbidity), events can no longer succeed each other:
whatever happens, while it may happen in connection
with some other perfectly distinct happening, does not
happen in a scale of temporal priorities—each happening
is self-sufficient, irrespective of minutes, months and the
other treasures of freedom.

It is for this reason that I do not purpose to inflict upon
the reader a diary of my alternative aliveness and non-
existence at La Ferté—not because such a diary would
unutterably bore him, but because the diary or time
method is a technique which cannot possibly do justice
to timelessness. I shall (on the contrary) lift from their
grey box at random certain (to me) more or less astonishing toys; which may or may not please the reader, but
whose colours and shapes and textures are a part of that
actual Present—without future and past—whereof they
alone are cognizant who, so to speak, have submitted to
an amputation of the world.

I have already stated that La Ferté was a *Porte de Triage*
—that is to say, a place where suspects of all varieties
were herded by *le gouvernement français* preparatory to
their being judged as to their guilt by a Commission. If
the Commission found that they were wicked persons,
or dangerous persons, or undesirable persons, or puzzling
persons, or persons in some way insusceptible of analysis,
they were sent from La Ferté to a 'regular' prison, called
Précigné, in the province of Sarthe. About Précigné the

most awful rumours were spread. It was whispered that it had a huge moat about it, with an infinity of barbed-wire fences thirty feet high, and lights trained on the walls all night to discourage the escape of prisoners. Once in Précigné you were 'in' for good and all, *pour la durée de la guerre*, which *durée* was a subject of occasional and dismal speculation—occasional for reasons (as I have mentioned) of mental health; dismal for unreasons of diet, privation, filth, and other trifles. La Ferté was, then, a stepping-stone either to freedom or to Précigné, the chances in the former case being—no speculation here—something less than the now celebrated formula made famous by the 18th amendment. But the excellent and inimitable and altogether benignant French government was not satisfied with its own generosity in presenting one merely with Précigné—beyond that lurked a *cauchemar* called by the singularly poetic name, Isle de Groix. A man who went to Isle de Groix was done.

As the *Surveillant* said to us all, leaning out of a littlish window, and to me personally upon occasion—

'You are not prisoners. Oh, no. No indeed. I should say not. Prisoners are not treated like this. You are lucky.'

I had *de la chance* all right, but that was something which *pauvre M. le Surveillant* wot altogether not of. As for my fellow-prisoners, I am sorry to say that he was —it seems to my humble personality—quite wrong. For who was eligible to La Ferté? Anyone whom the police could find in the lovely country of France (*a*) who was not guilty of treason, (*b*) who could not prove that he was not guilty of treason. By treason I refer to any little annoying habits of independent thought or action which *en temps de guerre* are put in a hole and covered over, with the somewhat naïve idea that from their cadavers

violets will grow whereof the perfume will delight all
good men and true and make such worthy citizens forget
their sorrows. Fort Leavenworth, for instance, emanates
even now a perfume which is utterly delightful to certain
Americans. Just how many La Fertés France boasted (and
for all I know may still boast) God Himself knows. At
least, in that Republic, amnesty has been proclaimed, or
so I hear.—But to return to the *Surveillant's* remark.

J'avais de la chance. Because I am by profession a
painter and a writer. Whereas my very good friends, all
of them deeply suspicious characters, most of them trai-
tors, without exception lucky to have the use of their
cervical vertebræ, etc., etc., could (with a few exceptions) write not a word and read not a word; neither
could they *faire la photographie* as Monsieur Auguste
chucklingly called it (at which I blushed with pleasure):
worst of all, the majority of these dark criminals who
had been caught in nefarious plots against the honour of
France were totally unable to speak French. Curious
thing. Often I pondered the unutterable and inextin-
guishable wisdom of the police, who—undeterred by
facts which would have deceived less astute intelligences
into thinking that these men were either too stupid or too
simple to be connoisseurs of the art of betrayal—swooped
upon their helpless prey with that indescribable courage
which is the prerogative of policemen the world over,
and bundled same prey into the La Fertés of that mighty
nation upon some, at least, of whose public buildings it
seems to me that I remember reading

Liberté. Egalité. Fraternité.

And I wondered that France should have a use for
Monsieur Auguste, who had been arrested (because he

was a Russian) when his fellow munition workers made
la grève, and whose wife wanted him in Paris because she
was hungry and because their child was getting to look
queer and white. Monsieur Auguste, that desperate ruf-
fian exactly five feet tall who—when he could not keep
from crying (one must think about one's wife or even
one's child once or twice, I merely presume, if one loves
them) *'et ma femme est très gen-tille, elle est fran-çaise
et très belle, très, très belle, vrai-ment elle n'est pas comme
moi, un pe-tit homme laid, ma femme est grande et
belle, elle sait bien lire et é-crire, vrai-ment; et notre fils
... vous de-vez voir notre pe-tit fils ...'*—used to start
up and cry out, taking B. by one arm and me by the
other:

'*Al-lons, mes amis! Chan-tons "Quackquackquack."* '

Whereupon we would join in the following song, which
Monsieur Auguste had taught us with great care, and
whose renditions gave him unspeakable delight:

'Un canard, déployant ses ailes
>
> (Quackquackquack)

Il disait à sa canarde fidèle
>
> (Quackquackquack)

Il chantait (Quackquackquack)

Il faisait (Quackquackquack)

Quand' (spelling mine)

'finirons nos desseins,
>
> Quack.
>
> Quack.
>
> Quack.
>
> Qua-
>
> ck.'

I suppose I will always puzzle over the ecstasies of That
Wonderful Duck. And how Monsieur Auguste, the

merest gnome of a man, would bend backwards in absolute laughter at this song's spirited conclusion upon a
note so low as to wither us all.

Then too the Schoolmaster.

A little fragile old man. His trousers were terrifically
too big for him. When he walked (in an insecure and
frightened way) his trousers did the most preposterous
wrinkles. If he leaned against a tree in the *cour*, with a
very old and also fragile pipe in his pocket—the stem
(which looked enormous in contrast to the owner) protruding therefrom—his three-sizes-too-big collar would
leap out so as to make his wizened neck appear no thicker
than the white necktie which flowed upon his two-sizes-
too-big shirt. He wore always a coat which reached below
his knees, which coat with which knees perhaps some one
had once given him. It had huge shoulders which sprouted,
like wings, on either side of his elbows when he sat in
The Enormous Room quietly writing at a tiny three-
legged table, a very big pen walking away with his weak
bony hand. His too big cap had a little button on top
which looked like the head of a nail, and suggested that
this old doll had once lost its poor grey head and had been
repaired by means of tacking its head upon its neck, where
it should be and properly belonged. Of what hideous crime
was this being suspected? By some mistake he had three
moustaches, two of them being eyebrows. He used to
teach school in Alsace-Lorraine, and his sister is there.
In speaking to you his kind face is peacefully reduced
to triangles. And his tie buttons on every morning with
a Bang! And off he goes; led about by his celluloid collar, gently worried about himself, delicately worried
about the world. At eating time he looks sidelong as he
stuffs soup into stiff lips. There are two holes where cheeks

might have been. Lessons hide in his wrinkles. Bells ding
in the oldness of eyes. Did he, by any chance, tell the children that there are such monstrous things as peace and
goodwill ... a corrupter of youth, no doubt ... he is altogether incapable of anger, wholly timid and tintinnabu-
lous. And he had always wanted so much to know—if
there were wild horses in America?

Yes, probably the Schoolmaster was a notorious sedi-
tionist. The all-wise French government has its ways,
which, like the ways of God, are wonderful. But how
about Emile?

Emile the Bum. Is the reader acquainted with the car-
toons of Mr. F. Opper? If not, he cannot properly relish
this personage. Emile the Bum was a man of thought.
In chasing his legs, his trousers seat scoots intriguingly
up-and-to-the-side. How often, Emile the Bum, *après
la soupe,* have I ascended behind thee; going slowly up
and up and up the miserable stairs behind thy pants'
timed slackness. Emile possesses a scarf which he winds
about his ample thighs, thereby connecting his otherwise
elusively independent trousers with that very important
individual—his stomach. His face is unshaven. He is
unshorn. Like all Belgians, he has a quid in his gums
night and day, which quid he buys outside in the town;
for in his capacity of Somethingorother (perhaps assistant
sweeper) he journeys (under proper surveillance) occasionally from the gates which unthoughtful men may
not leave. His F. Opper soul peeps from slippery little
eyes. Having entered an argument—be its subject the
rights of humanity, the price of potatoes, or the wisdom
of warfare—Emile the Bum sticks to his theme and his
man. He is, curiously enough, above all things sincere.
He is almost treacherously sincere. Having argued a man

to a standstill and won from him an abject admission of complete defeat, Emile stalks rollingly away. Upon reaching a distance of perhaps five metres he suddenly makes a rush at his victim—having turned around with the velocity of lightning, in fact so quickly that no one saw him do it;—his victim writhes anew under the lash of Emile the Bum's insatiate loquacity,—admits, confesses, begs pardon—and off Emile stalks rollingly . . . to turn again and dash back at his almost weeping opponent, thundering sputteringly with rejuvenated vigour, a vigour which annihilates everything (including reason) before it. Otherwise, considering that he is a Belgian, he is extraordinarily good-natured and minds his business rollingly and sucks his quid happily. Not a tremendously harmful individual, one would say . . . and why did the French Government need him behind lock and key, I wonder? It was his fatal eloquence, doubtless, which betrayed him to the clutches of *La Misère*. Gendarmes are sensitive in peculiar ways; they do not stand for any misleading information upon the probable destiny of the price of potatoes—since it is their duty and their privilege to resent all that is seditious to the Government, and since The Government includes the Minister of Agriculture (or something), and since the Minister of Something includes, of course, potatoes, and that means that no one is at liberty to in any way (however slightly or insinuatingly) insult a potato. I bet Emile the Bum insulted two potatoes.

We still have, however, the problem of the man in the Orange Cap. The man in the Orange Cap was, optically as well as in every other respect, delightful. Until the Zulu came (of which more later) he was a little and quietly lonely. The Zulu, however, played with him. He was always chasing the Zulu around trees in the *cour;* dodging, peeping, tagging him on his coat, and sometimes doing something like laughing. Before the Zulu came he was lonely because nobody would have anything to do with the little man in the Orange Cap. This was not because he had done something unpopular; on the contrary, he was perfectly well behaved. It was because he could not speak. Perhaps I should say with more accuracy that he could not articulate. This fact did not prevent the little man in the Orange Cap from being shy. When I asked him one day, what he had been arrested for, he replied GOO in the shyest manner imaginable. He was altogether delightful. Subconsciously every one was, of course, fearful that he himself would go nuts—every one with the exception of those who had already gone nuts, who were in the wholly pleasant situation of having no fear. The still sane were therefore inclined to snub and otherwise affront their luckier fellow-sufferers—unless, as in the case of Bathhouse John, the insane was fully protected by a number of unbeatable gentlemen of his own nationality. The little person was snubbed and affronted at every turn. He didn't care the littlest personal bit, beyond being quietly lonely so far as his big, blue, expressionless eyes were concerned, and keeping out of the way when fights were on. Which fights he sometimes caught himself enjoying, whereupon he would go sit under a very small apple-tree and ruminate thoroughly upon non-existence until he had sufficiently punished himself. I still don't see how the *gouvernement français* decided to need him at La Ferté, unless—ah! that's it . . . he was really a super-intelligent crook who had robbed the cabinet of the greatest cabinet-minister of the greatest cabinet-minister's cabinet papers, a crime involving the remarkable and demoralizing disclosure that President Poincaré had, the night before, been discovered in an unequal hand to hand battle with a défaitistically-minded bed-bug ... and all the apparent idiocy of the little man with the Orange Cap was a skilfully executed bluff ... and probably he was, even when I knew him, gathering evidence of a nature so derogatory as to be well-nigh unpublishable even by the disgusting *Défaitiste* Organ itself; evidence about the innocent and faithful *plantons* ... yes, now I remember, I asked him in French if it wasn't a fine day (because, as always, it was raining, and he and I alone had dared the promenade together) and he looked me straight in the eyes, and said WOO, and smiled shyly. That would seem to corroborate the theory that he was a master mind, for (obviously) the letters, W, O, O, stand for Wilhelm, Ober, Olles, which again is Austrian for Down With Yale. Yes, yes. *Le gouvernement français* was right, as always. Somebody once told me that the little person was an Austrian, and that The Silent Man was an Austrian, and that—whisper it—they were both Austrians! And that was why they were arrested; just as So-and-so (being a Turk) was naturally arrested, and So-and-so, a Pole, was inevitably naturally and of course (*en temps de guerre*) arrested. And me, an American; wasn't me arrested? I said Me certainly was, and Me's friend, too.

Once I did see the Orange Cap walk shyly up to The Silent Man. They looked at each other, both highly embarrassed, both perhaps conscious that they ought to say something Austrian to each other. The Silent Man looked away. The little person's face became vacant and lonely, and he tip-toed quietly back to his apple-tree.

'So-and-so, being a Turk' moved in one night, *paillasse* and all—having arrived from Paris on a very late train, heavily guarded by three gendarmes—to a vacant spot temporarily which separated my bed from the next bed on my right. Of the five definite and confirmed amusements which were established at La Ferté Macé—to wit, (1) spitting, (2) playing cards, (3) insulting *plantons*, (4) writing to the girls, and (5) fighting—I possessed a slight aptitude for the first only. By long practice, leaning with various more accomplished artists from a window and attempting to hit either the sentinel below or a projecting window-ledge or a spot of mud which, after refined and difficult intellectual exercise, we all had succeeded in agreeing upon, I had become not to be sure a master of the art of spitting but a competitor to be reckoned with so far as accuracy was concerned. Spitting in bed was not only amusing, it was—for climatic and other reasons—a necessity. The vacant place to my right made a very agreeable not to say convenient spittoon. Not every one, in fact only two or three, had my advantage. But every one had to spit at night. As I lay in bed, having for the third time spit into my spittoon, I was roused by a vision in neatly pressed pyjamas which had arisen from the darkness directly beside me. I sat up and confronted a small and, as nearly as I could make out, Jewish ghost, with sensitive eyes and an expression of mild protest centred in his talking cheeks. The language, said I, is Arabian—but who ever heard of an Arab in pyjamas? So I humbly apologized in French, explaining that his advent was to me as unexpected as it was pleasant. Next morning we exchanged the visiting-cards which prisoners use, that is to say he smoked one of my cigarettes and I one of his, and I learned that he was a Turk whose brother worked in Paris for a confectioner. With a very graceful and polite address he sought in his not over-

copious baggage and produced, to my delight and astonishment, the most delicious sweetmeats which I have ever
sampled. His generosity was as striking as his refinement.
We were fast friends in fifteen minutes. Of an evening,
subsequently, he would sit on B.'s bed or mine and tell
us about how he could not imagine that he could have
been arrested; tell it with a restrained wonderment which
we found extraordinarily agreeable. He was not at all
annoyed when we questioned him about the Arabian,
Turkish and Persian languages, and when pressed he wrote
a little for us with a simplicity and elegance that were
truly enchanting. I have spent many contented minutes
sitting alone copying certain of these rhythmic fragments. We hinted that he might perhaps sing, at which
he merely blushed as if he were remembering (or possibly dreaming of) something distant and too pleasant for
utterance.

He was altogether too polite not to have been needed
at La Ferté.

In supposing that we needed a professor of dancing the
French government made, perhaps, one little mistake—
I am so bold as to say this because I recall that the extraordinary being in question was with us only a short while.
Whither he went the Lord knows, but he left with great
cheerfulness. A vain blond boy of perhaps eighteen in
blue velvet corduroy pantaloons, who wore a big sash, and
exclaimed to us all in confidence:

'Moi, j'suis professeur de danse.'
Adding that he held at that minute 'vingt diplômes.' The
Hollanders had no use for him but we rather liked him—
as you would like a somewhat absurd peacock who, for
some reason, lit upon the sewer in which you were living
for the eternal nonce. About him I remember nothing

else; save that he talked boxing with an air of bravado and addressed every one as 'mon vieux.' When he left, clutching his baggage lightly and a little pale, it was as if our dung-heap were minus a butterfly. I imagine that Monsieur Malvy was fond of collecting butterflies—until he got collected himself. Some day I must visit him, at the Santé or whatever health resort he inhabits, and (introducing myself as one of those whom he sent to La Ferté Macé) question him upon the subject.

I had almost forgotten The Bear—number two, not to be confused with the seeker of cigarette-ends. A big, shaggy person, a farmer, talked about 'mon petit jardin,' an anarchist, wrote practically all the time (to the gentle annoyance of The Schoolmaster) at the queer-legged table; wrote letters (which he read aloud with evident satisfaction to himself) addressing 'my confrères,' stimulating them to even greater efforts, telling them that the time was ripe, that the world consisted of brothers, etc. I liked The Bear. He had a sincerity which, if somewhat startlingly uncouth, was always definitely compelling. His French itself was both uncouth and startling. I hardly think he was a dangerous bear. Had I been the French government I should have let him go berrying, as a bear must and should, to his heart's content. Perhaps I liked him best for his great awkward way of presenting an idea —he scooped it out of its environment with a hearty paw in a way which would have delighted anyone save *le gouvernement français*. He had, I think,

VIVE LA LIBERTÉ

tattooed in blue and green on his big, hairy chest. A fine bear. A bear whom no twitchings at his muzzle nor any starvation or yet any beating could ever teach to dance . . .

but then, I am partial to bears. Of course none of this bear's letters ever got posted—*Le Directeur* was not that sort of person; nor did this bear ever expect that they would go elsewhere than into the official waste-basket of La Ferté, which means that he wrote because he liked to; which again means that he was essentially an artist—for which reason I liked him more than a little. He lumbered off one day—I hope to his brier-patch, and to his children, and to his confrères, and to all things excellent and livable and highly desirable to a bruin.

The Young Russian and The Barber escaped while I was enjoying my little visit at Orne. The former was an immensely tall and very strong boy of nineteen or under, who had come to our society by way of solitary confine-ment, bread and water for months, and other reminders that to err is human, etc. Unlike Harree, whom if any-thing he exceeded in strength, he was very quiet. Every one let him alone. I 'caught water' in the town with him several times and found him an excellent companion. He taught me the Russian numerals up to ten, and was very kind to my struggles over 10 and 9. He picked up the cannon-ball one day and threw it so hard that the wall separating the men's *cour* from the *cour des femmes* shook, and a piece of stone fell off. At which the cannon-ball was taken away from us (to the grief of its daily wielders, Harree and Fritz) by four perspiring *plantons* who almost died in the performance of their highly pa-triotic duty. His friend, The Barber, had a little shelf in The Enormous Room, all tricked out with an astonishing array of bottles, atomisers, tonics, powders, scissors, razors and other deadly implements. It has always been a *mystère* to me that our captors permitted this array of obviously dangerous weapons when we were searched almost weekly for knives. Had I not been in the habit of using B.'s safety-razor I should probably have become better acquainted with The Barber. It was not his price, nor yet his technique, but the fear of contamination which made me avoid these instruments of hygiene. Not that I shaved to excess. On the contrary, the *Surveillant* often, nay bi-weekly (so soon as I began drawing certain francs from Norton Harjes) reasoned with me upon the subject of appearance; saying that I was come of a good family, that I had enjoyed (unlike my companions) an education, and that I should keep myself neat and clean and be a shining example to the filthy and ignorant—adding slyly that the 'hospital' would be an awfully nice place for me and my friend to live, and that there we could be by ourselves like gentlemen and have our meals served in the room, avoiding the *salle à manger;* moreover the food would be what we liked, delicious food, especially cooked ... all (quoth the *Surveillant* with the itching palm of a Grand Central Porter awaiting his tip) for a mere trifle or so, which if I liked I could pay him on the spot—whereat I scornfully smiled, being inhibited by a somewhat selfish regard for my own welfare from kicking him through the window. To The Barber's credit be it said: he never once solicited my trade, although the *Surveillant's* 'Soi-même' lectures (as B. and I referred to them) were the delight of our numerous friends and must, through them, have reached his alert ears. He was a good-looking quiet man of perhaps thirty, with razor-keen eyes—and that's about all I know of him except that one day The Young Russian and The Barber, instead of passing from the *cour* directly to the building, made use of a little door in an angle between the stone wall and the kitchen; and that to such good effect that we never saw them again. Nor were the ever-watchful guardians of our safety, the lion-hearted *plan-tons*, aware of what had occurred until several hours after; despite the fact that a ten-foot wall had been scaled, some lesser obstructions vanquished, and a run in the open made almost (one unpatriotically-minded might be tempted to say) before their very eyes. But then—who knows? May not the French government deliberately have allowed them to escape, after—through its incomparable spy system—learning that The Barber and his young friend were about to attempt the life of the *Surveillant* with an atomiser brim-full of T.N.T.? Nothing could after all be more highly probable. As a matter of fact, a couple of extra-fine razors (presented by the *Soi-même*-minded *Surveillant* to the wily coiffeur in the interests of public health) as well as a knife which belonged to the *cuisine* and had been lent to The Barber for the purpose of peeling potatoes—he having complained that the extraordinary safety-device with which, on alternate days, we were ordinarily furnished for that purpose, was an insult to himself and his profession—vanished into the rather thick air of Orne along with The Barber *lui-même*. I remember him perfectly in The Enormous Room, cutting apples deliberately with his knife and sharing them with the Young Russian. The night of the escape—in order to keep up our morale—we were helpfully told that both refugees had been snitched e'er they had got well without the limits of the town, and been remanded to a punishment consisting, among other things, in *travaux forcés à perpétuité*— *verbum sapientibus*, he that hath ears, etc. Also a nightly inspection was instituted; consisting of our being counted thrice by a *planton*, who then divided the total by 3 and vanished.

Soi-même reminds me of a pleasant spirit who graced

our little company with a good deal of wit and elegance. He was called by B. and myself, after a somewhat exciting incident which I must not describe but rather outline, by the agreeable title of *Même le Balayeur*. Only a few days after my arrival the incident in question happened. It seems (I was in *la cour* promenading for the afternoon) that certain more virile inhabitants of The Enormous Room, among them Harree and Pom Pom *bien entendu*, declined *se promener* and kept their habitat. Now this was in fulfilment of a little understanding with three or more girls—such as Celina, Lily and Renée—who, having also declined the promenade, managed in the course of the afternoon to escape from their quarters on the second floor, rush down the hall and upstairs, and gain that landing on which was the only and well-locked door to The Enormous Room. The next act of this little comedy (or tragedy, as it proved for the participants, who got *cabinot* and *pain sec*—male and female alike—for numerous days thereafter) might well be entitled 'Love will find a way.' Just how the door was opened, the lock picked, etc., from the inside is (of course) a considerable mystery to anyone possessing a limited acquaintance with the art of burglary. Anyway, it was accomplished, and that in several fifths of a second. Now let the curtain fall, and the reader be satisfied with the significant word 'Asbestos' which is part of all first-rate performances.

The *Surveillant*, I fear, distrusted his *balayeur*. *Balayeurs* were always being changed because *balayeurs* were (in shameful contrast to the *plantons*) invariably human beings. For this deplorable reason they inevitably carried notes to and fro between *les hommes* and *les femmes*. Upon which ground the *balayeur* in this case—a well-knit, keen-eyed, agile man, with a sense of humour and

sharp perception of men, women and things in particular
and in general—was called before the bar of an im-
promptu court, held by M. *le Surveillant* in The Enormous
Room after the promenade. I shall not enter in detail into
the nature of the charges pressed in certain cases, but
confine myself to quoting the close of a peroration which
would have done Demosthenes credit:

'*Même le balayeur a tiré un coup!*'

The individual in question mildly deprecated M. *le
Surveillant's* opinion, while the audience roared and
rocked with laughter of a somewhat ferocious sort. I have
rarely seen the *Surveillant* so pleased with himself as after
producing this *bon mot*. Only fear of his superior, the
ogre-like *Directeur*, kept him from letting off entirely all
concerned in what after all (from the European point of
view) was an essentially human proceeding. As nobody
could prove anything about *Même*, he was not locked up
in a dungeon; but he lost his job of sweeper—which was
quite as bad, I am sure, from his point of view—and from
that day became a common inhabitant of The Enormous
Room like any of the rest of us.

His successor, Garibaldi, was a corker.

How the Almighty French government in its Almighty
Wisdom ever found Garibaldi a place among us is more
than I understand or ever will. He was a little tot in a
faded blue-grey French uniform; and when he perspired
he pushed a *képi* up and back from his worried forehead
which a lock of heavy hair threateningly overhung. As I
recollect Garibaldi's terribly difficult not to say complicated lineage, his English mother had presented him to his
Italian father in the country of France. However this trilogy may be, he had served at various times in the Italian,
French and English armies. As there was (unless we call

Garibaldi Italian, which he obviously was not) nary a subject of King Ponzi or Caruso or whatever be his name residing at La Ferté Macé, nor yet a suitable citizen of Merry England, Garibaldi was in the habit of expressing himself—chiefly at the card table, be it said—in a curious language which might have been mistaken for French. To B. and me he spoke an equally curious language, but a perfectly recognizable one, i.e., Cockney Whitechapel English. He showed us a perfectly authentic mission-card which certified that his family had received a pittance from some charitable organization situated in the White-chapel neighbourhood, and that, moreover, they were in the habit of receiving same pittance; and that, finally, their claim to such pittance was amply justified by the poverty of their circumstances. Beyond this valuable certificate, Garibaldi (which every one called him) at-tained great incoherence. He had been wronged. He was always being misunderstood. His life had been a series of mysterious tribulations. I for one have the merest idea that Garibaldi was arrested for the theft of some peculiarly worthless trifle, and sent to the Limbo of La Ferté as a penance. This merest idea is suggested by something which happened when the Clever Man instituted a search for his missing knife—but I must introduce the Clever Man to my reader before describing that rather beguiling incident.

Conceive a tall, well-dressed, rather athletic, carefully kept, clean and neat, intelligent, not for a moment de-spondent, altogether superior man fairly young (perhaps twenty-nine) and quite bald. He wins enough every night at *banque* to enable him to pay the less fortunate to per-form his *corvée d'eau* for him. As a consequence he takes his vile coffee in bed every morning, then smokes a ciga-

rette or two lazily, then drops off for a nap, and gets up
about the middle of the morning promenade. Upon arising
he strops a razor of his own (nobody knows how he gets
away with a regular razor), carefully lathers his face and
neck—while gazing into a rather classy mirror which
hangs night and day over his head, above a little shelf on
which he displays at such times a complete toilet outfit—
and proceeds to annihilate the inconsiderable growth of
beard which his mirror reveals to him. Having completed
the annihilation, he performs the most extensive ablutions
per one of the three or four pails which The Enormous
Room boasts, which pail is by common consent dedicated
to his personal and exclusive use. All this time he has been
singing loudly and musically the following sumptuously
imaginative ditty:

> 'mEEt me to-nIght in DREamland,
> UNder the SIL-v'ry mOOn,
> meet me in DREAmland,
> sweet dreamy DREAmland—
> there all my DRE-ams come trUE.'

His English accent is excellent. He pronounces his native
language, which is the language of the Hollanders, crisply
and firmly. He is not given to Gottverdummering. In
addition to Dutch and English he speaks French clearly
and Belgian distinctly. I dare say he knows half a dozen
languages in all. He gives me the impression of a man who
would never be at a loss, in whatever circumstances he
might find himself. A man capable of extricating himself
from the most difficult situation; and that with the greatest ease. A man who bides his time, and improves the present by separating, one after one, his moneyed fellow-
prisoners from their bank-notes. He is, by all odds, the

coolest player that I have ever watched. Nothing worries him. If he loses two hundred francs to-night, I am sure he will win it and fifty in addition to-morrow. He accepts opponents without distinction—the stupid, the wily, the vain, the cautious, the desperate, the hopeless. He has not the slightest pity, not the least fear. In one of my numerous notebooks I have this perfectly direct paragraph:

Card table: 4 stares play banque with 2 cigarettes (1 dead) & A pipe the clashing faces yanked by a leanness of one candle bottle-stuck (Birth of X) where sits The Clever Man who pyramids, sings (mornings) 'Meet Me . . .'

which specimen of telegraphic technique, being interpreted, means: Judas, Garibaldi, and The Holland Skipper (whom the reader will meet *de suite*)—Garibaldi's cigarette having gone out, so greatly is he absorbed—play *banque* with four intent and highly focused individuals who may or may not be The Schoolmaster, Monsieur Auguste, The Barber, and Même; with The Clever Man (as nearly always) acting as banker. The candle by whose somewhat uncorpulent illumination the various physiognomies are yanked into a ferocious unity is stuck into the mouth of a bottle. The lighting of the whole, the rhythmic disposition of the figures, construct a sensuous integration suggestive of The Birth of Christ by one of the Old Masters. The Clever Man, having had his usual morning warble, is extremely quiet. He will win, he pyramids— and he pyramids because he has the cash and can afford to make every play a big one. All he needs is the rake of a *croupier* to complete his disinterested and wholly nerveless poise. He is a born gambler, is The Clever Man—and I dare say that to play cards in time of war constituted a heinous crime and I am certain that he played cards before he arrived at La Ferté; moreover, I suppose that to win at cards in time of war is an unutterable crime, and I know that he has won at cards before in his life—so now we have a perfectly good and valid explanation of the presence of The Clever Man in our midst. The Clever Man's chief opponent was Judas. It was a real pleasure to us whenever of an evening Judas sweated and mopped and sweated and lost more and more and was finally cleaned out.

But The Skipper, I learned from certain prisoners who escorted the baggage of The Clever Man from The Enormous Room when he left us one day (as he did for some reason, to enjoy the benefits of freedom), paid the master-mind of the card table 150 francs at the *gare*—poor Skipper! upon whose vacant bed lay down luxuriously the Lobster, immediately to be wheeled fiercely all around The Enormous Room by the *Garde-Champêtre* and Judas, to the boisterous plaudits of *tout le monde*—but I started to tell about the afternoon when the master-mind lost his knife; and tell it I will forthwith. B. and I were lying prone upon our respective beds when—presto, a storm arose at the further end of The Enormous Room. We looked, and beheld The Clever Man, thoroughly and efficiently angry, addressing, threatening and frightening generally a constantly increasing group of fellow-prisoners. After dismissing with a few sharp linguistic cracks of the whip certain theories which seemed to be advanced by the bolder auditors with a view to palliating, persuading and tranquillizing his just wrath, he made for the nearest *paillasse*, turned it topsy-turvy, slit it neatly and suddenly from stem to stern with a jack-knife, hanged the hay about, and then went with careful haste through the pitifully minute baggage of the *paillasse's* owner. Silence fell. No one, least of all the owner, said anything. From this bed The Clever Man turned to the next, treated it in the same fashion, searched it thoroughly, and made for the third. His motions were those of a perfectly oiled machine. He proceeded up the length of the room, varying his procedure only by sparing an occasional mattress, throwing *paillasses* about, tumbling *sacs* and boxes inside out; his face somewhat paler than usual but otherwise immaculate and expressionless. B. and I waited with some interest to see what would happen to our belongings. Arriving at our beds he paused, seemed to consider a moment, then not touching our *paillasses* proper, proceeded to open our duffle bags and hunt half-heartedly, remarking that 'somebody might have put it in'; and so passed on. 'What in hell is the matter with that guy?' I asked of Fritz, who stood near us with a careless air, some scorn and considerable amusement in his eyes. 'The bloody fool's lost his knife,' was Fritz's answer. After completing his rounds The Clever Man searched almost every one except ourselves and Fritz, and absolutely subsided on his own *paillasse* muttering occasionally 'if he found it' what he'd do. I think he never did find it. It was a beautiful knife, John the *Baigneur* said. 'What did it look like?' I demanded with some curiosity. 'It had a naked woman on the handle,' Fritz said, his eyes sharp with amusement.

And every one agreed that it was a great pity that The Clever Man had lost it, and every one began timidly to restore order and put his personal belongings back in place and say nothing at all.

But what amused me was to see the little tot in a bluish-grey French uniform, who—about when the search approached his *paillasse*—suddenly hurried over to B. (his perspiring forehead more perspiring than usual, his *képi* set at an angle of insanity) and hurriedly presented B. with a long-lost German-silver folding camp-knife, purchased by B. from a fellow-member of *Vingt-et-Un* who was known to us as 'Lord Algie'—a lanky, effeminate, brittle, spotless creature who was *en route* to becoming an officer and to whose finicky tastes the fat-jowled A. tirelessly pandered for, doubtless, financial considerations —which knife according to the trembling and altogether miserable Garibaldi had 'been found' by him that day in the *cour;* which was eminently and above all things curious, as the treasure had been lost weeks before.

Which again brings us to The Skipper, whose elaborate couch has already been mentioned—he was a Hollander and one of the strongest, most gentle and altogether most pleasant of men, who used to sit on the water-wagon under the shed in the *cour* and smoke his pipe quietly of an afternoon. His stocky, even tightly-knit person, in its heavy trousers and jersey sweater, culminated in a bronzed face which was at once as kind and firm a piece of supernatural work as I think I ever knew. His voice was agreeably modulated. He was utterly without affectation. He had three sons. One evening a number of gendarmes came to his house and told him that he was arrested, 'so my three sons and I threw them all out of the window into the canal.'

I can still see the opening smile, squared kindness of cheeks, eyes like cool keys—his heart always with the Sea.

The little Machine-Fixer (*le petit bonhomme avec le bras cassé* as he styled himself, referring to his little paralysed left arm) was so perfectly different that I must let you see him next. He was slightly taller than Garibaldi, about of a size with Monsieur Auguste. He and Monsieur

Auguste together were a fine sight, a sight which made me feel that I came of a race of giants. I am afraid it was more or less as giants that B. and I pitied the Machine-Fixer—still this was not really our fault, since the Machine-Fixer came to us with his troubles much as a very minute and helpless child comes to a very large and omnipotent one. And God knows we did not only pity him, we liked him—and if we could in some often ridiculous manner assist the Machine-Fixer I think we nearly always did. The assistance to which I refer was wholly spiritual; since the minute Machine-Fixer's colossal self-pride eliminated any possibility of material assistance. What we did, about every other night, was to entertain him (as we entertained our other friends) *chez nous*; that is to say, he would come up late every evening or every other evening, after his day's toil—for he worked as co-*balayeur* with Garibaldi and he was a tremendous worker; never have I seen a man who took his work so seriously and made so much of it—to sit, with great care and very respectfully, upon one or the other of our beds at the upper end of The Enormous Room, and smoke a black small pipe, talking excitedly and strenuously and fiercely about *La Misère* and himself and ourselves, often crying a little but very bitterly, and from time to time striking matches with a short angry gesture on the sole of his big, almost square boot. His little, abrupt, conscientious, relentless, difficult self lived always in a single dimension—the somewhat beautiful dimension of Sorrow. He was a Belgian, and one of two Belgians in whom I have ever felt the least or slightest interest; for the Machine-Fixer might have been a Polak or an Idol or an Esquimo so far as his nationality affected his soul. By and large, that was the trouble—the Machine-Fixer had a soul. Put the bracelets

on an ordinary man, tell him he's a bad egg, treat him
rough, shove him into the jug or its equivalent (you see
I have regard always for M. *le Surveillant's* delicate but
no doubt necessary distinction between La Ferté and
Prison), and he will become one of three animals—a rab-
bit, that is to say timid; a mole, that is to say stupid; or a
hyena, that is to say Harree the Hollander. But if, by some
fatal, some incomparably fatal accident, this man has a
soul—ah, then we have and truly have and have most
horribly what is called in La Ferté Macé by those who
have known it, *La Misère*. Monsieur Auguste's valiant attempts at cheerfulness and the natural buoyancy of his
gentle disposition in a slight degree protected him from
La Misère. The Machine-Fixer was lost. By nature he was
tremendously *sensible*, he was the very apotheosis of *l'âme
sensible* in fact. His *sensibilité* made him shoulder not only
the inexcusable injustice which he had suffered but the
incomparable and overwhelming total injustice which
every one had suffered and was suffering *en masse* day
and night in The Enormous Room. His woes, had they
not sprung from perfectly real causes, might have suggested a persecution complex. As it happened there was
no possible method of relieving them—they could be relieved in only one way: by Liberty. Not simply by his
personal liberty, but by the liberation of every single
fellow-captive as well. His extraordinarily personal anguish could not be selfishly appeased by a merely partial
righting, in his own case, of the Wrong—the ineffable
and terrific and to be perfectly avenged Wrong—done to
those who ate and slept and wept and played cards within
that abominable and unyielding Symbol which enclosed
the immutable vileness of our common life. It was necessary, for its appeasement, that a shaft of bright lightning

suddenly and entirely should wither the human and material structures which stood always between our filthy
and pitiful selves and the unspeakable cleanness of Liberty.

B. recalls that the little Machine-Fixer said or hinted
that he had been either a socialist or an anarchist when he
was young. So that is doubtless why we had the privilege
of his society. After all, it is highly improbable that this
poor socialist suffered more at the hands of the great and
good French government than did many a C.O. at the
hands of the great and good American government; or—
since all great governments are *per se* good and vice versa
—than did many a man in general who was cursed with
a talent for thinking during the warlike moments recently
passed; during that is to say an epoch when the g. and g.
nations demanded of their respective peoples the exact
antithesis to thinking; said antithesis being vulgarly called
Belief. Lest which statement prejudice some members of
the American Legion in the disfavour of the Machine-
Fixer or rather of myself—awful thought—I hasten to
assure every one that the Machine-Fixer was a highly
moral person. His morality was at times almost gruesome;
as when he got started on the inhabitants of the women's
quarters. Be it understood that the Machine-Fixer was
human, that he would take a letter—provided he liked the
sender—and deliver it to the sender's *adorée* without a
murmur. That was simply a good deed done for a friend;
it did not imply that he approved of the friend's choice,
which for strictly moral reasons he invariably and to the
friend's very face violently deprecated. To this little man
of perhaps forty-five, with a devoted wife waiting for
him in Belgium (a wife whom he worshipped and loved
more than he worshipped and loved anything in the world,
a wife whose fidelity to her husband and whose trust and

confidence in him echoed in the letters which—when we
three were alone—the little Machine-Fixer tried always
to read to us, never getting beyond the first sentence or
two before he broke down and sobbed from his feet to his
eyes), to such a little person his reaction to *les femmes*
was more than natural. It was in fact inevitable.

Women, to him at least, were of two kinds and two
kinds only. There were *les femmes honnêtes* and there
were *les putains*. In La Ferté, he informed us—and as
balayeur he ought to have known whereof he spoke—
there were as many as three ladies of the former variety.
One of them he talked with often. She told him her story.
She was a Russian, of a very fine education, living peacefully in Paris up to the time that she wrote to her relatives
a letter containing the following treasonable sentiment:

'Je m'ennuie pour les neiges de la Russie.'

The letter had been read by the French censor, as had B.'s
letter; and her arrest and transference from her home in
Paris to La Ferté Macé promptly followed. She was as intelligent as she was virtuous and had nothing to do with
her frailer sisters, so the Machine-Fixer informed us with
a quickly passing flash of joy. Which sisters (his little forehead knotted itself and his big bushy eyebrows plunged
together wrathfully) were wicked and indecent and utterly despicable disgraces to their sex—and this relentless
Joseph fiercely and jerkily related how only the day before
he had repulsed the painfully obvious solicitations of a
Madame Potiphar by turning his back, like a good Christian, upon temptation and marching out of the room,
broom tightly clutched in virtuous hands.

'*M'sieu Jean*' (meaning myself) '*savez-vous*'—with a

terrific gesture which consisted in snapping his thumb-nail between his teeth—'ÇA PUE!'

Then he added: 'And what would my wife say to me, if I came home to her and presented her with that which this creature had presented to me? They are animals—' cried the little Machine-Fixer—'all they want is a man, they don't care who he is, they want a man. But they won't get me!'—and he warned us to beware.

Especially interesting, not to say valuable, was the Machine-Fixer's testimony concerning the more or less regular 'inspections' (which were held by the very same doctor who had 'examined' me in the course of my first day at La Ferté) for *les femmes;* presumably in the interests of public safety. *Les femmes,* quoth the Machine-Fixer, who had been many times an eye-witness of this proceeding, lined up talking and laughing and—crime of crimes—smoking cigarettes, outside the *bureau* of M. le Médecin Major. *'Une femme entre. Elle se lève les jupes jusqu'au menton et se met sur le banc. Le médecin major la regarde. Il dit de suite "Bon. C'est tout." Elle sort. Une autre entre. La même chose. "Bon. C'est fini"* ... *M'sieu Jean: prenez garde!'*

And he struck a match fiercely on the black, almost square boot which lived on the end of his little worn trouser-leg, bending his small body forward as he did so, and bringing the flame upward in a violent curve. And the flame settled on his little black pipe. And his cheeks sucked until they must have met, and a slow unwilling noise arose, and with the return of his cheeks a small colourless wisp of possibly smoke came upon the air.— That's not tobacco. Do you know what it is? It's wood! And I sit here smoking wood in my pipe when my wife is sick with worrying ... *'M'sieu Jean'*—leaning forward with jaw protruding and a oneness of bristly eyebrows, *'Ces grands messieurs qui ne se foutent pas mal si l'on CREVE de faim, savez-vous, ils croient chacun qu'il est Le Bon Dieu LUI-Même. Et M'sieu Jean, savez-vous, ils sont tous'*—leaning right in my face, the withered hand making a pitiful fist of itself—*'Ils. Sont. Des. CRAPULES!'*

And his ghastly and toy-like wizened and minute arm would try to make a pass at their lofty lives. O *gouvernement français*, I think it was not very clever of You to put this terrible doll in La Ferté; I should have left him in Belgium with his little doll-wife if I had been You; for when Governments are found dead there is always a little doll on top of them, pulling and tweaking with his little hands to get back the microscopic knife which sticks firmly in the quiet meat of their hearts.

One day only did I see him happy or nearly happy— when a Belgian baroness for some reason arrived, and was bowed and fed and wined by the delightfully respectful and perfectly behaved Official Captors—'and I know of her in Belgium, she is a great lady, she is very powerful and she is generous; I fell on my knees before her, and implored her in the name of my wife and *Le Bon Dieu* to intercede in my behalf; and she has made a note of it, and she told me she would write the Belgian King and I will be free in a few weeks, FREE!'

The little Machine-Fixer, I happen to know, did finally leave La Ferté—for Précigné.

. . . In the kitchen worked a very remarkable person. Who wore sabots. And sang continuously in a very subdued way to himself as he stirred the huge black kettles. We, that is to say B. and I, became acquainted with Afrique very gradually. You did not know Afrique suddenly. You became cognizant of Afrique gradually. You were in the *cour*, staring at ooze and dead trees, when a figure came striding from the *cuisine* lifting its big wooden feet after it rhythmically, unwinding a parti-coloured scarf from its waist as it came, and singing to itself in a subdued manner a jocular and I fear unprintable ditty concerning Paradise. The figure entered the little gate to the *cour* in a business-like way, unwinding continuously, and made stridingly for the *cabinet* situated up against the stone-wall which separated the promenading sexes— dragging behind it on the ground a tail of ever-increasing dimensions. The *cabinet* reached, tail and figure parted company; the former fell inert to the limitless mud, the latter disappeared into the contrivance with a Jack-in-the-box rapidity. From which contrivance the continuing ditty,

'*le paradis est une maison . . .*'

—Or again, it's a lithe pausing poise, intensely intelligent, certainly sensitive, delivering dryingly a series of sure and rapid hints that penetrate the fabric of stupidity accurately and whisperingly; dealing one after another brief and poignant instupidities, distinct and uncompromising, crisp and altogether arrowlike. The poise has a cigarette in its hand, which cigarette it has just pausingly rolled from material furnished by a number of carefully saved butts (whereof Afrique's pockets are invariably full). Its neither old nor young but rather keen face hoards a pair of greyish-blue witty eyes, which face and eyes are directed upon us through the open door of a little room. Which little room is in the rear of the *cuisine;* a little room filled with the inexpressibly clean and soft odour of newly-cut wood. Which wood we are pretending to split and pile for kindling. As a matter of fact we are enjoying Afrique's conversation, escaping from the bleak and profoundly muddy *cour*, and (under the watchful auspices of the Cook, who plays sentinel) drinking something approximating coffee with something approximating sugar therein. All this because the Cook thinks we're *boches* and being the Cook and a *boche lui-même* is consequently peculiarly concerned for our welfare.

Afrique is talking about *les journaux*, and to what prodigious pains they go to not tell the truth; or he is telling how a native stole upon him in the night armed with a spear two metres long, once on a time in a certain part of the world; or he is predicting that the Germans will march upon the French by way of Switzerland; or he is teaching us to count and swear in Arabic; or he is having a very good time in the Midi as a tinker, sleeping under a tree outside of a little town ...

And Le Chef is grunting, without lifting his old eyes from the dissection of an obstreperous cabbage,

'*Dépêche-toi, voici le planton*'

and we are something like happy. For it is singularly and pleasantly warm in the cuisine. And Afrique's is an alert kind of mind, which has been and seen and observed and penetrated and known—a bit there, somewhat here, chiefly everywhere. Its specialty being politics in which case Afrique has had the inestimable advantage of observing without being observed—until La Ferté; whereupon Afrique goes on uninterruptedly observing, recognizing that a significant angle of observation has been presented to him gratis. *Les journaux* and politics in general are topics upon which Afrique can say more, without the slightest fatigue, than a book as big as my two thumbs—

'*Mais oui, ils ont cherché de l'eau et puis je leur donne
l'u café*,' Monsieur, or more properly Mynheer *le chef*, is

expostulating; the *planton* is stupidly protesting that we are supposed to be upstairs; Afrique is busily stirring a huge black pot, winking gravely at us and singing softly:

'*Le Bon Dieu, Saoûl comme un cochon . . .*'

Now that I have mentioned the pleasures of the kitchen, it is perhaps à propos that I say a word upon the displeasures of Brown Bread. He was a Belgian, and therefore chewed and spat juice night and day from the unutterably stolid face of an overgrown farmer. The only words in English which he was able to articulate were 'Me too'—when cigarettes were handed round by somebody who had got some money from somewhere. I hasten to say that the name which we gave him is a contraction of an occult sound, or rather rumbling shout, uttered by the *Surveillant* when he leaned from a little window which faced the *cour* and announced the names of those *fortunati* for whom letters (duly opened, read, and their contents approved by the *Secrétaire*, alias the weak-eyed biped) had somehow emanated from the *mystère* of the outer world. The *Surveillant*, his glasses having tremulously inspected a letter or a *carte postale*—while all *les hommes* breathlessly attended, in the mud, upon his slightest murmur—successfully would (to the great disappointment of everyone else) pronounce

'boo-r-OWNbread,'

whereat this ten-foot personage would awkwardly advance in his squeaky black puttees, shifting his quid with a violent effort in order to reply simperingly:

'*Oui, Monsieur le Surveillant.*'

For the rest, he was perfectly stupid, inclined to be morose, and had friends very much like himself who shared his nationality and whose moroseness and stupidity I do not particularly care to remember. He was a Belgian,

and that's all. By which I mean that I am uncharitable
enough to not care what happened to him or for what
stupid and morose crime he was doing penance at La
Ferté under the benignant auspices of the French government.

Just as well perhaps, since my search for causes in this
connection has proved futile; a fact which by this time
the reader realizes. Better to have let a sleeping *mystère*
lie, I suppose—or no I don't, for The Man Who Played
Too Late did that very thing and thereby shrouded the
inexplicable in a nimbus of inaccuracy. Perhaps because
he felt, in his blond, hungrily cadaverous way, that to
have been arrested for functioning (as a member of an
orchestra) after closing time in Paris was a humiliation
too obvious to require analysis. Be that as it may, I con-
clude this particular group of portraits with his own
remark, which frames them after all rather nicely:

'Every one is here for something.'

VI

APOLLYON

THE inhabitants of The Enormous Room whose portraits I have attempted in the preceding chapter were, with one or two exceptions, inhabiting at the time of my arrival. Now the thing which above all things made death worth living and life worth dying at La Ferté Macé was the kinetic aspect of that institution; the arrivals, singly or in groups, of *nouveaux* of sundry nationalities whereby our otherwise more or less simple existence was happily complicated, our putrescent placidity shaken by a fortunate violence. Before, however, undertaking this aspect I shall attempt to represent for my own benefit as well as the reader's certain more obvious elements of that stasis which greeted the candidates for disintegration upon their admittance to our select, not to say distinguished, circle. Or: I shall describe, briefly, Apollyon and the instruments of his power, which instruments are three in number: Fear, Women, and Sunday.

By Apollyon I mean a very definite fiend. A fiend who, secluded in the sumptuous and luxurious privacy of his own personal *bureau* (which as a rule no one of lesser rank than the *Surveillant* was allowed, so far as I might observe—and I observed—to enter) compelled to the unimaginable meanness of his will, by means of the three potent instruments in question, all—within the sweating walls of La Ferté—that was once upon a time human. I mean a very complete Apollyon, a Satan whose word is dreadful not because it is painstakingly unjust but because it is incomprehensibly omnipotent. I mean, in short, *Monsieur le Directeur*.

I shall discuss first of all *Monsieur le Directeur's* most obvious weapon.

Fear was instilled by three means into the erstwhile human entities whose presence at La Ferté gave Apollyon his job. The three means were: his subordinates, who being one and all fearful of his power directed their energies to but one end—the production in ourselves of a similar emotion; two forms of punishment, which supplied said subordinates with a weapon over any of us who refused to find room for this desolating emotion in his heart of hearts; and, finally, direct contact with his unutterable personality.

Beneath the Demon was the *Surveillant*. I have already described the *Surveillant*. I wish to say, however, that in my opinion the *Surveillant* was the most decent official at La Ferté. I pay him this tribute gladly and honestly. To me, at least, he was kind: to the majority he was inclined to be lenient. I honestly and gladly believe that the *Surveillant* was incapable of that quality whose innateness, in the case of his superior, rendered that gentleman a (to my mind) perfect representative of the Almighty French Government: I believe that the *Surveillant* did not enjoy being cruel, that he was not absolutely without pity or understanding. As a personality I therefore pay him my respects. I am myself incapable of caring whether, as a tool of the Devil, he will find the bright firelight of Hell too warm for him or no.

Beneath the *Surveillant* were the *Secrétaire*, Monsieur Richard, the Cook, and the *plantons*. The first I have described sufficiently, since he was an obedient and nega-

tive—albeit peculiarly responsible—cog in the machine
of decomposition. Of Monsieur Richard, whose portrait
is included in the account of my first day at La Ferté,
I wish to say that he had a very comfortable room of his
own filled with primitive and otherwise imposing
medicines; the walls of this comfortable room being
beauteously adorned by some fifty magazine covers
representing the female form in every imaginable state
of undress, said magazine-covers being taken chiefly from
such amorous periodicals as *Le Sourire* and the old stand-by
of indecency, *La Vie Parisienne*. Also Monsieur Richard
kept a pot of geraniums upon his window-ledge, which
haggard and aged-looking symbol of joy he doubtless (in
his spare moments) peculiarly enjoyed watering. The
Cook is by this time familiar to my reader. I beg to say
that I highly approve of The Cook; exclusive of the fact
that the coffee, which went up to The Enormous Room
tous les matins, was made every day with the same grounds
plus a goodly injection of checkerberry—for the simple
reason that the Cook had to supply our captors and
especially Apollyon with real coffee, whereas what he
supplied to *les hommes* made no difference. The same is
true of sugar: our morning coffee, in addition to being a
water-thin, black, muddy, stinking liquid, contained not
the smallest suggestion of sweetness, whereas the coffee
which went to the officials—and the coffee which B. and
I drank in recompense for 'catching water'—had all the
sugar you could possibly wish for. The poor Cook was
fined one day as a result of his economies, subsequent to a
united action on the part of the fellow-sufferers. It was a
day when a gent immaculately dressed appeared—after
duly warning the Fiend that he was about to inspect the
Fiend's ménage—an, I think, public official of Orne.

Judas (at the time *chef de chambre*), supported by the sole and unique indignation of all his fellow-prisoners save two or three out of whom Fear had made rabbits or moles, early carried the pail (which by common agreement not one of us had touched that day) downstairs, along the hall, and up one flight—where he encountered the *Directeur, Surveillant* and Handsome Stranger all amicably and pleasantly conversing. Judas set the pail down; bowed; and begged, as spokesman for the united male gender of La Ferté Macé, that the quality of the coffee be examined. 'We won't any of us drink it, begging your pardon, Messieurs,' he claims that he said. What happened then is highly amusing. The *petit balayeur*, an eye-witness of the proceeding, described it to me as follows:

'The *Directeur* roared "COMMENT"? He was horribly angry. "*Oui, Monsieur*," said the *maître de chambre* humbly.—"*Pourquoi?*" thundered the *Directeur.*—"Because it's undrinkable," the *maître de chambre* said quietly.—"Undrinkable? Nonsense!" cried the *Directeur* furiously.—"Be so good as to taste it, *Monsieur le Directeur.*"—"*I* taste it? Why should I taste it? The coffee is perfectly good, plenty good for you men. This is ridiculous—"—"Why don't we all taste it?" suggested the *Surveillant* ingratiatingly.—"Why, yes," said the Visitor mildly.—"Taste it? Of course not. This is ridiculous and I shall punish—"—"I should like, if you don't mind, to try a little," the Visitor said.—"Oh well, of course, if you like," the *Directeur* mildly agreed. "Give me a cup of that coffee, you!"—"With pleasure, sir," said the *maître de chambre*. The *Directeur*—M'sieu' Jean, you would have burst laughing—seized the cup, lifted it to his lips, swallowed with a frightful expression (his eyes almost pop-

ping out of his head) and cried fiercely, "DELICIOUS!"
The *Surveillant* took a cupful; sipped; tossed the coffee
away, looking as if he had been hit in the eyes, and remarked, "Ah." The *maître de chambre*—M'sieu' Jean he
is clever—scooped the third cupful from the very bottom
of the pail, and very politely, with a big bow, handed it
to the Visitor; who took it, touched it to his lips, turned
perfectly green, and cried out *"Impossible!"* M'sieu' Jean,
we all thought—the *Directeur* and the *Surveillant* and
the *maître de chambre* and myself—that he was going
to vomit. He leaned against the wall a moment, quite
green; then recovering said faintly—"The Kitchen." The
Directeur looked very nervous and shouted, trembling all
over, "Yes indeed! We'll see the Cook about this perfectly
impossible coffee. I had no idea that my men were getting
such coffee. It's abominable! That's what it is, an outrage!"—And they all tottered downstairs to the Cook;
and, M'sieu' Jean, they searched the kitchen; and what do
you think? They found ten pounds of coffee and twelve
pounds of sugar all neatly hidden away, that the Cook had
been saving for himself out of our allowance. He's a beast,
the Cook!'

I must say that, although the morning coffee improved
enormously for as much as a week, it descended afterwards to its original level of excellence.

The Cook, I may add, officiated three times a week at a
little table to the left as you entered the dining-room.
Here he stood, and threw at every one (as every one
entered) a hunk of the most extraordinary *viande* which
I have ever had the privilege of trying to masticate—it
could not be tasted. It was pale and leathery. B. and myself often gave ours away in our hungriest moments;
which statement sounds as if we were generous to others,

whereas the reason for these donations was that we couldn't eat, let alone stand the sight of, this staple of diets. We had to do our donating on the sly, since the *chef* always gave us choice pieces and we were anxious not to hurt the *chef's* feelings. There was a good deal of spasmodic protestation à propos *la viande,* but the Cook always bullied it down—nor was the meat his fault; since, from the miserable carcasses which I have often seen carried into the kitchen from without, the Cook had to select something which would suit the meticulous stomach of the Lord of Hell, as also the less meticulous digestive organs of his minions; and it was only after every *planton* had got a piece of *viande* to his plantonic taste that the captives, female and male, came in for consideration.

On the whole, I think I never envied the Cook his strange and difficult, not to say gruesome, job. With the men *en masse* he was bound to be unpopular. To the goodwill of those above he was necessarily more or less a slave. And on the whole I liked the Cook very much, as did B.— for the very good and sufficient reason that he liked us both.

About the *plantons* I have something to say, something which it gives me huge pleasure to say. I have to say, about the *plantons,* that as a bunch they struck me at the time and will always impress me as the next to the lowest species of human organism; the lowest, in my experienced estimation, being the gendarme proper. The *plantons* were, with one exception—he of the black holster with whom I collided on the first day—changed from time to time. Again with this one exception, they were (as I have noted) apparently *réformés* who were enjoying a vacation from the trenches in the lovely environs of Orne. Nearly all of them were witless. Every one of them had something the matter with him physically as well. For instance, one *planton* had a large wooden hand. Another was possessed of a long unmanageable left leg made, as nearly as I could discover, of tin. A third had a huge glass eye.

These peculiarities of physique, however, did not inhibit the *plantons* from certain essential and normal desires. On the contrary. The *plantons* probably realized that, in competition with the male world at large, their glass legs and tin hands and wooden eyes would not stand a Chinaman's chance of winning the affection and admiration of the fair sex. At any rate they were always on the alert for opportunities to triumph over the admiration and affection of *les femmes* at La Ferté, where their success was not endangered by competition. They had the bulge on everybody; and they used what bulge they had to such good advantage that one of them, during my stay, was pursued with a revolver by their sergeant, captured, locked up, and shipped off for court-martial on the charge of disobedience and threatening the life of a superior officer. He had been caught with the goods—that is to say, in the girl's *cabinot*—by said superior: an incapable, strutting, undersized, bepimpled person in a bright uniform who spent his time assuming the poses of a general for the benefit of the ladies; of his admiration for whom and his intentions toward whom he made no secret. By all means one of the most disagreeable petty bullies whom I ever beheld. This arrest of a *planton* was, so long as I inhabited La Ferté, the only case in which abuse of the weaker sex was punished. That attempts at abuse were frequent I know from allusions and direct statements made in the letters which passed by way of the *balayeur* from the girls to their captive admirers. I might say that the senders of these letters, whom I shall attempt to portray presently, have my unmitigated and unqualified admiration. By all odds they possessed the most terrible vitality and bravery of any human beings, women or men, whom it has ever been my extraordinary luck to encounter, or ever will be (I am absolutely sure) in this world.

The duties of the *plantons* were those simple and obvious duties which only very stupid persons can perfectly fulfil, namely: to take turns guarding the building and its inhabitants; to not accept bribes, whether in the form of matches, cigarettes or conversation, from their prisoners; to accompany anyone who went anywhere outside the walls (as did occasionally the *balayeurs*, to transport baggage; the men who did *corvée*; and the catchers of water for the cook, who proceeded as far as the hydrant situated on the outskirts of the town—a momentous distance of perhaps five hundred feet); and finally to obey any and all orders from all and any superiors without thinking. *Plantons* were supposed—but only supposed— to report any schemes for escaping which they might overhear during their watch upon *les femmes et les hommes en promenade*. Of course they never overheard any, since the least intelligent of the watched was a paragon of wisdom by comparison with the watchers. B. and I had a little ditty about *plantons*, of which I can quote (unfortunately) only the first line and refrain,

'A planton loved lady once
(Cabbages and cauliflowers!)'

It was a very fine song. In considering my remarks upon *plantons* I must, in justice to my subject, mention the three prime plantonic virtues—they were (1) beauty, as regards face and person and bearing, (2) chivalry, as regards women, (3) heroism, as regards males.

The somewhat unique and amusing appearance of the *plantons* rather militated against than served to inculcate Fear—it was therefore not wonderful that they and the desired emotion were supported by two strictly enforced punishments, punishments which were meted out with equal and unflinching severity to both sexes alike. The less undesirable punishment was known as *pain sec*—which Fritz, shortly after my arrival, got for smashing a window-pane by accident; and which Harree and Pompom, the incorrigibles, were getting most of the time. This punishment consisted in denying to the culprit all nutriment save two stone-hard morsels of dry bread per diem. The culprit's intimate friends, of course, made a point of eating only a portion of their own morsels of soft heavy sour bread (we got two a day, with each *soupe*) and presenting the culprit with the rest. The common method of getting *pain sec* was also a simple one—it was for a man to wave, shout or make other signs audible or visible to an inhabitant of the women's quarters; and, for a girl, to be seen at her window by the *Directeur* at any time during the morning and afternoon promenades of the men. The punishment for sending a letter to a girl might possibly be *pain sec*, but was more often—I pronounce the word even now with a sinking of the heart, though curiously enough I escaped that for which it stands—*cabinot*.

There were (as already mentioned) a number of *cabinots*, sometimes referred to as *cachots* by persons of linguistic propensities. To repeat myself slightly: at least three were situated on the ground floor; and these were used whenever possible in preference to the one or ones upstairs, for the reason that they were naturally more damp and chill and dark and altogether more dismal and unhealthy. Dampness and cold were considerably increased by the substitution, for a floor, of two or three planks resting here and there in mud. I am now describing what my eyes saw, not what was shown to the inspectors on their rare visits to the *Directeur's* little shop for making criminals. I know what these occasional visitors beheld, because it, too, I have seen with my own eyes: seen the two *balayeurs* staggering downstairs with a bed (consisting of a high iron frame, a huge mattress of delicious thickness, spotless sheets, warm blankets, and a sort of quilt neatly folded over all) ; seen this bed placed by the panting sweepers in the thoroughly cleaned and otherwise immaculate *cabinot* at the foot of the stairs and opposite the *cuisine,* the well-scrubbed door being left wide open. I saw this done as I was going to dinner. While *les hommes* were upstairs recovering from *la soupe,* the gentlemen-inspectors were invited downstairs to look at a specimen of the *Directeur's* kindness—a kindness which he could not restrain even in the case of those who were guilty of some terrible wrong. (The little Belgian with the Broken Arm, alias the Machine-Fixer, missed not a word nor a gesture of all this; and described the scene to me with an indignation which threatened his sanity.) —Then, while *les hommes* were in the *cour* for the afternoon, the *balayeurs* were rushed to The Enormous Room, which they cleaned to beat the band with the fear of Hell in them; after which, the *Directeur* led his amiable guests leisurely upstairs and showed them the way the men kept their quarters; kept them without dictation on the part of the officials, so fond were they of what was to them one and all more than a delightful temporary residence— was in fact a home. From The Enormous Room the procession wended a gentle way to the women's quarters (scrubbed and swept in anticipation of their arrival) and

so departed; conscious—no doubt—that in the *Directeur*
France had found a rare specimen of whole-hearted and
efficient generosity.

Upon being sentenced to *cabinot*, whether for writing
an intercepted letter, fighting, threatening a *planton*, or
committing some minor offence for the *n*th time, a man
took one blanket from his bed, carried it downstairs to
the *cachot*, and disappeared therein for a night or many
days and nights as the case might be. Before entering he
was thoroughly searched and temporarily deprived of the
contents of his pockets, whatever they might include. It
was made certain that he had no cigarettes or tobacco in
any other form upon his person, and no matches. The
door was locked behind him and double and triple locked
—to judge by the sound—by a *planton*, usually the Black
Holster, who on such occasions produced a ring of enormous keys suggestive of a burlesque jailor. Within the
stone walls of his dungeon (into which a beam of light
no bigger than a ten-cent piece, and in some cases no
light at all, penetrated) the culprit could shout and scream
his or her heart out if he or she liked, without serious
annoyance to His Majesty King Satan. I wonder how
many times, *en route* to *la soupe* or The Enormous Room
or promenade, I have heard the unearthly smouldering
laughter of girls or of men entombed within the drooling
greenish walls of La Ferté Macé. A dozen times, I suppose, I have seen a friend of the entombed stoop adroitly
and shove a cigarette or a *morceau* of *chocolat* under the
door, to the girls or the men or the girl or man screaming,
shouting, and pommelling faintly behind that very door
—but, you would say by the sound, a good part of a mile
away ... Ah well, more of this later, when we come to
les femmes on their own account.

The third method employed to throw Fear into the minds of his captives lay, as I have said, in the sight of the Captor Himself. And this was by far the most efficient method.

He loved to suddenly dash upon the girls when they were carrying their slops along the hall and down-stairs, as (in common with the men) they had to do at least twice every morning and twice every afternoon. The *corvée* of girls and men were of course arranged so as not to coincide; yet somehow or other they managed to coincide on the average about once a week, or if not coincide, at any rate approach coincidence. On such occasions, as often as not under the *planton's* very stupid nose, a kiss or an embrace would be stolen—provocative of much fierce laughter and some scurrying. Or else, while the moneyed captives (including B. and Cummings) were waiting their turn to enter the *bureau de M. le Gestionnaire,* or even were ascending the stairs with a *planton* behind them, *en route* to Mecca, along the hall would come five or six women staggering and carrying huge pails full to the brim of everyone knew what; five or six heads, lowered, ill-dressed bodies tense with effort, free arms rigidly extended from the shoulder downward and outward in a plane at right angles to their difficult progress, and thereby helping to balance the disconcerting load—all embarrassed, some humiliated, others desperately at ease—along they would come under the steady sensual gaze of the men, under a gaze which seemed to eat them alive ... and then one of them would laugh with the laughter which is neither pitiful nor terrible, but horrible ...

And BANG! would a door fly open, and ROAR! a well-dressed animal about five feet six inches in height, with prominent cuffs and a sportive tie, the altogether decently and neatly clothed thick-built figure squirming from top to toe with anger, the large head trembling and white-faced beneath a flourishing mane of coarse blackish bristly perhaps hair, the arm crooked at the elbow and shaking a huge fist of pinkish, well-manicured flesh, the distinct, cruel, brightish eyes sprouting from their sockets under bushily enormous black eyebrows, the big, weak, coarse mouth extended almost from ear to ear and spouting invective, the soggy, brutal lips clinched upward and backward showing the huge horse-like teeth to the froth-shot gums.

And I saw once a little girl eleven years old scream in terror and drop her pail of slops, spilling most of it on her feet; and seize it in a clutch of frail child's fingers, and stagger, sobbing and shaking, past the Fiend—one hand held over her contorted face to shield her from the Awful Thing of Things—to the head of the stairs; where she collapsed, and was half-carried, half-dragged by one of the older ones to the floor below, while another older one picked up her pail and lugged this and her own hurriedly downward.

And after the last head had disappeared, *Monsieur le Directeur* continued to rave and shake and tremble for as much as ten seconds, his shoe-brush mane crinkling with black anger—then, turning suddenly upon *les hommes* (who cowered up against the wall as men cower up against a material thing in the presence of the supernatural) he roared and shook his pinkish fist at us till the gold stud in his immaculate cuff walked out upon the wad of clenching flesh:

'ET VOUS—PRENEZ GARDE—SI JE VOUS AT-TRAPPE AVEC LES FEMMES UNE AUTRE FOIS

JE VOUS FOUS AU CABINOT POUR QUINZE
JOURS, TOUS—TOUS—'

for as much as half a minute; then turning suddenly his
round-shouldered big back he adjusted his cuffs, muttering PROSTITUTES and WHORES and DIRTY
FILTH OF WOMEN, crammed his big fists into his
trousers, pulled in his chin till his fattish jowl rippled
along the square jaws, panted, grunted, very completely
satisfied, very contented, rather proud of himself, took a
strutting stride or two in his expensive shiny boots, and
shot all at once through the open door which he
SLAMMED after him.

A propos the particular incident described for the purposes of illustration, I wish to state that I believe in
miracles: the miracle being that I did not knock the
spit-covered mouthful of teeth and jabbering, brutish,
out-thrust jowl (which certainly were not farther than
eighteen inches from me) through the bull neck bulging
in its spotless collar. For there are times when one almost
decides not to merely observe . . . besides which, never in
my life before had I wanted to kill, to thoroughly extinguish and to entirely murder. Perhaps some day. Unto
God I hope so.

Amen.

Now I will try to give the reader a glimpse of the
Women of La Ferté Macé.

The little Machine-Fixer, as I said in the preceding
chapter, divided them into Good and Bad. He said there
were as much as three Good ones, of which three he had
talked to one and knew her story. Another of the three
Good Women obviously was Margherite—a big, strong
female who did washing, and who was a permanent resi-
dent because she had been careless enough to be born of

German parents. I think I spoke with number three on the day I waited to be examined by the Commission—a Belgian girl, whom I shall mention later along with that incident. Whereat, by process of elimination, we arrive at *les putains,* whereof God may know how many there were at La Ferté, but I certainly do not. To *les putains* in general I have already made my deep and sincere bow. I should like to speak here of four individuals. They are Celina, Lena, Lily, Renée.

Celina Tek was an extraordinarily beautiful animal. Her firm girl's body emanated a supreme vitality. It was neither tall nor short, its movements nor graceful nor awkward. It came and went with a certain sexual velocity, a velocity whose health and vigour made everyone in La Ferté seem puny and old. Her deep sensual voice had a coarse richness. Her face, dark and young, annihilated easily the ancient and greyish walls. Her wonderful hair was shockingly black. Her perfect teeth, when she smiled, reminded you of an animal. The cult of Isis never worshipped a more deep luxurious smile. This face, framed in the night of its hair, seemed (as it moved at the window overlooking the *cour des femmes*) inexorably and colossally young. The body was absolutely and fearlessly alive. In the impeccable and altogether admirable desolation of La Ferté and the Normandy autumn, Celina, easily and fiercely moving, was a kinesis.

The French Government must have already recognized this; it called her *incorrigible.*

Lena, also a Belgian, always and fortunately just missed being a type which in the American language (sometimes called 'Slang') has a definite nomenclature. Lena had the makings of an ordinary broad. And yet, thanks to *La Misère,* a certain indubitable personality became gradually rescued. A tall hard face about which was loosely pitched some hay-coloured hair. Strenuous and mutilated hands. A loose, raucous way of laughing, which contrasted well with Celina's definite gurgling titter. Energy rather than vitality. A certain power and roughness about her laughter. She never smiled. She laughed loudly and obscenely and always. A woman.

Lily was a German girl, who looked unbelievably old, wore white or once white dresses, had a sort of drawling scream in her throat besides a thick deadly cough, and floundered leanly under the eyes of men. Upon the skinny neck of Lily a face had been set for all the world to look upon and be afraid. The face itself was made of flesh green and almost putrescent. In each cheek a bloody spot. Which was not rouge, but the flower which consumption plants in the cheek of its favourite. A face vulgar and vast and heavy-featured, about which a smile was always flopping uselessly. Occasionally Lily grinned, showing several monstrously decayed and perfectly yellow teeth, which teeth usually were smoking a cigarette. Her bluish hands were very interestingly dead; the fingers were nervous, they lived in cringing bags of freckled skin, they might almost be alive.

She was perhaps eighteen years old.

Renée, the fourth member of the circle, was always well-dressed and somehow chic. Her silhouette had character, from the waved coiffure to the enormously high heels. Had Renée been able to restrain a perfectly toothless smile she might possibly have passed for a *jeune gonzesse*. She was not. The smile was ample and black. You saw through it into the back of her neck. You felt as if her life was in danger when she smiled, as it probably was. Her skin was not particularly tired. But Renée was old, older than Lena by several years; perhaps twenty-five, which for a lady of her profession is very old. Also about Renée there was a certain dangerous fragility of unhealth. And yet Renée was hard, immeasurably hard. And accurate. Her exact movements were the movements of a mechanism. Including her voice, which had a purely mechanical timbre. She could do two things with this voice and two only—screech and boom. At times she tried to chuckle and almost fell apart. Renée was in fact dead. In looking at her for the first time, I realized that there may be something stylish about death.

This first time was interesting in the extreme. It was Lily's birthday. We looked out of the windows which composed one side of the otherwise windowless Enormous Room; looked down, and saw—just outside the wall of the building—Celina, Lena, Lily and a new girl who was Renée. They were all individually intoxicated. Celina was joyously tight. Renée was stiffly bunnied. Lena was raucously pickled. Lily, floundering and staggering and tumbling and whirling, was utterly soused. She was all tricked out in an erstwhile dainty dress, white, and with ribbons. Celina (as always) wore black. Lena had on a rather heavy striped sweater and skirt. Renée was immaculate in tight-fitting satin or something of the sort; she seemed to have somehow escaped from a doll's house overnight. About the group were a number of *plantons*, roaring with laughter, teasing, insulting, encouraging, from time to time attempting to embrace the ladies. Celina gave one of them a terrific box on the ear. The mirth of the others was redoubled. Lily spun about and fell down, moaning and coughing, and screaming about her fiancé in Belgium; what a handsome young fellow he was, how he had promised to marry her ... shouts of enjoyment from the *plantons*. Lena had to sit down or else fall down, so she sat down with a good deal of dignity, her back against the wall, and in that position attempted to execute a kind of dance. *Les plantons* rocked and applauded. Celina smiled beautifully at the men who were staring from every window of The Enormous Room, and, with a supreme effort, went over and dragged Renée (who had neatly and accurately folded up with machine-like rapidity in the mud) through the doorway and into the house. Eventually Lena followed her example, capturing Lily *en route*. The scene must have consumed all of twenty minutes. The *plantons* were so mirth-stricken that they had to sit down and rest under the washing-shed. Of all the inhabitants of The Enormous Room, Fritz and Harree and Pompom and Bathhouse John enjoyed it most. I should include Jan, whose chin nearly rested on the window-sill with the little body belonging to it fluttering in an ugly interested way all the time. That Bathhouse John's interest was largely cynical is evidenced by the remarks which he threw out between spittings—'*Une section mesdames!*' '*A la gare!*' '*Aux armes tout le monde!*' etc. With the exception of these enthusiastic watchers, the other captives evidenced vague amusement—excepting Count Bragard, who said with lofty disgust that it was 'no better than a bloody knocking 'ouse, Mr. Cummings,' and Monsieur Petairs, whose annoyance amounted to agony. Of course these twain were, comparatively speaking, old men . . .

The four female incorrigibles encountered less difficulty in attaining *cabinot* than any four specimens of incorrigibility among *les hommes*. Not only were they placed in dungeon vile with a frequency which amounted to continuity; their sentences were far more severe than those handed out to the men. Up to the time of my little visit to La Ferté I had innocently supposed that in referring to women as 'the weaker sex' a man was strictly within his rights. La Ferté, if it did nothing else for my intelligence, rid it of this over-powering error. I recall, for example, a period of sixteen days and nights spent (during my stay) by the woman Lena in the *cabinot*. It was either toward the latter part of October or the early part of November that this occurred, I will not be sure which. The dampness of the autumn was as terrible, under normal conditions— that is to say in The Enormous Room—as any climatic eccentricity which I have ever experienced. We had a wood-burning stove in the middle of the room, which antiquated apparatus was kept going all day, to the vast discomfort of eyes and noses not to mention throats and lungs—the pungent smoke filling the room with an at- mosphere next to unbreathable, but tolerated for the simple reason that it stood between ourselves and death. For even with the stove going full blast the walls never ceased to sweat and even trickle, so overpowering was the dampness. By night the chill was to myself—fortunately bedded at least eighteen inches from the floor and sleeping in my clothes; bed-roll, blankets, and all, under and over me and around me—not merely perceptible but desolat- ing. Once my bed broke, and I spent the night perforce on the floor with only my *paillasse* under me; to awake finally in the whitish dawn perfectly helpless with rheu- matism. Yet with the exception of my bed and B.'s bed and a wooden bunk which belonged to Bathhouse John, every *paillasse* lay directly on the floor; moreover the men who slept thus were three-quarters of them miserably clad, nor had they anything beyond their light-weight blankets —whereas I had a complete outfit including a big fur coat, which I had taken with me (as previously described) from the *Section Sanitaire*. The morning after my night spent on the floor I pondered, having nothing to do and being unable to move, upon the subject of my physical endurance—wondering just how the men about me, many of them beyond middle age, some extremely delicate, in all not more than five or six as rugged constitutionally as myself, lived through the nights in The Enormous Room. Also I recollected glancing through an open door into the women's quarters, at the risk of being noticed by the *planton* in whose charge I was at the time (who, fortunately, was stupid even for a *planton*, else I should have been well punished for my curiosity) and beholding *paillasses* identical in all respects with ours reposing on the floor; and I thought, If it is marvellous that old men and sick men can stand this and not die, it is certainly miraculous that girls of eleven and fifteen, and the baby which I saw once being caressed out in the women's *cour* with unspeakable gentleness by a little *putain* whose name I do not know, and the dozen or so oldish females whom I have often seen on promenade—can stand this and not die. These things I mention not to excite the reader's pity nor yet his indignation; I mention them because I do not know of any other way to indicate—it is no more than indicating—the significance of the torture perpetrated under the *Directeur's* direction in the case of the girl Lena. If incidentally it throws light on the personality of the torturer I shall be gratified.

Lena's confinement in the *cabinot*—which dungeon I have already attempted to describe but to whose filth and slime no words can begin to do justice—was in this case solitary. Once a day, of an afternoon and always at the time when all the men were upstairs after the second

promenade (which gave the writer of this history an exquisite chance to see an atrocity at first-hand), Lena was
taken out of the *cabinot* by three *plantons* and permitted
a half-hour promenade just outside the door of the building, or in the same locality—delimited by barbed-wire on
one side and the washing-shed on another—made famous
by the scene of inebriety above described. Punctually at
the expiration of thirty minutes she was shoved back into
the *cabinot* by the *plantons*. Every day for sixteen days I
saw her; noted the indestructible bravado of her gait and
carriage, the unchanging timbre of her terrible laughter
in response to the salutation of an inhabitant of The Enormous Room (for there were at least six men who spoke to
her daily, and took their *pain sec* and their *cabinot* in
punishment therefor with the pride of a soldier who takes
the *médaille militaire* in recompense for his valour); noted
the increasing pallor of her flesh; watched the skin gradually assume a distinct greenish tint (a greenishness which
I cannot describe save that it suggested putrefaction);
heard the coughing to which she had been always subject
grow thicker and deeper till it doubled her up every few
minutes, creasing her body as you crease a piece of paper
with your thumb-nail, preparatory to tearing it in two—
and I realized fully and irrevocably and for perhaps the
first time the meaning of civilization. And I realized that
it was true—as I had previously only suspected it to be
true—that in finding us unworthy of helping to carry
forward the banner of progress, alias the tricolour, the
inimitable and excellent French Government was con-
ferring upon B. and myself—albeit with other intent—
the ultimate compliment.

And the Machine-Fixer, whose opinion of this blonde
putain grew and increased and soared with every day of

her martyrdom till the Machine-Fixer's former classifica-
tion of *les femmes* exploded and disappeared entirely—the
Machine-Fixer who would have fallen on his little knees
to Lena had she given him a chance, and kissed the hem of
her striped skirt in an ecstasy of adoration—told me that
Lena on being finally released walked upstairs herself,
holding hard to the banister without a look for anyone,
'having eyes as big as tea-cups.' He added, with tears in
his own eyes:

'M'sieu' Jean, a woman.'

I recall perfectly being in the kitchen one day, hiding
from the eagle-eye of the Black Holster and enjoying a
talk on the economic consequences of war, said talk being
delivered by Afrique. As a matter of fact, I was not in the
cuisine proper, but in the little room which I have mentioned previously. The door into the *cuisine* was shut. The
sweetly soft odour of newly cut wood was around me.
And all the time that Afrique was talking I heard clearly,
through the shut door and through the kitchen wall and
through the locked door of the *cabinot* situated directly
across the hall from *la cuisine*, the insane, gasping voice of
a girl singing and yelling and screeching and laughing.
Finally I interrupted my speaker to ask what on earth was
the matter in the *cabinot*?—'*C'est la femme allemande qui
s'appelle Lily*,' Afrique briefly answered. A little later
BANG went the *cabinot* door, and ROAR went the familiar coarse voice of the *Directeur*. It disturbs him, the
noise, Afrique said. The *cabinot* door slammed. There was
silence. Heavily steps ascended. Then the song began
again, a little more insane than before; the laughter a little
wilder. . . . 'You can't stop her,' Afrique said admiringly.
'A great voice Mademoiselle has, eh? So, as I was saying,
the national debt being conditioned—'

But the experience, à propos *les femmes,* which meant
and will always mean more to me than any other, the
scene which is a little more unbelievable than perhaps any
scene that it has ever been my privilege to witness, the
incident which (possibly more than any other) revealed
to me those unspeakable foundations upon which are
builded with infinite care such at once ornate and comfortable structures as *La Gloire* and *Le Patriotisme*—occurred in this wise.

Les hommes, myself among them, were leaving *la cour*
for The Enormous Room under the watchful eye (as always) of a *planton.* As we defiled through the little gate
in the barbed-wire fence we heard, apparently just inside
the building whither we were proceeding on our way to
The Great Upstairs, a tremendous sound of mingled
screams, curses and crashings. The *planton* of the day was
not only stupid—he was a little deaf; to his ears this
hideous racket had not, as nearly as one could see, penetrated. At all events he marched us along toward the
door with utmost plantonic satisfaction and composure.
I managed to insert myself in the fore of the procession,
being eager to witness the scene within; and reached the
door almost simultaneously with Fritz, Harree and two
or three others. I forget which of us opened it. I will never
forget what I saw as I crossed the threshold.

The hall was filled with stifling smoke; the smoke which
straw makes when it is set on fire, a peculiarly nauseous,
choking, whitish-blue smoke. This smoke was so dense
that only after some moments could I make out, with
bleeding eyes and wounded lungs, anything whatever.
What I saw was this: five or six *plantons* were engaged in
carrying out of the nearest *cabinot* two girls, who looked
perfectly dead. Their bodies were absolutely limp. Their

hands dragged foolishly along the floor as they were carried. Their upward white faces dangled loosely upon their necks. Their crumpled figures sagged in the *plantons'* arms. I recognized Lily and Renée. Lena I made out at a little distance tottering against the door of the *cuisine* opposite the *cabinot*, her hay-coloured head drooping and swaying slowly upon the open breast of her shirt-waist, her legs far apart and propping with difficulty her hinging body, her hands spasmodically searching for the knob of the door. The smoke proceeded from the open *cabinot* in great ponderous murdering clouds. In one of these clouds, erect and tense and beautiful as an angel—her wildly shouting face framed in its huge night of dishevelled hair, her deep sexual voice, hoarsely strident above the din and smoke, shouting fiercely through the darkness—stood, triumphantly and colossally young, Celina. Facing her, its clenched pinkish fists raised high above its savagely bristling head in a big brutal gesture of impotence and rage and anguish—the Fiend Himself paused, quivering, on the fourth stair from the bottom of the flight leading to the women's quarters. Through the smoke the great bright voice of Celina rose at him, hoarse and rich and sudden and intensely luxurious, a quick throaty accurate slaying deepness:

CHIEZ, SI VOUS VOULEZ, CHIEZ,

and over and beneath and around the voice I saw frightened faces of women hanging in the smoke, some screaming with their lips apart and their eyes closed, some staring with wide eyes; and among the women's faces I discovered the large placid interested expression of the *Gestionnaire* and the nervous clicking eyes of the *Surveillant*. And there was a shout—it was the Black Holster shouting at us as we stood transfixed—

'Who the devil brought *les hommes* in here? Get up with you where you belong, you . . .'

—And he made a rush at us, and we dodged in the smoke and passed slowly up the hall, looking behind us, speechless to a man with the admiration of Terror, till we reached the further flight of stairs; and mounted slowly with the din falling below us, ringing in our ears, beating upon our brains—mounted slowly with quickened blood and pale faces—to the peace of The Enormous Room.

I spoke with both *balayeurs* that night. They told me, independently, the same story: the four incorrigibles had been locked in the *cabinot* ensemble. They made so much noise, particularly Lily, that the *plantons* were afraid the *Directeur* would be disturbed. Accordingly the *plantons* got together and stuffed the contents of a *paillasse* in the cracks around the door, and particularly in the crack under the door wherein cigarettes were commonly inserted by friends of the entombed. This process made the *cabinot* air-tight. But the *plantons* were not taking any chances on disturbing *Monsieur le Directeur*. They carefully lighted the *paillasse* at a number of points and stood back to see the result of their efforts. So soon as the smoke found its way inward the singing was supplanted by coughing; then the coughing stopped. Then nothing was heard. Then Celina began crying out within—'Open the door, Lily and Renée are dead'—and the *plantons* were frightened. After some debate they decided to open the door—out poured the smoke, and in it Celina, whose voice in a fraction of a second roused everyone in the building. The Black Holster wrestled with her and tried to knock her down by a blow on the mouth; but she escaped, bleeding a little, to the foot of the stairs—simultaneously with the advent of the *Directeur*, who for once had found someone beyond the power of his weapon— Fear, someone in contact with whose indescribable Youth the puny threats of death withered between his lips, someone finally completely and unutterably Alive whom the Lie upon his slavering tongue could not kill.

I do not need to say that, as soon as the girls who had fainted could be brought to, they joined Lena in *pain sec* for many days to come; and that Celina was overpowered by six *plantons*—at the order of *Monsieur le Directeur*—and reincarcerated in the *cabinot* adjoining that from which she had made her velocitous exit—reincarcerated without food for twenty-four hours. 'Mais, M'sieu' Jean,' the Machine-Fixer said trembling, '*Vous savez elle est forte.* She gave the six of them a fight, I tell you. And three of them went to the doctor as a result of their efforts, including *le vieux* (The Black Holster). But of course they succeeded in beating her up, six men upon one woman. She was beaten badly, I tell you, before she gave in. *M'sieu' Jean, ils sont tous—les plantons et le Directeur Lui-Même et le Surveillant et le Gestionnaire et tous—ils sonts des—*' and he said very nicely what they were, and lit his little black pipe with a crisp curving upward gesture, and shook like a blade of grass.

With which specimen of purely mediæval torture I leave the subject of Women, and embark upon the quieter if no less enlightening subject of Sunday.

Sunday, it will be recalled, was *Monsieur le Directeur's* third weapon. That is to say: lest the ordinarily tantalizing proximity of *les femmes* should not inspire *les hommes* to deeds which placed the doers automatically in the clutches of himself, his subordinates, and *la punition*, it was arranged that once a week the tantalizing proximity aforesaid should be supplanted by a positively maddening approach to coincidence. Or in other words, *les hommes* and *les femmes* might for an hour or less enjoy the same exceedingly small room; for purposes of course of devotion —it being obvious to *Monsieur le Directeur* that the representatives of both sexes at La Ferté Macé were inherently of a strongly devotional nature. And lest the temptation to err in such moments be deprived, through a certain aspect of compulsion, of its complete force, the attendance of such strictly devotional services was made optional.

The uplifting services to which I refer took place in that very room which (the night of my arrival) had yielded me my *paillasse* under the *Surveillant's* direction. It may have been thirty feet long and twenty wide. At one end was an altar at the top of several wooden stairs, with a large candle on each side. To the right as you entered a number of benches were placed to accommodate *les femmes*. *Les hommes* upon entering took off their caps and stood over against the left wall so as to leave between them and *les femmes* an alley perhaps five feet wide. In this alley stood the Black Holster with his *képi* firmly resting upon his head, his arms folded, his eyes spying to left and right in order to intercept any signals exchanged between the sheep and goats. Those who elected to enjoy spiritual things left the *cour* and their morning promenade after about an hour of promenading, while the materially minded remained to finish the promenade; or if one declined the promenade entirely (as frequently occurred owing to the fact that weather conditions on Sunday were invariably more indescribable than usual) a *planton* mounted to The Enormous Room and shouted
'*La Messe!*'

several times; whereat the devotees lined up and were carefully conducted to the scene of spiritual operations.

The priest was changed every week. His assistant (whom I had the indescribable pleasure of seeing only upon Sundays) was always the same. It was his function to pick the priest up when he fell down after tripping upon his robe, to hand him things before he wanted them, to ring a huge bell, to interrupt the peculiarly divine portions of the service with a squeaking of his shoes, to gaze about from time to time upon the worshippers for purposes of intimidation, and finally—most important of all—to blow out the two big candles at the very earliest opportunity, in the interests (doubtless) of economy. As he was a short, fattish, ancient, strangely soggy creature, and as his longish black suit was somewhat too big for him, he executed a series of profound efforts in extinguishing the candles. In fact he had to climb part-way up the candles before he could get at the flame; at which moment, he looked very much like a weakly and fat boy (for he was obviously in his second or fourth childhood) climbing a flag-pole. At moments of leisure he abased his fatty whitish jowl and contemplated with watery eyes the floor in front of his highly polished boots, having first placed his ugly chubby hands together behind his most ample back.

Dimanche: green murmurs in coldness. Surplice fiercely fearful, praying on his bony both knees, crossing himself ... The Fake French Soldier, alias Garibaldi, beside him, a little face filled with terror ... the Bell cranks the sharp-nosed *curé* on his knees ... titter from bench of whores— and that reminds me of a Sunday afternoon on our backs spent with the wholeness of a hill in Chevancourt, discovering a great apple pie, B. and Jean Stahl and Maurice *le*

Menuisier and myself; and the sun falling roundly before us.

—And then one *Dimanche* a new high old man with a sharp violet face and green hair—'*Vous êtes libres, mes enfants, de faire l'immortalité—Songez, songez donc—L'Eternité est une existence sans durée—Toujours le Paradis, toujours l'Enfer*' (to the silently roaring whores) '*Le ciel est fait pour vous*'—and the Belgian ten-foot farmer spat three times and wiped them with his foot, his nose dripping; and the nigger shot a white oyster into a far-off scarlet handkerchief—and the Man's strings came untied and he sidled crab-like down the steps—the two candles wiggle a strenuous softness . . .

In another chapter I will tell you about the nigger.

And another Sunday I saw three tiny old females stumble forward, three very formerly and even once bonnets perched upon three wizened skulls, and flop clumsily before the Man, and take the wafer hungrily into their leathery faces.

VII

AN APPROACH TO THE DELECT-
ABLE MOUNTAINS

'Sunday' (says Mr. Pound, with infinite penetration)
  'is a dreadful day,
Monday is much pleasanter.
Then let us muse a little space
Upon fond Nature's morbid grace.'

IT is a great and distinct pleasure to have penetrated
and arrived upon the outside of *Le Dimanche*. We may
now—Nature's morbid grace being a topic whereof the
reader has already heard much and will necessarily hear
more—turn to the 'much pleasanter,' the in fact 'Monday,' aspect of La Ferté; by which I mean *les nouveaux*,
whose arrivals and reactions constituted the actual or
kinetic aspect of our otherwise merely real Non-existence.
So let us tighten our belts (everyone used to tighten his
belt at least twice a day at La Ferté, but for another reason
—to follow and keep track of his surely shrinking anatomy), seize our staffs into our hands, and continue the
ascent begun with the first pages of the story.

One day I found myself expecting *La Soupe*, Number 1
with something like avidity. My appetite faded, however,
upon perceiving a vision *en route* to the empty place at
my left. It slightly resembled a tall youth not more than
sixteen or seventeen years old, having flaxen hair, a face
whose whiteness I have never seen equalled, and an ex-

pression of intense starvation which might have been well enough in a human being, but was somewhat unnecessarily uncanny in a ghost. The ghost, floatingly and slenderly, made for the place beside me, seated himself suddenly and gently like a morsel of white wind, and regarded the wall before him. *La Soupe* arrived. He obtained a plate (after some protest on the part of certain members of our table to whom the advent of a new-comer meant only that everyone would get less for lunch), and after gazing at his portion for a second in apparent wonderment at its size caused it gently and suddenly to disappear. I was no sluggard as a rule, but found myself outclassed by minutes —which, said I to myself, is not to be worried over since 'tis sheer vanity to compete with the supernatural. But (even as I lugged the last spoonful of lukewarm greasy water to my lips) this ghost turned to me for all the world as if I too were a ghost, and remarked softly:

'*Voulez-vous me prêter dix sous? Je vais acheter du tabac à la cantine.*'

One has no business crossing a spirit, I thought; and produced the sum cheerfully—which sum disappeared, the ghost arose slenderly and soundlessly, and I was left with emptiness beside me.

Later I discovered that this ghost was called Pete.

Pete was a Hollander, and therefore found firm and staunch friends in Harree, John o' the Bathhouse and the other Hollanders. In three days Pete discarded the immateriality which had constituted the exquisite definiteness of his advent, and donned the garb of flesh-and-blood. This change was due equally to *La Soupe* and the canteen, and to the finding of friends. For Pete had been in solitary confinement for three months, and had had nothing to eat but bread and water during that time, having been told by the jailors (as he informed us, without a trace of bitterness) that they would shorten his sentence provided he did not partake of *La Soupe* during his incarceration—that is to say, *le gouvernement français* had a little joke at Pete's expense. Also he had known nobody during that time but the five fingers which deposited said bread and water with conscientious regularity on the ground beside him. Being a Hollander neither of these things killed him —on the contrary, he merely turned into a ghost, thereby fooling the excellent French Government within an inch of its foolable life. He was a very excellent friend of ours —I refer as usual to B. and myself—and from the day of his arrival until the day of his departure to Précigné along with B. and three others I never ceased to like and to admire him. He was naturally sensitive, extremely the antithesis of coarse (which 'refined' somehow does not imply), had not in the least suffered from a 'good,' as we say, education, and possessed an at once frank and unobstreperous personality. Very little that had happened to Pete's physique had escaped Pete's mind. This mind of his quietly and firmly had expanded, in proportion as its owner's trousers had become too big around the waist—altogether not so extraordinary as was the fact that, after being physically transformed as I have never seen a human being transformed by food and friends, Pete thought and acted with exactly the same quietness and firmness as before. He was a rare spirit, and I salute him wherever he is.

Mexique was a good friend of Pete's, as he was of ours. He had been introduced to us by a man we called One-Eyed David, who was married and had a wife downstairs, with which wife he was allowed to live all day—being conducted to and from her society by a *planton*. He spoke

Spanish well and French passably; had black hair, bright
Jewish eyes, a dead-fish expression, and a both amiable
and courteous disposition. One-Eyed Dah-veed (as it was
pronounced, of course) had been in prison at Noyon
during the German occupation, which he described fully
and without hyperbole—stating that no one could have
been more considerate or just than the commander of the
invading troops. Dah-veed had seen with his own eyes a
French girl extend an apple to one of the common soldiers
as the German army entered the outskirts of the city:
'Prenez, dit elle; vous êtes fatigué.—Madame, répondit
le soldat allemand en français, je vous remercie—et il
cherchait dans sa poche et trouvait dix sous. Non, non, dit
la jeune fille, je ne veux pas d'argent; je vous donne de
bonne volonté—Pardon, madame, dit le soldat, il vous
faut savoir qu'il est défendu pour un soldat allemand de
prendre quelque chose sans payer.'—And before that,
One-Eyed Dah-veed had talked at Noyon with a barber
whose brother was an aviator with the French Army:
'Mon frère, me dit le coiffeur, m'a raconté une belle his-
toire il y a quelques jours. Il volait au-dessus des lignes, et
s'étonnait, un jour, de remarquer que les cannons français
ne tiraient pas sur les boches mais sur les français eux-
mêmes. Précipitamment il atterissait, sautait de l'appareil,
allait de suite au bureau du général. Il donnait le salut, et
criait, bien excité: Mon général, vous tirez sur les français!
Le général le regardait sans intérêt, sans bouger, puis il
disait tout simplement: On a commencé, il faut finir.'
Which is why perhaps, said One-Eyed Dah-veed, looking
two ways at once with his uncorrelated eyes, the Germans
entered Noyon . . . But to return to Mexique.

One night we had a soirée, as Dah-veed called it, à
propos a pot of hot tea which Dah-veed's wife had given

him to take upstairs, it being damnably damp and cold (as usual) in The Enormous Room. Dah-veed, cautiously and in a low voice, invited us to his *paillasse* to enjoy this extraordinary pleasure; and we accepted, B. and I, with huge joy; and sitting on Dah-veed's *paillasse* we found somebody who turned out to be Mexique—to whom, by his right name, our host introduced us with all the poise and courtesy vulgarly associated with a French salon.

For Mexique I cherish and always will cherish unmitigated affection. He was perhaps nineteen years old, very chubby, extremely good-natured; and possessed of an unruffled disposition which extended to the most violent and obvious discomforts a subtle and placid illumination. He spoke beautiful Spanish, had been born in Mexico, and was really called Philippe Burgos. He had been in New York. He criticized some one for saying 'Yes' to us, one day, stating that no American said 'Yes' but 'Yuh'; which —whatever the reader may think—is to my mind a very profound observation. In New York he had worked nights as a fireman in some big building or other and slept days, and this method of seeing America he had enjoyed extremely. Mexique had one day taken ship (being curious to see the world) and worked as *chauffeur*—that is to say in the stoke-hole. He had landed in, I think, Havre; had missed his ship; had inquired something of a gendarme in French (which he spoke not at all, with the exception of a phrase or two like '*quelle huere qu'il est?*'); had been kindly treated and told that he would be taken to a ship *de suite*—had boarded a train in the company of two or three kind gendarmes, ridden a prodigious distance, got off the train finally with high hopes, walked a little distance, come in sight of the grey perspiring wall of La Ferté, and—'So, I ask one of them: Where is the Ship?

He point to here and tell me, There is the ship. I say: This is a God Dam Funny Ship'—quoth Mexique, laughing.

Mexique played dominoes with us (B. having devised a set from cardboard), strolled The Enormous Room with us, telling of his father and brother in Mexico, of the people, of the customs; and—when we were in the *cour*— wrote the entire conjugation of *tengo* in the deep mud with a little stick, squatting and chuckling and explaining. He and his brother had both participated in the revolution which made Carranza president. His description of which affair was utterly delightful.

'Every-body run a-round with guns,' Mexique said. 'And by-and-by no see to shoot everybody, so everybody go home.' We asked if he had shot anybody himself. 'Sure. I shoot everybody I do'no,' Mexique answered, laughing. 'I t'ink every-body no hit me,' he added, regarding his stocky person with great and quiet amusement. When we asked him once what he thought about the war, he replied, 'I t'ink lotta bullsh-t,' which, upon copious reflection, I decided absolutely expressed my own point of view.

Mexique was generous, incapable of either stupidity or despondency, and mannered as a gentleman is supposed to be. Upon his arrival he wrote almost immediately to the Mexican or is it Spanish consul—'He know my fader in Mexico'—stating in perfect and unambiguous Spanish the facts leading to his arrest; and when I said good-bye to *La Misère*, Mexique was expecting a favourable reply at any moment, as indeed he had been cheerfully expecting for some time. If he reads this history I hope he will not be too angry with me for whatever injustice it does to one of the altogether pleasantest companions I have ever had. My notebooks, one in particular, are covered with conjugations which bear witness to Mexique's ineffable good-nature. I also have a somewhat superficial portrait of his back sitting on a bench by the *poêle*. I wish I had another of Mexique out in *le jardin* with a man who worked there, who was a Spaniard, and whom the *Surveillant* had considerately allowed Mexique to assist; with the perfectly correct idea that it would be pleasant for Mexique to talk to some one who could speak Spanish—if not as well as he, Mexique, could, at least passably well. As it is, I must be content to see my very good friend sitting with his hands in his pockets by the stove with Bill the Hollander beside him. And I hope it was not many days after my departure that Mexique went free. Somehow I feel that he went free . . . and if I am right, I will only say about Mexique's freedom what I have heard him slowly and placidly say many times concerning not only the troubles which were common property to us all but his own peculiar troubles as well.

'That's fine.'

The Young (or Holland) Skipper—not to be confused with The Skipper whom I have already tried to describe—was a real contribution to our midst. On his own part he contributed his mate—a terribly tall, rather round-shouldered individual, of whom I said to myself immediately: 'By Jove, here's a tough guy and a murderer all in one.' Of course I was wrong; I say 'of course,' since to judge an arrival by the arrival's exterior was (as I discovered in practically every case) equivalent to judging a motor by its horse-power instead of what it did when confronted by a hill. As it turned out, the mate was a taciturn and very gentle youth who had committed no greater crime than that of being a member of The Young Skipper's crew. That this was far from a crime was proved by The Young Skipper himself, than whom I have never met a jollier, more open-hearted and otherwise both generous and genuine man in my life. He wore a collarless shirt gaily striped, a vest and trousers calculated to withstand the ravages of time, a jaunty cap, a big signet ring on his fourth finger, and a pair of seaworthy boots which were the envy and admiration of every one, including myself. He used to sit on an extraordinarily small wooden stool by the stove, thereby exaggerating his almost round five-feet exactly of bone and muscle. The Hollanders, especially John, made a great deal of him. He was ready without being rough, had a pair of frank, good-humoured eyes, a tiny happy nose somewhat uppish and freckled, and large strong hard hands which seemed always rather embarrassed to find themselves on land. He told us confidentially that Pete had run away to sea; that Pete came of a very good family in Holland, who were worried to death about Pete's whereabouts; that Pete was too proud to let them know he had been arrested; and that he, The Young Skipper, if and when he got back to Holland, would make a point of going immediately to Pete's parents and telling them where Pete was, which would make them move earth and heaven for their son's liberty. Of a Sunday, The Young or Holland Skipper got himself up to beat the cars and joined the immaculate Holland Delegation at *la messe* —being, from the instant of his arrival, assoted upon a fair lady who invariably attended all functions of a religious nature. I must add (for the benefit of the highly moral readers of this chronicle) that this admiration served merely to while away the moments of The Young Skipper's captivity—and that The Young Skipper never seriously deviated from an intense devotion to 'my girl' as he called her, whose photograph he always carried over his heart. A large-faced and plump person, with apparently a very honest heart of her own—I wish I could say more for her . . . but then, photographs are always untrustworthy. He told us some very vivid incidents in his voyages, which (the war being on) were accomplished with some danger and a great deal of excitement. I remember how his eyes twinkled when he said his ship passed directly under a huge Zeppelin: 'And the fellers waved to us, and we gave 'em a cheer and waved too, and all the fellers in the Zeppelin keeked'—due to which word in particular I conceived a great fondness for The Young Skipper. He told about the multitudinous English deserters in Holland, how 'The girls were crazy about 'em, and if a Hollander comes up and asks 'em to go skating with him on the canal they won't, for the English soldiers don't know how to skate'—and later when the haughty misses had been 'left' by their flames, 'Up we'd come and give 'em the laugh.' . . . He spoke first-rate English, clear rousing Dutch, some I should say, faulty but fluent German, and no French. 'This language is too bloody much for me,' said The Young Skipper with perfect candour, smiling. 'The john-darmz ask me a lotta questions and I say no parlezvous so they take me and my mate'—with a gesture toward the mild and monumental youth by the stove—'and puts us on trains and everywhere and where the Gottverdummer bloody Hell are we all agoing I don't know till we gets here'—at which he laughed heartily. 'Thanks,' he said when I offered a Scarferlati *Jaune,* 'I'll get some myself to-night at the canteen and pay you back'—for in common with Pete he shared a great conscientiousness in respect to receiving favours. 'They're made of bloody dust, these,' he said, smiling pleasantly after the first inhalation. I asked him what did he carry in the way of cargo? 'Coal,' he replied with great emphasis. And he told me they got it clear from Norway, and that it was a good business bringing it (for the French needed it and would pay anything) —'Provided you can stand the excitement.' His utter and absolute contempt for the john-darmz was, to B. and myself in particular, considerably more than delightful. 'Them fellers with their swords and little coats cape-like' were not to be spoken of in the same breath with a man. As B. says, one of the nicest things anyone ever did in La Ferté (I almost said in prison) was done by The Young Skipper one night: who came up to our beds where we were cooking cocoa, or rather chocolate (for we sliced up a cake of imitation Menier purchased at the canteen, added water, and heated the ensemble in a tin cup suspended by a truly extraordinary series of wires (B. fecit) directly above a common *bougie*), and said to us, with a sticking of his thumb behind him—'There's a poor feller lying sick over there and I wondered will you give me a bit o' hot chocolate for him; he wouldn't ask for it himself.' Naturally we were peculiarly happy to give it—happier when we saw The Young Skipper stride over to the bed of The Silent Man, to whom he spoke very gently and persuadingly in (as I guess) German—happiest, when we saw The Silent Man half-rise from his *paillasse* and drink, with The Young Skipper standing over him smiling from ear to ear. Anyone who could with utmost ease conquer the irrevocable diffidence of The Silent Man is insusceptible of portraiture. I hereby apologize to The Young Skipper, and wish him well with his girl in Holland, where I hope with all my heart he is. And maybe some day we'll all of us go skating on the canals; and maybe we'll talk about what happens when the dikes break, and about the houses and the flowers and the windmills.

Here let me introduce the *Garde-champêtre*, whose name I have already taken more or less in vain. A little sharp, hungry-looking person who, subsequent to being a member of a rural police force (of which membership he seemed rather proud), had served his *patrie*—otherwise known as *La Belgique*—in the capacity of motor-cyclist. As he carried dispatches from one end of the line to the other his disagreeably big eyes had absorbed certain peculiarly inspiring details of civilized warfare. He had, at one time, seen a bridge hastily constructed by *les alliés* over the Yser River, the cadavers of the faithful and the enemy alike being thrown in helter-skelter to make a much needed foundation for the timbers. This little procedure had considerably outraged the *Garde-champêtre's* sense of decency. The Yser, said he, flowed perfectly red for a long time. 'We were all together: Belgians, French, English ... we Belgians did not see any good reason for continuing the battle. But we continued. O indeed we continued. Do you know why?'

I said that I was afraid I didn't.

'Because in front of us we had *les obus allemands, en arrière les mitrailleuses françaises, toujours les mitrailleuses françaises, mon vieux.*'

'*Je ne comprends pas bien,*' I said in confusion, recalling all the highfalutin rigmarole which Americans believed— (little martyred Belgium protected by the allies from the inroads of the aggressor, etc.)—'why should the French put machine-guns behind you?'

The *Garde-champêtre* lifted his big empty eyes nervously. The vast hollows in which they lived darkened. His little rather hard face trembled within itself. I thought for a second he was going to throw a fit at my feet—

instead of doing which he replied pettishly, in a sunken bright whisper:

'To keep us going forward. At times a company would drop its guns and turn to run. Pupupupupupupupup . . .' his short unlovely arm described gently the swinging of a *mitrailleuse* . . . 'finish. The Belgian soldiers to left and right of them took the hint. If they did not—pupupupu-pupupupupup. . . . O we went forward. Yes. *Vive le patriotisme.*'

And he rose with a gesture which seemed to brush away these painful trifles from his memory, crossed the end of the room with short rapid steps, and began talking to his best friend Judas, who was at that moment engaged in training his wobbly moustachios. . . . Toward the close of my visit to La Ferté the *Garde-champêtre* was really happy for a period of two days—during which time he moved in the society of a rich, intelligent, mistakenly arrested and completely disagreeable youth in bone spectacles, copious hair and spiral puttees, whom B. and I named JoJo the Lion-Faced Boy, thereby partially contenting ourselves. Had the charges against JoJo been stronger my tale would have been longer—fortunately for *tout le monde* they had no basis; and back went JoJo to his native Paris, leaving the *Garde-champêtre* with Judas and attacks of only occasionally interesting despair.

The reader may suppose that it is about time another Delectable Mountain appeared upon his horizon. Let him keep his eyes wide open, for here one comes . . .

Whenever our circle was about to be increased, a bell from somewhere afar (as a matter of fact the gate which had admitted my weary self to La Ferté upon a memorable night, as already has been faithfully recounted) tanged audibly—whereat up jumped the more strenuous inhabitants of The Enormous Room and made pellmell for the common peep-hole, situated at the door end or nearer end of our habitat and commanding a somewhat fragmentary view of the gate together with the arrivals, male and female, whom the bell announced. In one particular case the watchers appeared almost unduly excited, shouting 'four!'—'big box'—'five gendarmes!' and other incoherencies with a loudness which predicted great things. As nearly always, I had declined to participate in the mêlée; and was still lying comfortably horizontal on my bed (thanking God that it had been well and thoroughly mended by a fellow prisoner whom we called The Frog and Le Coiffeur—a tremendously keen-eyed man with a large drooping black moustache, whose boon companion, chiefly on account of his shape and gait, we knew as The Lobster) when the usual noises attendant upon the unlocking of *la porte* began with exceptional violence. I sat up. The door shot open, there was a moment's pause, a series of grunting remarks uttered by two rather terrible voices; then in came four *nouveaux* of a decidedly interesting appearance. They entered in two ranks of two each. The front rank was made up of an immensely broadshouldered hipless and consequently triangular man in blue trousers belted with a piece of ordinary rope, plus a thick-set ruffianly personage the most prominent part of whose accoutrements were a pair of hideous whiskers. I leaped to my feet and made for the door, thrilled in spite of myself. By the, in this case, shifty blue eyes, the pallid hair, the well-knit form of the rope's owner I knew instantly a Hollander. By the coarse brutal features half-hidden in the piratical whiskers, as well as by the heavy mean wandering eyes, I recognized with equal speed a Belgian. Upon its shoulders the front rank bore a large box, blackish, well-made, obviously very weighty, which box it set down with a grunt of relief hard by the *cabinet*. The rear rank marched behind in a somewhat asymmetrical manner: a young stupid-looking clear-complexioned fellow (obviously a farmer, and having expensive black puttees and a handsome cap with a shiny black leather visor) slightly preceded a tall gliding thinnish unjudgeable personage who peeped at every one quietly and solemnly from beneath the visor of a somewhat large slovenly cloth cap, showing portions of a lean, long incognizable face upon which sat or rather drooped a pair of moustachios identical in character with those which are sometimes pictorially attributed to a Chinese dignitary—in other words, the moustachios were exquisitely narrow, homogeneously downward, and made of something like black corn-silk. Behind *les nouveaux* staggered four *paillasses* motivated mysteriously by two pair of small legs belonging (as it proved) to Garibaldi and the little Machine-Fixer; who, coincident with the tumbling of the *paillasses* to the floor, perspiringly emerged to sight.

The first thing the shifty-eyed triangular Hollander did was to exclaim Gottverdummer. The first thing the whiskery Belgian did was to grab his *paillasse* and stand guard over it. The first thing the youth in the leggings did was to stare helplessly about him, murmuring something whimperingly in Polish. The first thing the fourth *nouveau* did was pay no attention to anybody; lighting a cigarette in an unhurried manner as he did so, and puffing silently and slowly as if in all the universe nothing whatever save the taste of tobacco existed.

A bevy of Hollanders were by this time about the triangle, asking him all at once, Was he from so and so? What was in his box? How long had he been in coming?

etc. Half a dozen stooped over the box itself, and at least three pair of hands were on the point of trying the lock —when suddenly with incredible agility the unperturbed smoker shot a yard forward landing quietly beside them, and exclaimed rapidly and briefly through his nose

'Mang.'

He said it almost petulantly, or as a child says 'Tag! You're it.'

The onlookers recoiled, completely surprised. Whereat the frightened youth in black puttees sidled over and explained with a pathetically at once ingratiating and patronizing accent:

'Il n'est pas méchant. C'est un bonhomme. C'est mon ami. Il veut dire que c'est à lui, la caisse. Il parle pas français.'

'It's the Gottverdummer Polak's box,' said the Triangular Man, exploding in Dutch—'They're a pair of Polakers; and this man' (with a twist of his pale blue eyes in the direction of the Bewhiskered One) 'and I had to carry it all the Gottverdummer way to this Gottverdummer place.'

All this time the incognizable *nouveau* was smoking slowly and calmly, and looking at nothing at all with his black button-like eyes. Upon his face no faintest suggestion of expression could be discovered by the hungry minds which focused unanimously upon its almost stern contours. The deep furrows in the cardboard-like cheeks (furrows which resembled slightly the gills of some extraordinary fish, some unbreathing fish) moved not an atom. The moustache drooped in something like mechanical tranquillity. The lips closed occasionally with a gesture at once abstracted and sensitive upon the lightly and carefully held cigarette; whose curling smoke accentuated the poise of the head, at once alert and uninterested.

Monsieur Auguste broke in, speaking as I thought Russian—and in an instant he and the youth in puttees and the Unknowable's cigarette and the box and the Unknowable had disappeared through the crowd in the direction of Monsieur Auguste's *paillasse*, which was also the direction of the *paillasse* belonging to the *Cordonnier* as he was sometimes called—a diminutive man with immense moustachios of his own who promenaded with Monsieur Auguste, speaking sometimes French and as a general rule Russian or Polish.

Which was my first glimpse, and is the reader's, of the Zulu; he being one of the Delectable Mountains. For which reason I shall have more to say of him later, when I ascend the Delectable Mountains in a separate chapter or chapters; till when the reader must be content with the above however unsatisfactory description. . . .

One of the most utterly repulsive personages whom I have met in my life—perhaps (and on second thought I think certainly) the most utterly repulsive—was shortly after this presented to our midst by the considerate French Government. I refer to The Fighting Sheeney. Whether or no he arrived after the Spanish Whore-master I cannot say. I remember that Bill The Hollander—which was the name of the triangular rope-belted man with shifty blue eyes (co-*arrivé* with the whiskery Belgian; which Belgian, by the way, from his not to be exaggerated brutal look, B. and myself called The Babysnatcher)—upon his arrival told great tales of a Spanish millionaire with whom he had been in prison just previous to his discovery of La Ferté. 'He'll be here too in a couple o' days,' added Bill The Hollander, who had been four-

teen years in These United States, spoke the language to
a T, talked about 'The America Lakes' and was otherwise
amazingly well acquainted with The Land of the Free.
And sure enough in less than a week one of the fattest
men whom I have ever laid eyes on, over-dressed, much
beringed, and otherwise wealthy-looking, arrived—and
was immediately played up to by Judas (who could smell
cash almost as far as *le gouvernement français* could smell
sedition) and, to my somewhat surprise, by the utterly
respectable Count Bragard. But most emphatically NOT
by Mexique, who spent a half-hour talking to the *nouveau*
in his own tongue, then drifted placidly over to our beds
and informed us:

'You see dat feller over dere, dat fat feller? I speak
Spanish to him. He no good. Tell me he make fifty-
tousand francs last year runnin' whore-house in' (I think
it was) 'Brest. Son of bitch!'

Dat fat feller lived in a perfectly huge bed which he
contrived to have brought up for him immediately upon
his arrival. The bed arrived in a knock-down state and
with it a mechanician from *la ville* who set about putting
it together, meanwhile indulging in many glances expressive not merely of interest but of amazement and
even fear. I suppose the bed had to be of special size
in order to accommodate the circular millionaire, and
being an extraordinary bed required the services of a
skilled artisan—at all events, dat fat feller's couch put
The Skipper's altogether in the shade. As I watched the
process of construction it occurred to me that after all
here was the last word in luxury—to call forth from
the metropolis not only a special divan but with it a special slave, the Slave of the Bed. . . . Dat fat feller had one
of the prisoners perform his *corvée* for him. Dat fat feller

bought enough at the canteen twice every day to stock a transatlantic liner for seven voyages, and never ate with the prisoners. I will mention him again à propos the Mecca of respectability, the Great White Throne of purity, Three rings Three—alias Count Bragard, to whom I have long since introduced my reader.

So we come, willy-nilly, to The Fighting Sheeney.

The Fighting Sheeney arrived carrying the expensive suit-case of a livid, strangely unpleasant-looking Roumanian gent, who wore a knit sweater of a strangely ugly red hue, impeccable clothes, and an immaculate velour hat which must have been worth easily fifty francs. We called this gent Rockyfeller. His personality might be faintly indicated by the adjective Disagreeable. The porter was a creature whom Ugly does not even slightly describe. There are some specimens of humanity in whose presence one instantly and instinctively feels a profound revulsion, a revulsion which—perhaps because it is profound—cannot be analysed. The Fighting Sheeney was one of these specimens. His face (or to use the good American idiom, his mug) was exceedingly coarse-featured and had an indefatigable expression of sheer brutality—yet the impression which it gave could not be traced to any particular plane or line. I can and will say, however, that this face was most hideous—perhaps that is the word—when it grinned. When The Fighting Sheeney grinned you felt that he desired to eat you, and was prevented from eating you only by a superior desire to eat everybody at once. He and Rockyfeller came to us from I think it was the *Santé*; both accompanied B. to Précigné. During the weeks which The Fighting Sheeney spent at La Ferté Macé, the non-existence of the inhabitants of The Enormous Room was rendered something more than miserable. It was rendered wellnigh unbearable.

The night Rockyfeller and his slave arrived was a night to be remembered by every one. It was one of the wildest and strangest and most perfectly interesting nights I, for one, ever spent. Rockyfeller had been corralled by Judas, and was enjoying a special bed to our right at the upper end of The Enormous Room. At the canteen he had purchased a large number of candles in addition to a great assortment of dainties which he and Judas were busily enjoying—when the *planton* came up, counted us thrice, divided by three, gave the order '*Lumières éteintes,*' and descended locking the door behind him. Every one composed himself for miserable sleep. Every one except Judas, who went on talking to Rockyfeller, and Rockyfeller, who proceeded to light one of his candles and begin a pleasant and conversational evening. The Fighting Sheeney lay stark-naked on a *paillasse* between me and his lord. The Fighting Sheeney told every one that to sleep stark-naked was to avoid bugs (whereof everybody including myself had a goodly portion). The Fighting Sheeney was, however, quieted by the *planton's* order; whereas Rockyfeller continued to talk and munch to his heart's content. This began to get on everybody's nerves. Protests in a number of languages arose from all parts of The Enormous Room. Rockyfeller gave a contemptuous look around him and proceeded with his conversation. A curse emanated from the darkness. Up sprang The Fighting Sheeney, stark-naked; strode over to the bed of the curser, and demanded ferociously:

'*Boxe? Vous?*'

The curser was apparently fast asleep, and even snoring. The Fighting Sheeney turned away disappointed, and

had just reached his *paillasse* when he was greeted by a
number of uproariously discourteous remarks uttered in
all sorts of tongues. Over he rushed, threatened, received
no response, and turned back to his place. Once more
ten or twelve voices insulted him from the darkness. Once
more The Fighting Sheeney made for them, only to find
sleeping innocents. Again he tried to go to bed. Again
the shouts arose, this time with redoubled violence and
in greatly increased number. The Fighting Sheeney was
at his wit's end. He strode about challenging everyone to
fight, receiving not the slightest recognition, cursing, re-
viling, threatening, bullying. The darkness always waited
for him to resume his *paillasse*, then burst out in all sorts
of maledictions upon his head and the sacred head of
his lord and master. The latter was told to put out his
candle, go to sleep, and give the rest a chance to enjoy
what pleasure they might in forgetfulness of their woes.
Whereupon he appealed to The Sheeney to stop this. The
Sheeney (almost weeping) said he had done his best, that
everyone was a pig, that nobody would fight, and that it
was disgusting. Roars of applause. Protests from the less
strenuous members of our circle against the noise in general: Let him have his *foutue* candle, Shut up, Go to sleep
yourself, etc. Rockyfeller kept on talking (albeit visibly
annoyed by the ill-breeding of his fellow-captives) to
the smooth and oily Judas. The noise or rather noises increased. I was for some reason angry at Rockyfeller—I
think I had a curious notion that if I couldn't have a light
after '*lumières éteintes*,' and if my very good friends
were none of them allowed to have one, then by God
neither should Rockyfeller. At any rate I passed a few
remarks calculated to wither the by this time a little nervous Übermensch; got up, put on some enormous sabots

(which I had purchased from a horrid little boy whom the French Government had arrested with his parent, for some cause unknown—which horrid little boy told me that he had 'found' the sabots 'in a train' on the way to La Ferté) shook myself into my fur coat, and banged as noisemakingly as I knew how over to One-Eyed Dah-veed's *paillasse*, where Mexique joined us. 'It is useless to sleep,' said One-Eyed Dah-veed in French and Spanish. 'True,' I agreed, 'therefore let's make all the noise we can.'

Steadily the racket bulged in the darkness. Human cries, quips and profanity had now given place to wholly inspired imitations of various not to say sundry animals. Afrique exclaimed—with great pleasure I recognized his voice through the impenetrable gloom—

'Agahagahagahagahagah!'

—perhaps, said I, he means a machine gun; it sounds like either that or a monkey. The Wanderer crowed beautifully. Monsieur Auguste's bosom friend, *le Cordonnier*, uttered an astonishing

'Meeee-oooooOW!'

which provoked a tornado of laughter and some applause. Mooings, chirpings, cacklings—there was a superb hen—neighings, he-hawings, roarings, bleatings, growlings, quackings, peepings, screamings, bellowings, and—something else, of course—set The Enormous Room suddenly and entirely alive. Never have I imagined such a menagerie as had magically instated itself within the erstwhile soggy and dismal four walls of our *chambre*. Even such staid characters as Count Bragard set up a little bawling. Monsieur Pet-airs uttered a tiny aged crowing, to my immense astonishment and delight. The dying, the sick, the ancient, the mutilated, made their contributions to the common pandemonium. And then, from the lower left darkness, sprouted one of the very finest noises which ever fell on human ears—the noise of a little dog with floppy ears who was tearing after something on very short legs and carrying his very fuzzy tail straight up in the air as he tore; a little dog who was busier than he was wise, louder than he was big; a red-tongued, foolish, breathless, intent little dog with black eyes and a great smile and woolly paws—which noise, conceived and executed by The Lobster, sent The Enormous Room into an absolute and incurable hysteria.

The Fighting Sheeney was at a stand-still. He knew not how to turn. At last he decided to join with the insurgents, and wailed brutally and dismally. That was the last straw. Rockyfeller, who could no longer (even by shouting to Judas) make himself heard, gave up conversation and gazed angrily about him; angrily yet fearfully, as if he expected some of these numerous bears, lions, tigers and baboons to leap upon him from the darkness. His livid, super-disagreeable face trembled with the flickering cadence of the *bougie*. His lean lips clenched with mortification and wrath. '*Vous êtes chef de chambre*,' he said fiercely to Judas; 'why don't you make the men stop this? *C'est emmerdant*.'—'Ah,' replied Judas smoothly and insinuatingly, 'they are only men, and boors at that; you can't expect them to have any manners.' A tremendous group of Something Elses greeted this remark together with cries, insults, groans and linguistic trumpetings. I got up and walked the length of the room to the *cabinet* (situated as always by this time of night in a pool of urine which was in certain places six inches deep, from which pool my sabots somewhat protected me) and returned, making as loud a clattering as I was able. Sud-

denly the voice of Monsieur Auguste leaped through the
din in an

'*Alors! c'est as-sez.*'

The next thing we knew he had reached the window just
below the *cabinet* (the only window, by the way, not
nailed up with good long wire nails for the sake of
warmth) and was shouting in a wild high gentle angry
voice to the sentinel below—

'*Plan-ton! C'est im-possi-ble de dor-mir!*'

A great cry 'OUI! JE VIENS!' floated up—every single
noise dropped—Rockyfeller shot out his hand for the
candle, seized it in terror, blew it out as if blowing it out
were the last thing he would do in this life—and The
Enormous Room hung silent; enormously dark, enormously expectant . . .

BANG! Open flew the door. '*Alors, qui m'appelle?
Qu'est-ce qu'on fout ici.*' And The Black Holster, revolver in hand, flashed his torch into the inky stillness of
the *chambre*. Behind him stood two *plantons* white with
fear; their trembling hands clutching revolvers, the bar-
rels of which shook ludicrously.

'*C'est moi, plan-ton!*' Monsieur Auguste explained that
no one could sleep because of the noise, and that the noise
was because '*ce monsieur là*' would not extinguish his
bougie when everyone wanted to sleep. The Black Holster
turned to the room at large and roared: 'You children of
Merde, don't let this happen again or I'll fix you, everyone of you.'—Then he asked if anyone wanted to dispute
this assertion (he brandishing his revolver the while) and
was answered by peaceful snorings. Then he said by X, Y
and Z he'd fix the noisemakers in the morning and fix
them good—and looked for approbation to his trembling
assistants. Then he swore twenty or thirty times for luck,

turned, and thundered out on the heels of his fleeing confrères who almost tripped over each other in their haste
to escape from The Enormous Room. Never have I seen
a greater exhibition of bravery than was afforded by The
Black Holster, revolver in hand, holding at bay the snoring and weaponless inhabitants of The Enormous Room.
Vive les plantons. He should have been a gendarme.

Of course Rockyfeller, having copiously tipped the officials of La Ferté upon his arrival, received no slightest
censure nor any hint of punishment for his deliberate
breaking of an established rule—a rule for the breaking
of which any one of the common scum (e.g. thank God,
myself) would have got *cabinot de suite*. No indeed. Several of *les hommes*, however, got *pain sec*—not because
they had been caught in an act of vociferous protestation
by The Black Holster, which they had not—but just on
principle, as a warning to the rest of us and to teach us
a wholesome respect for (one must assume) law and order. One and all, they heartily agreed that it was worth it.
Everyone knew, of course, that the Spy had peached.
For, by Jove, even in The Enormous Room there was a
man who earned certain privileges and acquired a complete
immunity from punishments by squealing on his fellow-
sufferers at each and every opportunity. A really ugly
person, with a hard knuckling face and treacherous hands,
whose daughter lived downstairs in a separate room apart
from *les putains* (against which 'dirty,' filthy,' 'whores'
he could not say enough—'Hi'd rather die than 'ave my
daughter with them stinkin' 'ores,' remarked once to me
this strictly moral man, in Cockney English) and whose
daughter (aged thirteen) was generally supposed to serve
the *Directeur* in a pleasurable capacity. One did not need
to be warned against the Spy (as both B. and I were

warned, upon our arrival)—a single look at that phiz was enough for anyone partially either intelligent or sensitive. This phiz or mug, had, then, squealed. Which everyone took as a matter of course and admitted among themselves that hanging was too good for him.

But the vast and unutterable success achieved by the *Ménagerie* was this—Rockyfeller, shortly after, left our ill-bred society for '*l'hôpital*'; the very same 'hospital' whose comforts and seclusion *Monsieur le Surveillant* had so dexterously recommended to B. and myself. Rockyfeller kept The Fighting Sheeney in his pay, in order to defend him when he went on promenade; otherwise our connection with him was definitely severed; his new companions being Muskowitz the Cock-eyed Millionaire, and The Belgian Song Writer—who told everyone to whom he spoke that he was a government official ('*de la blague*,' cried the little Machine-Fixer, '*c'est un menteur!*' Adding that he knew of this person in Belgium and that this person was a man who wrote popular ditties). Would to Heaven we had got rid of the slave as well as the master —but unfortunately The Fighting Sheeney couldn't afford to follow his lord's example. So he went on making a nuisance of himself, trying hard to curry favour with B. and me, getting into fights, and bullying everyone generally.

Also this lion-hearted personage spent one whole night shrieking and moaning on his *paillasse* after an injection by Monsieur Richard—for syphilis. Two or three men were, in the course of a few days, discovered to have had syphilis for some time. They had it in their mouths. I don't remember them particularly, except that at least one was a Belgian. Of course they and The Fighting Sheeney had been using the common dipper and drinking-water pail.

Le gouvernement français couldn't be expected to look out for a little thing like venereal disease among prisoners: didn't it have enough to do curing those soldiers who spent their time on *permission* trying their best to infect themselves with both gonorrhœa and syphilis? Let not the reader suppose I am day-dreaming: let him rather recall that I had had the honour of being a member of *Section Sanitaire Vingt-et-Un*, which helped evacuate the venereal hospital at Ham, with whose inhabitants (in odd moments) I talked and walked and learned several things about *la guerre*. Let the reader—if he does not realize it already—realize that This Great War For Humanity, etc., did not agree with some people's ideas, and that some people's ideas made them prefer to the glories of the front line the torments (I have heard my friends at Ham screaming a score of times) attendant upon venereal diseases. Or as one of my aforesaid friends told me—after discovering that I was, in contrast to *les américains*, not bent upon making France discover America but rather upon discovering France and *les français* myself—

'*Mon vieux, c'est tout-à-fait simple. Je m'en vais en permission. Je demande à aller à Paris, parce qu'il y a des gonzesses là-bas qui sont toutes malades! J'attrappe le syphilis, et, quand il est possible, la gonnorrhée aussi. Je reviens. Je pars pour la première ligne. Je suis malade. L'hôpital. Le médecin me dit: Il ne faut ni fumer ni boire, comme ça vous serez bientôt guéri. "Merci, monsieur le médecin!" Je fume toujours et je bois toujours et je ne suis pas guéri. Je reste cinq, six, sept semaines. Peut-être des mois. Enfin, je suis guéri. Je rejoins mon regiment. Et maintenant, c'est mon tour de'aller en permission. Je m'en vais. Encore la même chose. C'est joli ça, tu sais.*'

But about the syphilitics at La Ferté: they were, somewhat tardily to be sure, segregated in a very small and
dirty room—for a matter of, perhaps, two weeks. And
the *Surveillant* actually saw to it that during this period
they ate *la soupe* out of individual china bowls.

I scarcely know whether The Fighting Sheeney made
more of a nuisance of himself during his decumbiture or
during the period which followed it—which period houses
an astonishing number of fights, rows, bullyings, etc. He
must have had a light case for he was *guéri* in no time,
and on everyone's back as usual. Well, I will leave him for
the nonce; in fact I will leave him until I come to The
Young Pole, who wore black puttees and spoke of The
Zulu as '*mon ami*'—The Young Pole whose troubles I
will recount in connection with the second Delectable
Mountain itself. I will leave The Sheeney with the observation that he was almost as vain as he was vicious;
for with what ostentation, one day when we were in the
kitchen, did he show me a post-card received that afternoon from Paris, whereon I read '*Comme vous êtes beau*'
and promises to send more money as fast as she earned
it and, hoping that he had enjoyed her last present, the
signature (in a big, adoring hand)

'*Ta môme. Alice.*'

and when I had read it—sticking his mug up into my face,
The Fighting Sheeney said with emphasis:

'*No travailler moi. Femme travaille, fait la noce, tout
le temps. Toujours avec officiers anglais. Gagne beaucoup,
cent francs, deux cent francs, trois cent francs, toutes
les nuits. Anglais riches. Femme me donne tout. Moi no
travailler. Bon, eh?*'

Grateful for this little piece of information, and with
his leer an inch from my chin, I answered slowly and

calmly that it certainly was. I might add that he spoke Spanish by preference (according to Mexique very bad Spanish); for The Fighting Sheeney had made his home for a number of years in Rio, his opinion whereof may be loosely translated by the expressive phrase, 'it's a swell town.'

A charming fellow, The Fighting Sheeney.

Now, I must tell you what happened to the poor Spanish Whoremaster. I have already noted the fact that Count Bragard conceived an immediate fondness for this roly-poly individual, whose belly—as he lay upon his back of a morning in bed—rose up with the sheets, blankets and quilts as much as two feet above the level of his small stupid head studded with chins. I have said that this admiration on the part of the admirable Count and R.A. for a personage of the Spanish Whoremaster's profession somewhat interested me. The fact is, a change had recently come in our own relations with Vanderbilt's friend. His cordiality toward B. and myself had considerably withered. From the time of our arrivals the good nobleman had showered us with favours and advice. To me, I may say, he was even extraordinarily kind. We talked painting, for example: Count Bragard folded a piece of paper, tore it in the centre of the folded edge, unfolded it carefully, exhibiting a good round hole, and remarking —'Do you know this trick? It's an English trick, Mr. Cummings'—held the paper before him and gazed profoundly through the circular aperture at an exceptionally disappointing section of the altogether gloomy landscape, visible thanks to one of the ecclesiastical windows of The Enormous Room. 'Just look at that, Mr. Cummings,' he said with quiet dignity. I looked. I tried my best to find something to the left—'No, no, straight

through,' Count Bragard corrected me. 'There's a lovely
bit of landscape,' he said sadly. 'If I only had my paints
here. I thought, you know, of asking my housekeeper to
send them on from Paris—but how can you paint in a
bloody place like this with all these bloody pigs around
you? It's ridiculous to think of it. And it's tragic, too,'
he added grimly, with something like tears in his grey tired
eyes.

Or we were promenading The Enormous Room after
supper—the evening promenade in the *cour* having been
officially eliminated owing to the darkness and the cold of
the autumn twilight—and through the windows the dull
bloating colours of sunset pouring faintly; and the Count
stops dead in his tracks and regards the sunset without
speaking for a number of seconds. Then—'It's glorious,
isn't it?' he asks quietly. I say 'Glorious indeed.' He re-
sumes his walk with a sigh, and I accompany him. '*Ce
n'est pas difficile à peindre, un coucher du soleil,* it's not
hard,' he remarks gently. 'No?' I say with deference. 'Not
hard a bit,' the Count says, beginning to use his hands.
'You only need three colours, you know. Very simple.'—
'Which colours are they?' I inquire ignorantly. 'Why,
you know of course,' he says surprised. 'Burnt sienna, cad-
mium yellow, and—er—there! I can't think of it. I know
it as well as I know my own face. So do you. Well, that's
stupid of me.'

Or, his worn eyes dwelling benignantly upon my duf-
flebag, he warns me (in a low voice) of Prussian Blue.

'Did you notice the portrait hanging in the *bureau* of
the *Surveillant*?' Count Bragard inquired one day. 'That's
a pretty piece of work, Mr. Cummings. Notice it when
you get a chance. The green moustache, particularly fine.
School of Cézanne.'—'Really?' I said in surprise.—'Yes,

indeed,' Count Bragard said, extracting his tired looking hands from his tired looking trousers with a cultured gesture. 'Fine young fellow painted that, I knew him. Disciple of the master. Very creditable piece of work.'—'Did you ever see Cézanne?' I ventured.—'Bless you, yes, scores of times,' he answered almost pityingly.—'What did he look like?' I asked, with great curiosity.—'Look like? His appearance, you mean?' Count Bragard seemed at a loss. 'Why, he was not extraordinary looking. I don't know how you could describe him. Very difficult in English. But you know a phrase we have in French, *"l'air pesant"*; I don't think there's anything in English for it; *il avait l'air pesant,* Cézanne, if you know what I mean.'

'I should work, I should not waste my time,' the Count would say almost weepingly. 'But it's no use, my things aren't here. And I'm getting old too; couldn't concentrate in this stinking hole of a place, you know.'

I did some hasty drawings of Monsieur Pet-airs washing and rubbing his bald head with a great towel in the dawn. The R.A. caught me in the act and came over shortly after, saying, 'Let me see them.' In some perturbation (the subject being a particular friend of his) I showed one drawing. 'Very good, in fact, excellent'; the R.A. smiled whimsically. 'You have a real talent for caricature, Mr. Cummings, and you should exercise it. You really got Peters. Poor Peters, he's a fine fellow, you know; but this business of living in the muck and filth, *c'est malheureux*. Besides, Peters is an old man. It's a dirty bloody shame, that's what it is. A bloody shame that all of us here should be forced to live like pigs with this scum!'

'I tell you what, Mr. Cummings,' he said with something like fierceness, his weary eyes flashing, 'I'm getting

out of here shortly, and when I do get out (I'm just waiting for my papers to be sent on by the English consul)
I'll not forget my friends. We've lived together and suffered together and I'm not a man to forget it. This hideous mistake is nearly cleared up, and when I go free I'll
do anything for you and Mr. B. Anything I can do for
you I'd be only too glad to do it. If you want me to
buy you paints when I'm in Paris, nothing would give
me more pleasure. I know French as well as I know my
own language' (he most certainly did) 'and whereas you
might be cheated, I'll get you everything you need *à bon
marché*. Because you see they know me there, and I know
just where to go. Just give me the money for what you
need and I'll get you the best there is in Paris for it.
You needn't worry'—I was protesting that it would be
too much trouble—'my dear fellow, it's no trouble to do
a favour for a friend.'

And to B. and myself ensemble he declared, with tears
in his eyes, 'I have some marmalade at my house in Paris;
real marmalade, not the sort of stuff you buy these days.
We know how to make it. You can't get an idea how
delicious it is. In big crocks'—the Count said simply—
'well, that's for you boys.' We protested that he was too
kind. 'Nothing of the sort,' he said, with a delicate smile.
'I have a son in the English army,' and his face clouded
with worry, 'and we send him some now and then, and
he's crazy about it. I know what it means to him. And
you shall share in it too. I'll send you six crocks.' Then,
suddenly looking at us with a pleasant expression, 'By
Jove,' the Count said, 'do you like whisky? Real Bour-
bon whisky? I see by your look that you know what it is.
But you never tasted anything like this. Do you know
London?' I said no, as I had said once before. 'Well, that's

a pity,' he said, 'for if you did you'd know this bar. I know the bar-keeper well, known him for thirty years. There's a picture of mine hanging in his place. Look at it when you're in London, drop in to —— Street, you'll find the place, anyone will tell you where it is. This fellow would do anything for me. And now I'll tell you what I'll do: you fellows give me whatever you want to spend and I'll get you the best whisky you ever tasted. It's his own private stock, you understand. I'll send it on to you—God knows you need it in this place. I wouldn't do this for anyone else, you understand,' and he smiled kindly, 'but we've been prisoners together, and we understand each other, and that's enough for gentlemen. I won't forget you.' He drew himself up. 'I shall write,' he said slowly and distinctly, 'to Vanderbilt about you. I shall tell him it's a dirty bloody shame that two young Americans, gentlemen born, should be in this foul place. He's a man who's quick to act. He'll not tolerate a thing like this—an outrage, a bloody outrage, upon two of his own countrymen. We shall see what happens then.'

It was during this period that Count Bragard lent us for our personal use his greatest treasure, a water-glass. 'I don't need it,' he said simply and pathetically.

Now, as I have said, a change in our relations came.

It came at the close of one soggy, damp raining afternoon. For this entire hopeless grey afternoon Count Bragard and B. promenaded The Enormous Room. Bragard wanted the money—for the whisky and the paints. The marmalade and the letter to Vanderbilt were, of course, gratis. Bragard was leaving us. Now was the time to give him money for what we wanted him to buy in Paris and London. I spent my time rushing about, falling over things, upsetting people, making curious and secret signs

to B.—which signs, being interpreted, meant: Be careful!
—But there was no need of telling B. this particular thing.
When the *planton* announced *la soupe* a fiercely weary
face strode by me *en route* to his *paillasse* and his spoon.
I knew that B. had been careful. A minute later he joined
me, and told me as much. . . .

On the way downstairs we ran into the *Surveillant*.
Bragard stepped from the ranks and poured upon the
Surveillant a torrent of French, of which the substance
was: You told them not to give me anything. The *Surveillant* smiled and bowed and wound and unwound his
hands behind his back and denied anything of the sort.

It seems that B. had heard that the kindly nobleman
wasn't going to Paris at all.

Moreover, Monsieur Pet-airs had said to B. something
about Count Bragard being a suspicious personage—Monsieur Pet-airs, the R.A.'s best friend.

Moreover, as I have said, Count Bragard had been playing up to the poor Spanish Whoremaster to beat the band.
Every day had he sat on a little stool beside the roly-poly
millionaire, and written from dictation letter after letter
in French—with which language the roly-poly was sadly
unfamiliar. . . . And when next day Count Bragard took
back his treasure of treasures, his personal water-glass, remarking briefly that he needed it once again, I was not
surprised. And when, a week or so later, he left—I was
not surprised to have Mexique come up to us and placidly
remark:

'I give dat feller five francs. Tell me he send me overcoat, very good overcoat. But say: Please no tell anybody
come from me. Please tell everybody your family send it.'
And with a smile, 'I t'ink dat feller fake.'

Nor was I surprised to see, some weeks later, the poor

Spanish Whoremaster rending his scarce hair as he lay in bed of a morning. And Mexique said with a smile:

'Dat feller give dat English feller one hundred franc. Now he sorry.'

All of which meant merely that Count Bragard should have spelt his name, not Bra— but with an l.

And I wonder to this day that the only letter of mine which ever reached America and my doting family should have been posted by this highly entertaining personage *en ville*, whither he went as a trusted inhabitant of La Ferté to do a few necessary errands for himself; whither he returned with a good deal of colour in his cheeks and a good deal of *vin rouge* in his guts; going and returning with Tommy, the *planton* who brought him the *Daily Mail* every day until Bragard couldn't afford it, after which either B. and I, or Jean le Nègre took it off Tommy's hands—Tommy for whom we had a delightful name which I sincerely regret being unable to tell, Tommy who was an Englishman for all his French *planton's* uniform and worshipped the ground on which the Count stood, Tommy who looked like a boiled lobster and had tears in his eyes when he escorted his idol back to captivity. . . . *Mirabile dictu*, so it was.

Well, such was the departure of a great man from among us.

And now, just to restore the reader's faith in human nature, let me mention an entertaining incident which occurred during the latter part of my stay at La Ferté Macé. Our society had been gladdened—or at any rate galvanized—by the biggest single contribution in its history; the arrival simultaneously of seven purely extraordinary persons, whose names alone should be of more than general interest: The Magnifying Glass, The Trick

Raincoat Sheeney, The Messenger Boy, The Hat, The Alsatian, The Whitebearded Raper and His Son. In order to give the aforesaid reader an idea of the situation created by these *arrivés*, which situation gives the entrance of the Washing-Machine Man—the entertaining incident, in other words—its full and unique flavour, I must perforce sketch briefly each member of a truly imposing group. Let me say at once that, so terrible an impression did the members make, each inhabitant of The Enormous Room rushed at break-neck speed to his *paillasse;* where he stood at bay, assuming as frightening an attitude as possible. The Enormous Room was full enough already in all conscience. Between sixty and seventy *paillasses,* with their inhabitants and in nearly every case baggage, occupied it so completely as scarcely to leave room for *le poêle* at the further end and the card-table in the centre. No wonder we were struck with terror upon seeing the seven *nouveaux.* Judas immediately protested to the *planton* who brought them up that there were no places, getting a roar in response and the door slammed in his face to boot. But the reader is not to imagine that it was the number alone of the arrivals which inspired fear and distrust— their appearance was enough to shake anyone's sanity. I do protest that never have I experienced a feeling of more profound distrust than upon this occasion; distrust of humanity in general and in particular of the following individuals:

First, an old man shabbily dressed in a shiny frock coat, upon whose peering and otherwise very aged face a pair of dirty spectacles rested. The first thing he did, upon securing a place, was to sit upon his *paillasse* in a professorial manner, tremulously extract a journal from his left coat-pocket, tremblingly produce a large magnifying-glass from his upper right vest-pocket, and forget everything. Subsequently, I discovered him promenading the room with an enormous expenditure of feeble energy, taking tiny steps flat-footedly and leaning in when he rounded a corner as if he were travelling at terrific speed. He suffered horribly from rheumatism, could scarcely move after a night on the floor, and must have been at least sixty-seven years old.

Second, a palish, foppish, undersized, prominent-nosed creature who affected a deep musical voice and the cut of whose belted raincoat gave away his profession—he was a pimp, and proud of it, and immediately upon his arrival boasted thereof, and manifested altogether as disagreeable a species of bullying vanity as I ever (save in the case of The Fighting Sheeney) encountered. He got his from Jean le Nègre, as the reader will learn later.

Third, a super-Western-Union-Messenger type of ancient-youth, extraordinarily unhandsome if not positively ugly. He had a weak pimply grey face, was clad in a brownish uniform, puttees (on pipe-stem calves), and a regular Messenger Boy cap. Upon securing a place he instantly went to the card-table, seated himself hurriedly, pulled out a batch of blanks, and wrote a telegram to (I suppose) himself. Then he returned to his *paillasse*, lay down with apparently supreme contentment, and fell asleep.

Fourth, a tiny old man who looked like a caricature of an East-side second-hand clothes dealer—having a long beard, a long worn and dirty coat reaching just to his ankles, and a small derby hat on his head. The very first night his immediate neighbour complained that '*Le Chapeau*' (as he was christened by The Zulu) was guilty of fleas. A great tempest ensued immediately. A *planton* was

hastily summoned. He arrived, heard the case, inspected
The Hat (who lay on his *paillasse* with his derby on, his
hand far down the neck of his shirt, scratching busily
and protesting occasionally his entire innocence), uttered
(being the Black Holster) an oath of disgust, and ordered The Frog to '*couper les cheveux de suite et la barbe
aussi; après il va au bain, le vieux.*' The Frog approached
and gently requested The Hat to seat himself upon a
chair—the better of two chairs boasted by The Enormous
Room. The Frog, successor to The Barber, brandished his
scissors. The Hat lay and scratched. '*Allez, Nom de Dieu,*'
the *planton* roared. The poor Hat arose trembling, assumed a praying attitude; and began to talk in a thick
and sudden manner. '*Asseyez-vous là, tête de cochon.*'
The pitiful Hat obeyed, clutching his derby to his head
in both withered hands. 'Take off your hat, you son of
a bitch,' the *planton* yelled. 'I don't want to,' the tragic
Hat whimpered. BANG! the derby hit the floor, bounded
upward and lay still. 'Proceed,' the *planton* thundered to
The Frog; who regarded him with a perfectly inscrutable
expression on his extremely keen face, then turned to his
subject, snickered with the scissors, and fell to. Locks,
ear-long, fell in crisp succession. Pete the Shadow, standing beside The Barber, nudged me; and I looked; and
I beheld upon the floor the shorn locks rising and curling
with a movement of their own.... 'Now for the beard,'
said The Black Holster.—'No, no, Monsieur, *s'il vous
plait, pas ma barbe, monsieur*'—the Hat wept, trying to
kneel.—'*Ta gueule* or I'll cut your throat,' the *planton* replied amiably; and The Frog, after another look, obeyed.
And lo, the beard squirmed gently upon the floor, alive
with a rhythm of its own; squirmed and curled crisply
as it lay ... When The Hat was utterly shorn, he was

bathed and became comparatively unremarkable, save for the worn long coat which he clutched about him, shivering. And he borrowed five francs of me twice, and paid me punctually each time when his own money arrived, and presented me with chocolate into the bargain, tipping his hat quickly and bowing (as he always did whenever he addressed anyone). Poor Old Hat, B. and I and The Zulu were the only men at La Ferté who liked you.

Fifth, a fat, jolly, decently dressed man.—He had been to a camp where everyone danced, because an entire ship's crew was interned there, and the crew were enormously musical, and the captain (having sold his ship) was rich and tipped the Director regularly; so everyone danced night and day, and the crew played, for the crew had brought their music with them.—He had a way of borrowing the paper (*Le Matin*) which we bought from one of the lesser *plantons* who went to the town and got the *Matin* there; borrowing it before we had read it—by the sunset. And his favourite observations were:

'*C'est un mauvais pays. Sale temps.*'

Sixth and seventh, a vacillating, staggering, decrepit creature with wildish white beard and eyes, who had been arrested—incredibly enough—for 'rape.' With him his son, a pleasant youth quiet of demeanour, inquisitive of nature, with whom we sometimes conversed on the subject of the English Army.

Such were the individuals whose concerted arrival taxed to its utmost the capacity of The Enormous Room. And now for my incident—

Which incident is not peculiarly remarkable, but may (as I hope) serve to revive the reader's trust in humanity—

In the doorway, one day shortly after the arrival of the

gentlemen mentioned, quietly stood a well-dressed, hand-
somely middle-aged man, with a sensitive face culminat-
ing in a groomed Van Dyck beard. I thought for a moment that the Mayor of Orne, or whatever his title is, had
dropped in for an informal inspection of The Enormous
Room. Thank God, I said to myself, it has never looked
so chaotically filthy since I have had the joy of inhabiting
it. And *sans blague*, The Enormous Room *was* in a state
of really supreme disorder; shirts were thrown everywhere, a few twine clothes-lines supported various pants,
handkerchiefs and stockings, the *poêle* was surrounded
by a gesticulating group of nearly undressed prisoners,
the stink was actually sublime.

As the door closed behind him, the handsome man
moved slowly and vigorously up The Enormous Room.
His eyes were as big as turnips. His neat felt hat rose
with the rising of his hair. His mouth opened in a gesture of unutterable astonishment. His knees trembled
with surprise and terror, the creases of his trousers quivering. His hands lifted themselves slowly outward and
upward till they reached the level of his head; moved
inward till they grasped his head: and were motionless.
In a deep awe-struck resonant voice he exclaimed simply
and sincerely:

'*Nom de nom de nom de nom de nom de DIEU!*'

Which introduces the reader to The Washing-Machine
Man, the Hollander, owner of a store at Brest where he
sold the highly *utile* contrivances which gave him his
name. He, as I remember, had been charged with aiding
and abetting in the case of escaping Holland deserters—
but I know a better reason for his arrest: undoubtedly
le gouvernement français caught him one day in the act
of inventing a super-washing-machine, in fact a white-

washing machine, for the private use of the Kaiser and His Family . . .

Which brings us, if you please, to the first Delectable Mountain.

VIII

THE WANDERER

ONE day somebody and I were 'catching water' for Monsieur the Chef.

'Catching water' was ordinarily a mixed pleasure. It consisted, as I have mentioned, in the combined pushing and pulling of a curiously primitive two-wheeled cart over a distance of perhaps three hundred yards to a kind of hydrant situated in a species of square upon which the mediæval structure known as *Porte* (or *Camp*) *de Triage* faced stupidly and threateningly. A *planton* always escorted the catchers through the big door, between the stone wall, which backed the men's *cour,* and the end of the building itself or in other words the canteen. The ten-foot stone wall was, like every other stone wall connected with La Ferté, topped with three feet of barbed-wire. The door by which we exited with the water-wagon to the street outside was at least eight feet high, adorned with several large locks. One pushing behind, one pulling in the shafts, we rushed the wagon over a sort of threshold or sill and into the street; and were immediately yelled at by the *planton,* who commanded us to stop until he had locked the door aforesaid. We waited until told to proceed; then yanked and shoved the reeling vehicle up the street to our right, that is to say along the wall of the building, but on the outside. All this was pleasant and astonishing. To feel oneself, however temporarily, outside the eternal walls in a street connected with a rather selfish and placid-looking little town (whereof not more than a dozen houses were visible) gave the prisoner an at once silly and uncanny sensation, much like the sensation one must get when he starts to skate for the first time in a dozen years or so. The street met two others in a moment, and here was a very flourishing sumach bush (as I guess) whose berries shocked the stunned eye with a savage splash of vermilion. Under this colour one discovered the Mecca of water-catchers in the form of an iron contrivance operating by means of a stubby lever which, when pressed down, yielded grudgingly a spout of whiteness. The contrivance was placed in sufficiently close proximity to a low wall so that one of the catchers might conveniently sit on the wall and keep the water spouting with a continuous pressure of his foot, while the other catcher manipulated a tin pail with telling effect. Having filled the barrel which rode on the two wagon-wheels, we turned it with some difficulty and started it down the street with the tin pail on top; the man in the shafts leaning back with all his might to offset a certain velocity promoted by the down-grade, while the man behind tugged helpingly at the barrel itself. On reaching the door we skewed the machine skilfully to the left, thereby bringing it to a complete standstill, and waited for the *planton* to unlock the locks; which done, we rushed it violently over the threshold, turned left, still running, and came to a final stop in front of the *cuisine*. Here stood three enormous wooden tubs. We backed the wagon around; then one man opened the spigot in the rear of the barrel, and at the same time the other elevated the shafts in a clever manner, inducing the *jet d'eau* to hit one of the tubs. One tub filled, we switched the stream wittily to the next. To fill the three tubs (they were not always all of them empty) required as many as six or eight delightful trips. After which one entered the *cuisine* and got his well-earned reward—coffee with sugar.

I have remarked that catching water was a mixed pleasure. The mixedness of the pleasure came from certain highly respectable citizens, and more often citizenesses, of *la ville de* La Ferté Macé, who had a habit of endowing the poor water-catchers with looks which I should not like to remember too well, at the same moment clutching whatever infants they carried or wore or had on leash spasmodically to them. Honestly, I never ceased to be surprised by the scorn, contempt, disgust, and frequently sheer ferocity manifested in the male and particularly in the female faces. All the ladies wore, of course, black; they were wholly unbeautiful of face or form, some of them actually repellent; not one should I, even under more favourable circumstances, have enjoyed meeting. The first time I caught water everybody in the town was returning from church, and a terrific sight it was. *Vive la bourgeoisie,* I said to myself, ducking the shafts of censure by the simple means of hiding my face behind the moving water-barrel.

But one day—as I started to inform the reader—somebody and I were catching water, and in fact had caught our last load, and were returning with it down the street; when I, who was striding rapidly behind (trying to lessen with both hands the impetus of the machine) suddenly tripped and almost fell with surprise—

On the kerb of the little unbeautiful street a figure was sitting, a female figure dressed in utterly barbaric pinks and vermilions, having a dark shawl thrown about her shoulders; a positively Arabian face delimited by a bright coif of some tenuous stuff, slender golden hands holding with extraordinary delicacy what appeared to be a baby of not more than three months old; and beside her a black-haired child of perhaps three years and beside this child a girl of fourteen, dressed like the woman in crashing hues, with the most exquisite face I had ever known.

Nom de dieu, I thought vaguely. Am I or am I not completely asleep? And the man in the shafts craned his neck in stupid amazement, and the *planton* twirled his moustache and assumed that intrepid look which only a *planton* (or a gendarme) perfectly knows how to assume in the presence of female beauty.

That night The Wanderer was absent from *la soupe*, having been called by Apollyon to the latter's office upon a matter of superior import. Every one was abuzz with the news. The gypsy's wife and three children, one a baby at the breast, were outside demanding to be made prisoners. Would the *Directeur* allow it? They had been told a number of times by *plantons* to go away, as they sat patiently waiting to be admitted to captivity. No threats, pleas nor arguments had availed. The wife said she was tired of living without her husband—roars of laughter from all the Belgians and most of the Hollanders, I regret to say Pete included—and wanted merely and simply to share his confinement. Moreover, she said, without him she was unable to support his children; and it was better that they should grow up with their father as prisoners than starve to death without him. She would not be moved. The Black Holster told her he would use force—she answered nothing. Finally she had been admitted pending judgment. Also sprach, highly excited, the *balayeur*.

'Looks like a f——g hoor,' was the Belgian-Dutch ver-

dict, a verdict which was obviously due to the costume of
the lady in question almost as much as to the untempera-
mental natures sojourning at La Ferté. B. and I agreed
that she and her children were the most beautiful people
we had ever seen, or would ever be likely to see. So *la
soupe* ended, and everybody belched and gasped and
trumpeted up to The Enormous Room as usual.

That evening, about six o'clock, I heard a man crying
as if his heart were broken. I crossed The Enormous Room.
Half-lying on his *paillasse*, his great beard pouring upon
his breast, his face lowered, his entire body shuddering
with sobs, lay The Wanderer. Several of *les hommes* were
about him, standing in attitudes ranging from semi-
amusement to stupid sympathy, listening to the anguish
which—as from time to time he lifted his majestic head
—poured slowly and brokenly from his lips. I sat down
beside him. And he told me '*Je l'ai acheté pour six cent
francs et je l'ai vendu pour quatre cent cinquante*—it was
not a horse of this race but of the race' (I could not
catch the word) 'as long as from here to that post—*j'ai
pleuré un quart d'heure comme si j'avais une gosse morte*
—and it is seldom I weep over horses—*je dis: Bijou,
quittes; au r'oir et bon jour*' ...

The vain little dancer interrupted about '*réformé*'
horses.... '*Excuses donc*—this was no *réformé* horse,
such as goes to the front—these are some horses—pardon,
whom you give eat, this, it is *colique*, that, the other, it's
colique—this never—he could go forty kilometres a
day ....'

One of the strongest men I have seen in my life is
crying because he has had to sell his favourite horse. No
wonder *les hommes* in general are not interested. Some

one said: 'Be of good cheer, Demestre, your wife and kids are well enough.'

'Yes—they were not cold; they have a bed like that' (a high gesture toward the quilt of many colours on which we were sitting, such a quilt as I have not seen since; a feathery deepness soft to the touch as air in Spring) *'qui vaut trois fois* this of mine—but *tu comprends, le matin il ne fait pas chaud'*—then he dropped his head, and lifted it again, crying:

'*Et mes outils,* I had many—and my garments—where are they put, *où—où? Kis!* And I had *chemises* . . . this is poor' (looking at himself as a prince might look at his disguise)—'and like this, that—where?

'*Si* the *voiture* is not sold . . . I never will stay here for *la durée de la guerre.* No—*bahsht!* To resume, that is why.'

(More than upright in the priceless bed—the twice-streaming darkness of his beard, his hoarse sweetness of voice—his immense perfect face and deeply softnesses eyes—pouring voice)

'. . . my wife sat over there, she spoke to No one and bothered Nobody—why was my wife taken here and shut up? Had she done anything? There is a wife who *fait la putain* and turns to every one and another, whom I bring another to-morrow . . . but a woman *qui n'aime que son mari, qui n'attend que son mari.'*

(The tone bulged, and the eyes together.)

'—*Ces cigarettes ne tirent pas!'* I added an apology, having presented him with the package. 'Why do you *dépenser pour* these? They cost fifteen sous, you may spend for them if you like, you understand what I'm saying? But some time when you have nothing' (extraordinarily gently), 'what then? Better to save for that day

... better to buy *du tabac* and *faire* yourself; these *sont fait de la poussière du tabac.*'

And there was some one to the right who was saying: '*Demain, c'est Dimanche alors*'—wearily. The King lying upon his huge quilt, sobbing now only a little, heard:

'So—ah—*il est tombé un dimanche—ma femme est en nourrice, elle donne la petite à têter*' (the gesture charmed) 'she said to them she would not eat if they gave her that—*ça ne vaut rien du tout—il faut de la viande, tous les jours ...*' he mused. I tried to go.

'*Assieds-toi là*' (graciousness of complete gesture. The sheer kingliness of poverty. He creased the indescribably soft *couverture* for me and I sat and looked into his forehead bounded by the cube of square sliced hair. Blacker than Africa. Than imagination.)

After this evening I felt that possibly I knew a little of The Wanderer, or he of me.

The Wanderer's wife and his two daughters and his baby lived in the women's quarters. I have not described and cannot describe these four. The little son of whom he was tremendously proud slept with his father in the great quilts in The Enormous Room. Of The Wanderer's little son I may say that he had lolling buttons of eyes sewed on gold flesh, that he had a habit of turning cartwheels in one-third of his father's trousers, that we called him The Imp. He ran, he teased, he turned handsprings, he got in the way, and he even climbed the largest of the scraggly trees in the *cour* one day. 'You will fall,' Monsieur Pet-airs (whose old eyes had a fondness for this irrepressible creature) remarked with conviction.—'Let him climb,' his father said quietly. 'I have climbed trees. I have fallen out of trees. I am alive.' The Imp shinnied like a monkey, shouting and crowing, up a lean gnarled limb

—to the amazement of the very *planton* who later tried
to rape Celina and was caught. This *planton* put his gun
in readiness and assumed an eager attitude of immutable
heroism. 'Will you shoot?' the father inquired politely.
'Indeed it would be a big thing of which you might boast
all your life: I, a *planton*, shot and killed a six-year-old
child in a tree.'—'*C'est emmerdant*,' the *planton* countered, in some confusion—'he may be trying to escape.
How do I know?'—'Indeed, how do you know anything?'
the father murmured quietly. 'It's a *mystère*.' The Imp,
all at once, fell. He hit the muddy ground with a disagreeable thud. The breath was utterly knocked out of
him. The Wanderer picked him up kindly. His son began,
with the catching of his breath, to howl uproariously.
'Serves him right, the—jackanapes,' a Belgian growled.—
'I told you so, didn't I?' Monsieur Pet-airs worryingly
cried: 'I said he would fall out of that tree!'—'Pardon,
you were right, I think,' the father smiled pleasantly.
'Don't be sad, my little son, everybody falls out of trees,
they're made for that by God,' and he patted The Imp,
squatting in the mud and smiling. In five minutes The
Imp was trying to scale the shed. 'Come down or I fire,'
the *planton* cried nervously . . . and so it was with The
Wanderer's son from morning till night. 'Never,' said
Monsieur Pet-airs with solemn desperation, 'have I seen
such an incorrigible child, a perfectly incorrigible child,'
and he shook his head and immediately dodged a missile
which had suddenly appeared from nowhere.

Night after night The Imp would play around our
beds, where we held court with our *chocolat* and our
bougie; teasing us, cajoling us, flattering us, pretending
tears, feigning insult, getting lectures from Monsieur
Pet-airs on the evil of cigarette smoking, keeping us in a

state of perpetual inquietude. When he couldn't think of anything else to do he sang at the top of his clear bright voice:

> 'C'est la guerre
> faut pas t'en faire'

and turned a handspring or two for emphasis . . . Mexique once cuffed him for doing something peculiarly mischievous, and he set up a great crying—instantly The Wanderer was standing over Mexique, his hands clenched, his eyes sparkling—it took a good deal of persuasion to convince the parent that the son was in error, meanwhile Mexique placidly awaited his end . . . and neither B. nor I, despite The Imp's tormentings, could keep from laughing when he all at once with a sort of crowing cry rushed for the nearest post, jumped upon his hands, arched his back, and poised head-downward; his feet just touching the pillar. Bare-footed, in a bright chemise and one third of his father's trousers . . .

Being now in a class with 'les hommes mariés,' The Wanderer spent most of the day downstairs, coming up with his little son every night to sleep in The Enormous Room. But we saw him occasionally in the cour; and every other day when the dreadful cry was raised

> 'Allez, tout-le-monde, plucher les pommes!'

and we descended to, in fair weather, the lane between the building and the cour, and in foul (very foul I should say) the dinosaur-coloured sweating walls of the dining-room—The Wanderer would quietly and slowly appear, along with the other hommes mariés, and take up the peeling of the amazingly cold potatoes which formed the pièce de résistance (in guise of Soupe) for both women and men at La Ferté. And if the wedded males did not all

of them show up for this unagreeable task, a dreadful
hullabaloo was instantly raised:

'LES HOMMES MARIÉS!'
and forth would more or less sheepishly issue the delin-
quents.

And I think The Wanderer, with his wife and children,
whom he loved as never have I seen a man love anything in
this world, was partly happy; walking in the sun when
there was any, sleeping with his little boy in a great gulp
of softness. And I remember him pulling his fine beard
into two darknesses—huge-sleeved, pink-checked chemise
—walking kindly like a bear—corduroy bigness of trousers, waist-line always amorous of knees—finger-ends just
catching tops of enormous pockets. When he feels, as I
think, partly happy, he corrects our pronunciation of the
ineffable Word—saying:

'O, May-errr-DE!'
and smiles. And once Jean le Nègre said to him, as he
squatted in the *cour* with his little son beside him, his
broad strong back as nearly always against one of the
gruesome and minute *pommiers*—

'*Barbu! j'vais te couper la barbe, barbu!*' Whereat the
father answered, slowly and seriously:

'*Quand vous arrachez ma barbe, il faut couper ma tête,*'
regarding Jean le Nègre with unspeakably sensitive, tremendously deep, peculiarly soft eyes. 'My beard is finer
than that; you have made it too coarse,' he gently remarked one day, looking attentively at a piece of
photographie which I had been caught in the act of per-
petrating; whereat I bowed my head in silent shame.

'Demestre, Josef (*femme, née* Feliska),' I read another
day in the Gestionnaire's book of judgment. O *Monsieur
le Gestionnaire*, I should not have liked to have seen those

names in my book of sinners, in my album of filth and
blood and incontinence, had I been you . . . O little, very
little, *gouvernement français*, and you the great and comfortable *messieurs* of the world, tell me why you have
put a gypsy who dresses like To-morrow among the squab-
bling pimps and thieves of yesterday . . .

He had been in New York one day.

One child died at sea.

'*Les landes*,' he cried, towering over The Enormous
Room suddenly one night in Autumn, '*je les connais
comme ma poche—Bordeaux? Je sais où que c'est. Madrid?
Je sais où que c'est. Tolède? Séville? Naples? Je sais où que
c'est. Je les connais comme ma poche.*'

He could not read. 'Tell me what it tells,' he said briefly
and without annoyance, when once I offered him the journal. And I took pleasure in trying to do so.

One fine day, perhaps the finest day, I looked from a
window of The Enormous Room and saw (in the same
spot that Lena had enjoyed her half-hour promenade
during confinement in the *cabinot*, as related) the wife
of The Wanderer, '*née* Feliska,' giving his baby a bath
in a pail, while The Wanderer sat in the sun smoking.
About the pail an absorbed group of *putains* stood. Several
plantons (abandoning for one instant their plantonic
demeanour) leaned upon their guns and watched. Some
even smiled a little. And the mother, holding the brownish, naked, crowing child tenderly, was swimming it
quietly to and fro, to the delight of Celina in particular.
To Celina it waved its arms greetingly. She stooped and
spoke to it. The mother smiled. The Wanderer, looking
from time to time at his wife, smoked and pondered by
himself in the sunlight.

This baby was the delight of the *putains* at all times.

They used to take turns carrying it when on promenade. The Wanderer's wife, at such moments, regarded them with a gentle and jealous weariness.

There were two girls, as I said. One, the littlest girl I ever saw walk and act by herself, looked exactly like a golliwog. This was because of the huge mop of black hair. She was very pretty. She used to sit with her mother and move her toes quietly for her own private amusement. The older sister was as divine a creature as God in his skilful and infinite wisdom ever created. Her intensely sexual face greeted us nearly always as we descended *pour la soupe*. She would come up to B. and me slenderly and ask, with the brightest and darkest eyes in the world:

'*Chocolat, M'sieu'?*'

and we would present her with a big or small, as the case might be, *morceau de chocolat*. We even called her *Chocolat*. Her skin was nearly sheer gold; her fingers and feet delicately formed; her teeth wonderfully white; her hair incomparably black and abundant. Her lips would have seduced, I think, *le gouvernement français* itself. Or any saint.

Well . . .

Le gouvernement français decided in its infinite but unskilful wisdom that The Wanderer, being an inexpressibly bad man (guilty of who knows what gentleness, strength and beauty) should suffer as much as he was capable of suffering. In other words, it decided (through its Three Wise Men, who formed the visiting Commission whereof I speak anon) that the wife, her baby, her two girls, and her little son should be separated from the husband by miles and by stone walls and by barbed wire and by Law. Or perhaps (there was a rumour to this effect)

the Three Wise Men discovered that the father of these
incredibly exquisite children was not her lawful husband.
And of course, this being the case, the utterly and incomparably moral French Government saw its duty plainly;
which duty was to inflict the ultimate anguish of separation upon the sinners concerned. I know that The Wanderer came from *la commission* with tears of anger in his
great eyes. I know that some days later he, along with
that deadly and poisonous criminal Monsieur Auguste,
and that aged arch-traitor Monsieur Pet-airs, and that
incomparably wicked person Surplice, and a ragged
gentle being who one day presented us with a broken
spoon which he had found somewhere—the gift being a
purely spontaneous mark of approval and affection—who
for this reason was known to us as The Spoonman, had
the vast and immeasurable honour of departing for
Précigné *pour la durée de la guerre*. If ever I can create
by some occult process of imagining a deed so perfectly
cruel as the deed perpetrated in the case of Joseph
Demestre, I shall consider myself a genius. Then let us
admit that the Three Wise Men were geniuses. And let us,
also and softly, admit that it takes a good and great government perfectly to negate mercy. And let us, bowing
our minds smoothly and darkly, repeat with *Monsieur le
Curé*—'*toujours l'enfer . . .*'

The Wanderer was almost insane when he heard the
judgment of *la commission*. And hereupon I must pay
my respects to Monsieur Pet-airs; whom I had ever liked,
but whose spirit I had not, up to the night preceding The
Wanderer's departure, fully appreciated. Monsieur Pet-
airs sat for hours at the card-table, his glasses continually
fogging, censuring The Wanderer in tones of apparent

annoyance for his frightful weeping (and now and then himself sniffing faintly with his big red nose); sat for hours pretending to take dictation from Joseph Demestre, in reality composing a great letter or series of great letters to the civil and I guess military authorities of Orne on the subject of the injustice done to the father of four children, one a baby at the breast, now about to be separated from all he held dear and good in this world. 'I appeal' (Monsieur Pet-airs wrote, in his boisterously careful, not to say elegant, script) 'to your sense of mercy and of fair play and of honour. It is not merely an unjust thing which is being done, not merely an unreasonable thing, it is an unnatural thing. . . .' As he wrote I found it hard to believe that this was the aged and decrepit and fussing biped whom I had known, whom I had caricatured, with whom I had talked upon ponderous subjects (a comparison between the Belgian and French cities with respect to their location as favouring progress and prosperity, for example); who had with a certain comic shyness revealed to me a secret scheme for reclaiming inundated territories by means of an extraordinary pump 'of my invention.' Yet this was he, this was Monsieur Pet-airs *Lui-Même;* and I enjoyed peculiarly making his complete acquaintance for the first and only time.

May the Heavens prosper him.

The next day The Wanderer appeared in the *cour* walking proudly in a shirt of solid vermilion.

He kissed his wife—excuse me, Monsieur Malvy, I should say the mother of his children—crying very bitterly and suddenly.

The *plantons* yelled for him to line up with the rest, who were waiting outside the gate, bag and baggage. He covered his great king's eyes with his long golden hands and went.

With him disappeared unspeakable sunlight, and the dark, keen, bright strength of the earth.

IX

ZOO-LOO

THIS is the name of the second Delectable Mountain.
Zulu is he called, partly because he looks like what I
have never seen, partly because the sounds somehow re-
late to his personality and partly because they seemed
to please him.

He is, of all the indescribables whom I have known,
definitely the most completely or entirely indescribable.
Then (quoth my reader) you will not attempt to describe him, I trust.—Alas, in the medium which I am
now using a certain amount or at least quality of description is disgustingly necessary. Were I free with a
canvas and some colours ... but I am not free. And so
I will buck the impossible to the best of my ability.
Which, after all, is one way of wasting your time.

He did not come and he did not go. He drifted.

His angular anatomy expended and collected itself
with an effortless spontaneity which is the prerogative of
perhaps fairies, or at any rate of those things in which
we no longer believe. But he was more. There are certain
things in which one is unable to believe for the simple
reason that he never ceases to feel them. Things of this
sort—things which are always inside of us and in fact
are us and which consequently will not be pushed off or
away where we can begin thinking about them—are no
longer things; they, and the us which they are, equals
A Verb; an IS. The Zulu, then, I must perforce call an IS.

In this chapter I shall pretend briefly to describe cer-

tain aspects and attributes of an IS. Which IS we have
called The Zulu, who Himself intrinsically and indu-
bitably escapes analysis. *Allons!*

Let me first describe a Sunday morning when we lifted
our heads to the fight of the stove-pipes.

I was awakened by a roar, a human roar, a roar such as
only a Hollander can make when a Hollander is honestly
angry. As I rose from the domain of the subconscious, the
idea that the roar belonged to Bill the Hollander became
conviction. Bill the Hollander, alias America Lakes, slept
next to The Young Pole (by whom I refer to that young
stupid-looking farmer with that peaches-and-cream complexion and those black puttees who had formed the
rear rank, with the aid of The Zulu Himself, upon the
arrival of Baby-snatcher, Bill, Box, Zulu, and Young
Pole aforesaid). Now this same Young Pole was a case.
Insufferably vain and self-confident was he. Monsieur
Auguste palliated most of his conceited offensiveness on
the ground that he was *un garçon;* we, on the ground
that he was obviously and unmistakably The Zulu's friend.
This Young Pole, I remember, had me design upon the
wall over his *paillasse* (shortly after his arrival) a virile
soldat clutching a somewhat dubious flag—I made the
latter from descriptions furnished by Monsieur Auguste
and The Young Pole himself—intended, I may add, to
be the flag of Poland. Underneath which beautiful picture I was instructed to perpetrate the flourishing in-
scription:

'*Vive la Pologne,*'

which I did to the best of my limited ability and for
Monsieur Auguste's sake. No sooner was the *photographie*
complete than The Young Pole, patriotically elated, set
out to demonstrate the superiority of his race and nation

by making himself obnoxious. I will give him this credit:
he was *pas méchant*, he was in fact a stupid boy. The
Fighting Sheeney temporarily took him down a peg by
flooring him in the nightly '*Boxe*' which The Fighting
Sheeney instituted immediately upon the arrival of The
Trick Raincoat—a previous acquaintance of The Sheeney's at La Santé; the similarity of occupations (or non-
occupation; I refer to the profession of pimp) having
cemented a friendship between these two. But, for all
that The Young Pole's Sunday-best clothes were covered with filth, and for all that his polished puttees were
soiled and scratched by the splintery floor of The Enormous Room (he having rolled well off the blanket upon
which the wrestling was supposed to occur), his spirit
was dashed but for the moment. He set about cleaning
and polishing himself, combing his hair, smoothing his
cap—and was as cocky as ever next morning. In fact I
think he was cockier; for he took to guying Bill the Hollander in French, with which tongue Bill was only faintly
familiar and of which, consequently, he was doubly suspicious. As The Young Pole lay in bed of an evening
after *lumières éteintes*, he would guy his somewhat mas-
sive neighbour in a childish, almost girlish voice, shouting with laughter when The Triangle rose on one arm
and volleyed Dutch at him, pausing whenever The Triangle's good-nature threatened to approach the breaking-
point, resuming after a minute or two when The Triangle
appeared to be on the point of falling into the arms of
Morpheus. This sort of blaguing had gone on for several
nights without dangerous results. It was, however, inevitable that sooner or later something would happen—
and as we lifted our heads on this particular Sunday morn
we were not surprised to see The Hollander himself stand-

ing over The Young Pole, with clenched paws, wringing shoulders, and an apocalyptic face whiter than Death's horse.

The Young Pole seemed incapable of realizing that the climax had come. He lay on his back, cringing a little and laughing foolishly. The Zulu (who slept next to him on our side) had, apparently, just lighted a cigarette which projected upward from a slender holder. The Zulu's face was as always, absolutely expressionless. His chin, with a goodly growth of beard, protruded tranquilly from the blanket which concealed the rest of him with the exception of his feet—feet which were ensconced in large, somewhat clumsy leather boots. As The Zulu wore no socks, the X's of the rawhide lacings on his bare flesh (blue, of course, with cold) presented a rather fascinating kinesis. The Zulu was, to all intents and purposes, gazing at the ceiling . . .

Bill the Hollander, clad only in his shirt, his long, lean, muscled legs planted far apart, shook one fist after another at the recumbent Young Pole, thundering (curiously enough in English):

'Come on, you Gottverdummer son-of-a-bitch of a Polak bastard, and fight! Get up out o' there, you Polak hoor, and I'll kill you, you Gottverdummer bastard you! I stood enough o' your Gottverdummer nonsense, you Gottverdummer,' etc.

As Bill the Hollander's thunder crescendoed steadily, cramming the utmost corners of The Enormous Room with Gottverdummers which echoingly telescoped one another, producing a dim, huge, shaggy mass of vocal anger, The Young Pole began to laugh less and less; began to plead and excuse and palliate and remonstrate—and all the while the triangular tower in its naked legs

and its palpitating chemise brandished its vast fists nearer
and nearer, its ghastly yellow lips hurling cumulative volumes of rhythmic profanity, its blue eyes snapping like
fire-crackers, its enormous hairy chest heaving and tumbling like a monstrous hunk of sea-weed, its flat soiled feet
curling and uncurling their ten sour mutilated toes.

The Zulu puffed gently as he lay.

Bill the Hollander's jaw, sticking into the direction of
The Young Pole's helpless gestures, looked (with the piti-
less scorching face behind it) like some square house carried in the fore of a white cyclone. The Zulu depressed
his chin; his eyes (poking slowly from beneath the visor
of the cap which he always wore, in bed or out of it) regarded the vomiting tower with an abstracted interest.
He allowed one hand delicately to escape from the blanket
and quietly to remove from his lips the holder with its
gently-burning cigarette—

'You won't, eh? You bloody Polak coward!'
and with a speed in comparison to which lightning is
snail-like the tower reached twice for the peaches-and-
cream cheeks of the prone victim, who set up a tragic
bellowing of his own, writhed upon his somewhat dislocated *paillasse,* raised his elbows shieldingly, and started
to get to his feet by way of his trembling knees—to be
promptly knocked flat. Such a howling as The Young
Pole set up I have rarely heard: he crawled sideways; he
got on one knee; he made a dart forward—and was caught
cleanly by an uppercut, lifted through the air a yard,
and spread-eagled against the stove which collapsed with
an unearthly crash, yielding an inky shower of soot upon
the combatants and almost crowning The Hollander
simultaneously with three four-foot sections of pipe. The
Young Pole hit the floor, shouting, on his head at the

apogee of a neatly executed back-somersault, collapsed; rose yelling, and with flashing eyes picked up a length of the ruined *tuyau* which he lifted high in air—at which the Hollander seized in both fists a similar piece, brought it instantly forward and sideways with incognizable velocity and delivered such an immense wallop as smoothed The Young Pole horizontally to a distance of six feet; where he suddenly landed, stove-pipe and all, in a crash of entire collapse, having passed clear over The Zulu's bed. The Zulu, remarking:

'Muh,'

floated hingingly to a sitting position and was saluted by 'Lie down, you Gottverdummer Polaker, I'll get you next'—in spite of which he gathered himself to rise upward, catching as he did so a swish of The Hollander's pipe-length which made his cigarette leap neatly, holder and all, upward and outward. The Young Pole had by this time recovered sufficiently to get upon his hands and knees behind The Zulu, who was hurriedly but calmly propelling himself in the direction of the cherished cigarette-holder, which had rolled under the remains of the stove. Bill the Hollander made for his enemy, raising perpendicularly ten feet in air the unrecognizably dented summit of the pipe which his colossal fists easily encompassed, the muscles in his tree-like arms rolling beneath the chemise like balloons. The Young Pole with a shriek of fear climbed The Zulu—receiving just as he had compassed this human hurdle a crack on the seat of his black pants that stood him directly upon his head. Pivoting slightly for an instant he fell loosely at full length on his own *paillasse*, and lay sobbing and roaring, one elbow protectingly raised, interspersing the inarticulations of woe with a number of sincerely uttered *Assez!*'s. Meanwhile

The Zulu had discovered the whereabouts of his treasure, had driftingly resumed his original position; and was quietly inserting the also-captured cigarette which appeared somewhat confused by its violent aerial journey. Over The Young Pole stood toweringly Bill the Hollander, his shirt almost in ribbons about his thick, bulging neck, thundering as only Hollanders thunder:

'Have you got enough, you Gottverdummer Polak?'
and The Young Pole, alternating nursing the mutilated pulp where his face had been and guarding it with futile and helpless and almost infantile gestures of his quivering hands, was sobbing:

'*Oui, Oui, Oui, Assez!*'
And Bill the Hollander hugely turned to The Zulu, stepping accurately to the *paillasse* of that individual, and demanded:

'And you, you Gottverdummer Polaker, do you want t' fight?'
at which The Zulu gently waved in recognition of the compliment and delicately and hastily replied, between slow puffs:

'Mog.'
Whereat Bill the Hollander registered a disgusted kick in The Young Pole's direction and swearingly resumed his *paillasse*.

All this, the reader understands, having taken place in the terribly cold darkness of the half-dawn.

That very day, after a great deal of examination (on the part of the *Surveillant*) of the participants in this Homeric struggle—said examination failing to reveal the particular guilt or the particular innocence of either—Judas, immaculately attired in a white coat, arrived from downstairs with a step-ladder and proceeded with every one's assistance to reconstruct the original *tuyau*. And a pretty picture Judas made. And a pretty bum job he made. But anyway the stove-pipe drew; and every one thanked God and fought for places about *le poêle*. And Monsieur Pet-airs hoped there would be no more fights for awhile.

One might think that The Young Pole had learned a lesson. But no. He had learned (it is true) to leave his immediate neighbour, America Lakes, to himself; but that is all he had learned. In a few days he was up and about, as full *de la blague* as ever. The Zulu seemed at times almost worried about him. They spoke together in Polish frequently and—on The Zulu's part—earnestly. As subsequent events proved, whatever counsel The Zulu imparted was wasted upon his youthful friend. But let us turn for a moment to The Zulu himself.

He could not, of course, write any language whatever. Two words of French he knew: they were *fromage* and *chapeau*. The former he pronounced 'grumidge.' In English his vocabulary was even more simple, consisting of the single word 'po-lees-man.' Neither B. nor myself understood a syllable of Polish (though we subsequently learned *jin-dobri*, *nima-zatz*, *zampni-pisk* and *shimay pisk*, and used to delight The Zulu hugely by giving him

'*Jin-dobri, pan*'

every morning, also by asking him if he had a '*papierosa*') ; consequently in that direction the path of communication was to all intents shut. And withal—I say this not to astonish my reader but merely in the interests of truth—I have never in my life so perfectly understood (even to the most exquisite nuances) whatever idea another human being desired at any moment to communicate to me, as I have in the case of The Zulu. And if

I had one-third the command over the written word that he had over the unwritten and the unspoken—not merely that; over the unspeakable and the unwritable—God knows this history would rank with the deep art of all time.

It may be supposed that he was master of an intricate and delicate system whereby ideas were conveyed through signs of various sorts. On the contrary. He employed signs more or less, but they were in every case extraordinarily simple. The secret of his means of complete and unutterable communication lay in that very essence which I have only defined as an IS; ended and began with an innate and unlearnable control over all which one can only describe as the homogeneously tactile. The Zulu, for example, communicated the following facts in a very few minutes, with unspeakable ease, one day shortly after his arrival:

He had been formerly a Polish farmer, with a wife and four children. He had left Poland to come to France, where one earned more money. His friend (The Young Pole) accompanied him. They were enjoying life placidly in it may have been Brest—I forget—when one night the gendarmes suddenly broke into their room, raided it, turned it bottom-side up, handcuffed the two arch-criminals wrist to wrist, and said, 'Come with us.' Neither The Zulu nor The Young Pole had the ghost of an idea what all this meant or where they were going. They had no choice but to obey, and obey they did. Every one boarded a train. Every one got out. Bill the Hollander and The Baby-snatcher appeared under escort, handcuffed to each other. They were immediately re-handcuffed to the Polish delegation. The four culprits were hustled, by rapid stages, through several small prisons to La Ferté

Macé. During this journey (which consumed several nights and days) the handcuffs were not once removed. The prisoners slept sitting up or falling over one another. They urinated and defecated with the handcuffs on, all of them hitched together. At various times they complained to their captors that the agony caused by the swelling of their wrists was unbearable—this agony, being the result of over-tightness of the handcuffs, might easily have been relieved by one of the *plantons* without loss of time or prestige. Their complaints were greeted by commands to keep their mouths shut or they'd get it worse than they had it. Finally they hove in sight of La Ferté and the handcuffs were removed in order to enable two of the prisoners to escort The Zulu's box upon their shoulders, which said prisoners were only too happy to do under the circumstances. This box, containing not only The Zulu's personal effects but also a great array of cartridges, knives and heaven knows what extraordinary souvenirs which he had gathered from God knows where, was a strong point in the disfavour of The Zulu from the beginning; and was consequently brought along as evidence. Upon arriving all had been searched, the box included, and sent to The Enormous Room. The Zulu (at the conclusion of this dumb and eloquent recital) slipped his sleeve gently above his wrist and exhibited a bluish ring, at whose persistence upon the flesh he evinced great surprise and pleasure, winking happily to us. Several days later I got the same story from The Young Pole in French; but after some little difficulty due to linguistic misunderstandings, and only after a half-hour's intensive conversation. So far as directness, accuracy and speed are concerned, between the method of language and the

method of The Zulu there was not the slightest comparison.

Not long after The Zulu arrived I witnessed a mystery:
it was toward the second *Soupe,* and B. and I were
proceeding (our spoons in our hands) in the direction
of the door, when beside us suddenly appeared The Zulu
—who took us by the shoulders gently and (after carefully looking about him) produced from, as nearly as
one could see, his right ear a twenty-franc note, asking
us in a few well-chosen silences to purchase with it *confiture, fromage,* and *chocolat* at the canteen. He silently
apologized for encumbering us with these errands, aver-
ring that he had been found when he arrived to have
no money upon him and consequently wished to keep
intact this little tradition. We were only too delighted
to assist so remarkable a prestidigitator—we scarcely
knew him at that time—and *après la soupe* we bought as
requested, conveying the treasures to our bunks and
keeping guard over them. About fifteen minutes after
the *planton* had locked every one in The Zulu driftingly
arrived before us; whereupon we attempted to give him
his purchases—but he winked and told us wordlessly
that we should (if we would be so kind) keep them for
him, immediately following this suggestion by a request
that we open the marmalade or jam or whatever it might
be called—preserve is perhaps the best word. We com-
plied with alacrity. Now (he said soundlessly), you may
if you like offer me a little. We did. Now have some yourselves, The Zulu commanded. So we attacked the *confiture* with a will, spreading it on pieces, or rather chunks,
of the brownish bread, whose faintly rotten odour is one
element of the life at La Ferté which I, for one, find it
easier to remember than to forget. And next, in similar

fashion, we opened the cheese and offered some to our visitor; and finally the chocolate. Whereupon The Zulu rose up, thanked us tremendously for our gifts, and—winking solemnly—floated off.

Next day he told us that he wanted us to eat all we could of the delicacies we had purchased, whether or no he happened to be in the vicinity. He also informed us that when they were gone we should buy more until the twenty francs gave out. And, so generous were our appetites, it was not more than two or three weeks later that The Zulu, having discovered that our supplies were exhausted, produced from his back hair a neatly folded twenty-franc note; wherewith we invaded the canteen with renewed violence. About this time The Spy got busy and The Zulu, with The Young Pole for interpreter, was summoned to *Monsieur le Directeur*, who stripped The Zulu and searched every wrinkle and crevice of his tranquil anatomy for money (so The Zulu vividly informed us)—finding not a sou. The Zulu, who vastly enjoyed the discomfiture of Monsieur, cautiously extracted (shortly after this) a twenty-franc note from the back of his neck, and presented it to us with extreme care. I may say that most of his money went for cheese, of which The Zulu was almost abnormally fond. Nothing more suddenly delightful has happened to me than happened, one day, when I was leaning from the next to the last window—the last being the property of users of the *cabinet*—of The Enormous Room, contemplating the muddy expanse below, and wondering how the Hollanders had ever allowed the last two windows to be opened. Margherite passed from the door of the building proper to the little washing shed. As the sentinel's back was turned I saluted her, and she locked up and smiled pleasantly. And then—a hand leapt quietly outward from the wall, just to my right; the fingers clenched gently upon one half a newly-broken cheese; the hand moved silently in my direction cheese and all, pausing when perhaps six inches from my nose. I took the cheese from the hand, which departed as if by magic; and a little later had the pleasure of being joined at my window by The Zulu, who was brushing cheese crumbs from his long slender Mandarin moustaches, and who expressed profound astonishment and equally profound satisfaction upon noting that I too had been enjoying the pleasures of cheese. Not once, but several times, this Excalibur appearance startled myself and B.: in fact the extreme modesty and incomparable shyness of The Zulu found only in this procedure a satisfactory method of bestowing presents upon his two friends ... I would I could see that long hand once more, the sensitive fingers poised upon a half-Camembert; the bodiless arm swinging gently and surely with a derrick-like grace and certainty in my direction. ...

Not very long after The Zulu's arrival occurred an incident which I give with pleasure because it shows the dauntless and indomitable, not to say intrepid, stuff of which *plantons* are made. The single *seau* which supplied the (at this time) sixty-odd inhabitants of The Enormous Room with drinking water had done its duty, shortly after our arrival from the first *Soupe*, with such thoroughness as to leave a number of unfortunates (among whom I was one) waterless. The interval between *soupe* and promenade loomed darkly and thirstily before said unfortunates. As the minutes passed, it loomed with greater and greater distinctness. At the end of twenty minutes our thirst—stimulated by an especially salty dose of lukewarm water for lunch—attained truly desperate proportions. Several of the bolder thirsters leaned from the various windows of the room and cried

   'De l'eau, planton; de l'eau, s'il vous plait'

upon which the guardian of the law looked up suspiciously; pausing a moment as if to identify the scoundrels whose temerity had so far got the better of their understanding as to lead them to address him, a *planton*, in familiar terms—and then grimly resumed his walk, gun on shoulder, revolver on hip, the picture of simple and unaffected majesty. Whereat, seeing that entreaties were of no avail, we put our seditious and dangerous heads together and formulated a very great scheme: to wit, the lowering of an empty tin-pail about eight inches high, which tin-pail had formerly contained *confiture*, which *confiture* had long since passed into the guts of Monsieur Auguste, The Zulu, B., myself, and—as The Zulu's friend—The Young Pole. Now this fiendish imitation of The Old Oaken Bucket That Hung In The Well was to be lowered to the good-hearted Margherite (who went to and fro from the door of the building to the washing-shed); who was to fill it for us at the pump situated directly under us in a cavernous chilly cave on the ground-floor, then re-hitch it to the rope, and guide its upward beginning. The rest was in the hands of Fate.

   Bold might the *planton* be; we were no *fainéants*. We made a little speech to everyone in general desiring them to lend us their belts. The Zulu, the immensity of whose pleasure in this venture cannot be even indicated, stripped off his belt with unearthly agility—Monsieur Auguste gave his, which we tongue-holed to The Zulu's—somebody else contributed a necktie—another a shoe-string—The Young Pole his scarf, of which he was impossibly proud—etc. The extraordinary rope so constructed was

now tried out in The Enormous Room, and found to be
about thirty-eight feet long; or in other words of ample
length, considering that the window itself was only three
stories above terra firma. Margherite was put on her guard
by signs, executed when the *planton's* back was turned
(which it was exactly half the time, as the *planton's* pa-
trol stretched at right angles to the wing of the building
whose *troisième étage* we occupied). Having attached
the minute bucket to one end (the stronger looking end,
the end which had more belts and less neckties and handkerchiefs) of our improvised rope, B., Harree, myself and
The Zulu bided our time at *la fenêtre*—then seizing a
favourable opportunity, in enormous haste began paying
out the infernal contrivance. Down went the sinful tin-
pail, safely past the window-ledge just below us, straight
and true into the waiting hands of the faithful Margherite—who had just received it and was on the point of
undoing the bucket from the first belt when, lo! who
should come in sight around the corner but the pimply-
faced, brilliantly-uniformed, glitteringly-putteed *sergent
de plantons lui-même*. Such amazement as dominated his
puny features I have rarely seen equalled. He stopped
dead in his tracks; for one second stupidly contemplated
the window, ourselves, the wall, seven neckties, five belts,
three handkerchiefs, a scarf, two shoe-strings, the jam-
pail, and Margherite—then, wheeling, noticed the *planton* (who peacefully and with dignity was pursuing a
course which carried him further and further from the
zone of operations) and finally, spinning around again,
cried shrilly:

'*Qu'est-ce que vous avez foutu avec cette machine-là?*'
At which cry the *planton* staggered, rotated, brought his

gun clumsily off his shoulder, and stared, trembling all over with emotion, at his superior.

'*Là-bas!*' screamed the pimply *sergent de plantons*, pointing fiercely in our direction.

Margherite, at his first command, had let go the jam-pail and sought shelter in the building. Simultaneously with her flight we all began pulling on the rope for dear life, making the bucket bound against the wall.

Upon hearing the dreadful exclamation '*Là-bas!*' the *planton* almost fell down. With a supreme effort he turned toward the wing of the building. The sight which greeted his eyes caused him to excrete a single mouthful of vivid profanity, made him grip his gun like a hero, set every nerve in his noble and faithful body tingling. Apparently, however, he had forgotten completely his gun, which lay faithfully and expectingly in his two noble hands.

'Attention!' screamed the sergeant.

The *planton* did something to his gun very aimlessly and rapidly.

'FIRE!' shrieked the sergeant, scarlet with rage and mortification.

The *planton*, cool as steel, raised his gun.

'*NOM DE DIEU TIREZ!*'

The bucket, in big merry sounding jumps, was approaching the window below us.

The *planton* took aim, falling fearlessly on one knee, and closing both eyes. I confess that my blood stood on tip-toe; but what was death to the loss of that jam-bucket, let alone everyone's apparel which everyone had so generously lent? We kept on hauling silently. Out of the corner of my eye I beheld the *planton*—now on both knees, musket held to his shoulder by his left arm and pointing unflinchingly at us one and all—hunting with his right arm and hand in his belt for cartridges! A few seconds after this fleeting glimpse of heroic devotion had penetrated my considerably heightened sensitivity—UP suddenly came the bucket and over backwards we all went together on the floor of The Enormous Room. And as we fell I heard a cry like the cry of a boiler announcing noon—

'Too late!'

I recollect that I lay on the floor for some minutes, half on top of The Zulu and three-quarters smothered by Monsieur Auguste, shaking with laughter . . .

Then we all took to our hands and knees, and made for our bunks.

I believe no one (curiously enough) got punished for this atrocious misdemeanour—except the *planton;* who was punished for not shooting us, although God knows he had done his very best.

And now I must chronicle the famous duel which took place between The Zulu's compatriot, The Young Pole, and that herebefore introduced pimp, The Fighting Sheeney; a duel which came as a climax to a vast deal of teasing on the part of The Young Pole—who, as previously remarked, had not learned his lesson from Bill the Hollander with the thoroughness which one might have expected of him.

In addition to a bit of French and considerable Spanish, Rockyfeller's valet spoke Russian very (I did not have to be told) badly. The Young Pole, perhaps sore at being rolled on the floor of The Enormous Room by the worthy Sheeney, set about nagging him just as he had done in the case of neighbour Bill. His favourite epithet for the conqueror was 'moshki' or 'moski,' I never was sure which. Whatever it meant (The Young Pole

and Monsieur Auguste informed me that it meant 'Jew'
in a highly derogatory sense) its effect upon the noble
Sheeney was definitely unpleasant. But when coupled
with the word 'moskosi,' accent on the second syllable
or long o, its effect was more than unpleasant—it was
really disagreeable. At intervals throughout the day, on
promenade, of an evening, the ugly phrase

'MOS-ki mosKOsi'

resounded through The Enormous Room. The Fighting
Sheeney, then rapidly convalescing from syphilis, bided
his time. The Young Pole, moreover, had a way of jesting
upon the subject of The Sheeney's infirmity. He would,
particularly during the afternoon promenade, shout various none too subtle allusions to Moshki's physical condition for the benefit of *les femmes*. And in response
would come peals of laughter from the girls' windows,
shrill peals and deep guttural peals intersecting and breaking joints like overlapping shingles on the roof of Crazi-
ness. So hearty did these responses become one afternoon
that, in answer to loud pleas from the injured Moshki,
the pimply *sergent de plantons* himself came to the gate
in the barbed-wire fence and delivered a lecture upon
the seriousness of venereal ailments (heart-felt, I should
judge by the looks of him) as follows:

'*Il ne faut pas rigoler de ça. Savez-vous? C'est une
maladie, ça,*' which little sermon contrasted agreeably
with his usual remarks concerning and in the presence
of *les femmes*, whereof the essence lay in a single phrase
of prepositional significance:

'*bonne pour coucher avec*'

he would say shrilly, his puny eyes assuming an expression of amorous wisdom which was most becoming. . . .
The Sheeney looked sheepish, and waited.

One day we were all upon afternoon promenade, it being *beau temps* (for that part of the world), under the auspices of by all odds one of the littlest and mildest and most delicate specimens of mankind that ever donned the high and dangerous duties of a *planton*. As B. says: 'He always looked like a June bride.' This mannikin could not have been five feet high, was perfectly proportioned (unless we except the musket upon his shoulder and the bayonet at his belt), and minced to and fro with a feminine grace which suggested—at least to *les deux citoyens* of These United States—the extremely authentic epithet 'fairy.' He had such a pretty face! and so cute a moustache! and such darling legs! and such a wonderful smile! For plantonic purposes the smile—which brought two little dimples into his pink cheeks—was for the most part suppressed. However, it was impossible for this little thing to look stern: the best he could do was to look poignantly sad. Which he did with great success, standing like a tragic last piece of uneaten candy in his big box at the end of the *cour*, and eyeing the sinful *hommes* with sad eyes. Won't anyone eat me?—he seemed to ask.—I'm really delicious, you know, perfectly delicious, really I am.

To resume: everyone being in the *cour* the *cour* was well filled, not only from the point of view of space but of sound. A barn-yard crammed with pigs, cows, horses, ducks, geese, hens, cats and dogs could not possibly have produced one-fifth of the racket that emanated, spontaneously and inevitably, from the *cour*. Above which racket I heard *tout à coup* a roar of pain and surprise; and looking up, with some interest and also in some alarm, beheld The Young Pole backing and filling and slipping in the deep ooze under the strenuous jolts, jabs and even haymakers of The Fighting Sheeney; who, with his coat off and his cap off and his shirt open at the neck, was swatting luxuriously and for all he was worth that round helpless face and that peaches-and-cream complexion. From where I stood, at a distance of six or eight yards, the impact of The Sheeney's fist on The Young Pole's jaw and cheeks was disconcertingly audible. The latter made not the slightest attempt to defend himself, let alone retaliate; he merely skidded about, roaring, and clutching desperately out of harm's way his long white scarf, of which (as I have mentioned) he was extremely proud. But for the sheer brutality of the scene it would have been highly ludicrous. The Sheeney was swinging like a wind-mill and hammering like a blacksmith. His ugly head lowered, the chin protruding, lips drawn back in a snarl, teeth sticking forth like a gorilla's, he banged and smote that moon-shaped physiognomy as if his life depended upon utterly annihilating it. And annihilate it he doubt-less would have, but for the prompt (not to say punctual) heroism of The June Bride—who, lowering his huge gun, made a rush for the fight; stopped at a safe distance; and began squeaking at the very top and even summit of his faint girlish voice:

'*Aux armes! Aux armes!*'

which plaintive and intrepid utterance by virtue of its very fragility penetrated the building and released The Black Holster—who bounded through the gate, roaring a salutation as he bounded, and in a jiffy had cuffed the participants apart. 'All right, whose fault is this!' he roared. And a number of highly reputable spectators such as Judas and The Fighting Sheeney himself said it was The Young Pole's fault. '*Allez! Au cabinot! De suite!*' —and off trickled the sobbing Young Pole, winding his great scarf comfortingly about him, to the dungeon.

Some few minutes later we encountered The Zulu
speaking with Monsieur Auguste. Monsieur Auguste was
very sorry. He admitted that The Young Pole had brought
his punishment upon himself. But he was only a boy. The
Zulu's reaction to the affair was absolutely profound:
he indicated *les femmes* with one eye, his trousers with
another, and converted his utterly plastic personality into
an amorous machine for several seconds, thereby vividly
indicating the root of the difficulty—then drifting softly
off began playing hide-and-seek with the much delighted
Little Man In The Orange Cap. That the stupidity of his
friend The Young Pole hurt The Zulu deeply I discovered by looking at him as he lay in bed the next morning, limply and sorrowfully prone; beside him the empty
paillasse which meant *cabinot* . . . his perfectly extraordinary face (a face perfectly at once fluent and angular,
expressionless and sensitive) told me many things whereof
even The Zulu might not speak, things which in order
entirely to suffer he kept carefully and thoroughly
ensconced behind his rigid and mobile eyes.

From the day that The Young Pole emerged from
cabinot he was our friend. The blague had been at last
knocked out of him, thanks to *Un Mangeur de Blanc*, as
the little Machine-Fixer expressively called The Fighting Sheeney. Which *mangeur*, by the way (having been
exonerated from all blame by the more enlightened spectators of the unequal battle) strode immediately and ferociously over to B. and me, a hideous grin crackling
upon the coarse surface of his mug, and demanded—
hiking at the front of his trousers—

'*Bon, eh? Bien fait, eh?*'

and a few days later asked us for money, even hinting

that he would be pleased to become our special protector. I think, as a matter of fact, we 'lent' him one-eighth of what he wanted (perhaps we lent him five cents) in order to avoid trouble and get rid of him. At any rate he didn't bother us particularly afterwards; and if a nickel could accomplish that a nickel should be proud of itself.

And always, through the falling greyness of the desolate Autumn, The Zulu was beside us, or wrapped around a tree in the *cour*, or melting in a post after tapping Mexique, or suffering from toothache—God, I wish I could see him expressing for us the wickedness of toothache—or losing his shoes and finding them under Garibaldi's bed (with a huge perpendicular wink which told tomes about Garibaldi's fatal propensities for ownership), or marvelling silently at the power of *les femmes* à propos his young friend—who, occasionally resuming his former bravado, would stand in the black evil rain with his white warm scarf twined about him, singing as of old:

> '*Je suis content*
> *pour mettre dedans*
> *suis pas pressé*
> *pour tirer*
> *ah-la-la-la* . . .'

. . . And The Zulu came out of *la commission* with identically the expressionless expression which he had carried into it; and God knows what the Three Wise Men found out about him, but (whatever it was) they never found and never will find that Something whose discovery was worth to me more than all the round and powerless money of the world—limbs' tin grace, wooden wink, shoulderless, unhurried body, velocity of a grasshopper, soul up

under his arm-pits, mysteriously falling over the own-
ness of two feet, floating fish of his slimness half a
bird. . . .

Gentlemen, I am inexorably grateful for the gift of
these ignorant and indivisible things.

X

SURPLICE

LET us ascend the third Delectable Mountain, which is called Surplice.

I will admit, in the beginning, that I never knew Surplice. This for the simple reason that I am unwilling to know except as a last resource. And it is by contrast with Harree the Hollander, whom I knew, and Judas, whom I knew, that I shall be able to give you (perhaps) a little of Surplice, whom I did not know. For that matter I think Monsieur Auguste was the only person who might possibly have known him; and I doubt whether Monsieur Auguste was capable of descending to such depths in the case of so fine a person as Surplice.

Take a sheer animal of a man. Take the incredible Hollander with cobalt-blue breeches, shock of orange hair, pasted over forehead, pink long face, twenty-six years old, had been in all the countries of all the world: 'Australia girl fine girl—Japanese girl cleanest girl of the world—Spanish girl all right—English girl no good, no face—everywhere these things: Norway sailors, German girls, Swedisher matches, Holland candles' . . . had been to Philadelphia, worked on a yacht for a millionaire; knew and had worked in the Krupp factories; was on two boats torpedoed and one which struck a mine when in sight of shore through the 'looking-glass': 'Holland almost no soldier—India' (the Dutch Indies) 'nice place, always warm there, I was in cavalry; if you kill a man

or steal one hundred franc or anything, in prison twenty-
four hours; every week black girl sleep with you because
government want white children, black girl fine girl, always doing something, your finger-nails or clean your
ears or make wind because it's hot.... No one can beat
German people; if Kaiser tell man to kill his father and
mother he do it quick!'—the tall, strong, coarse vital
youth who remarked:

'I sleep with black girl who smoke a pipe in the night.'

Take this animal. You hear him, you are afraid of him,
you smell and you see him and you know him—but you
do not touch him.

Or a man who makes us thank God for animals, Judas
as we called him: who keeps his moustaches in press during the night (by means of a kind of transparent frame
which is held in place by a band over his head); who
grows the nails of his two little fingers with infinite care;
has two girls with both of whom he flirts carefully and
wisely, without ever once getting into trouble; talks in
French; converses in Belgian; can speak eight languages,
and is therefore always useful to *Monsieur le Surveillant*
—Judas with his shining horrible forehead, pecked with
little indentures; with his Reynard full-face—Judas with
his pale almost putrescent fatty body in the *douche*—
Judas with whom I talked one night about Russia, he
wearing my *pelisse*—the frightful and impeccable Judas:
take this man. You see him, you smell the hot stale odour
of Judas's body; you are not afraid of him, in fact you
hate him; you hear him and you know him. But you do
not touch him.

And now take Surplice, whom I see and hear and smell
and touch and even taste, and whom I do not know.

Take him in dawn's soft squareness, gently stooping to

pick chewed cigarette-ends from the spitty floor . . . hear
him, all night; retchings which light into the dark . . . see
him all day and all days, collecting his soaked ends and
stuffing them gently into his round pipe (when he can
find none he smokes tranquilly little splinters of wood)
. . . watch him scratching his back (exactly like a bear)
on the wall . . . or in the *cour*, speaking to no one, sunning
his soul. . . .

He is, we think, Polish. Monsieur Auguste is very kind
to him, Monsieur Auguste can understand a few words
of his language and thinks they mean to be Polish. That
they are trying hard to be and never can be Polish.

Everyone else roars at him, Judas refers to him before
his face as a dirty pig, Monsieur Peters cries angrily:

'*Il ne faut pas cracher par terre,*'
eliciting a humble not to say abject apology; the Belgians
spit on him; the Hollanders chaff him and bulldoze him
now and then, crying 'Syph'lis'—at which he corrects
them with offended majesty

'*Pas syph'lis, Surplice*'
causing shouts of laughter from everyone—of nobody
can he say My Friend, of no one has he ever said or will
he ever say My Enemy.

When there is labour to do he works like a dog . . . the
day we had *nettoyage de chambre,* for instance, and Surplice and The Hat did most of the work; and B. and I
were caught by the *planton* trying to stroll out into the
cour . . . every morning he takes the pail of solid excrement down, without anyone's suggesting that he take it;
takes it as if it were his, empties it in the sewer just beyond
the *cour des femmes,* or pours a little (just a little) very
delicately on the garden where *Monsieur le Directeur* is
growing a flower for his daughter—he has, in fact, an

unobstreperous affinity for excrement; he lives in it; he is shaggy and spotted and blotched with it; he sleeps in it; he puts it in his pipe and says it is delicious. . . .

And he is intensely religious, religious with a terrible and exceedingly beautiful and absurd intensity . . . every Friday he will be found sitting on a little kind of stool by his *paillasse*, reading his prayer-book upside down; turning with enormous delicacy the thin difficult leaves, smiling to himself as he sees and does not read. Surplice is actually religious, and so are Garibaldi, and I think The Woodchuck (a little dark sad man who spits blood with regularity); by which I mean they go to *la messe* for *la messe*, whereas everyone else goes *pour voir les femmes*. And I don't know for certain why The Woodchuck goes, but I think it's because he feels entirely sure he will die. And Garibaldi is afraid, immensely afraid. And Surplice goes in order to be surprised, surprised by the amazing gentleness and delicacy of God—Who put him, Surplice, upon his knees in La Ferté Macé, knowing that Surplice would appreciate His so doing.

He is utterly ignorant. He thinks America is out of a particular window on your left as you enter The Enormous Room. He cannot understand the submarine. He does not know that there is a war. On being informed upon these subjects he is unutterably surprised, he is inexpressibly astonished. He derives huge pleasure from this astonishment. His filthy rather proudly noble face radiates the pleasure he receives upon being informed that people are killing people for nobody knows what reason, that boats go under water and fire six-foot-long bullets at ships, that America is not really just outside this window close to which we are talking, that America is in fact over the sea. The sea: is that water?—'*c'est de l'eau, monsieur?*'

Ah: a great quantity of water; enormous amounts of water, water and then water; water and water and water and water and water. 'Ah! You cannot see the other side of this water, monsieur? Wonderful, monsieur!'—He meditates it, smiling quietly; its wonder, how wonderful it is, no other side, and yet—the sea. In which fish swim. Wonderful.

He is utterly curious. He is utterly hungry. We have bought cheese with The Zulu's money. Surplice comes up, bows timidly and ingratiatingly with the demeanour of a million-times whipped but somewhat proud dog. He smiles. He says nothing, being terribly embarrassed. To help his embarrassment, we pretend we do not see him. That makes things better:

'*Fromage, monsieur?*'

'*Oui, c'est du fromage.*'

'*Ah-h-h-h-h-h-h. . . .*'

his astonishment is supreme. *C'est du fromage.* He ponders this. After a little

'*Monsieur, c'est bon, monsieur?*'

asking the question as if his very life depended on the answer—'Yes, it is good,' we tell him reassuringly.

'*Ah-h-h. Ah-h.*'

He is once more superlatively happy. It is good, *le fromage*. Could anything be more superbly amazing? After perhaps a minute:

'*Monsieur—monsieur—c'est cher le fromage?*'

'Very,' we tell him truthfully. He smiles, blissfully astonished. Then, with extreme delicacy and the utmost timidity conceivable:

'*Monsieur, combien ça coute, monsieur?*'

We tell him. He totters with astonishment and happiness.

Only now, as if we had just conceived the idea, we say carelessly:

'*En voulez-vous?*'

He straightens, thrilled from the top of his rather beautiful filthy head to the soleless slippers with which he promenades in rain and frost:

'*Merci, Monsieur!*'

We cut him a piece. He takes it quiveringly, holds it a second as a king might hold and contemplate the best and biggest jewel of his realm, turns with profuse thanks to us—and disappears. . . .

He is perhaps most curious of this pleasantly sounding thing which everyone around him, everyone who curses and spits upon and bullies him, desires with a terrible desire—*Liberté*. When anyone departs Surplice is in an ecstasy of quiet excitement. The lucky man may be Fritz; for whom Bathhouse John is taking up a collection as if he, Fritz, were a Hollander and not a Dane—for whom Bathhouse John is striding hither and thither, shaking a hat into which we drop coins for Fritz; Bathhouse John, chipmunk-cheeked, who talks Belgian, French, English and Dutch in his dreams, who has been two years in La Ferté (and they say he declined to leave, once, when given the chance), who cries '*baigneur de femmes, moi,*' and every night hoists himself into his wooden bunk crying 'goo-dni-te'; whose favourite joke is '*une section pour les femmes*'; which he shouts occasionally in the *cour* as he lifts his paper-soled slippers and stamps in the freezing mud, chuckling and blowing his nose on the Union Jack . . . and now Fritz, beaming with joy, shakes hands and thanks us all and says to me, 'Good-bye, Johnny,' and waves and is gone for ever—and behind me I hear a timid voice:

'*Monsieur, Liberté?*'

and I say Yes, feeling that Yes in my belly and in my head at the same instant; and Surplice stands beside me, quietly marvelling, extremely happy, uncaring that *le parti* did not think to say good-bye to him. Or it may be Harree and Pom-pom, who are running to and fro shaking hands with everybody in the wildest state of excitement, and I hear a voice behind me:

'*Liberté, monsieur? Liberté?*'

and I say No, Précigné, feeling weirdly depressed, and Surplice is standing to my left, contemplating the departure of the incorrigibles with interested disappointment—Surplice of whom no man takes any notice when that man leaves, be it for Hell or Paradise. . . .

And once a week the *maître de chambre* throws soap on the *paillasses*, and I hear a voice:

'*Monsieur, voulez pas?*'

and Surplice is asking that we give him our soap to wash with.

Sometimes, when he has made *quelques sous* by washing for others, he stalks quietly to The Butcher's chair (everyone else who wants a shave having been served) and receives with shut eyes and a patient expression the blade of The Butcher's dullest razor—for The Butcher is not the man to waste a good razor on Surplice; he, The Butcher as we call him, the successor of the Frog (who one day somehow managed to disappear like his predecessor The Barber), being a thug and a burglar fond of telling us pleasantly about German towns and prisons, prisons where men are not allowed to smoke, clean prisons where there is a daily medical inspection, where anyone who thinks he has a grievance of any sort has the right of immediate and direct appeal; he, The Butcher, being perhaps happiest when he can spend an evening showing us little parlour-tricks fit for children of four and three years old; quite at his best when he remarks:

'Sickness doesn't exist in France,'
meaning that one is either well or dead; or

'If they (the French) get an inventor they put him in prison.'

—So The Butcher is stooping heavily upon Surplice and slicing and gashing busily and carelessly, his thick lips stuck a little pursewise, his buried pig's eyes glistening— and in a moment he cries *Fini!* and poor Surplice rises unsteadily, horribly slashed, bleeding from at least three two-inch cuts and a dozen large scratches; totters over to his couch holding on to his face as if he were afraid it would fall off any moment; and lies down gently at full length, sighing with pleasurable surprise, cogitating the inestimable delights of cleanness. . . .

It struck me at the time as intensely interesting that, in the case of a certain type of human being, the more cruel are the miseries inflicted upon him the more cruel does he become toward anyone who is so unfortunate as to be weaker or more miserable than himself. Or perhaps I should say that nearly every human being, given sufficiently miserable circumstances, will from time to time react to those very circumstances (whereby his own personality is mutilated) through a deliberate mutilation on his own part of a weaker or already more mutilated personality. I daresay that this is perfectly obvious. I do not pretend to have made a discovery. On the contrary, I merely state what interested me peculiarly in the course of my sojourn at La Ferté: I mention that I was extremely moved to find that, however busy sixty men may be kept suffering in common, there is always one man or two or

three men who can always find time to make certain of
their comrades enjoying a little extra suffering. In the case
of Surplice, to be the butt of everyone's ridicule could not
be called precisely suffering; inasmuch as Surplice, being
unspeakably lonely, enjoyed any and all insults for the
simple reason that they constituted or at least implied a
recognition of his existence. To be made a fool of was, to
this otherwise completely neglected individual, a mark of
distinction; something to take pleasure in; to be proud
of. The inhabitants of The Enormous Room had given to
Surplice a small but essential part in the drama of *La
Misère:* he would play that part to the utmost of his
ability; the cap-and-bells should not grace a head unworthy of their high significance. He would be a great
fool, since that was his function; a supreme entertainer,
since his duty was to amuse. After all, men in *La Misère*
as well as anywhere else rightly demand a certain amount
of amusement; amusement is, indeed, peculiarly essential
to suffering; in proportion as we are able to be amused
we are able to suffer; I, Surplice, am a very necessary
creature after all.

I recall one day when Surplice beautifully demonstrated
his ability to play the fool. Someone had crept up behind
him as he was stalking to and fro, head in air proudly,
hands in pockets, pipe in teeth, and had (after several
heart-breaking failures) succeeded in attaching to the
back of his jacket by means of a pin a huge placard carefully prepared beforehand, bearing the numerical inscrip-
tion

606

in vast writing. The attacher, having accomplished his
difficult feat, crept away. So soon as he reached his *pail-*

lasse a volley of shouts went up from all directions, shouts in which all nationalities joined, shouts or rather jeers which made the pillars tremble and the windows rattle—

'*SIX CENT SIX! SYPH'LIS!*'

Surplice started from his reverie, removed his pipe from his lips, drew himself up proudly, and—facing one after another the sides of The Enormous Room—blustered in his bad and rapid French accent:

'*Pas syph'lis! Pas syph'lis!*'

at which, rocking with mirth, everyone responded at the top of his voice

'*SIX CENT SIX!*'

Whereat, enraged, Surplice made a dash at Pete the Shadow and was greeted by:

'Get away, you bloody Polak, or I'll give you something you'll be sorry for'—this from the lips of America Lakes. Cowed, but as majestic as ever, Surplice attempted to resume his promenade and his composure together. The din bulged:

'*Six cent six! Syph'lis! Six cent six!*'

—increasing in volume with every instant. Surplice, beside himself with rage, rushed another of his fellow-captives (a little old man, who fled under the table) and elicited threats of:

'Come on now, you Polak hoor, and quit that business or I'll kill you,' upon which he dug his hands into the pockets of his almost transparent pantaloons and marched away in a fury, literally frothing at the mouth.

'*Six cent six!*'

everyone cried. Surplice stamped with wrath and mortification. '*C'est dommage,*' Monsieur Auguste said gently beside me. '*C'est un bon-homme, le pauvre, il ne faut pas l'em-merd-er.*'

'Look behind you!'

somebody yelled. Surplice wheeled, exactly like a kitten trying to catch its own tail, and provoked thunders of laughter. Nor could anything at once more pitiful and ridiculous, more ludicrous and horrible, be imagined.

'On your coat!' 'Look on your jacket!'

Surplice bent backward, staring over his left then his right shoulder, pulled at his jacket first one way then the other—thereby making his improvised tail to wag, which sent The Enormous Room into spasms of merriment— finally caught sight of the incriminating appendage, pulled his coat to the left, seized the paper, tore it off, threw it fiercely down, and stamped on the crumpled 606; spluttering and blustering and waving his arms; slavvering like a mad dog. Then he faced the most prominently vociferous corner and muttered thickly and crazily:

"Wuhwuhwuhwuhwuh. . . .'

Then he strode rapidly to his *paillasse* and lay down; in which position I caught him, a few minutes later, smiling and even chuckling ... very happy ... as only an actor is happy whose efforts have been greeted with universal applause. . . .

In addition to being called 'Syph'lis' he was popularly known as '*Chaude-Pisse*, the Pole.' If there is anything particularly terrifying about prisons, or at least imitations of prisons such as La Ferté, it is possibly the utter obviousness with which (quite unknown to themselves) the prisoners demonstrate willy-nilly certain fundamental psychological laws. The case of Surplice is a very exquisite example: everyone, of course, is afraid of *les maladies vénériennes*—accordingly all pick an individual (of whose inner life they know and desire to know nothing, whose external appearance satisfies the requirements of the mind

à propos what is foul and disgusting) and, having tacitly
agreed upon this individual as a Symbol of all that is evil,
proceed to heap insults upon him and enjoy his very natural discomfiture . . . but I shall remember Surplice on his
both knees sweeping sacredly together the spilled sawdust
from a spittoon-box knocked over by the heel of the
omnipotent *planton*; and smiling as he smiled at *la messe*
when *Monsieur le Curé* told him that there was always
Hell. . . .

He told us one day a great and huge story of an important incident in his life, as follows:

'*Monsieur, réformé moi—oui monsieur—réformé—
travaille, beaucoup de monde, maison, très haute, troisième
étage, tout le monde, planches, en haut—planches pas
bonnes—chancelle, tout*'—(here he began to stagger and
rotate before us) '*commence à tomber—tombe, tombe,
tout, tous, vingt-sept hommes-briques-planches-brouettes-
tous—dix mètres—zuhzuhzuhzuhzuh POOM!—tout le
monde blessé, tout le monde tué, pas moi, réformé—oui
monsieur*'—and he smiled, rubbing his head foolishly.
Twenty-seven men, bricks, planks and wheelbarrows. . . .

Also he told us, one night, in his gentle, crazy, shrugging voice, that once upon a time he played the fiddle
with a big woman in Alsace-Lorraine for fifty francs a
night; '*C'est la misère*'—adding quietly, 'I can play well,
I can play anything, I can play *n'importe quoi*.'

Which I suppose and guess I scarcely believed—until
one afternoon a man brought up a harmonica which he
had purchased *en ville*; and the man tried it; and everyone tried it; and it was perhaps the cheapest instrument
and the poorest that money can buy, even in the fair
country of France; and everyone was disgusted—but,

about six o'clock in the evening, a voice came from behind the last experimenter; a timid hasty voice:

'*Monsieur, monsieur, permettez?*'

the last experimenter turned, and to his amazement saw
Chaude-Pisse the Pole, whom everyone had (of course)
forgotten—

The man tossed the harmonica on the table with a
scornful look (a menacingly scornful look) at the object
of universal execration; and turned his back. Surplice,
trembling from the summit of his filthy and beautiful
head to the naked soles of his filthy and beautiful feet,
covered the harmonica delicately and surely with one
shaking paw; seated himself with a surprisingly deliberate
and graceful gesture; closed his eyes, upon whose lashes
there were big filthy tears . . .

. . . and suddenly:

He put the harmonica softly upon the table. He rose.
He went quickly to his *paillasse*. He neither moved nor
spoke nor responded to the calls for more music, to the
cries of '*Bis!*'—'*Bien joué!*'—'*Allez!*'—'*Va-z-y!*' He was
crying, quietly and carefully, to himself . . . quietly and
carefully crying, not wishing to annoy anyone . . . hoping
that people could not see that Their Fool had temporarily
failed in his part.

The following day he was up as usual before anyone
else, hunting for chewed cigarette-ends on the spitty,
slippery floor of The Enormous Room; ready for insult,
ready for ridicule, for buffets, for curses.

Alors—

One evening, some days after everyone who was fit for
la commission had enjoyed the privilege of examination
by that inexorable and delightful body—one evening very
late, in fact just before *lumières éteintes,* a strange *planton*

arrived in The Enormous Room and hurriedly **read a list**
of five names, adding:

'*partir demain de bonne heure,*'

and shut the door behind him. Surplice was, as usual, very
interested, enormously interested. So were we: for the
names respectively belonged to Monsieur Auguste, Monsieur Pet-airs, The Wanderer, Surplice, and The Spoonman. These men had been judged. These men were going
to Précigné. These men would be *prisonniers pour la durée
de la guerre.*

I have already told how Monsieur Pet-airs sat with the
frantically weeping Wanderer writing letters, and sniffing
with his big red nose, and saying from time to time: 'Be a
man, Demestre, don't cry, crying does no good.'—Monsieur Auguste was broken-hearted. We did our best to
cheer him; we gave him a sort of Last Supper at our bed-
side, we heated some red wine in the tin-cup and he drank
with us. We presented him with certain tokens of our
love and friendship, including—I remember—a huge
cheese . . . and then, before us, trembling with excitement,
stood Surplice—

We asked him to sit down. The onlookers (there were
always onlookers at every function, however personal,
which involved Food or Drink) scowled and laughed. *Le
con*, Surplice, *chaude-pisse*—how could he sit with men
and gentlemen? Surplice sat down gracefully and lightly
on one of our beds, taking care not to strain the somewhat
capricious mechanism thereof; sat very proudly; erect;
modest but unfearful. We offered him a cup of wine. A
kind of huge convulsion gripped, for an instant, fiercely
his entire face: then he said in a whisper of sheer and
unspeakable wonderment, leaning a little toward us with-

out in any way suggesting that the question might **have** an affirmative answer:

'*Pour moi, monsieur?*'

We smiled at him and said, '*Prenez, monsieur.*' His eyes opened. I have never seen eyes since. He remarked quietly, extending one hand with majestic delicacy:

'*Merci, monsieur.*'

. . . Before he left B. gave him some socks and I presented him with a flannel shirt, which he took softly and slowly and simply and otherwise not as an American would take a million dollars.

'I will not forget you,' he said to us, as if in his own country he were a more than very great king . . . and I think I know where that country is, I think I know this; I, who never knew Surplice, know.

For he has the territory of harmonicas, the acres of flutes, the meadows of clarinets, the domain of violins. And God says: Why did they put you in prison? What did you do to the people? 'I made them dance and they put me in prison. The soot-people hopped; and to twinkle like sparks on a chimney-back and I made 80 francs every *dimanche*, and beer and wine, and to eat well. *Maintenant . . . c'est fini. . . . Et tout de suite*' (gesture of cutting himself in two) '*la tête.*' And He says: O you who put the jerk into joys, come up hither. There's a man up here called Christ who likes the violin.

XI

JEAN LE NÈGRE

ON a certain day, the ringing of the bell and accompanying rush of men to the window facing the entrance gate was supplemented by an unparalleled volley of enthusiastic exclamations in all the languages of La Ferté Macé—provoking in me a certainty that the queen of fair women had arrived. This certainly thrillingly withered when I heard the cry: '*Il y a un noir!*' Fritz was at the best peep-hole, resisting successfully the onslaughts of a dozen fellow-prisoners, and of him I demanded in English, 'Who's come?'—'Oh, a lot of girls,' he yelled, 'and there's a NIGGER too'—hereupon writhing with laughter.

I attempted to get a look, but in vain; for by this at least two dozen men were at the peep-hole, fighting and gesticulating and slapping each other's backs with joy. However, my curiosity was not long in being answered. I heard on the stairs the sound of mounting feet, and knew that a couple of *plantons* would before many minutes arrive at the door with their new prey. So did everyone else—and from the farthest beds uncouth figures sprang and rushed to the door, eager for the first glimpse of the *nouveau*: which was very significant, as the ordinary procedure on arrival of prisoners was for everybody to rush to his own bed and stand guard over it.

Even as the *plantons* fumbled with the locks I heard the inimitable, unmistakable divine laugh of a negro. The door opened at last. Entered a beautiful pillar of black strutting muscle topped with a tremendous display of the whitest teeth on earth. The muscle bowed politely in our direction, the grin remarked musically; 'Bo'jour, tou'l'monde'; then came a cascade of laughter. Its effect on the spectators was instantaneous: they roared and danced with joy. 'Comment vous appelez-vous?' was fired from the hubbub.—'J'm'appelle Jean, moi,' the muscle rapidly answered with sudden solemnity, proudly gazing to left and right as if expecting a challenge to this statement: but when none appeared, it relapsed as suddenly into laughter—as if hugely amused at itself and everyone else including a little and tough boy, whom I had not previously noted, although his entrance had coincided with the muscle's.

Thus into the misère of La Ferté Macé stepped lightly and proudly Jean Le Nègre.

Of all the fine people in La Ferté, Monsieur Jean ('le noir' as he was entitled by his enemies) swaggers in my memory as the finest.

Jean's first act was to complete the distribution (begun, he announced, among the plantons who had escorted him upstairs) of two pockets full of Cubebs. Right and left he gave them up to the last, remarking carelessly, 'J'ne veux, moi.'

Après la soupe (which occurred a few minutes after le noir's entry) B. and I and the greater number of prisoners descended to the cour for our afternoon promenade. The cook spotted us immediately, and desired us to 'catch water'; which we did, three cartfulls of it, earning our usual café sucré. On quitting the cuisine after this delicious repast (which as usual mitigated somewhat the effects of the swill that was our official nutriment) we entered the *cour*. And we noticed at once a well-made figure standing conspicuously by itself, and poring with extraordinary intentness over the pages of a London *Daily Mail* which it was holding upside-down. The reader was culling choice bits of news of a highly sensational nature, and exclaiming from time to time—'*Est-ce vrai! V'la, le roi d'Angleterre est malade. Quelque chose!— Comment? La reine aussi? Bon Dieu! Qu'est-ce que c'est? —Mon père est mort! Merde!—Eh, b'en! La guerre est fini. Bon.*'—It was Jean Le Nègre, playing a little game with himself to beguile the time.

When we had mounted *à la chambre,* two or three tried to talk with this extraordinary personage in French; at which he became very superior and announced: '*J'suis anglais, moi. Parlez anglais. Comprends pas français, moi.*' At this a crowd escorted him over to B. and me—anticipating great deeds in the English language. Jean looked at us critically and said, '*Vous parlez anglais? Moi parlez anglais.*'—'We are Americans, and speak English,' I answered.—'*Moi anglais,*' Jean said. '*Mon père, capitaine de gendarmerie, Londres. Comprends pas français, moi. SPEE-Kingliss*'—he laughed all over himself.

At this display of English on Jean's part the English-speaking Hollanders began laughing. 'The son of a bitch is crazy,' one said.

And from that moment B. and I got on famously with Jean.

His mind was a child's. His use of language was sometimes exalted fibbing, sometimes the purely picturesque. He courted above all the sound of words, more or less disdaining their meaning. He told us immediately (in pidgin-French) that he was born without a mother because his mother died when he was born, that his father was (first) sixteen (then) sixty years old, that his father *gagnait cinq cent francs par jour* (later, *par année*), that he was born in London and not in England, that he was in the French army and had never been in any army.

He did not, however, contradict himself in one statement: '*Les français sont des cochons*'—to which we heartily agreed, and which won him the approval of the Hollanders.

The next day I had my hands full acting as interpreter for '*le noir qui comprend pas français.*' I was summoned from the *cour* to elucidate a great grief which Jean had been unable to explain to the *Gestionnaire*. I mounted with a *planton* to find Jean in hysterics; speechless; his eyes starting out of his head. As nearly as I could make out, Jean had had sixty francs when he arrived, which money he had given to a *planton* upon his arrival, the *planton* having told Jean that he would deposit the money with the *Gestionnaire* in Jean's name (Jean could not write). The *planton* in question, who looked particularly innocent, denied this charge upon my explaining Jean's version; while the *Gestionnaire* puffed and grumbled, disclaiming any connection with the alleged theft and protesting sonorously that he was hearing about Jean's sixty francs for the first time. The *Gestionnaire* shook his thick piggish finger at the book wherein all financial transactions were to be found—from the year one to the present year, month, day, hour and minute (or words to that effect). '*Mais c'est pas là,*' he kept repeating stupidly. The *Surveillant* was uh-ahing at a great rate and attempting to pacify Jean in French. I myself was somewhat fearful for Jean's sanity and highly indignant at the *planton*. The matter ended with the *planton's* being sent about his business; simultaneously with Jean's dismissal to the *cour,* whither I accompanied him. My best efforts to comfort Jean in this matter were quite futile. Like a child who has been unjustly punished he was inconsolable. Great tears welled in his eyes. He kept repeating 'Sees-tee franc —*planton voleur*,' and—absolutely like a child who in anguish calls itself by the name which has been given itself by grown-ups—'steel Jean munee.' To no avail I called the *planton* a *menteur*, a *voleur*, a *fils de chienne* and various other names. Jean felt the wrong itself too keenly to be interested in my denunciation of the mere agent through whom injustice had (as it happened) been consummated.

But—again like an inconsolable child who weeps his heart out when no human comfort avails and wakes the next day without an apparent trace of the recent grief— Jean Le Nègre, in the course of the next twenty-four hours, had completely recovered his normal buoyancy of spirit. The sees-tee franc were gone. A wrong had been done. But that was yesterday. To-day—

And he wandered up and down, joking, laughing, singing:

'*après la guerre fini.*' . . .

In the *cour* Jean was the mecca of all female eyes. Handkerchiefs were waved to him; phrases of the most amorous nature greeted his every appearance. To all these demonstrations he by no means turned a deaf ear; on the contrary, Jean was irrevocably vain. He boasted of having been enormously popular with the girls wherever he went and of having never disdained their admiration. In Paris one day—(and thus it happened that we discovered why *le gouvernement français* had arrested Jean)—

One afternoon, having *rien à faire*, and being flush (owing to his success as a thief, of which vocation he

made a great deal, adding as many ciphers to the amounts
as fancy dictated) Jean happened to cast his eyes in a
store window where were displayed all possible appurtenances for the *militaire*. Vanity was rooted deeply in Jean's
soul. The uniform of an English captain met his eyes.
Without a moment's hesitation he entered the store,
bought the entire uniform, including leather puttees and
belt (of the latter purchase he was especially proud), and
departed. The next store contained a display of medals of
all descriptions. It struck Jean at once that a uniform
would be incomplete without medals. He entered this
store, bought one of every decoration—not forgetting
the Colonial, nor yet the Belgian Cross (which on account
of its size and colour particularly appealed to him)—and
went to his room. There he adjusted the decorations on
the chest of his blouse, donned the uniform, and sallied
importantly forth to capture Paris.

Everywhere he met with success. He was frantically
pursued by women of all stations from *les putains* to *les
princesses*. The police salaamed to him. His arm was
wearied with the returning of innumerable salutes. So far
did his medals carry him that, although on one occasion a
gendarme dared to arrest him for beating in the head of a
fellow English officer (who being a mere lieutenant, should
not have objected to Captain Jean's stealing the affections
of his lady), the *sergent de gendarmerie* before whom Jean
was arraigned on a charge of attempting to kill refused
to even hear the evidence, and dismissed the case with
profuse apologies to the heroic Captain. ' "*Le gouvernement français, Monsieur*, extends to you through me its
profound apology for the insult which your honour has
received." *Ils sont des cochons, les français*,' said Jean, and
laughed throughout his entire body.

Having had the most blue-blooded ladies of the capital cooing upon his heroic chest, having completely beaten up with the full support of the law whosoever of lesser rank attempted to cross his path or refused him the salute—having had 'great fun' saluting generals on *les grands boulevards* and being in turn saluted (*'tous les généraux, tous,* salute me, Jean have more medal'), and this state of affairs having lasted for about three months—Jean began to be very bored (*'me très ennuyé'*). A fit of temper (*'me très fâché'*) arising from this ennui led to a *rixe* with the police, in consequence of which (Jean, though outnumbered three to one, having almost killed one of his assailants) our hero was a second time arrested. This time the authorities went so far as to ask the heroic captain to what branch of the English army he was at present attached; to which Jean first replied, *'Parle pas français, moi,'* and immediately after announced that he was a Lord of the Admiralty, that he had committed robberies in Paris to the tune of sees-meel-i-own franc, that he was a son of the Lord Mayor of London by the Queen, that he had lost a leg in Algeria, and that the French were *cochons.* All of which assertions being duly disproved, Jean was remanded to La Ferté for psychopathic observation and safe keeping on the technical charge of wearing an English officer's uniform.

Jean's particular girl at La Ferté was 'LOO-Loo.' With Lulu it was the same as with *les princesses* in Paris—'me no *travaille, ja MAIS. Les femmes travaillent,* geev Jean mun-ee, sees, sees-tee, see-*cent francs. Jamais travaille, moi.'* Lulu smuggled Jean money; and not for some time did the woman who slept next Lulu miss it. Lulu also sent Jean a lace embroidered handkerchief, which Jean would squeeze and press to his lips with a beatific smile of perfect contentment. The affair with Lulu kept Mexique and Pete the Hollander busy writing letters; which Jean dictated, rolling his eyes and scratching his head for words.

At this time Jean was immensely happy. He was continually playing practical jokes on one of the Hollanders, or Mexique, or the Wanderer, or in fact anyone of whom he was particularly fond. At intervals between these demonstrations of irrepressibility (which kept everyone in a state of laughter) he would stride up and down the filth-sprinkled floor with his hands in the pockets of his stylish jacket, singing at the top of his lungs his own version of the famous song of songs:

> *après la guerre fini,*
> *soldat anglais parti*
> *mademoiselle que je laissai en France*
> *avec des pickaninee. PLENTY!*

and laughing till he shook and had to lean against a wall.

B. and Mexique made some dominoes. Jean had not the least idea of how to play, but when we three had gathered for a game he was always to be found leaning over our shoulders, completely absorbed, once in a while offering us sage advice, laughing utterly when some one made a cinque or a multiple thereof.

One afternoon, in the interval between *la soupe* and promenade, Jean was in especially high spirits. I was lying down on my collapsible bed when he came up to my end of the room and began showing off exactly like a child. This time it was the game of *l'armée française* which Jean was playing.—'*Jamais soldat, moi. Connais toute l'armée française.*' John the Bathman, stretched comfortably in his bunk near me, grunted. '*Tous,*' Jean repeated.—And he stood in front of us; stiff as a stick in imitation of a

French lieutenant with an imaginary company in front of him. First he would be the lieutenant giving commands, then he would be the Army executing them. He began with the manual of arms.

'*Com-pag-nie* . . .' then, as he went through the manual holding his imaginary gun—'htt, htt, htt.'—Then as the officer commending his troops: '*Bon. Très bon. Très bien fait*'—laughing with head thrown back and teeth aglitter at his own success. John Le Baigneur was so tremendously amused that he gave up sleeping to watch. *L'armée* drew a crowd of admirers from every side. For at least three-quarters of an hour this game went on. . . .

Another day Jean, being angry at the weather and having eaten a huge amount of *soupe*, began yelling at the top of his voice '*MERDE à la France*,' and laughing heartily. No one paying especial attention to him, he continued (happy in this new game with himself) for about fifteen minutes. Then The Sheeney With The Trick Raincoat (that undersized specimen, clad in feminine-fitting raiment with flashy shoes), who was by trade a pimp, being about half Jean's height and a tenth of his physique, strolled up to Jean—who had by this time got as far as my bed—and, sticking his sallow face as near Jean's as the neck could reach, said in a solemn voice: '*Il ne faut pas dire ça.*' Jean, astounded, gazed at the intruder for a moment; then demanded, '*Qui dit ça? Moi? Jean? Jamais, ja-MAIS. MERDE à la France!*' nor would he yield a point, backed up as he was by the moral support of every one present except the Sheeney—who found discretion the better part of valour and retired with a few dark threats; leaving Jean master of the situation and yelling for the Sheeney's particular delectation: '*MAY-RRR-DE à la France!*' more loudly than ever.

A little after the epic battle with stovepipes between The Young Pole and Bill the Hollander, the wrecked *poêle* (which was patiently waiting to be repaired) furnished Jean with perhaps his most brilliant inspiration. The final section of pipe (which conducted the smoke through a hole in the wall to the outer air) remained in place all by itself, projecting about six feet into the room at a height of seven or eight feet from the floor. Jean noticed this; got a chair; mounted on it, and by applying alternately his ear and his mouth to the end of the pipe created for himself a telephone, with the aid of which he carried on a conversation with The Wanderer (at that moment visiting his family on the floor below) to this effect:

—Jean, grasping the pipe and speaking angrily into it, being evidently nettled at the poor connection—'Heh-loh, hello, hello, hello'—surveying the pipe in consternation—'*Merde. Ça marche pas*'—trying again with a deep frown—'heh-LOH!'—tremendously agitated—'HEH-LOH!'—a beatific smile supplanting the frown—'hello *Barbu. Est-ce que tu es là? Qui? Bon!*'—evincing tremendous pleasure at having succeeded in establishing the connection satisfactorily—'*Barbu? Est-ce que tu m'écoutes? Qui? Qu'est-ce que c'est Barbu? Comment? Moi? Qui, MOI? JEAN? jaMAIS! jamais, jaMAIS, Barbu. J'ai jamais dit que vous avez des puces. C'était pas moi, tu sais. JaMAIS, c'était un autre. Peut-être c'était Mexique*'—turning his head in Mexique's direction and roaring with laughter—'Hello, HEH-LOH. *Barbu? Tu sais, Barbu, j'ai jamais dit ça. Au contraire, Barbu. J'ai dit que vous avez des totos*'—another roar of laughter—'*Comment? C'est pas vrai? Bon. Alors. Qu'est-ce que vous avez, Barbu? Des poux*—OHHHHHHHHH. *Je comprends. C'est mieux*'—shaking with laughter, then suddenly tre-

mendously serious—'Hellohellohellohello HEHLOH!'—
addressing the stovepipe—'*C'est une mauvaise machine, ça*
—speaking into it with the greatest distinctness—'HEL-
L-LOH. *Barbu? Liberté, Barbu. Oui. Comment? C'est
ça. Liberté pour tou'l'monde. Quand? Après la soupe. Oui.
Liberté pour tou'l'monde après la soupe!*'—to which jest
astonishingly reacted a certain old man known as the
West Indian Negro (a stocky, credulous creature with
whom Jean would have nothing to do, and whose tales
of Brooklyn were indeed outclassed by Jean's *histoires
d'amour*) who leaped rheumatically from his *paillasse* at
the word '*Liberté*' and rushed limpingly hither and thither
inquiring Was it true?—to the enormous and excruciating
amusement of The Enormous Room in general.

After which Jean, exhausted with laughter, descended
from the chair and lay down on his bed to read a letter
from Lulu (not knowing a syllable of it). A little later
he came rushing up to my bed in the most terrific state of
excitement, the whites of his eyes gleaming, his teeth
bared, his kinky hair fairly standing on end, and cried:

'You f— me, me f— you? Pas bon. You f— you, me
f—me:—bon. Me f— me, you f—you!' and went away
capering and shouting with laughter, dancing with great
grace and as great agility and with an imaginary partner
the entire length of the room.

There was another game—a pure child's game—which
Jean played. It was the name game. He amused himself
for hours together by lying on his *paillasse*, tilting his head
back, rolling up his eyes, and crying in a high quavering
voice—'JAW-neeeeeee.' After a repetition or two of his
own name in English, he would demand sharply '*Qui
m'appelle? Mexique? Est-ce que tu m'appelle,* Mexique?'
and if Mexique happened to be asleep, Jean would rush

over and cry in his ear shaking him thoroughly—*'Est-ce
tu m'appelle, toi?'* Or it might be *Barbu*, or Pete the Hollander, or B. or myself, of whom he sternly asked the
question—which was always followed by quantities of
laughter on Jean's part. He was never perfectly happy
unless exercising his inexhaustible imagination. . . .

Of all Jean's extraordinary selves, the moral one was at
once the most rare and most unreasonable. In the matter
of *les femmes* he could hardly have been accused by his
bitterest enemy of being a Puritan. Yet the Puritan streak
came out one day, in a discussion which lasted for several
hours. Jean, as in the case of France, spoke in dogma. His
contention was very simple: *'La femme qui fume n'est
pas une femme.'* He defended it hotly against the attacks
of all the nations represented; in vain did Belgian and
Hollander, Russian and Pole, Spaniard and Alsatian,
charge and counter-charge—Jean remained unshaken. A
woman could do anything but smoke—if she smoked she
ceased automatically to be a woman and became something unspeakable. As Jean was at this time sitting alternately on B.'s bed and mine, and as the alternations became
increasingly frequent as the discussion waxed hotter, we
were not sorry when the *planton's* shout, *'A la promenade
les hommes!'* scattered the opposing warriors. Then up
leaped Jean (who had almost come to blows innumerable
times) and rushed laughing to the door, having already
forgotten the whole thing.

Now we come to the story of Jean's undoing, and may
the gods which made Jean Le Nègre give me grace to tell
it as it was.

The trouble started with Lulu. One afternoon, shortly
after the telephoning, Jean was sick at heart and couldn't
be induced either to leave his couch or to utter a word.

Every one guessed the reason—Lulu had left for another camp that morning. The *planton* told Jean to come down with the rest and get *soupe*. No answer. Was Jean sick? '*Oui*, me seek.' And steadfastly he refused to eat, till the disgusted *planton* gave it up and locked Jean in alone. When we ascended after *la soupe* we found Jean as we had left him, stretched on his couch, big tears on his cheeks. I asked him if I could do anything for him; he shook his head. We offered him cigarettes—no, he did not wish to smoke. As B. and I went away we heard him moaning to himself, 'Jawnee no see Loo-Loo no more.' With the exception of ourselves, the inhabitants of La Ferté Macé took Jean's desolation as a great joke. Shouts of Lulu! rent the welkin on all sides. Jean stood it for an hour; then he leaped up, furious; and demanded (confronting the man from whose lips the cry had last issued)—'Feeneesh Loo-Loo?" The latter coolly referred him to the man next to him; he in turn to some one else; and round and round the room Jean stalked, seeking the offender, followed by louder and louder shouts of Lulu! and Jawnee! the authors of which (so soon as he challenged them) denied with innocent faces their guilt and recommended that Jean look closer next time. At last Jean took to his couch in utter misery and disgust.—The rest of *les hommes* descended as usual for the promenade—not so Jean. He ate nothing for supper. That evening not a sound issued from his bed.

Next morning he awoke with a broad grin, and to the salutations of Lulu! replied, laughing heartily at himself, 'FEENEESH LooLoo.' Upon which the tormentors (finding in him no longer a victim) desisted; and things resumed their normal course. If an occasional Lulu! upraised itself, Jean merely laughed, and repeated (with a wave of his arm) 'FEENEESH.' Finished Lulu seemed to be.

But *un jour* I had remained upstairs during the promenade, both because I wanted to write and because the weather was worse than usual. Ordinarily, no matter how deep the mud in the *cour,* Jean and I would trot back and forth, resting from time to time under the little shelter out of the drizzle, talking of all things under the sun. I remember on one occasion we were the only ones to brave the rain and slough—Jean in paper-thin soled slippers (which he had recently succeeded in drawing from the *Gestionnaire*) and I in my huge sabots—hurrying back and forth with the rain pouring on us, and he very proud. On this day, however, I refused the challenge of the *boue.*

The promenaders had been singularly noisy, I thought. Now they were mounting to the room making a truly tremendous racket. No sooner were the doors opened than in rushed half a dozen frenzied friends, who began telling me all at once about a terrific thing which my friend the *noir* had just done. It seems that The Sheeney With The Trick Raincoat had pulled at Jean's handkerchief (Lulu's gift in other days) which Jean wore always conspicuously in his outside breast pocket; that Jean had taken the Sheeney's head in his two hands, held it steady, abased his own head, and rammed the helpless Sheeney as a bull would do—the impact of Jean's head upon the Sheeney's nose causing that well-known feature to occupy a new position in the neighbourhood of the right ear. B. corroborated this description, adding the Sheeney's nose was broken and that everyone was down on Jean for fighting in an unsportsmanlike way. I found Jean still very angry, and moreover very hurt because every one was now shunning him. I told him that I personally was glad of what he'd done; but nothing would cheer him up. The Sheeney now entered, very terrible to see, having been patched up by Monsieur Richard with copious plasters. His nose was not broken, he said thickly, but only bent. He hinted darkly of trouble in store for *le noir;* and received the commiserations of everyone present except Mexique, The Zulu, B. and me. The Zulu, I remember, pointed to his own nose (which was not unimportant), then to Jean, then made a *moue* of excruciating anguish, and winked audibly.

Jean's spirit was broken. The wellnigh unanimous verdict against him had convinced his minutely sensitive soul that it had done wrong. He lay quietly, and would say nothing to anyone.

Some time after the soup, about eight o'clock, The Fighting Sheeney and The Trick Raincoat suddenly set upon Jean Le Nègre à propos nothing; and began pommelling him cruelly. The conscience-stricken pillar of beautiful muscle—who could have easily killed both his assailants at one blow—not only offered no reciprocatory violence but refused even to defend himself. Unresistingly, wincing with pain, his arms mechanically raised and his head bent, he was battered frightfully to the window by his bed, thence into the corner (upsetting the stool in the *pissoir*), thence along the wall to the door. As the punishment increased he cried out like a child: '*Laissez-moi tranquille!*'—again and again; and in his voice the insane element gained rapidly. Finally, shrieking in agony, he rushed to the nearest window; and while the Sheeneys together pommelled him yelled for help to the *planton* beneath.—

The unparalleled consternation and applause produced by this one-sided battle had long since alarmed the authorities. I was still trying to break through the five-deep ring of spectators—among whom was The Messenger Boy, who advised me to desist and got a piece of advice in return—when with a tremendous crash open burst the door, and in stepped four *plantons* with drawn revolvers, looking frightened to death, followed by the *Surveillant* who carried a sort of baton and was crying faintly: '*Qu'est-ce que c'est!*'

At the first sound of the door the two Sheeneys had fled, and were now playing the part of innocent spectators. Jean alone occupied the stage. His lips were parted. His eyes were enormous. He was panting as if his heart would break. He still kept his arms raised as if seeing everywhere before him fresh enemies. Blood spotted here and there the wonderful chocolate carpet of his skin, and his whole body glistened with sweat. His shirt was in ribbons over his beautiful muscles.

Seven or eight persons at once began explaining the fight to the *Surveillant*, who could make nothing out of their accounts and therefore called aside a trusted older man in order to get his version. The two retired from the room. The *plantons*, finding the expected wolf a lamb, flourished their revolvers about Jean and threatened him in the insignificant and vile language which *plantons* use to anyone whom they can bully. Jean kept repeating dully, '*Laissez-moi tranquille. Ils voulaient me tuer.*' His chest shook terribly with vast sobs.

Now the *Surveillant* returned and made a speech, to the effect that he had received independently of each other the stories of four men, that by all counts *le nègre* was absolutely to blame, that *le nègre* had caused an inexcusable trouble to the authorities and to his fellow-prisoners by this wholly unjustified conflict, and that as a punishment the *nègre* would now suffer the consequences of his guilt in the *cabinot*.—Jean had dropped his arms to his sides. His face was twisted with anguish. He made a child's gesture, a pitiful hopeless movement with his slender hands. Sobbing, he protested: '*C'est pas ma faute, monsieur le surveillant! Ils m'attaquaient! J'ai rien fait! Ils voulaient me tuer! Demandez à lui*'—he pointed to me desperately. Before I could utter a syllable the *Surveillant* raised his hand for silence: *le nègre* had done wrong. He should be placed in the *cabinot*.

—Like a flash, with a horrible tearing sob, Jean leaped from the surrounding *plantons* and rushed for the coat which lay on his bed screaming—'AHHHHH—*mon couteau!*'—'Look out or he'll get his knife and kill himself!' some one yelled; and the four *plantons* seized Jean by both arms just as he made a grab for his jacket. Thwarted in this hope and burning with the ignominy of his situation, Jean cast his enormous eyes up at the nearest pillar, crying hysterically: '*Tout le monde me fout au cabinot parce que je suis noir.*'—In a second, by a single movement of his arms, he sent the four *plantons* reeling to a distance of ten feet; leaped at the pillar: seized it in both hands like a Samson, and (gazing for another second with a smile of absolute beatitude at its length) dashed his head against it. Once, twice, thrice he smote himself, before the *plantons* seized him—and suddenly his whole strength wilted; he allowed himself to be overpowered by them and stood with bowed head, tears streaming from his eyes—while the smallest pointed a revolver at his heart.

This was a little more than the *Surveillant* had counted on. Now that Jean's might was no more, the bearer of the *croix de guerre* stepped forward and in a mild placating

voice endeavoured to soothe the victim of his injustice.
It was also slightly more than I could stand, and slamming
aside the spectators I shoved myself under his honour's
nose. 'Do you know,' I asked, 'whom you are dealing with
in this man? A child. There are a lot of Jeans where I
come from. You heard what he said? He is black, is he
not, and gets no justice from you. You heard that. I saw
the whole affair. He was attacked, he put up no resistance
whatever, he was beaten by two cowards. He is no more
to blame than I am.—The *Surveillant* was waving his
wand and cooing, '*Je comprends, je comprends, c'est malheureux.*'—'You're god damn right it's *malheureux*,' I
said, forgetting my French. '*Quand même*, he has resisted
authority.' The *Surveillant* gently continued: 'Now, Jean,
be quiet, you will be taken to the *cabinot*. You may as well
go quietly and behave yourself like a good boy.'

At this I am sure my eyes started out of my head. All
I could think of to say was: '*Attends, un petit moment.*'
To reach my own bed took but a second. In another second I was back, bearing my great and sacred pelisse. I
marched up to Jean. 'Jean,' I remarked with a smile, '*tu
vas au cabinot, mais tu vas revenir tout de suite. Je sais
bien que tu as parfaitement raison. Mets cela*'—and I
pushed him gently into my coat. '*Voici mes cigarettes,
Jean; tu peux fumer comme tu veux*'—I pulled out all I
had, one full *paquet jaune* of Marylands and half a dozen
loose ones, and deposited them carefully in the right-hand
pocket of the pelisse. Then I patted him on the shoulder
and gave him the immortal salutation—'*Bonne chance,
mon ami!*'

He straightened proudly. He stalked like a king through
the doorway. The astounded *plantons* and the embarrassed

Surveillant followed, the latter closing the doors behind him. I was left with a cloud of angry witnesses.

An hour later the doors opened, Jean entered quietly, and the doors shut. As I lay on my bed I could see him perfectly. He was almost naked. He laid my pelisse on his mattress, then walked calmly up to a neighbouring bed and skilfully and unerringly extracted a brush from under it. Back to his own bed he tiptoed, sat down on it, and began brushing my coat. He brushed it for a half-hour, speaking to no one, spoken to by no one. Finally he put the brush back, disposed the pelisse carefully on his arm, came to my bed, and as carefully laid it down. Then he took from the right-hand outside pocket a full *paquet jaune* and six loose cigarettes, showed them for my approval, and returned them to their place. *'Merci,'* was his sole remark. B. got Jean to sit down beside him on his bed and we talked for a few minutes, avoiding the subject of the recent struggle. Then Jean went back to his own bed and lay down.

It was not till later that we learned the climax—not till *le petit belge avec le bras cassé, le petit balayeur,* came hurrying to our end of the room and sat down with us. He was bursting with excitement, his well arm jerked and his sick one stumped about and he seemed incapable of speech. At length words came.

'Monsieur Jean' (now that I think of it, I believe some one had told him that all male children in America are named Jean at their birth) *'j'ai vu QUELQUE CHOSE! le nègre, vous savez?—il est FORT! Monsieur Jean, c'est un GÉANT, croyez moi! C'est pas un homme, tu sais? Je l'ai vu, moi'*—and he indicated his eyes.

We pricked our ears.

The *balayeur*, stuffing a pipe nervously with his tiny

thumb said: 'You saw the fight up here? So did I. The whole of it. *Le noir avait raison.* Well, when they took him downstairs, I slipped out too—*Je suis le balayeur, savez-vous?* and the *balayeur* can go where other people can't.'

—I gave him a match, and he thanked me. He struck it on his trousers with a quick pompous gesture, drew heavily on his squeaky pipe, and at last shot a minute puff of smoke into the air; then another, and another. Satisfied, he went on; his good hand grasping the pipe between its index and second fingers and resting on one little knee, his legs crossed, his small body hunched forward, wee unshaven face close to mine—went on in the confidential tone of one who relates an unbelievable miracle to a couple of intimate friends:

'Monsieur Jean, I followed. They got him to the *cabinot.* The door stood open. At this moment *les femmes descendaient,* it was their *corvée d'eau, vous savez.* He saw them, *le noir.* One of them cried from the stairs, Is a Frenchman stronger than you, Jean? The *plantons* were standing around him, the *Surveillant* was behind. He took the nearest *planton,* and tossed him down the corridor so that he struck against the door at the end of it. He picked up two more, one in each arm, and threw them away. They fell on top of the first. The last tried to take hold of Jean, and so Jean took him by the neck'—(the *balayeur* strangled himself for our benefit)—'and that *planton* knocked down the other three, who had got on their feet by this time. You should have seen the *Surveillant.* He had run away and was saying, "Capture him, capture him." The *plantons* rushed Jean; all four of them. He caught them as they came and threw them about. One knocked down the *Surveillant.* The *femmes* cried "*Vive, Jean,*" and clapped their hands. The *Surveillant* called to the *plantons* to take Jean, but they wouldn't go near Jean; they said he was a black devil. The women kidded them. They were so sore. And they could do nothing. Jean was laughing. His shirt was almost off him. He asked the *plantons* to come and take him, please. He asked the *Surveillant,* too. The women had set down their pails and were dancing up and down and yelling. The *Directeur* came down and sent them flying. The *Surveillant* and his *plantons* were as helpless as if they had been children. Monsieur Jean—*quelque chose.*'

I gave him another match. '*Merci,* Monsieur Jean.' He struck it, drew on his pipe, lowered it, and went on:

'They were helpless, and men. I am little. I have only one arm, *tu sais.* I walked up to Jean and said, "Jean, you know me, I am your friend." He said, "Yes." I said to the *plantons,* "Give me that rope." They gave me the rope that they would have bound him with. He put out his wrists for me. I tied his hands behind his back. He was like a lamb. The *plantons* rushed up and tied his feet together. Then they tied his hands and feet together. They took the lacings out of his shoes for fear he would use them to strangle himself. They stood him up in an angle between two walls in the *cabinot.* They left him there for an hour. He was supposed to have been in there all night; but The *Surveillant* knew that he would have died, for he was almost naked, and *vous savez,* Monsieur Jean, it was cold in there. And damp. A fully-clothed man would have been dead in the morning. And he was naked . . . Monsieur Jean—*un géant!*'

—This same *petit belge* had frequently protested to me that *Il est fou, le noir.* He is always playing when sensible men try to sleep. The last few hours (which had made

of the *fou* a *géant*) made of the scoffer a worshipper. Nor
did *'le bras cassé'* ever from that time forth desert his
divinity. If as *balayeur* he could lay hands on a *morceau de
pain* or *de viande*, he bore it as before to our beds; but
Jean was always called over to partake of the forbidden
pleasure.

As for Jean, one would hardly have recognized him. It
was as if the child had fled into the deeps of his soul, never
to reappear. Day after day went by, and Jean (instead of
courting excitement as before) cloistered himself in soli-
tude; or at most sought the company of B. and me and
Le Petit Belge for a quiet chat or a cigarette. The morning after the three fights he did not appear in the *cour* for
early promenade along with the rest of us (including The
Sheeneys). In vain did *les femmes* strain their necks and
eyes to find the *noir qui était plus fort que six français*.
And B. and I noticed our bed-clothing airing upon the
windowsills. When we mounted, Jean was patting and
straightening our blankets, and looking for the first time
in his life guilty of some enormous crime. Nothing however had disappeared. Jean said, 'Me feeks, *lits tous les
jours.*' And every morning he aired and made our beds
for us, and we mounted to find him smoothing affection-
ately some final ruffle, obliterating with enormous solemnity some microscopic crease. We gave him cigarettes
when he asked for them (which was almost never) and
offered them when we knew he had none or when we saw
him borrowing from some one else whom his spirit held
in less esteem. Of us he asked no favours. He liked us too
well.

When B. went away, Jean was almost as desolate as I.

About a fortnight later, when the grey dirty snow-
slush hid the black filthy world which we saw from our

windows, and when people lived in their ill-smelling beds, it came to pass that my particular *amis*—The Zulu, Jean, Mexique—and I and all the remaining miserables of La Ferté descended at the decree of Cæsar Augustus to endure our bi-weekly *bain*. I remember gazing stupidly at Jean's chocolate-coloured nakedness as it strode to the tub, a rippling texture of muscular miracle. *Tout le monde* had *baigné* (including The Zulu, who tried to escape at the last minute and was nabbed by the *planton* whose business it was to count heads and see that none escaped the ordeal) and now *tout le monde* was shivering all together in the ante-room, begging to be allowed to go upstairs and get into bed—when *Le Baigneur*, Monsieur Richard's strenuous successor that is, set up a hue and cry that one *serviette* was lacking. The Fencer was sent for. He entered; heard the case; and made a speech. If the guilty party would immediately return the stolen towel, he, The Fencer, would guarantee that party pardon; if not, everyone present should be searched, and the man on whose person the *serviette* was found *va attraper quinze jours de cabinot*. This eloquence yielding no results, The Fencer exhorted the culprit to act like a man and render to Cæsar what is Cæsar's. Nothing happened. Everyone was told to get in single file and make ready to pass out the door. One after one we were searched; but so general was the curiosity that as fast as they were inspected the erstwhile bed-enthusiasts, myself included, gathered on the side-lines to watch their fellows instead of availing themselves of the opportunity to go upstairs. One after one we came opposite The Fencer, held up our arms, had our pockets run through and our clothing felt over from head to heel, and were exonerated. When Cæsar came to Jean, Cæsar's eyes lighted, and Cæsar's hitherto perfunctory proddings and pokings became inspired and methodical. Twice he went over Jean's entire body, while Jean, his arms raised in a bored gesture, his face completely expressionless, suffered loftily the examination of his person. A third time the desperate Fencer tried; his hands, starting at Jean's neck, reached the calf of his leg —and stopped. The hands rolled up Jean's right trouser leg to the knee. They rolled up the underwear on his leg —and there, placed perfectly flat to the skin, appeared the missing *serviette*. As The Fencer seized it, Jean laughed— the utter laughter of old days—and the onlookers cackled uproariously, while with a broad smile The Fencer proclaimed: 'I thought I knew where I should find it.' And he added, more pleased with himself than anyone had ever seen him—'*Maintenant, vous pouvez tous monter à la chambre.*' We mounted, happy to get back to bed; but none so happy as Jean le Nègre. It was not that the *cabinot* threat had failed to materialize—at any minute a *planton* might call Jean to his punishment: indeed this was what everyone expected. It was that the incident had absolutely removed that inhibition which (from the day when Jean *le noir* became Jean *le géant*) had held the child, which was Jean's soul and destiny, prisoner. From that instant till the day I left him he was the old Jean—joking, fibbing, laughing, and always playing—Jean L'Enfant.

And I think of Jean Le Nègre ... you are something to dream over, Jean; summer and winter (birds and darkness) you go walking into my head; you are a sudden and chocolate-coloured thing, in your hands you have a habit of holding six or eight *plantons* (which you are about to throw away) and the flesh of your body is like the flesh of a very deep cigar. Which I am still and always quietly smoking: always and still I am inhaling its very fragrant and remarkable muscles. But I doubt if ever I am quite through with you, if ever I will toss you out of my heart into the sawdust of forgetfulness. Kid, Boy, I'd like to tell you: *la guerre est finie*.

O yes, Jean: I do not forget, I remember Plenty; the snow's coming, the snow will throw again a very big and gentle shadow into The Enormous Room and into the eyes of you and me walking always and wonderfully up and down. . . .

—Boy, Kid, Nigger with the strutting muscles—take me up into your mind once or twice before I die (you know why: just because the eyes of me and you will be full of dirt some day). Quickly take me up into the bright child of your mind, before we both go suddenly all loose and silly (you know how it will feel). Take me up (carefully; as if I were a toy) and play carefully with me, once or twice, before I and you go suddenly all limp and foolish. Once or twice before you go into great Jack roses and ivory—(once or twice Boy before we together go wonderfully down into the Big Dirt laughing, bumped with the last darkness).

XII

THREE WISE MEN

It must have been late in November when *la commission* arrived. *La commission*, as I have said, visited La Ferté *tous les trois mois*. That is to say B. and I (by arriving when we did) had just escaped its clutches. I consider this one of the luckiest things in my life.

La commission arrived one morning, and began work immediately.

A list was made of *les hommes* who were to pass *la commission*, another of *les femmes*. These lists were given to the *planton* with The Wooden Hand. In order to avert any delay, those of *les hommes* whose names fell in the first half of the list were not allowed to enjoy the usual stimulating activities afforded by La Ferté's supreme environment: they were, in fact, confined to The Enormous Room, subject to instant call—moreover they were not called one by one, or as their respective turns came, but in groups of three or four; the idea being that *la commission* should suffer no smallest annoyance which might be occasioned by loss of time. There were always, in other words, eight or ten men waiting in the upper corridor opposite a disagreeably crisp door, which door belonged to that mysterious room wherein *la commission* transacted its inestimable affairs. Not more than a couple of yards away ten or eight women waited their turns. Conversation between *les hommes* and *les femmes* had been forbidden in the fiercest terms by *Monsieur le Directeur*:

nevertheless conversation spasmodically occurred, thanks
to the indulgent nature of The Wooden Hand. The
Wooden Hand must have been cuckoo—he looked it. If
he wasn't I am totally at a loss to account for his in-
dulgence.

B. and I spent a morning in The Enormous Room without results, an astonishing acquisition of nervousness excepted. *Après la soupe* (noon) we were conducted *en
haut,* told to leave our spoons and bread (which we did)
and—in company with several others whose names were
within a furlong of the last man called—were descended
to the corridor. All that afternoon we waited. Also we
waited all next morning. We spent our time talking
quietly with a buxom, pink-cheeked Belgian girl who was
in attendance as translator for one of *les femmes.* This
Belgian told us that she was a permanent inhabitant of
La Ferté, that she and another *femme honnête* occupied
a room by themselves, that her brothers were at the front
in Belgium, that her ability to speak fluently several languages (including English and German) made her
invaluable to *Messieurs la commission,* that she had committed no crime, that she was held as a *suspecte,* that she
was not entirely unhappy. She struck me immediately as
being not only intelligent but alive. She questioned us in
excellent English as to our offences, and seemed much
pleased to discover that we were—to all appearances—
innocent of wrong-doing.

From time to time our subdued conversation was interrupted by admonitions from the amiable Wooden Hand.
Twice the door SLAMMED open, and *Monsieur le Directeur* bounced out frothing at the mouth and threatening
everyone with infinite *cabinot,* on the ground that everyone's deportment or lack of it was menacing the aplomb

of the commissioners. Each time The Black Holster appeared in the background and carried on his master's bullying until everyone was completely terrified—after which we were left to ourselves and The Wooden Hand once again.

B. and I were allowed by the latter individual—he was that day, at least, an individual and not merely a *planton* —to peek over his shoulder at the men's list. The Wooden Hand even went so far as to escort our seditious minds to the nearness of their examination by the simple yet efficient method of placing one of his human fingers opposite the name of him who was (even at that moment) within, submitting to the inexorable justice of *le gouvernement français.* I cannot honestly say that the discovery of this proximity of ourselves to our respective fates wholly pleased us; yet we were so weary of waiting that it certainly did not wholly terrify us. All in all, I think I have never been so utterly un-at-ease as while waiting for the axe to fall, metaphorically speaking, upon our squawking heads.

We were still conversing with the Belgian girl when a man came out of the door unsteadily, looking as if he had submitted to several strenuous fittings of a wooden leg upon a stump not quite healed. The Wooden Hand, nodding at B., remarked hurriedly in a low voice:

'*Allez!*'

And B. (smiling at *La Belge* and at me) entered. He was followed by The Wooden Hand, as I suppose for greater security.

The next twenty minutes or whatever it was were by far the most nerve-racking which I had as yet experienced. *La Belge* said to me:

'*Il est gentil, votre ami,*'

and I agreed. And my blood was bombarding the roots of
my toes and the summits of my hair.

After (I need not say) two or three million æons, B.
emerged. I had not time to exchange a look with him—let
alone a word—for The Wooden Hand said from the doorway:

'*Allez, l'autre américain,*'
and I entered in more confusion than can easily be imagined; entered the torture chamber, entered the inquisi-
tion, entered the tentacles of that sly and beaming polyp,
le gouvernement français. . . .

As I entered I said, half-aloud: The thing is this, to look
'em in the eyes and keep cool whatever happens, not for
the fraction of a moment forgetting that they are made
of *merde,* that they are all of them composed entirely of
merde—I don't know how many inquisitors I expected
to see; but I guess I was ready for at least fifteen, among
them President Poincaré lui-même. I hummed noiselessly:

'si vous passez par ma vil-le
n'oubliez pas ma maison:
on y mange de bonne sou-pe Ton Ton Tay-ne;
faite de merde et des onions, Ton Ton Tayne Ton Ton
Ton,'

remembering the fine *forgeron* of Chevancourt who used
to sing this, or something very like it, upon a table.—Entirely for the benefit of *les deux américains,* who would
subsequently render 'Eats uh lonje wae to Tee-pear-raer-
ee,' wholly for the gratification of a roomful of what Mr.
A. liked to call 'them bastards,' alias 'dirty' Frenchmen,
alias *les poilus, les poilus divins.* . . .

A little room. The *Directeur's* office? Or the *Surveillant's?* Comfort. O yes, very, very comfortable. On my

right a table. At the table three persons. Reminds me of
Noyon a bit, not unpleasantly of course. Three persons:
reading from left to right as I face them—a soggy, sleepy,
slumpy lump in a gendarme's cape and cap, quite old,
captain of gendarmes, not at all interested, wrinkled
coarse face, only semi-*méchant*, large hard clumsy hands
floppingly disposed on table; wily, tidy man in civilian
clothes, pen in hand, obviously lawyer, *avocat* type, little
bald on top, sneaky civility, smells of bad perfume or at
any rate sweetish soap; tiny red-headed person, also civilian, creased, worrying, excited face, amusing little body
and hands, brief and jumpy, must be a Dickens character,
ought to spend his time sailing kites of his own construction over other people's houses in gusty weather. Behind
the Three, all tied up with deference and inferiority, mild
and spineless, Apollyon.

Would the reader like to know what I was asked?

Ah, would I could say! Only dimly do I remember those
moments—only dimly do I remember looking through
the lawyer at Apollyon's clean collar—only dimly do I
remember the gradual collapse of the *capitaine de gendarmerie,* his slow but sure assumption of sleepfulness, the
drooping of his soggy *tête de cochon* lower and lower till
it encountered one hand whose elbow, braced firmly
upon the table, sustained its insensate limpness—only
dimly do I remember the enthusiastic antics of the little
red-head when I spoke with patriotic fervour of the
wrongs which La France was doing *mon ami et moi*—
only dimly do I remember, to my right, the immobility
of The Wooden Hand, reminding one of a clothing-
dummy, or a life-size doll which might be made to move
only by him who knew the proper combination. . . . At
the outset I was asked: Did I want a translator? I looked

and saw the *secrétaire*, weak-eyed and lemon-pale, and I said 'Non.' I was questioned mostly by the *avocat*, somewhat by the Dickens, never by either the captain (who was asleep) or The *Directeur* (who was timid in the presence of these great and good delegates of hope, faith, and charity per the French Government). I recall that, for some reason, I was perfectly cool. I put over six or eight hot shots without losing in the least this composure, which surprised myself and pleased myself and altogether increased myself. As the questions came for me I met them half-way, spouting my best or worst French in a manner which positively astonished the tiny red-headed demigod. I challenged with my eyes and with my voice and with my manner Apollyon Himself, and Apollyon Himself merely cuddled together, depressing his hairy body between its limbs as a spider sometimes does in the presence of danger. I expressed immense gratitude to my captors and to *le gouvernement français* for allowing me to see and hear and taste and smell and touch the things which inhabited La Ferté Macé, Orne, France. I do not think that *la commission* enjoyed me much. It told me, through its sweetish-soap-leader, that my friend was a criminal—this immediately upon my entering—and I told it with a great deal of well-chosen politeness that I disagreed. In telling how and why I disagreed I think I managed to shove my shovel-shaped imagination under the refuse of their intellects. At least once or twice.

Rather fatiguing—to stand up and be told: Your friend is no good; have you anything to say for yourself?—And to say a great deal for yourself and for your friend and for *les hommes*—or try your best to—and be contradicted, and be told 'Never mind that, what we wish to know is,' and instructed to keep to the subject; et cetera, ad infinitum. At last they asked each other if each other wanted to ask the man before each other anything more, and each other not wanting to do so, they said:

'*C'est fini.*'

As at Noyon, I had made an indisputably favourable impression upon exactly one of my three examiners. I refer, in the present case, to the red-headed little gentleman who was rather decent to me. I do not exactly salute him in recognition of this decency; I bow to him, as I might bow to somebody who said he was sorry he couldn't give me a match but there was a cigar-store just around the corner you know.

At '*C'est fini,*' The *Directeur* leaped into the lime-light with a savage admonition to The Wooden Hand—who saluted, opened the door suddenly, and looked at me with (dare I say it?) admiration. Instead of availing myself of this means of escape I turned to the little kite-flying gentleman and said:

'If you please, sir, will you be so good as to tell me what will become of my friend?'

The little kite-flying gentleman did not have time to reply, for the perfumed presence stated drily and distinctly:

'We cannot say anything to you upon that point.'

I gave him a pleasant smile which said, If I could see your intestines very slowly embracing a large wooden drum rotated by means of a small iron crank turned gently and softly by myself, I should be extraordinarily happy —and I bowed softly and gently to *Monsieur le Directeur* and I went through the door using all the perpendicular inches which God had given me.

Once outside I began to tremble like a *peuplier* in *l'automne* .. '*L'automne humide et monotone.*'

—'*Allez en bas, pour la soupe,*' The Wooden Hand said not unkindly. I looked about me. 'There will be no more men before the commission until to-morrow,' The Wooden Hand said. 'Go get your dinner in the kitchen.'

I descended.

Afrique was all curiosity—what did they say? what did I say?—as he placed before me a huge, a perfectly huge, an inexcusably huge plate of something more than lukewarm grease. . . . B. and I ate at a very little table in *la cuisine,* excitedly comparing notes as we swallowed the red-hot stuff. . . . '*Du pain; prenez, mes amis,*' Afrique said. '*Mangez comme vous voulez,*' the Cook quoth benignantly, with a glance at us over his placid shoulder. . . . Eat we most surely did. We could have eaten the French Government.

The morning of the following day we went on promenade once more. It was neither pleasant nor unpleasant to promenade in the *cour* while somebody else was suffering in the Room of Sorrow. It was, in fact, rather thrilling.

The afternoon of this day we were all up in The Enormous Room when *la commission* suddenly entered with Apollyon strutting and lisping behind it, explaining, and poohpoohing, and graciously waving his thick wicked arms.

Everyone in The Enormous Room leaped to his feet, removing as he did so his hat—with the exception of *les deux américains,* who kept theirs on, and The Zulu, who couldn't find his hat and had been trying for some time to stalk it to its lair. *La commission* reacted interestingly to The Enormous Room: the captain of gendarmes looked soggily around and saw nothing with a good deal of contempt; the scented soap squinted up his face and said 'Faugh' or whatever a French bourgeois *avocat* says in the presence of a bad smell (*la commission* was standing by the door and consequently close to the *cabinet*); but the little red-head kite-flying gentleman looked actually horrified.

'Is there in the room anyone of Austrian nationality?'
The Silent Man stepped forward quietly.

'Why are you here?'

'I don't know,' The Silent Man said, with tears in his eyes.

'NONSENSE! You're here for a very good reason and you know what it is and you could tell it if you wished, you imbecile, you incorrigible, you criminal,' Apollyon shouted; then, turning to the *avocat* and the red-headed little gentleman, 'He is a dangerous alien, he admits it, he has admitted it—DON'T YOU ADMIT IT, EH? EH?' he roared at The Silent Man, who fingered his black cap without raising his eyes or changing in the least the simple and supreme dignity of his poise. 'He is incorrigible,' said (in a low snarl) The *Directeur*. 'Let us go, gentlemen, when you have seen enough.' But the red-headed man, as I recollect, was contemplating the floor by the door, where six pails of urine solemnly stood, three of them having overflowed slightly from time to time upon the reeking planks. . . . And The *Directeur* was told that *les hommes* should have a tin trough to urinate into, for the sake of sanitation; and that this trough should be immediately installed, installed without delay—'O yes indeed, sirs,' Apollyon simpered, 'a very good suggestion; it shall be done immediately; yes indeed. Do let me show you the—it's just outside—' and he bowed them out with no little skill. And the door SLAMMED behind Apollyon and the Three Wise Men.

This, as I say, must have occurred toward the last of November.

For a week we waited.

Jan had already left us. Fritz, having waited months for a letter from the Danish consul in reply to the letters which he, Fritz, wrote every so often and sent through *le bureau*—meaning the *secrétaire*—had managed to get news of his whereabouts to said consul by unlawful means; and was immediately, upon reception of this news by the consul, set free and invited to join a ship at the nearest port. His departure (than which a more joyous I have never witnessed) has been already mentioned in connection with the third Delectable Mountain, as has been the departure for Précigné of Pompom and Harree ensemble. Bill the Hollander, Monsieur Pet-airs, Mexique, The Wanderer, The little Machine-Fixer, Pete, Jean le Nègre, The Zulu and Monsieur Auguste (second time) were some of our remaining friends who passed the commission with us. Along with ourselves and these fine people were judged gentlemen like The Trick Raincoat and The Fighting Sheeney. One would think, possibly, that Justice— in the guise of the Three Wise Men—would have decreed different fates, to (say) The Wanderer and The Fighting Sheeney. *Au contraire.* As I have previously remarked, the ways of God and of the good and great French Government are alike inscrutable.

Bill the Hollander, whom we had grown to like whereas at first we were inclined to fear him, Bill the Hollander who washed some towels and handkerchiefs and what-nots for us and turned them a bright pink, Bill the Hollander who had tried so hard to teach The Young Pole the lesson which he could only learn from The Fighting Sheeney, left us about a week after *la commission.* As I understand it, they decided to send him back to Holland under guard in order that he might be jailed in his native land as a

deserter. It is beautiful to consider the unselfishness of
le gouvernement français in this case. Much as *le gouvernement français* would have liked to have punished Bill
on its own account and for its own enjoyment, it gave him
up—with a Christian smile—to the punishing clutches of
a sister or brother government: without a murmur denying itself the incense of his sufferings and the music of
his sorrows. Then too it is really inspiring to note the perfect collaboration of *la justice française* and *la justice hol-
landaise* in a critical moment of the world's history. Bill
certainly should feel that it was a great honour to be
allowed to exemplify this wonderful accord, this exquisite
mutual understanding, between the punitive departments
of two nations superficially somewhat unrelated—that is,
as regards customs and language. I fear Bill didn't appreciate the intrinsic usefulness of his destiny. I seem to
remember that he left in a rather Gottverdummerish
condition. Such is ignorance.

Poor Monsieur Pet-airs came out of the commission
looking extraordinarily *épaté*. Questioned, he averred that
his penchant for inventing force-pumps had prejudiced
ces messieurs in his disfavour; and shook his poor old head
and sniffed hopelessly. Mexique exited in a placidly cheerful condition, shrugging his shoulders and remarking:

"I no do nut'ing. Dese fellers tell me wait few days,
after you go free,' whereas Pete looked white and determined and said little—except in Dutch to The Young
Skipper and his mate; which pair took *la commission* more
or less as a healthy bull-calf takes nourishment: there was
little doubt that they would refind *la liberté* in a short
while, judging from the inability of the Three Wise Men
to prove them even suspicious characters. The Zulu
uttered a few inscrutable gestures made entirely of silence

and said he would like us to celebrate the accomplishment
of this ordeal by buying ourselves and himself a good fat
cheese apiece—his friend The Young Pole looked as if said
ordeal had scared the life out of him temporarily; he was
unable to say whether or no he and 'mon ami' would leave
us: la commission had adopted, in the case of these twain,
an awe-inspiring taciturnity. Jean le Nègre, who was one
of the last to pass, had had a tremendously exciting time,
due to the fact that le gouvernement français' polished
tools had failed to scratch his mystery either in French or
English—he came dancing and singing toward us; then,
suddenly suppressing every vestige of emotion, solemnly
extended for our approval a small scrap of paper on which
was written:

CALAIS

remarking: 'Qu'est-ce que ça veut dire?'—and when we
read the word for him, 'm'en vais à Calais, moi, travailler
à Calais, très bon!'—with a jump and a shout of laughter
pocketing the scrap and beginning the Song of Songs:

'après la guerre fini. . . .'

A trio which had been hit and hard hit by the Three
Wise Men were or was The Wanderer and The Machine-
Fixer and Monsieur Auguste—the former having been insulted in respect to Chocolat's mother (who also occupied
the witness-stand) and having retaliated, as nearly as we
could discover, with a few remarks straight from the
shoulder à propos Justice (O Wanderer, did you expect
honour among the honourable?); The Machine-Fixer
having been told to shut up in the midst of a passionate
plea for mercy, or at least fair-play, if not in his own
case in the case of the wife who was crazed by his absence;

Monsieur Auguste having been asked (as he had been asked three months before by the honourable commissioners), Why did you not return to Russia with your wife and your child at the outbreak of the war?—and having replied, with tears in his eyes and that gentle ferocity of which he was occasionally capable,

'Par-ce-que je n'en a-vais pas les moy-ens. Je ne suis pas un millio-naire, mes-sieurs.'

The Baby-Snatcher, The Trick Raincoat, The Messenger Boy, The Fighting Sheeney and similar gentry passed the commission without the slightest apparent effect upon their disagreeable personalities.

It was not long after Bill the Hollander's departure that we lost two Delectable Mountains in The Wanderer and Surplice. Remained The Zulu and Jean le Nègre. . . . B. and I spent most of our time when on promenade collecting rather beautifully hued leaves in *la cour*. These leaves we inserted in one of my note-books, along with all the colours which we could find on cigarette-boxes, chocolate-wrappers, labels of various sorts and even postage-stamps. (We got a very brilliant red from a certain piece of cloth.) Our efforts puzzled everyone (including the *plantons*) more than considerably; which was natural, considering that everyone did not know that by this exceedingly simple means we were effecting a study of colour itself, in relation to what is popularly called 'abstract' and sometimes 'non-representative' painting. Despite their natural puzzlement everyone (*plantons* excepted) was extraordinarily kind and brought us often valuable additions to our chromatic collection. Had I, at this moment and in the city of New York, the complete confidence of one-twentieth as many human beings I should not be so inclined to consider The Great American Public as the most æsthetically incapable organization ever created for the purpose of perpetuating defunct ideals and ideas. But of course The Great American Public has a handicap which my friends at La Ferté did not as a rule have—education. Let no one sound his indignant yawp at this. I refer to the fact that, for an educated gent or lady, to create is first of all to destroy—that there is and can be no such thing as authentic art until the *bons trucs* (whereby we are taught to see and imitate on canvas and in stone and by words this so-called world) are entirely and thoroughly and perfectly annihilated by that vast and painful process of Unthinking which may result in a minute bit of purely personal Feeling. Which minute bit is Art.

Ah well, the revolution—I refer of course to the intelligent revolution—is on the way; is perhaps nearer than some think, is possibly knocking at the front doors of The Great Mister Harold Bell Wright and The Great Little Miss Polyanna. In the course of the next ten thousand years it may be possible to find Delectable Mountains without going to prison—captivity I mean, *Monsieur Le Surveillant*—it may be possible, I dare say, to encounter Delectable Mountains who are not in prison. . . .

The Autumn wore on.

Rain did, from time to time, not fall: from time to time a sort of unhealthy almost-light leaked from the large uncrisp corpse of the sky, returning for a moment to our view the ruined landscape. From time to time the eye, travelling carefully with a certain disagreeable suddenly fear no longer distances of air, coldish and sweet, stopped upon the incredible nearness of the desolate without-motion autumn. Awkward and solemn clearness, making louder the unnecessary cries, the hoarse laughter, of the invisible harlots in their muddy yard, pointing a

cool actual finger at the silly and ferocious group of man-
shaped beings huddled in the mud under four or five
little trees, came strangely in my own mind pleasantly
to suggest the ludicrous and hideous and beautiful antics
of the insane. Frequently I would discover so perfect a
command over myself as to easily reduce *la promenade* to
a recently invented mechanism; or to the demonstration
of a collection of vivid and unlovely toys around and
around which, guarding them with impossible heroism,
funnily moved purely unreal *plantons,* always absurdly
marching, the maimed and stupid dolls of my imagination.
Once I was sitting alone on the long beam of silent iron
and suddenly had the gradual complete unique experience of death. . . .

It became amazingly cold.

One evening B. and myself and, I think it was, The
Machine-Fixer, were partaking of the warmth of a *bougie*
hard by and in fact between our ambulance beds, when
the door opened, a *planton* entered, and a list of names
(none of which we recognized) was hurriedly read off
with (as in the case of the last *partis* including The Wanderer and Surplice) the admonition:

'*Soyez prêts partir demain matin de bonne heure*'
—and the door shut loudly and quickly. Now one of the
names which had been called sounded somewhat like
'Broom,' and a strange inquietude seized us on this account. Could it possibly have been 'Brown'? We made
inquiries of certain of our friends who had been nearer
the *planton* than ourselves. We were told that Pete and
The Trick Raincoat and The Fighting Sheeney and
Rockyfeller were leaving—about 'Brown' nobody was
able to enlighten us. Not that opinions in this matter were
lacking. There were plenty of opinions—but they con-

tradicted each other to a painful extent. *Les hommes* were in fact about equally divided; half considering that the occult sound had been intended for 'Brown,' half that the somewhat asthmatic *planton* had unwittingly uttered a spontaneous grunt or sigh, which sigh or grunt we had mistaken for a proper noun. Our uncertainty was augmented by the confusion emanating from a particular corner of The Enormous Room, in which corner The Fighting Sheeney was haranguing a group of spectators on the pregnant topic: What I won't do to Précigné when I get there. In deep converse with Bathhouse John we beheld the very same youth who, some time since, had drifted to a place beside me at *la soupe*—Pete the Ghost, white and determined, blonde and fragile: Pete the Shadow. . . .

I forget who, but someone—I think it was the little Machine-Fixer—established the truth that an American was to leave the next morning. That, moreover, said American's name was *Brun*.

Whereupon B. and I became extraordinarily busy.

The Zulu and Jean le Nègre, upon learning that B. was among the *partis*, came over to our beds and sat down without uttering a word. The former, through a certain shy orchestration of silence, conveyed effortlessly and perfectly his sorrow at the departure; the latter, by his bowed head and a certain very delicate restraint manifested in the wholly exquisite poise of his firm alert body, uttered at least a universe of grief.

The little Machine-Fixer was extremely indignant; not only that his friend was going to a den of thieves and ruffians, but that his friend was leaving in such company as that of *cette crapule* (meaning Rockyfeller) and *les deux mangeurs de blanc* (to wit, The Trick Raincoat and The

Fighting Sheeney). 'C'est malheureux' he repeated over and over, wagging his poor little head in rage and despair —'it's no place for a young man who has done no wrong, to be shut up with pimps and cut-throats, *pour la durée de la guerre: le gouvernement français a bien fait!*' and he brushed a tear out of his eye with a desperate rapid little gesture. . . . But what angered The Machine-Fixer most was that B. and I were about to be separated— 'M'sieu' Jean' (touching me gently on the knee), 'they have no hearts, *la commission*; they are not simply unjust, they are cruel, *savez-vous?* Men are not like these; they are not men, they are Name of God I don't know what, they are worse than the animals; and they pretend to Justice' (shivering from top to toe with an indescribable sneer) 'Justice! My God, Justice!'

All of which, somehow or other, did not exactly cheer us.

And, the packing completed, we drank together for The Last Time. The Zulu and Jean le Nègre and The Machine-Fixer and B. and I—and Pete the Shadow drifted over, whiter than I think I ever saw him, and said simply to me:

'I'll take care o' your friend, Johnny,'

. . . and then at last it was *lumières éteintes*; and *les deux américains* lay in their beds in the cold rotten darkness, talking in low voices of the past, of Pétrouchka, of Paris, of that brilliant and extraordinary and impossible something: Life.

Morning. Whitish. Inevitable. Deathly cold.

There was a great deal of hurry and bustle in The Enormous Room. People were rushing hither and thither in the heavy half-darkness. People were saying good-bye to people. Saying good-bye to friends. Saying good-bye to themselves. We lay and sipped the black, evil, dull, certainly not coffee; lay on our beds, dressed, shuddering with cold, waiting. Waiting. Several of *les hommes* whom we scarcely knew came up to B. and shook hands with him and said good luck and good-bye. The darkness was going rapidly out of the dull, black, evil, stinking air. B. suddenly realized that he had no gift for The Zulu; he asked a fine Norwegian to whom he had given his leather belt if he, The Norwegian, would mind giving it back because there was a very dear friend who had been forgotten. The Norwegian, with a pleasant smile, took off the belt and said 'Certainly' ... he had been arrested at Bordeaux, where he came ashore from his ship, for stealing three cans of sardines when he was drunk ... a very great and dangerous criminal ... he said 'Certainly' and gave B. a pleasant smile, the pleasantest smile in the world. B. wrote his own address and name in the inside of the belt, explained in French to The Young Pole that any time The Zulu wanted to reach him all he had to do was to consult the belt; The Young Pole translated; The Zulu nodded; the Norwegian smiled appreciatively; The Zulu received the belt with a gesture to which words cannot do the faintest justice—

A *planton* was standing in The Enormous Room, a *planton* roaring and cursing and crying '*Dépêchez-vous, ceux qui von partir.*'—B. shook hands with Jean and Mexique and The Machine-Fixer and The Young Skipper, and Bathhouse John (to whom he had given his ambulance tunic, and who was crazy-proud in consequence), and The Norwegian and The Washing-Machine Man and

The Hat, and many of *les hommes* whom we scarcely knew.—The Black Holster was roaring:

'*Allez, nom de dieu, l'américain!*'

I went down the room with B. and Pete, and shook hands with both at the door. The other *partis*, alias The Trick Raincoat and The Fighting Sheeney, were already on the way downstairs. The Black Holster cursed us and me in particular and slammed the door angrily in my face—

Through the little peephole I caught a glimpse of them, entering the street. I went to my bed and lay down quietly in my great pelisse. The clamour and filth of the room brightened and became distant and faded. I heard the voice of the jolly Alsatian saying:

'*Courage, mon ami, votre camarade n'est pas mort; vous le verrez plus tard,*' and after that, nothing. In front of and on and within my eyes lived suddenly a violent and gentle and dark silence.

The Three Wise Men had done their work. But wisdom cannot rest. . . .

Probably at that very moment they were holding their court in another La Ferté committing to incomparable anguish some few merely perfectly wretched criminals: little and tall, tremulous and brave—all of them white and speechless, all of them with tight bluish lips and large whispering eyes, all of them with fingers weary and mutilated and extraordinarily old . . . desperate fingers; closing, to feel the final lukewarm fragment of life glide neatly and softly into forgetfulness.

XIII

I SAY GOOD-BYE TO LA MISÈRE

To convince the reader that this history is mere fiction (and rather vulgarly violent fiction at that) nothing perhaps is needed save that ancient standby of sob-story writers and thrill-artists alike—the Happy Ending. As a matter of fact, it makes not the smallest difference to me whether anyone who has thus far participated in my travels does or does not believe that they and I are (as that mysterious animal 'the public' would say) 'real.' I do however very strenuously object to the assumption, on the part of anyone, that the heading of this my final chapter stands for anything in the nature of happiness. In the course of recalling (in God knows a rather clumsy and perfectly inadequate way) what happened to me between the latter part of August 1917 and the first day of January 1918, I have proved to my own satisfaction (if not to anyone else's) that I was happier in La Ferté Macé, with The Delectable Mountains about me, than the very keenest words can pretend to express. I dare say it all comes down to a definition of happiness. And a definition of happiness I most certainly do not intend to attempt; but I can and will say this: to leave *La Misère* with the knowledge, and worse than that the feeling, that some of the finest people in the world are doomed to remain prisoners thereof for no one knows how long—are doomed to continue, possibly for years and tens of years and all the years which terribly are between them and their deaths, the grey and indivisible Non-existence which without apology you are quitting for Reality—cannot by any stretch of the imagination be conceived as constituting a Happy Ending to a great and personal adventure. That I write this chapter at all is due, purely and simply, to the I dare say unjustified hope on my part that—by recording certain events—it may hurl a little additional light into a very tremendous darkness. . . .

At the outset let me state that what occurred subsequent to the departure for Précigné of B. and Pete and The Sheeneys and Rockyfeller is shrouded in a rather ridiculous indistinctness; due, I have to admit, to the depression which this departure inflicted upon my altogether too human nature. The judgment of the Three Wise Men had—to use a peculiarly vigorous (not to say vital) expression of my own day and time—knocked me for a loop. I spent the days intervening between the separation from '*votre camarade*' and my somewhat supernatural departure for freedom in attempting to partially straighten myself. When finally I made my exit, the part of me popularly referred to as 'mind' was still in a slightly bent if not twisted condition. Not until some weeks of American diet had revolutionized my exterior did my interior completely resume the contours of normality. I am particularly neither ashamed nor proud of this (one might nearly say) mental catastrophe. No more ashamed or proud, in fact, than of the infection of three fingers which I carried to America as a little token of La Ferté's good-will. In the latter case I certainly have no right to boast, even should I find myself so inclined; for B. took with him to Précigné a case of what his father, upon B.'s arrival in The Home of The

Brave, diagnosed as scurvy—which scurvy made my mutilations look like thirty cents or even less. One of my vividest memories of La Ferté consists in a succession of crackling noises associated with the disrobing of my friend. I recall that we appealed to Monsieur Ree-chard together, B. in behalf of his scurvy and I in behalf of my hand plus a queer little row of sores, the latter having proceeded to adorn that part of my face which was trying hard to be graced with a moustache. I recall that Monsieur Ree-chard decreed a *bain* for B., with *bain* meant immersion in a large tin tub partially filled with not quite lukewarm water. I, on the contrary, obtained a speck of zinc ointment on a minute piece of cotton, and considered myself peculiarly fortunate. Which details cannot possibly offend the reader's æsthetic sense to a greater degree than have already certain minutiæ connected with the sanitary arrangements of the *Directeur's* little home for homeless boys and girls—therefore I will not trouble to beg the reader's pardon but will proceed with my story proper or improper.

'*Mais qu'est-ce que vous avez,*' *Monsieur le Surveillant* demanded, in a tone of profound if kindly astonishment, as I wended my lonely way to *la soupe* some days after the disappearance of *les partis.*

I stood and stared at him very stupidly without answering, having indeed nothing at all to say.

'But why are you so sad?' he asked.

'I suppose I miss my friend,' I ventured.

'*Mais—mais*—' he puffed and panted like a very old and fat person trying to persuade a bicycle to climb a hill—'*mais—vous avez de la chance!*'

'I suppose I have,' I said without enthusiasm.

'*Mais-mais-parfaitement—vous avez de la chance—uh-*

ah—uh-ah—parce que—comprenez-vous—votre cama-
rade—uh-ah—a attrapé prison!'

'Uh-ah,' I said wearily.

'Whereas,' continued Monsieur, 'you haven't. You
ought to be extraordinarily thankful and particularly
happy!'

'I should rather have gone to prison with my friend,' I
stated briefly; and went into the dining-room, leaving
the *Surveillant* uh-ahing in nothing short of complete
amazement.

I really believe that my condition worried him, incredible as this may seem. At the time I gave neither an extraordinary nor a particular damn about *Monsieur le
Surveillant*, nor indeed about *'l'autre américain,'* alias
myself. Dimly, through a fog of disinterested inappre-
hension, I realized that—with the exception of the
plantons and of course Apollyon—everyone was trying
very hard to help me; that The Zulu, Jean, The Machine-
Fixer, Mexique, The Young Skipper, even The Washing-
Machine Man (with whom I promenaded frequently
when no one else felt like taking the completely unagreeable air) were kind, very kind, kinder than I can possibly
say. As for Afrique and The Cook—there was nothing
too good for me at this time. I asked the latter's permission to cut wood, and was not only accepted as a sawyer
but encouraged with assurances of the best coffee there
was, with real sugar *dedans*. In the little space outside
the *cuisine*, between the building and *la cour*, I sawed
away of a morning to my great satisfaction, from time to
time clumping my saboted way into the chef's domain
in answer to a subdued signal from Afrique. Of an afternoon I sat with Jean or Mexique or The Zulu on the long
beam of silent iron, pondering very carefully nothing at

all, replying to their questions or responding to their observations in a highly mechanical manner. I felt myself to be, at last, a doll—taken out occasionally and played with and put back into its house and told to go to sleep. . . .

One afternoon I was lying on my couch, thinking of the usual Nothing, when a sharp cry sung through The Enormous Room:

'*Il tombe de la neige—Noël! Noël!*'

I sat up. The *Garde-Champêtre* was at the nearest window, dancing a little horribly and crying:

'*Noël! Noël!*'

I went to another window and looked out. Sure enough. Snow was falling, gradually and wonderfully falling, silently falling through the thick, soundless autumn. . . . It seemed to me supremely beautiful, the snow. There was about it something unspeakably crisp and exquisite, something perfect and minute and gentle and fatal. . . . The *Garde-Champêtre*'s cry began a poem in the back of my head, a poem about the snow, a poem in French, beginning *Il tombe de la neige, Noël, Noël.* I watched the snow. After a long time I returned to my bunk and I lay down, closing my eyes, feeling the snow's minute and crisp touch falling gently and exquisitely, falling perfectly and suddenly, through the thick, soundless autumn of my imagination. . . .

'*L'américain! L'américain!*'

Some one is speaking to me.

'*Le petit belge avec le bras cassé est là-bas, à la porte, il veut vous parler. . . .*'

I marched the length of the room. The Enormous Room is filled with a new and beautiful darkness, the darkness of the snow outside, falling and falling and

falling with the silent and actual gesture which has
touched the soundless country of my mind as a child
touches a toy it loves. . . .

Through the locked door I heard a nervous whisper:
'*Dis à l'américain que je veux parler avec lui.*'—'*Me
voici,*' I said.

'Put your ear to the key-hole, M'sieu' Jean,' said The
Machine-Fixer's voice. The voice of the little Machine-
Fixer, tremendously excited. I obey—'*Alors. Qu'est-ce
que c'est, mon ami?*'

'*M'sieu' Jean! Le Directeur va vous appeler tout de
suite!* You must get ready instantly! Wash and shave,
eh? He's going to call you right away. And don't forget!
Oloron! You will ask to go to Oloron Sainte-Marie,
where you can paint! Oloron Sainte-Marie, Basse Pyre-
nées! *N'oubliez pas, M'sieu' Jean! Et dépêchez-vous!*'

'*Merci bien, mon ami!*'—I remember now. The little
Machine-Fixer and I had talked. It seemed that *la commission* had decided that I was not a criminal, but only
a suspect. As a suspect I would be sent to some place in
France, any place I wanted to go provided it was not on or
near the sea-coast. That was in order that I should not
perhaps try to escape from France. The Machine-Fixer
had advised me to ask to go to Oloron Sainte-
Marie. I should say that, as a painter, the Pyrenees particularly appealed to me. '*Et qu'il fait beau, là-bas!* The
snow on the mountains! And it's not cold. And what
mountains! You can live there very cheaply. As a suspect
you will merely have to report once a month to the chief
of police of Oloron Sainte-Marie; he's an old friend of
mine! He's a fine, fat, red-cheeked man, very kindly. He
will make it easy for you, M'sieu' Jean, and will help you
out in every way, when you tell him you are a friend of

the little Belgian with the broken arm. Tell him I sent
you. You will have a very fine time, and you can paint:
such scenery to paint! My God—not like what you see
from these windows. I advise you by all means to ask
to go to Oloron.'

So thinking I lathered my face, standing before
Judas's mirror.

'You don't rub enough,' the Alsatian advised, *'il faut
frotter bien!'* A number of fellow-captives were regarding my toilet with surprise and satisfaction. I discovered
in the mirror an astounding beard and a good layer of
dirt. I worked busily, counselled by several voices, cen-
sured by the Alsatian, encouraged by Judas himself. The
shave and the wash completed, I felt considerably refreshed.

WHANG!

'L'américain en bas!' It was the Black Holster. I carefully adjusted my tunic and obeyed him.

The *Directeur* and the *Surveillant* were in consultation
when I entered the latter's office. Apollyon, seated at a
desk, surveyed me very fiercely. His subordinate swayed
to and fro, clasping and unclasping his hands behind his
back, and regarded me with an expression of almost
benevolence. The Black Holster guarded the doorway.

Turning on me ferociously—*'Votre ami est mauvais,
très mauvais,* SAVEZ-VOUS?' *Le Directeur* shouted.

I answered quietly, *'Oui? Je ne le savais pas.'*

'He is a bad fellow, a criminal, a traitor, an insult to
civilization,' Apollyon roared into my face.

'Yes?' I said again.

'You'd better be careful!' The *Directeur* shouted. 'Do
you know what's happened to your friend?'

'Sais pas,' I said.

'He's gone to prison where he belongs!' Apollyon roared. 'Do you understand what that means?'

'*Peut être,*' I answered, somewhat insolently I fear.

'You're lucky not to be there with him! Do you understand?' *Monsieur Le Directeur* thundered, 'and next time pick your friends better, take more care I tell you, or you'll go where he is—TO PRISON FOR THE REST OF THE WAR!'

'With my friend I should be well content in prison,' I said evenly, trying to keep looking through him and into the wall behind his black, big, spidery body.

'In God's Name what a fool!' The *Directeur* bellowed furiously—and The *Surveillant* remarked pacifyingly: '*Il aime trop son camarade, c'est tout.*'—'But his comrade is a traitor and a villain!' objected the Fiend, at the top of his harsh voice—'*Comprenez-vous: votre ami est UN SALAUD!*' he snarled at me.

He seems afraid that I don't get his idea, I said to myself. 'I understand what you say,' I assured him.

'And you don't believe it?' he screamed, showing his fangs and otherwise looking like an exceedingly dangerous maniac.

'*Je ne le crois pas, Monsieur.*'

'O God's name!' he shouted. 'What a fool, *quel idiot,* what a beastly fool!' And he did something through his froth-covered lips, something remotely suggesting laughter.

Hereupon The *Surveillant* again intervened. I was mistaken. It was lamentable. I could not be made to understand. Very true. But I had been sent for—'do you know, you have been decided to be a suspect,' *Monsieur le Surveillant* turned to me, 'and now you may choose where you wish to be sent.' Apollyon was blowing and wheezing and muttering . . . clenching his huge pinkish hands.

I addressed the *Surveillant,* ignoring Apollyon. 'I should like, if I may, to go to Oloron Sainte-Marie.'

'What do you want to go there for?' the *Directeur* exploded threateningly.

I explained that I was by profession an artist, and had always wanted to view the Pyrenees. 'The environment of Oloron would be most stimulating to an artist—'

'Do you know it's near Spain?' he snapped, looking straight at me.

I knew it was, and therefore replied with a carefully childish ignorance: 'Spain? Indeed! Very interesting.'

'You want to escape from France, that's it?' The *Directeur* snarled.

'Oh, I hardly should say that,' The *Surveillant* interposed soothingly, 'he is an artist, and Oloron is a very pleasant place for an artist. A very nice place. I hardly think his choice of Oloron a cause for suspicion. I should think it a very natural desire on his part.'—His superior subsided snarling.

After a few more questions I signed some papers which lay on the desk, and was told by Apollyon to get out.

'When can I expect to leave?' I asked The *Surveillant.*

'Oh, it's only a matter of days, of weeks perhaps,' he assured me benignantly.

'You'll leave when it's proper for you to leave!' Apollyon burst out. 'Do you understand?'

'Yes, indeed. Thank you very much,' I replied with a bow, and exited. On the way to The Enormous Room the Black Holster said to me sharply:

'*Vous allez partir?*'

'*Oui.*'

He gave me such a look as would have turned a mahogany piano leg into a mound of smoking ashes, and slammed the key into the lock.

Every one gathered about me. 'What news?'

'I have asked to go to Oloron as a suspect,' I answered.

'You should have taken my advice and asked to go to Cannes,' the fat Alsatian reproached me. He had indeed spent a great while advising me—but I trusted the little Machine-Fixer.

'*Parti?*' Jean le Nègre said with huge eyes, touching me gently.

'*Non, non. Plus tard, peut être. Pas maintenant,*' I assured him. And he patted my shoulder and smiled, '*Bon!*' And we smoked a cigarette in honour of the snow, of which Jean—in contrast to the majority of *les hommes* —highly and unutterably approved. '*C'est joli!*' he would say, laughing wonderfully. And next morning he and I went on an exclusive promenade, I in my sabots, Jean in a new pair of slippers which he had received (after many requests) from the *bureau*. And we strode to and fro in the muddy *cour* admiring *la neige,* not speaking.

One day, after the snow-fall, I received from Paris a complete set of Shakespeare in the Everyman edition. I had forgotten completely that B. and I—after trying and failing to get William Blake—had ordered and paid for the better known William; the ordering and communicating in general being done with the collaboration of Monsieur Pet-airs. It was a curious and interesting feeling which I experienced upon first opening to 'As You Like It'... the volumes had been carefully inspected, I learned, by the *secrétaire*, in order to eliminate the possibility of their concealing something valuable or dangerous. And in this connection let me add that the *secrétaire,* or (if not he) his superiors, were a good

judge of what is valuable—if not what is dangerous. I
know this because, whereas my family several times sent
me socks, in every case enclosing cigarettes, I received
invariably the former *sans* the latter. Perhaps it is not fair
to suspect the officials of La Ferté of this particularly
mean theft; I should, possibly, doubt the honesty of that
very same French censor whose intercepting of B.'s correspondence had motivated our removal from the *Section
Sanitaire*. Heaven knows I wish (like the Three Wise
Men) to give justice where justice is due.

Somehow or other, reading Shakespeare did not appeal
to my disordered mind. I tried 'Hamlet' and 'Julius
Cæsar' once or twice and gave it up, after telling a man
who asked 'Shah-kay-spare, who is Shah-kay-spare?' that
Mr. S. was the Homer of the English-speaking peoples—
which remark, to my surprise, appeared to convey a very
definite idea to the questioner and sent him away perfectly satisfied. Most of the timeless time I spent promenading in the rain and sleet with Jean le Nègre, or talking
with Mexique, or exchanging big gifts of silence with
The Zulu. For Oloron—I did not believe in it, and I did
not particularly care. If I went away, good; if I stayed,
so long as Jean and The Zulu and Mexique were with me,
good. '*M'en fous pas mal*' pretty nearly summed up my
philosophy.

At least The *Surveillant* let me alone on the *Soi-Même*
topic. After my brief visit to Satan I wallowed in a perfect luxury of dirt. And no one objected. On the contrary, every one (realizing that the enjoyment of dirt
may be made the basis of a fine art) beheld with something like admiration my more and more uncouth appearance. Moreover, my being dirtier than usual I was
protesting in a (to me) very satisfactory way against all

that was neat and tidy and bigoted and solemn and founded upon the anguish of my fine friends. And my fine friends, being my fine friends, understood. Simultaneously with my arrival at the summit of dirtiness—by the calendar, as I guess, December the twenty-first— came the Black Holster into The Enormous Room and with an excited and angry mien proclaimed loudly:

'*L'américain! Allez chez Le Directeur. De suite.*'

I protested mildly that I was dirty—

'*N'importe. Allez avec moi,*' and down I went to the amazement of every one and the great amusement of myself. 'By Jove, wait till he sees me this time,' I remarked half-audibly. . . .

The *Directeur* said nothing when I entered.

The *Directeur* extended a piece of paper, which I read.

The *Directeur* said, with an attempt at amiability, '*Alors, vous allez sortir.*'

I looked at him in eleven-tenths of amazement. I was standing in the *bureau de Monsieur le Directeur du Camp de Triage de la Ferté Macé,* Orne, France, and holding in my hand a slip of paper which said that if there was a man named Edward E. Cummings, he should report immediately to the American Embassy, Paris, and I had just heard the words:

'*Alors, vous allez sortir,*'

which words were pronounced in a voice so subdued, so constrained, so mild, so altogether ingratiating, that I could not imagine to whom it belonged. Surely not to the Fiend, to Apollyon, to the Prince of Hell, to Satan, to *Monsieur le Directeur du Camp de Triage de la Ferté Macé*—

'Get ready. You will leave immediately.'

Then I noticed the *Surveillant*. Upon his face I saw an almost smile. He returned my gaze and remarked:

'Uh-ah, uh-ah, *Oui*.'

'That's all,' The *Directeur* said. 'You will call for your money at the *bureau* of the *Gestionnaire* before leaving.'

'Go and get ready,' The Fencer said, and I certainly saw a smile. . . .

'I? Am? Going? To? Paris?' somebody who certainly wasn't myself remarked in a kind of whisper.

'*Parfaitement*.'—Pettish. Apollyon. But how changed. Who the devil is myself? Where in Hell am I? What is Paris—a place, a somewhere, a city, life, to live: infinitive. Present first singular I live. Thou livest. The *Directeur*. The *Surveillant*. La Ferté Macé, Orne, France. 'Edward E. Cummings will report immediately.' Edward E. Cummings. The *Surveillant*. A piece of yellow paper. The *Directeur*. A necktie. Paris. Life. *Liberté*. *La liberté*. '*La Liberté*'—I almost shouted in agony.

'*Dépêchez-vous. Savez-vous, vous allez partir de suite. Cet aprèsmidi. Pour Paris.*'

I turned, I turned so suddenly as almost to bowl over the Black Holster, Black Holster and all; I turned toward the door, I turned upon the Black Holster, I turned into Edward E. Cummings, I turned into what was dead and is now alive, I turned into a city, I turned into a dream—

I am standing in The Enormous Room for the last time. I am saying good-bye. No, it is not I who am saying good-bye. It is in fact somebody else, possibly myself. Perhaps myself has shaken hands with a little creature with a wizened arm, a little creature in whose eyes tears for some reason are; with a placid youth (Mexique?) who smiles and says shakily:

'Good-bye, Johnny, I no for-get you,'

with a crazy old fellow who somehow or other has got
inside B.'s tunic and is gesticulating and crying out and
laughing; with a frank-eyed boy who claps me on the
back and says:

'Good-bye and good-luck t' you'
(is he The Young Skipper, by any chance?); with a lot
of hungry, wretched, beautiful people—I have given my
bed to The Zulu, by Jove, and The Zulu is even now
standing guard over it, and his friend The Young Pole
has given me the address of '*mon ami*,' and there are tears
in The Young Pole's eyes, and I seem to be amazingly
tall and altogether tearless—and this is the nice Norwegian, who got drunk at Bordeaux and stole three (or
four was it?) cans of sardines . . . and now I feel before
me some one who also has tears in his eyes, some one who
is in fact crying, some one whom I feel to be very strong
and young as he hugs me quietly in his firm alert arms,
kissing me on both cheeks and on the lips. . . .

'Goo-bye, boy,'
—O good-bye, good-bye, I am going away, Jean; have
a good time, laugh wonderfully when *la neige* comes. . . .

And I am standing somewhere with arms lifted up.
'*Si tu as une lettre, sais-tu, il faut dire.* For if I find a
letter on you it will go hard with the man that gave it
to you to take out.' Black. The Black Holster even. Does
not examine my baggage. Wonder why? '*Allez!*' Jean's
letter to his *gonzesse* in Paris still safe in my little pocket
under my belt. Ha ha, by God, that's a good one on you,
you Black Holster, you Very Black Holster. That's a good
one. Glad I said good-bye to the cook. Why didn't I give
Monsieur Auguste's little friend, the *cordonnier*, more
than six francs for mending my shoes? He looked so injured. I am a fool, and I am going into the street, and I

am going by myself with no *planton* into the little street of the little city of La Ferté Macé which is a little, a very little city in France, where once upon a time I used to catch water for an old man. . . .

I have already shaken hands with the cook, and with the *cordonnier* who has beautifully mended my shoes. I am saying good-bye to *les deux balayeurs*. I am shaking hands with the little (the very little) Machine-Fixer again. I have given him a franc and I have given Garibaldi a franc. We had a drink a moment ago on me. The tavern is just opposite the *gare*, where there will soon be a train. I will get upon the soonness of the train and ride into the now of Paris. No, I must change at a station called Briouse did you say? Good-bye, *mes amis, et bonne chance!* They disappear, pulling and pushing at a cart, *les deux balayeurs . . . de mes couilles . . .* by Jove, what a tin noise is coming, see the wooden engineer, he makes a funny gesture utterly composed (composed silently and entirely) of *merde. Merde! Merde.* A wee, tiny, absurd whistle coming from nowhere, from outside of me. Two men opposite. Jolt. A few houses, a fence, a wall, a bit of *neige* float foolishly by and through a window. These gentlemen in my compartment do not seem to know that *La Misère* exists. They are talking politics. Thinking that I don't understand. By Jesus, that's a good one. 'Pardon me, gentlemen, but does one change at the next station for Paris?' Surprised, I thought so. 'Yes, Monsieur, the next station.' By Hell I surprised somebody. . . .

Who are a million, a trillion, a nonillion young men? All are standing. I am standing. We are wedged in and on and over and under each other. Sardines. Knew a man once who was arrested for stealing sardines. I, sardine, look at three sardines, at three million sardines, at a car-ful of sardines. How did I get here? O yes, of course. Briouse. Horrible name 'Briouse.' Made a bluff at riding *deuxième classe* on a *troisième classe* ticket bought for me by *les deux balayeurs*. Gentleman in the compartment talked French with me till conductor appeared. 'Tickets, gentleman?' I extended mine dumbly. He gave me a look. 'How? This is third class!' I look intelligently ignorant. '*Il ne comprend pas français*,' says the gentleman. 'Ah!' says the conductor, 'tease ease eye-ee thoorde claz tea-keat. You air een tea saycoend claz. You weel go eantoo tea thoorde claz weal you yes pleace at once?' So I got stung after all. Third is more amusing certainly, though god-damn hot with these sardines, including myself of course. Oh yes, of course. *Poilus en permission.* Very old some. Others mere kids. Once saw a *planton* who never saw a razor. Yet he was *réformé. C'est la guerre*. Several of us get off and stretch at a little tanktown-station. Engine thumping up front somewhere in the darkness. Wait. They get their *bidons* filled. Wish I had a *bidon*, a *dis-donc bidon n'est-ce pas. Faut pas t'en faire,* who sang or said that?

PEE-p. . . .

We're off.

I am almost asleep. Or myself. What's the matter here? Sardines writhing about, cut it out, no room for that sort of thing. Jolt.

'Paris.'

Morning. Morning in Paris. I found my bed full of fleas this morning, and I couldn't catch the fleas, though I tried hard because I was ashamed that anyone should find fleas in my bed which is at the Hotel des Saints Pères whither I went in a *fiacre* and the driver didn't know where it was. Wonderful. This is the American

embassy. I must look funny in my pelisse. Thank God for
the breakfast. I ate somewhere ... good-looking girl,
Parisienne, at the switch-board upstairs. 'Go right in,
sir.' A1 English, by God. So this is the person to whom
Edward E. Cummings is immediately to report.

'Is this Mr. Cummings?'

'Yes.' Rather a young man, very young in fact. Jove,
I must look queer.

'Sit down! We've been looking all over creation for
you.'

'Yes?'

'Have some cigarettes?'

'Yes,'

By God, he gives me a sac of Bull. Extravagant they are
at the American Embassy. Can I roll one? I can. I do.

Conversation. Pleased to see me. Thought I was lost
for good. Tried every means to locate me. Just discovered
where I was. What was it like? No, really? You don't
mean it! Well I'll be damned! Look here; this man B.,
what sort of a fellow is he? Well I'm interested to hear
you say that. Look at his correspondence. It seemed to
me that a fellow who could write like that wasn't dangerous. Must be a little queer. Tell me, isn't he a trifle
foolish? That's what I thought. Now I'd advise you to
leave France as soon as you can. They're picking up ambulance men left and right, men who've got no business
to be in Paris. Do you want to leave by the next boat?
I'd advise it. Good. Got money? If you haven't we'll pay
your fare. Or half of it. Plenty, eh? Norton Harjes, I
see. Mind going second class? Good. Not much difference
on this line. Now you can take these papers and go to
.... No time to lose, as she sails to-morrow. That's it.
Grab a taxi, and hustle. When you've got those signatures

bring them to me and I'll fix you all up. Get your ticket first, here's a letter to the manager of the Compagnie Generale. Then go through the police department. You can do it if you hurry. See you later. Make it quick, eh? Good-bye!

The streets. *Les rues de Paris*. I walked past Notre Dame. I bought tobacco. Jews are peddling things with American trade-marks on them, because in a day or two it's Christmas I suppose. Jesus, it is cold. Dirty snow. Huddling people. *La guerre*. Always *la guerre*. And chill. Goes through these big mittens. To-morrow I shall be on the ocean. Pretty neat the way that passport was put through. Rode all day in a taxi, two cylinders, running on one. Everywhere waiting lines. I stepped to the head and was attended to by the officials of the great and good French government. Gad, that's a good one. A good one on *le gouvernement français*. Pretty good. *Les rues sont tristes*. Perhaps there's no Christmas, perhaps the French Government has forbidden Christmas. Clerk at Norton Harjes seemed astonished to see me. O God it is cold in Paris. Every one looks hard under lamplight, because it's winter I suppose. Every one hurried. Every one hard. Every one cold. Every one huddling. Every one alive; alive; alive.

Shall I give this man five francs for dressing my hand? He said 'anything you like, monsieur.' Ship's doctor's probably well-paid. Probably not. Better hurry before I put my lunch. Awe-inspiring stink, because it's in the bow. Little member of the crew immersing his guess what in a can of some liquid or other, groaning from time to time, staggers when the boat tilts. '*Merci bien, Monsieur!*' That was the proper thing. Now for the—never can reach it—here's the *première classe* one—any port in a storm.

. . . Feel better now. Narrowly missed American officer but just managed to make it. Was it yesterday or day before saw the *Vaterland,* I mean the what deuce is it— that biggest in the world afloat boat. Damned rough. Snow falling. Almost slid through the railing that time. Snow. The snow is falling into the sea; which quietly receives it: into which it utterly and peacefully disappears. Man with a college degree returning from Spain, not disagreeable sort, talks Spanish with that fat man who's an Argentinian.—Tinian?—Tinish, perhaps. All the same. In other words Tin. Nobody at the table knows I speak English or am American. Hell, that's a good one on nobody. That's a pretty fat kind of a joke on nobody. Think I'm French. Talk mostly with those three or four Frenchmen going on *permission* to somewhere via New York. One has an accordion. Like second class. Wait till you see the *gratte-ciel,* I tell 'em. They say '*Oui?*' and don't believe. I'll show them. America. 'The land of the flea and the home of the dag'—short for dago of course. My spirits are constantly improving. Funny Christmas, second day out. Wonder if we'll dock New Year's Day. My God, what a list to starboard. They say a waiter broke his arm when it happened, ballast shifted. Don't believe it. Something wrong. I know I nearly fell downstairs. . . .

My God, what an ugly island. Hope we don't stay here long. All the red-bloods first-class much excited about land. Damned ugly, I think.

Hullo.

The tall, impossibly tall, incomparably tall, city shoulderingly upward into hard sunlight leaned a little through the octaves of its parallel edges, leaningly strode upward into firm, hard, snowy sunlight; the noises of America nearingly throbbed with smokes and hurrying dots which

are men and which are women and which are things new
and curious and hard and strange and vibrant and immense, lifting with a great ondulous stride firmly into
immortal sunlight. . . .